New Found Land

New Found Land

Lewis and Clark's
Voyage of Discovery

a novel by

ALLAN WOLF

CANDLEWICK PRESS

For Ginger, Simon, Ethan, and Jameson: co-captain and crew

Copyright © 2004 by Allan Wolf
Map illustrations copyright © 2004 by Malcolm Cullen

First paperback edition 2007

The Library of Congress has cataloged the hardcover edition as follows:

Wolf, Allan.
New found land: Lewis and Clark's voyage of discovery / a novel by Allan Wolf. — 1st ed.
p. cm.
Summary: The letters and thoughts of Thomas Jefferson, members of the Corps of Discovery,
their guide Sacagawea, and Captain Lewis's Newfoundland dog all tell of the historic
exploratory expedition to seek a water route to the Pacific Ocean.
ISBN 978-0-7636-2113-1 (hardcover)
1. Lewis and Clark Expedition (1804–1806)—Juvenile fiction.
[1. Lewis and Clark Expedition 1804–1806—Fiction.
2. Overland journeys to the Pacific—Fiction.
3. West (U.S)—Discovery and exploration—Fiction.]
I. Title.
PZ7.W8185513Ne 2004
[Fic]—dc22   2003065254

ISBN 978-0-7636-3288-5 (paperback)

13 14 15 16 17 18 MVP 10 9 8 7 6 5 4 3

Printed in York, PA, U.S.A.

This book was typeset in Bulmer.

Candlewick Press
99 Dover Street
Somerville, Massachusetts 02144

visit us at www.candlewick.com

The real voyage of discovery consists
not in seeking new landscapes,
but in having new eyes.

Marcel Proust

— Contents —

The Corps of Discovery

Meriwether Lewis: *The Explorer*

William Clark: *The Gentleman*

Oolum: *The Newfoundland*

Sacagawea: *The Bird Woman*

York: *The Slave*

George Shannon: *The Kid*

George Drouillard: *The Half-Breed*

John Colter: *The Hunter*

Pierre Cruzatte: *The Fiddler*

Hugh Hall: *The Drinker*

Patrick Gass: *The Carpenter*

Joseph and Reubin Field: *The Brothers*

Thomas Jefferson: *The President*

PART ONE

WASHINGTON, D.C., TO ST. CHARLES

JUNE 1803–MAY 1804

Iowa

MISSOURI RIVER

Illinois

MISSISSIPPI RIVER

Indiana

Missouri

RIVER DUBOIS

Clarksv

St. Charles

Camp Dubois

Falls of
the Ohio

St. Louis

Fort
Kaskaskia

OHIO RIVER

Louisville

Indian attempts
to purchase
Newfoundland
11·16·1803

Fort Massac

Arkansas

Tennessee

MISSISSIPPI RIVER

Mississippi · Alabama

Pennsylvania

Philadelphia

ALLEGHENY RIVER

Pittsburgh

Wheeling

MONONGAHELA RIVER

Zane's
Trace

Ohio

Newfoundland
catches squirrels
9·11·1803

Washington
D.C.

OHIO RIVER

Cincinnati

West
Virginia

Virginia

Maysville

Kentucky

APPALACHIAN MOUNTAINS

Fort South West
Point

North
Carolina

South
Carolina

Georgia

Sacagawea ◇ *the bird woman*

After my eleventh winter
I was kidnapped by our enemies
and made to be their slave.

My people, the Shoshone, were in hiding
in the Shining Mountains
at the place where three rivers become one.
In times of war, we never left the camp unescorted.
That day the young brave Split Feather
watched over my cousin and me.
Split Feather kept lookout from atop his horse
while we two girls crouched by a creek
mashing *pah-see-goo* roots with a heavy stone.

We were filled with hope. Spring had arrived.
We would soon return to the plains to hunt the buffalo.
Soon there would be skins to cover our tepees.
Soon there would be meat to fill our stomachs.

I was yet a young girl, but a strong one.
Cousin was older and due to marry Split Feather soon.
They brought joy to each other
and their union was a blessing to our family.
Long ago my father had promised me to Sitting Hawk,
an important Shoshone scout.
I was to become his wife,
but not until I reached womanhood.

Despite our hunger, Cousin and I were always laughing.
That day was no different.
She held her basket, filled with roots, against her stomach.

"Look, Watches the Sky," she said, joking.
"I am pregnant with many small children."
Even serious Split Feather cracked a smile.

Suddenly we heard the sound of the hawk.
It was Sitting Hawk, at watch in the forest,
signaling to the tribe that the enemy was near.

Every bird ceased its singing.
My cousin and I fell silent too.
We were still as the trees.
Split Feather raised his head to listen—

the high whine of a flying arrow.
The thud of arrow hitting flesh, cracking bone.
Split Feather's chest erupted in blood;
his eyes were wide; he died instantly.
The arrow passed through him as if
his body had been river mist.

Cousin ran across the water and vanished
into the woods at the far side of the creek.
I remained crouching by the stream.
Try as I might, I could not move.
Split Feather slumped onto his horse.
His eyes, open in death, watched me.
His body slid to the ground.

A Hidatsa warrior broke through the thicket.
He sat high atop a white horse.
In his left hand he held the rein.

In his right hand he held a long battle club.
He gestured with the club as if to say,
Now bow your head—you are mine.

Instead I stood.
I remembered the rock in my hand.
And I hurled it.
I managed to hit him between the eyes.
The warrior's expression was fear and surprise.

But then he smiled.
Blood streamed down his painted face,
across his white teeth.
He licked it from his lips,
his grin turning red.
As if in a dream I turned, like a doe, to leap
as the warrior on the white horse raised his club
and, still smiling,
brought it down
against my head.

Oolum ◈ *the newfoundland*

I mean to tell you this story in the only way I know how. That is to say, I will tell it like a river. It may meander here and there, but in the end it will always find its way to the sea.

Seaman is the name given to me by my human master, but my true name is Oolum. Every living thing has a true name, even though it may be buried under a lifetime of lies. Perk up your ears, open your eyes, lift your muzzle into the wind—eventually you will discover the true name of anything you wish. Maybe even your own.

As for me, Oolum is a name passed on through the ages. It was first given long ago by the Master of all Masters. Then it sailed across the water in search of new landscapes. I am the latest link in a lengthy chain.

My human master, Meriwether Lewis, purchased me for twenty dollars and trained me to accompany him on a dangerous expedition through an unknown wilderness. He named me Seaman because our ultimate destination was nothing less than the Pacific Ocean.

My appearance is typical of my breed. I am a Newfoundland. I am large (140 pounds, according to Captain Lewis). My coat is black as coal except for my front left paw, which is white from toe-tip to elbow, as if I were wearing a lady's dinner glove, and a diamond of white on my chest. I am stocky. Thick-furred. A water dog with webbed toes for swimming and a long, strong tail, tailor-made to be grabbed in a panic by drowning humans.

And I am a seer.

Though I cannot speak human languages, I understand them all, and on this journey there were many.

But there is one universal language shared by all living things. It is called Roloje. Ro-LO-jee. You feel it in your heart. You see it when you sleep. It is spoken through the eyes and carried on the air but never heard. It is the language of longing. It is the language of anticipation and exploration, hopes and dreams. This is how I speak. This is how I am speaking to you now.

Meriwether Lewis ◇ *the explorer*

The night after I brought the Newfoundland home
to my lodgings at the President's House,
I had the oddest dream.

I'm back East at Locust Hill, the old home place in Virginia,
dressed to go on a night hunt for raccoon and possum. I am my
present age, a grown man, and yet I'm in the same ridiculous hat I
used to wear as a child. I'm carrying the old British musket my
father would let me load for him, back before he died.

When I step outside my door, it is suddenly daylight, and
I'm standing alone on the edge of a river. The water level is high
and the current rapid and choppy. And my father is on the opposite bank—not my stepfather, but my natural father, William
Lewis. He is sitting straight in the saddle, and he is dressed in a
handsome officer's uniform.

Then he begins calling to me and riding toward me across
the river. He is smiling and glad to see me, and I am waving him
on. But his horse begins to lose its footing and slip. The water
swells and deepens. And almost in an instant, my father is gone
beneath the surface. The gray water bubbles and boils. Then all
is silent.

In the river, a final, single bubble rises. Nothing moves.
The water, the air, my own breath—everything is still.

A time goes by. Then a solitary bubble surfaces. To my
astonishment, an arm reaches up from the water. Then a second
arm, a head, and a body. The swollen river subsides, and the man
reemerges whole, stands, and begins to wade toward me. The
horse is gone. And the handsome uniform is gone. Instead the
man is in knee breeches and a fashionable jacket that reaches to
the tops of the high white woolen socks that cover his shins. He
wears slippers on his feet. There are white muslin ruffles at his

throat and wrists. In his hand, where there once was a sword, is now a book. His hair is white and his features are handsome. His face is resolute and he is looking at me and calling and walking quickly toward me as if nothing had happened. He is oblivious to the cold as if it were just a day in summer.

As he approaches more closely, I'm shocked to see that he is absolutely dry. And I'm shocked to see that he is not my father. And I'm shocked to see that he is in fact President Thomas Jefferson.

I call to him, "Are you all right?"

He doesn't hear me, and he answers only with, "Meriwether, my boy! Come quickly! And bring your gun. And bring your pen and inkstand. I have a very important job for you!"

Thomas Jefferson ◆ *the president*

To Captain Meriwether Lewis esq.
Captain of the 1ˢᵗ Regiment of Infantry of the U.S. of A.

The object of your mission is to explore the Missouri River, & such principal stream of it, as, by it's course and communication to discover the most direct & practicable all water route across this continent to the waters of the Pacific ocean (the so called Northwest Passage) for the purposes of commerce.

At all remarkable points on the river you are to take careful observations of latitude & longitude and compass. Along the way you should also endeavor to make yourself acquainted with the names and nature of any Indian nations you encounter. Treat them in the most friendly & conciliatory manner which their own conduct will admit and make them acquainted with the peaceable & commercial dispositions of the U.S.

As it is impossible for us to foresee in what manner you will be received by those people, whether with hospitality or hostility, to your own discretion therefore must be left the degree of danger you may risk, only saying we wish you to err on the side of your safety.

Given under my hand at the city of Washington
this 20ᵗʰ day of June 1803,
Thomas Jefferson
President, U.S. of A.

Meriwether Lewis ◈ *the explorer*

Washington
June 19, 1803

Dear Clark,

I have been intrusted by President Jefferson to lead an expedition across the continent, my main goal being to discover the elusive Northwest Passage. I say elusive since no living man in civilized society knows with certainty where it is located or indeed if it exists at all.

My plan is this: to travel by horse from Washington to Pittsburgh and once in Pittsburgh set out in a large keeled boat with a small crew, down the Ohio River. Along the way I will add recruits to my party and hopefully, my friend, you will join me as I pass through Kentucky. More soldiers will be waiting at Forts Massac and Kaskaskia farther downriver.

Together we will follow the Ohio to its end, turn into the Mississippi river and follow it northward to St. Louis, at which time we will turn up the Missouri River against its curent, westward and past the Mandan villages as far as possible untill our keelboat must be replaced by smaller canoes which will transport us to the headwaters of the Missouri in the Rocky Mountains.

Here we will seek out the Northwest Passage in order to execute portage across those mountains by foot or horseback. From the western side of the Rockies we will place our boats into whatever tributary will lead us to the Columbia River and thus the remainder of the way to the Pacific Ocean.

Along the way we are to write down extensive observations of any unusual plant and animal life we see and of the native people that we encounter. Celestial observations, weather patterns, geographical information & C. Your skill as a maker of maps would be invaluable.

I propose to you a joint command leading the expedition as equals in every way. Believe me there is no man on earth with whom I should feel equal pleasure in sharing the many fatigues, dangers, and honors of this mission.

My dear friend Clark.
We have been given the opportunity of a lifetime:
to fill in a thousand-mile gap in the map.
What we will find there, only God knows.
We shall leave civilization as simple officers.
We will return as national heroes.

With sincere and affectionate regard
Your friend & Humble Servant,
Meriwether Lewis

William Clark ◈ *the gentleman*

I am happily retired from the army now
and there is much to keep me here in Kentucky
but
today I received a very interesting letter,
a letter from my old friend Captain Meriwether Lewis.
After reading it over, I sat down on the porch
to contemplate and think.

There is much to keep me here in Kentucky
but
Lewis proposes that I accompany him
across the continent to the Pacific Ocean—
a mission from the president, he says.
I would be given the rank of captain
with a captain's pay and a large land grant
upon our return.
                    If we return.

And Lewis proposes that we be *co*-commanders.
Never in my experience in the military
have I heard of something so . . . unmilitary.

I like that.

Meriwether Lewis ◇ *the explorer*

Washington
July 2, 1803

Dear Mother,

The day after tomorrow I shall set out for the Western
Country; my absence will probably be equal to fifteen or
eighteen months; the nature of this expedition is by no
means dangerous, my rout will be altogether through tribes
of Indians who are perfectly friendly to the United States,
therefore consider the chances of life just as much in my
favor on this trip as I should conceive them were I to
remain at home for the same length of time. . . .

My mother will know that I'm lying.
Still, she will appreciate the gesture.

To explain to her the true nature of my mission
would not be prudent. There are spies everywhere,
and letters are not always read by friendly eyes.
I will be traveling much farther than I can confess to her,
all the way into the very heart of the continent
where no civilized man has ever been.

This is what I've been working toward all of my life.
My boyhood spent learning the ways of the wilderness.
My adulthood spent learning the ways of the military.
My time in Philadelphia
learning the ways of science:
botany, zoology, geography, celestial navigation.

Even my mother, so long ago,
taught me the medicinal nature of herbs.

I am meant to lead this expedition.
I am meant to discover what is out there.
So long as there is an empty space on the map
        there is an empty space in *me* as well.

Perhaps I will fill them both.

William Clark ◇ *the gentleman*

There is much to keep me here in Kentucky.
I have land and a plantation to oversee,
crops and livestock and slaves to tend.
Brother George is in bad health.
Brother George is in bad debt.
Brother Jonathan is newly moved here.
> And there is the young Miss J. H., in Virginia,
> whom I hope to make Mrs. W. C.
There is much to keep me here in Kentucky.

But then,
brother George *does* have brother Jonathan
and of course
the plantation may run *more* smoothly with*out* my help.
I am no farmer;
the crops will not weep for me.
> This journey would be an important public service.
> And to return a national hero
> would certainly further my campaign with Miss J. H.,
> not to mention her father.
My body servant, York,
is fat and could do with the exercise.

And I am a bit broad in the beam myself.

Oolum ⬦ *the newfoundland*

My paws ached. Master Lewis and I finally left Washington, and for a week we walked across the Appalachian Mountains, down a wide well-traveled road. Captain Lewis was mounted with a second packhorse in tow. I walked to the side of Lewis's horse, doing my best to keep up. I had never walked this much back in Washington. But each day, I felt a little stronger, and as we neared Pittsburgh, I began to forge ahead alone. I walked quickly, making a zigzag pattern across the trail. My thick coat was full of the dust that was everywhere. I panted in the hot sun and kept my nose low to the ground, picking up a thousand different scents.

After each exploration, I returned to Lewis wagging my tail and barking. I had never felt so alive. I was beginning to understand the force that drove Lewis to wander and explore.

The night before we arrived in Pittsburgh, we were camped just outside the city. I rose and left the circle of firelight to seek out a nearby spring. My nose told me it was there. The water was not cold, but it met the need. A slight breeze blew in from the west, and I raised my head to read the scents that it carried. I smelled livestock. Sweet cow dung. Dusty chicken feathers. The pungent stench of hogs. The rich mellow blood of slaughterhouses. The clean creosote smoke of wood burning hot in potbelly stoves. And the familiar bitter bite of human sewage.

There in the forest, alone in the dark, I had seen the entire city of Pittsburgh by simply lifting my head to sniff. I returned to the campfire to find Lewis asleep, a horse pistol loaded and primed nearby. I approached slowly and licked Lewis's lips, a gesture of respect more than affection.

At Lewis's feet, near the fire, I turned three times in a circle and rested my chin across my master's knees. I heard a wolf howling in the distance, so faintly that it may have been a dream.

Would wolves venture so close to a city filled with humans?

Sacagawea   ◇   *the bird woman*

Before I was taken from my people,
before the warrior on the white horse,
I was waiting every day to become a woman.

The blood had not yet begun to flow from inside me.
Until it did, I could not belong to Sitting Hawk.
When I was two, my father had promised me to him.
I was at peace with the match,
for though Sitting Hawk was much older than me,
he was an important scout who wore the skin of the wolf.
This was to bring great honor to my family.

But then our enemies came and took everything.
I was told that many in my family were killed:
My oldest brother, who was wise and well respected.
My mother, who taught me all that I know.
Is Sitting Hawk alive or dead?
I know not.

My captors treat me with kindness — mostly.
I live in the earth lodge
of the warrior on the white horse.
Living among the Indians here is a white man.
His name is Toussaint Charbonneau.
He is old and stinks of beaver musk.
I am told that Charbonneau wishes me to be his own.
But he is not like Sitting Hawk.
He is not of my people.

His face is hairy
and he never washes.

Oolum ◇ *the newfoundland*

Pittsburgh was a city of rivers. The Monongahela flowed in from the south, the Allegheny flowed in from the north, and where they met, the Ohio flowed west. The Ohio was the river down which my master wanted to go. But the boatwright, a Mr. Noah Johnson, was slow and difficult. He spent more time in the Green Tree Tavern than supervising the progress on Lewis's keelboat, which was already several weeks behind.

Captain Lewis's supplies were delivered to the fort where we stayed during our wait: food, clothing, equipment, guns, gifts for the Indians. A temporary crew of soldiers had been arranged to man the boat. Except for the boat itself, all was ready for departure.

Meanwhile, as each day passed, the rivers dropped lower and lower. Sandbars began to rise from the water like huge loaves of bread. Noah Johnson continued, at his slow and erratic pace, to build the keelboat. Lewis was left to simmer in his anger.

Only once during this time did I see my master smile. One day he burst from the post office, laughing and waving in the air a square of paper covered with human scribble. He gave me a pat on the head.

"Good news, Seaman," he said. "It is our letter from Kentucky."

William Clark ❖ *the gentleman*

Clarksville

July 18, 1803

Dear Lewis,

I received by yesterdays Mail, your letter of June 19th. The Contents of which I received with much pleasure. I will chearfully join you as co commander and partake of the dangers, difficulties, and fatigues, and I anticipate the honors & rewards of such an enterprise. This is an undertaking fraited with many difficulties, but My friend, I join you with hand & Heart and I do assure you that no man lives with whome I would perfur to undertake Such a Trip as yourself.

Word of your offer has Spred here and thus Several young men (Gentelmens sons) have applied to accompany us—as they are not accustomed to labour I am cautious in giveing them any encouragement. Instead I have engaged some men for the enterprise of a discription calculated to work & go thro' those labours & fatigues which will be necessary. Though they be Somewhat lacking in cultur I am confedent you will find them the best woodsmen & Hunters, of young men in this part of the Countrey, and of courageous and loyal disposition.

Oh hell,

I'll go.

Of *course* I'll go.

This is the opportunity of a lifetime.

Miss J. H., in Virginia, is not yet even of age.

My man York says he wants to shoot a buffalo.
And there is nothing in Kentucky that cannot keep.

And if I am killed?
Well, I suppose there are plenty of crops to ruin in heaven.
And my family members will join me there in time,

most of them.

> With every sincerity & frendship
> Your Obedient Servant,
> Wm. Clark

> Is it true what we read in the papers, that France has sold the entire Louisiana Country to the U.S.? Surely that gives our mission even greater importance and urgency, since this wold be the very country through which we are to travel. Pray let me here from you as Soon as possible.

Joseph and Reubin Field ◇ *the brothers*

Joseph   Reubin Field, I love you, Brother,
            but Lordy, you are dumber 'n a stump.
            Can't you see I'm tryin' t' git respectable?
            We ain't young boys any longer, you 'n I.

Reubin   I may not be smart as you, Brother Joe,
            but I know a once-in-a-lifetime oppertunity when I see it.
            And I see it now. William Clark says we'll see wonders
            beyond all imagination 'n be the toast o' Louisville.

Joseph   I got me a good honest trade
            and I got me a good woman,
            and I got me a good piece o' land right here on Pond Creek.
            Now, why would I want t' up and leave all that?
            So I can break my back rowin' a barge again' the current
            to God knows whar fer five dollars a month,
            sleeping on the ground with a bunch o' roughneck soldiers?

Reubin   What you got *here*, Joe?
            A job makin' salt fer Brother Zeek?
                  What kind o' work is *that* for a man?
            And you call Mary Myrtle a "good" woman?
                  Why she's more woman 'n you can handle
                      anyways!
                  Part wildcat, Mary Myrtle is.
            And if you're thinkin' that knob-hilled farm o' yours
                  is "a good piece o' land,"
                well, you're dumber 'n *I* am, Brother,
                  and that's some kind o' dumb!
            Owww! What'd you wallop me on the head fer?

Joseph That's fer yer words on Mary Myrtle.
Don't you talk sassy 'bout the woman I'm goin' t' marry,
Brother Reub, I swar t' Gawd.
All our lives you been draggin' me into trouble.

Reubin And jest think back on what fun we've had!
Oh Lordy, Joe,
don't grow up on me *now*!

Meriwether Lewis ◈ *the explorer*

Pittsburgh

August 3, 1803

Dear Clark,

Yours of July 18 has been duly received, and be assured I
feel myself much gratifyed with your decision; for I could
neither hope, wish, or expect from a union with any man
on earth, more perfect support or further aid in the discharge of the several duties of my mission, than that, which
I am confident I shall derive from being associated with
yourself.

    As to the purchase of Louisiana, your newspapers
are correct, it is now no secret; on the 14th of July President Jefferson received the treaty from Paris, by which
France has ceded to the U. States, not just the strategic
port of New Orleans as intended, but rather the whole of
Louisiana, for the price of 15 Millions of dollars. This territory includes all land east of the Rocky Mountains and
stretching to the farthest Northern tributaries of the Mississippi River.

And *that,* my fine Kentucky friend,
makes our voyage even more important than it already was.
President Jefferson has purchased Louisiana
and it is up to us and our maps to show him what he has bought.

In other words our mission has expanded.
Not only are we to search out the Northwest Passage (should it exist);
we are also now charged with determining
the very boundaries of the United States of America.

I feel as if I am setting out to determine
the very boundaries of myself as well.
As I define this country's borders
I shall also be defining Captain Meriwether Lewis.

That is if I'm ever allowed to leave Pittsburgh,
and I *will,* if I have to make the journey riding atop my dog, Seaman,
who has to date been the most reliable member of the expedition.

> I am detained here in Pittsburgh owing to the unpardonable
> negligence and inattention of the boat-builders who, unfor-
> tunately for me, are a set of most incorrigible drunkards.
>   I hope to be with you in Clarksville soon. Adieu and
> believe me your very sincere friend and associate,
> Meriwether Lewis

Meriwether Lewis ◇ *the explorer*

Mr. Johnson, you originally contracted to have my boat in readiness by July 20th. In this you failed me. You told me that you had trouble procuring timber. After the timber arrived, you were sick for nearly a week. The week after that, you returned to work drunk and quarreled with your assistants; half your crew quit on the spot. The drunken crew you *now* have is so far into their cups that they cannot tell the bow of the boat from the stern. My threats to deny you this contract have had no effect. And unfortunately there is no other boatwright within a hundred miles who can accommodate me at this late date. Shall I drop to my knees and beg? There is a drought on, Mr. Johnson, and the rivers are lower than most local folk recall them *ever* being. Please, sir. I am pleading with you, sir, in the name of Thomas Jefferson, the president of these United States, for whom I am working. *Please* finish this boat while there is yet water left in the river upon which to *float* it!

George Shannon ◇ *the kid*

I'm a talker.

My mom always said *George,*
if you were a blackberry,
you could talk your way out of a hungry bear's mouth.
   So I came to Pittsburgh to stay with Uncle Will
   while I went to school to study the law.
 At least that's what my mother thinks.
 The past few weeks I've been working
as an apprentice at the Tarascon Brothers Shipyard.
    My plan was to eventually hop on a ship
    bound for the open ocean.
   I figure I can always become a lawyer later
   but for now I want to live a little,
see the world,
  get my feet wet.

   Anybody can become a lawyer.
   I want to become something special.
   I want to accomplish
   something that no one else can top.

   I want to read my story in the history books.

Not like my father.
He worked like a dog doing ordinary things
and then he up and died just like that.
Well, that's not for me.

Now, today down at the Green Tree Tavern
the boys are all talking about this officer
        come to town to have a keelboat built
        to sail himself on an expedition of discovery
                to explore certain secret stretches of our great country
                that no other civilized man has yet seen.
Well, that sounds like the boat George Shannon has been waiting for.

Meriwether Lewis ◇ *the explorer*

The kid, George Shannon,
came to see me at my quarters.
He's got a big mouth, that boy,
but I like him nevertheless.
I sensed from his demeanor
that he may be a young man of breeding
so I asked after his lineage
and he spoke of an uncle
being the governor of Kentucky.
He was lying.
I asked him his age
and he said that he was eighteen years old,
another bold-faced lie, and I told him so.
I asked him about his parents
and he told me that his daddy had died.
I could tell he wasn't lying then.
I've agreed to take him onboard
for a seven-week trial period.
My dog seems to like him very much.

George Shannon ❖ *the kid*

Okay. So I altered a fact or two.
That was a mistake.
        Captain Lewis is nobody's fool.
        I just about ruined my chance there and then
but I thought fast and made him a deal.

I told Lewis I would
join on with Noah Johnson's crew for free!

           The river is so low that old man Tarascon
           wants to lay off workers till the shipyard picks up
           so he's glad to see me go.

Lewis gives me a sharp stare and says, "You get that keelboat
in the water and then we'll talk."

        So I get a couple of the other men
        from the yard to lend a hand,
        and before you know it, we got ourselves a boat
        and a whole mess of adventures ahead of us.

           And that old drunk Noah Johnson
           barely set foot outside the Green Tree Tavern.

When Captain Lewis saw his boat
ready for loading
and floating in the water as easy as a cork,

well, when Captain Lewis saw *that,*
he grinned and said
he'd sign me up "on trial."

Now, isn't that just grand.
My mother always wanted me to study law,
and now here I am . . . "on trial."

Oolum ◈ *the newfoundland*

During our long wait in Pittsburgh, I never left my master's side. The city was so different from our home in Washington. There were humans everywhere. The streets were well tended, some even paved in brick and stone. I smelled hat shops, shoe shops, and bakeries. The independent hogs, roaming freely, reminded me of Washington, and I always barked a greeting. There was much for a dog to see and do.

But with each passing day, Master Lewis grew more irritable. A less perceptive soul might have called him melancholy, moody, or depressed. But his anxiety was caused by simple lack of action. He had the heart of a boy and the body of a man. He was an explorer. He was a discoverer. Too long in any one place and he would turn his hungry gaze inward. Not even I could tell what he saw there—whatever it was, it brought him no joy.

Lewis filled his time as best he could, visiting the boat builders, gathering up stores, sizing up potential recruits, taking me out on an occasional hunt. During daylight hours he would write and write.

Finally, the boat was finished. In the privacy of his officer's quarters, on that night before we set out, Lewis bent over his maps. As if caressing the contours of a beloved child's face, my master traced his route with an ink-stained finger.

His finger moved along the line of the Ohio River, turned up at the Mississippi and sharply left along the Missouri, which bent upward in an arc. At the top of the map, his finger paused.

"The Mandan villages," he said. "Beyond this point, Seaman, no one knows. It will take a few months to get there, but once we leave the Mandan villages . . . once we leave the Mandans, we may as well be a flock of birds flying to the moon."

Then he smiled, turned out the lamp, and crawled into bed.

Sacagawea ◇ *the bird woman*

The Mandan villages are not far
from the Hidatsa village where I live.
If only my *own* people lived so close.
The Shoshone homeland where I come from
is located far to the west where the Missouri River ends
and the land of grass meets the Shining Mountains,
what the white men call the Rockies.
Among my people was a wise man named Swooping Eagle
who would tell tales of crossing those mountains
toward the place where the sun sets.
On the other side of the mountains, he said, is a great river.
He said the great river leads to an even greater lake
called the Lake of the Bad-Tasting Waters.
Swooping Eagle said that this lake
marks the place where the world ends.
He said there is nothing beyond its shore.
Many of my people thought that Swooping Eagle was lying.

But I believed.

I knew, because when I was a very young girl
I looked into the sky and saw a vision.
I saw a snow white brant flying west.
Then I leaped into the sky, and I *became* the bird.
And I flew over the Shining Mountains
in search of the place where the world ended.
But before I reached my destination
I was standing once again on the earth.
And I could see once again the white brant in the sky.
No matter how far up the white brant flies
it is always in my sight.

Patrick Gass ◇ *the carpenter*

I was sawing through a good straight poplar log,
patching the walls of the garrison
around the grounds of Fort Kaskaskia,
when Captain Bissell says the army is looking for volunteers
to go exploring way up the Missouri River.

Now, I hear tell that there is a tribe of Indians
up the Missouri, called the Mandans,
who farm crops and have huge gatherings
to sell and trade and meet and greet
and generally carry on
just like the county fairs back in Pennsylvania.
Not only that,
these Indians live in huge houses
built with thick wooden beams covered over in dirt.
I hear that their village is surrounded by a
blockade of wooden pillars for defense
just like the one I'm building here.

Wonder what kind of *trees* they've got out there.

York ◈ *the slave*

What's out there? Way out West?
Mister William says there's a whole mess o' freedom
for an industrious man to make use of.
>   *An industrious* white *man, he means.*
Sounds like a whole lot o' nothin' to me.
I've got everything *I* need right here in Kentucky.

I have belonged to Mister William long as I've been alive, I guess.
And he has always treated me with tenderness—mostly.
I've got to be the luckiest Negro man alive.
I wear nice clothes and good boots.
And I'm spared hard labor—mostly.
Why, across the river, in Louisville,
I've even got a wife 'n young'uns.
So when Mister William says we're going
to the end of the world and back,
I slap my knee and say, "Let's go!"
Just so long as I get back to Sally.
>   *'Course I don't say the Sally part out loud.*
>   *That wouldn't be my place.*
Yes, sir.
I've got about everything I could hope to have.
Except maybe my freedom.
>   *And I don't hope* much *for that.*
>   *What on earth would I do*
>   *with freedom?*

Hugh Hall ◇ *the drinker*

I'm telling you right here and right now,
there is not, there has never been, nor will there ever be
no damned Northwest Passage.
I know because it doesn't make any sense at all.
If it exists, some damned savage Indian
would have spilled the beans
a long, long time ago.
But now Captain Campbell tells us
some fancy-ass Virginia officers
are asking for volunteers
to find this passage that doesn't exist.
Well, I said, *count me in, Captain!*
'cause I'll do anything
I mean *anything*
to get out of this stinking latrine of a fort.
A man needs to stretch his legs.
And between you and me and the fence post,
I'm thinking that the army is just not the place for me.
Once I get far enough north,
why, I'll just go for a long walk,
and I won't stop until I'm back in Pennsylvania.
Back in civilization where a man
can get himself a proper bottle of whiskey.

Oolum   ♦ *the newfoundland*

Finally we left Pittsburgh. The boat builders had stayed sober long enough to fit the final plank into place and hammer home the last long-awaited nail. They had to season the hull in the river, allowing the water to swell the wood. Whatever seams still leaked afterward were sealed with pitch pine tar. The keelboat was complete. In just a few hours, Master Lewis had the boat loaded and ready for the river.

To lighten the load, Lewis sent a wagon containing provisions on to Wheeling, which we would pass through later. He also bought a large pirogue, an open boat with six oars and a small sail, to further ease the keelboat's burden.

The water was shallow and warm. Fun for me, but not for the men.

The crew was made up of seven soldiers, a local river pilot, and a few men from the shipyard, including the youngster, George Shannon. Shannon was tall and muscular, but still gawky. Somewhere between a puppy and a full-grown dog. Though he was young and inexperienced, he seemed intelligent beyond his years. He was educated, and most likable. He wore a fashionable overcoat and vest. Most gentlemen trusted him. Most ladies thought him rather good-looking. And though he talked more than any human I have met, Shannon always went out of his way to toss me a scrap or two.

Good kid.

George Shannon ◇ *the kid*

The entire town of Pittsburgh thinks we're loco.
And they're right.
> No one in his right mind
> would try to float a fifty-five-foot, twelve-ton barge
> down the Ohio with the water as low as it is.

Well, call us loco, 'cause we're doin' it.

> We've been at it now for a week.
> Seems like every hundred feet or so
> we run up on another sandbar.

So we hop in the river and rock the boat a bit
or else get out the shovels and start digging.

> If *that* doesn't work, we drag it along with ropes.

When *that* doesn't work,
Lewis hires some local farmer with a team of oxen
to tow us over the sand into deeper water.

> I have never worked so hard in all my life.

Captain Meriwether Lewis is a magician
and I'm watching him to see how he does it.

> I figure if he can turn an ox into a sailor,
> then maybe he can turn George Shannon
> into one too.

Oolum ◇ *the newfoundland*

*On the third day of our voyage down the Ohio, I had my first vision of
the bird woman.*

*During the night the temperature dropped. Cold air slid down the
slopes of the valley and slipped like a ghost across the river's warmer
waters. This cold air, heated and moistened from below, created rising
fog. It was as if the river was releasing whatever spirits it had captured
during the night.*

*It was in this thick mist that I saw her. She stood there, barely vis-
ible, hovering just above the water's surface in the middle of the river.
She wore a doeskin dress ornamented about the shoulders with an intri-
cate pattern of colored porcupine quills and glass beads. Otherwise
there was nothing remarkable about her attire. Her feet were bare.*

*She was watching our boat with hopeful eyes as if she was waiting
for us to bring her aboard. Then she smiled and began to place her fingers to her lips, repeating the gesture as if bringing food to her mouth.
She continued at this until she and the fog faded together.*

*My vision of her vanished just as Lewis declared that the crew
could safely see. My master grumbled about the delay he had been forced
to endure. It was late in the day, nearly eight A.M.*

*Just as the humans began their labor onward, a large flock of pas-
senger pigeons blotted out the sun—journeying to their winter home.*

Sacagawea ◇ *the bird woman*

For three winters I have lived among the enemy.
I have learned the Hidatsa language.
I have learned the Hidatsa ways.
I have learned to plant corn
and beans and squash.
Here no one goes hungry.
The hunters share their meat with all.
Here no one lives in fear.

Yet here I do not belong.
The Mandans and Hidatsa are a tall people
and their skin is fair.
I am small. My skin is dark.
And my heart is broken forever.
I will never see my family again.
I will never see Sitting Hawk again.
Hatred fights inside my chest
like two struggling wolves.

      I hate the Hidatsa for *bringing* me here.
      I hate myself for *liking* it here.

I never smile. I never laugh.
No man dares to touch me.
I do not love the Hidatsa boys
and they do not love me.

If only old, hairy Charbonneau
felt the same way.

Oolum ◇ *the newfoundland*

Fall had begun to work its magic. The cold mornings made me shiver through my fur, though the heat of the sun was unbearable by noon.

The birds continued to clutter the sky. On the ground the wingless animals were on the move as well, and once they reached the northern bank of the Ohio River, there was nothing to do but swim. In mid-September we began to see squirrels taking to the water. At first just a dozen or so. Then hundreds. And still more hundreds.

I am a water dog, after all. I know what to do around a river. Given my master's command, I jumped into the current and picked off the squirrels one after another. One after another, with a slight rush of savage adrenaline, I broke their backs with one swift bite. Then I swam back to Lewis, careful not to crush the lifeless creatures in my jaws.

Master Lewis and a few of the other men thought they were good eating. This is when I discovered that my master was a fair cook. With the same intensity he used to command the movement of his soldiers, he instructed a few of the men as to the proper way to fry squirrel.

Lewis was a man of the Enlightenment, so he had an inexhaustible need for knowledge. Even the mundane behavior of squirrels was a question to ponder, a riddle to answer. My master pensively picked at the squirrel meat. Then he stopped to dip the tip of a turkey feather into his inkwell. He narrowed his eyes. He began to scratch his human markings into his book.

I turned back to my meal. Fried squirrel is good. I ate mine bones and all.

Meriwether Lewis ◇ *the explorer*

Due to my observation
of hickory nuts and walnuts in abundance on both sides,
I deduced that the squirrels must have been migrating.
They certainly weren't swimming in search of food.
At first for sport, I would send my dog at them.
He would bring them back to me at the bow of the boat
and I would tie them all together with a bit of cord.
Later I would gut, skin, and fry the meat.
These squirrels were fat from the early autumn glut of nuts
and had a pleasant flavor. This migration went on for days.
Many of them were gray coated, though a good number
sported black fur. The clamor of hundreds of small bodies
darting across the river's surface was a sight to behold.

But on one occasion, as we navigated
down a stretch of the Ohio running south,
I chanced to see, among the frenzy of tiny swimmers,
one lone and determined squirrel
swimming west in opposition to all the others,
bumping noses now and then
with the rush of his oncoming brothers.
He alone was heading west,
swimming very light on the water
and making good speed.
My Newfoundland, Seaman, saw him
from a few yards away, and the chase was on.

George Shannon ◇ *the kid*

Tonight some of the men are tending to multiple
squirrels on spits, rotating them slowly over the fire.
Me, I'm frying mine in bear grease.
My buddy, Sea, caught nearly all of them himself
and it was easy pickin's.

But earlier today, Seaman lighted out
after this one loco squirrel trying to swim the wrong way!
Now, Lewis's dog is a natural swimmer.
He throws out his paws in front of his chest
with every stroke, like no dog I've ever seen.
His head is bobbing up and down
and with every bob he's gaining.
Meanwhile the poor squirrel is falling off in speed.

By this time all us men on the boat are whooping and hollering
and rooting for the dog just for the sport of it.
All the same
I'm rather hoping the dog doesn't catch him.

A few of the men are making wagers
one way or the other.
And just as that big dog is about to bite down
on the squirrel's tail, the little thing puts on a burst
of speed and bolts onto the riverbank!
SAFE!

All the men are clapping
        and spitting
                and stomping,
including those who lost their bets.

Even the dog is barking like he was happy for the chase,
not caring that the squirrel outran him.

And the squirrel,
wet as a fresh turd, is humping it up the slope
and twitching his tail like a victory dance
and chattering curses and chittering boasts
on account of his besting the big dog, I guess.

Oh, us boys were just beside ourselves!
It's been downright exhausting, all this tugging and pushing
on this heavy barge over these infernal sandbars
and with the rain pouring down hard all day
the boys were glad for a bit of mirth.

But then it all stops.

Suddenly we hear the hiss of powder flash
followed by a rifle blast.
Everyone shuts up quick.
And the little squirrel is lying,
shot dead,
under a young willow,
its bright white belly turned up to the sky
like a fallen flag of truce.

It's all silence, everywhere,
except for the creaking of the keelboat.

Even *I* don't know what to say.

That little critter was doing what I've always wanted.
It was swimming against the herd.
Going its own way.
Making a mark that distinguished it from all the others.

And we all look over to where the shot came from
and see Captain Lewis,
already reloading his rifle.
Lewis is all business as he packs a charge down the muzzle.

I guess he thought that dead squirrel
might just jump up

        and fire back.

Meriwether Lewis ◇ *the explorer*

I have gathered up the contrary squirrel
and examined it for clues.

What would make this particular individual
direct its movements against the migration?

I have cut the carcass open with my penknife
but its organs, bones, muscles, brain, blood:

none of these is irregular or ill shaped.
None of these speaks to me.

I can discover no evidence
that this individual was any different from the others.

It is as if this squirrel possessed something unseen
that escaped its skin as I made the incision.

Didn't I hear it whisper to me, after all?
Didn't I feel its spirit moving through me

as it fled?

Oolum ◇ *the newfoundland*

Lewis commanded that the crew stop at Wheeling to rest and gather the wagonload of supplies that had arrived overland from Pittsburgh. He purchased a second pirogue to carry the added weight.

After a week's rest, we set all three boats into the water and resumed the voyage. The water grew deeper and the river grew wider, and after that point, we were rarely slowed by sand. We made one hundred miles in a week, passing through Marietta, Parkersburg, and Huntington, until we finally reached Kentucky.

All this while my master was packing and repacking the boats, trying to keep his many possessions from getting wet. This is something humans do, unique to any other species of creature. Humans have possessions, which they attempt to carry with them at all costs. It is odd to me, but Captain Lewis would not consider leaving a single trinket behind.

Every other day, it seemed, my master would dismiss a crew member who displeased him. Every other day, it seemed, he would bring another volunteer onboard to replace the one he had just sent away. And so it went for days.

At Maysville, Kentucky, we brought aboard a scruffy-looking fellow named John Colter who was dressed in a buckskin hunting frock over a simple linen shirt and brown wool pants. His hair was oily under a crude skin cap. His fingers were black with gunpowder. In his arms, cradled like a baby, rested a Kentucky long rifle with a fine maple stock and brass fittings.

I could remember first seeing him back in Pittsburgh, with Shannon. I remember he hardly spoke (although when you are with Shannon, you do not get much chance). Colter was tall and strong and looked to be no stranger to the out-of-doors. He had blue eyes that he would turn on you only if there was a need.

John Colter ◇ *the hunter*

I grew up in Maysville, which ain't much more 'n
a couple log cabins 'n a ferryboat
that'll gitch you 'cross the Ohio
if'n you got someware t' go.
I've been livin' here in th' woods
near my whole life, no wife nor family
'cept fer Ma 'n Pa.

I been makin' good money
movin' goods up 'n down Zane's Trace,
between here 'n Wheeling,
then on to Pittsburgh,
an' I know these woods better 'n the bears do.
Now I'm near twenty-eight years old
an' I've had about enough o' goin' back 'n forth
along th' same ol' same ol'.

And it ain't the city life I's after.
Pittsburgh surely ain't fer me!
There's only hard labor to be found,
an' although they's plenty o' good whiskey,
they's just too many rules 'n laws 'n setch.
Now, I'm as honest as th' next man,
but I don't need no*body* tellin' me what t' do
'n when t' do it!
An' in the city they's just too many dang people.
Seems like you cain't spit without someone in yer business.

It's Pittsburgh where I first met Cap'n Lewis.
Met him on th' hunt. He's almost as good a shot as me—almost.
Lewis says t' get my business in order back home,

an' he'll pick me up on his way down th' Ohio.
Wants me t' be a soldier. Now, what about that?

I ain't much fer th' army life.
Me, I'd rather sit alone in th' woods, listenin'. Jest listenin'.
Jest me an' the trees, sittin' downwind of a white-tailed deer.
But the army's good steady pay. Five dollars a month!
Imagine gettin' that kind o' scratch fer rowin' a boat
an' seein' the world!

So I gathered up my gun 'n my good spare shirt
an' I climbed aboard today!
Private John Colter, haw!
I can shoot a chipmunk off a fence
at two hundred yards. It sure cain't be that hard
to cut m' hair,
shave m' whiskers,
larn t' salute
an' march about
in a fancy suit.

Pierre Cruzatte ◇ *the fiddler*

Ah, *merci.*
Thank you, *Madame La Rivière.*
Always give thanks to the river,
then watch well for clues.
Every set of rapids has a soft spot.
Even the most treacherous water
has hidden within it some secret easy path.
Watch it long enough, the path will show itself.
And as you travel through the foam,
be sure to say *pardonnez-moi,* river,
it is only I, your friend Pierre.
And once safely through, *mes amis,*
always say *merci.*

Oolum ❖ *the newfoundland*

On October 14 we pulled our boats ashore at the top of the Falls of the Ohio, a series of low limestone ledges that ran on some two miles before reaching the town of Clarksville below. The water ran fast and treacherous, and Lewis had to stop to hire local river men to guide us safely down.

Clarksville on one side of the river and Louisville on the other side marked the location of the old western frontier. Until recently this little outpost community was about as far west as any white settlers could safely go. Just one generation previous, William Clark's father had staked a claim here and fought dearly to keep it, as had every settler in the area. The citizens of Jefferson County were cut out of a rough cloth.

The banks were lined with cheering onlookers. Word had spread of our mission, and Clark, who had been awaiting our arrival for weeks, had been approached by several of the locals eager to sign up for the adventure.

None was as eager as Clark himself.

William Clark ◇ *the gentleman*

Today my good friend Lewis finally arrived.
York and I walked down to the foot of the falls
to meet the assortment of boats that was to be our little fleet.
The whole county must have been there
lining the banks to watch them come in.
Word gets around. I did my best to make the townsfolk
think that ours was a voyage to explore the northern Mississippi
but everyone knew it was more than that.
There was an excitement in the air not unlike the Fourth of July.

I first glimpsed Lewis as he was coming off the keelboat.
A huge black bear of a dog was at his heel.
I had not seen him in person for years but knew him instantly—
he was clothed in his military finery:
navy blue dress coat with silver lace
and the single silver epaulet on his shoulder,
which showed his rank—captain.
Black tasseled boots on his feet
and a bicorn hat atop his head.

> My man York says, "Mister William,
> we should have dressed proper for this meetin'.
> Here we stand in our breeches and shirtsleeves."

York was right; I was not dressed.
I must have appeared the ruffian.
And here came Lewis striding toward me,
the spitting image of Napoleon.
And a six-foot-tall Napoleon to boot.
That's about two feet more Napoleon than Napoleon himself.

Meriwether Lewis ◇ *the explorer*

I had dressed above the falls
in order to make the proper impression
when our boats landed below.
My meeting with Clark was, after all, a military matter.
And I wanted to send a message
to any locals with ideas of joining our crew:
this is not a pleasure trip nor a lark.

I knew Clark at once though he was dressed like the others.
He stood a few inches taller than most
and he had, of course, that head of red hair.
He was accompanied by his Negro servant.

I stepped off the boat with my dog at my side.
Clark strode over to face me and extended his hand.
He said nothing. Just smirked and spoke with his eyes.
I shook his hand and as I did, I felt a breeze rise up
and through me. I felt taller. Stronger. Wiser.
As though Clark and I were two minor gods
come down from Mount Olympus.
As though we two were the coachmen
and our cargo was mankind.

> Afterward Clark would lead the way up to his homestead,
> which would house our makeshift headquarters;
> there were local woodsmen to recruit,
> strategies to be devised;
> there was much to do.

But for the moment there was only our meeting
and just one word each:
"Lewis." "Clark."

In that instant,
with that handshake,
we two became as brothers.

Joseph and Reubin Field ♦ *the brothers*

Reubin   Come on now, Joe.
Why, out West they got monster buffalo t' hunt
and wildcats and big bull moose
and woolly mammoths with twenty-foot-long ivory tusks.
They got savage Indian warriors t' fight.
They got pretty Indian maidens t' woo—

Joseph   Now, you jest hold off there, Brother.
I done got a pretty maiden to woo
an' her name's Mary Myrtle.
Now, what do ya think,
that she'll jest set on her hands 'n wait
fer me to, *maybe*, drag whatever is left of me back home:
      shot up with Indian arrows
      and bald from bein' scalped?
      If I come home at all?
You think these Kentucky boys won't
be linin' up at her door stoop th' minute
I set off downriver?
A prize catch like Mary Myrtle?

Reubin   Now, you know your claim on Mary Myrtle will be safe
'cause you know the only man she really wants is *me*
and *I'll* be with *you*!
Owwww! What'd ya wallop me fer?

Joseph   Hush up about Mary Myrtle.
She won't give you th' time o' day, Reubin Field.

Reubin   Well, is that right? Jest this morning
she was downright chatty with me
an' told me if you was to bring her back a buffalo skin,
she guesses that she'd have you.
Though what she *sees* in you I jest can't tell.

Joseph   You jest shut up about Mary Myrtle.

Reubin   Hmf.

Joseph   Did she *really* say that—about th' buffalo?
What else'd she say?

William Clark ◇ *the gentleman*

Between Captain Lewis and myself,
Lewis is the better scientist and politician
and he can have all that.
It is I who have more experience on the river
and as a leader of troops.
And so command of the boats and men
will mostly fall to me.

It seems I was not meant to live
the easy life of a Kentucky planter,
      my wife at my side, my children running in the yard,
      a glass of brandy and a good cigar,
      York in knee breeches and fine white gloves
      holding a golden tray.

All in time, Clark. Family and fortune,
but first adventure and fame, eh?
And the life of a soldier.
Co-captain of the Corps of Discovery.

"York, man. Where are you?
There's someone at the door again!"

York ◇ *the slave*

The local boys have been coming by the house for days,
looking to join up with what Mister William has been calling
the Corps of Volunteers for Northwestern Discovery.
I've known some o' these men since they were *playing* soldier boy
killing redcoats 'n redskins with long sticks in place o' muskets.
Now here they all are joining the army for real.

There's Johnny Shields and Willy Bratton.
George Gibson and those crazy Field brothers, Joe'nReubin.
> *That's how it is with those brothers:*
> *Joe'nReubin is all one word.*
There's Nat Pryor and his cousin Charlie Floyd.
> *Now, Charlie is a good man.*
> *Black or white, Charlie Floyd*
> *may be the best of us all.*

All these men are unmarried on account o' they may get killed.
Mister William an' Captain Lewis wanted no husbands
nor daddies among them.

> So I say to Mister William,
> > *before I could stop myself*
> I say, "Mister William, what about *my* missus
> and *my* young'uns — all of 'em living across the river in
> Louisville?"

> He says back, "Easy now, York — watch your words."

And so I shall, Mister William. So I shall.
Besides, when I get way out west — with all that freedom,
> *I'm gonna shoot myself a fat buffalo.*

George Shannon ◇ *the kid*

Things are looking up for George Shannon.

I am getting an eyeful of new sights at every turn.
The Falls of the Ohio turned out to be nothing
but a long stretch o' white-water rapids.
No easy ride, but still not the monster they talk of back East.

It is interesting how your idea of things changes
with the benefit of firsthand experience:
The big becomes small. The small becomes big.
A waterfall becomes just a rapid. A rapid becomes just an eddy.
And a Negro becomes just a regular man.

By that last I refer to Clark's man, York.
There he was standing around talking
with all the other white boys
who were signing up for the tour.
There he was just shooting the breeze
as pretty as you please. Nothing unusual in that.
But I could not take my gaze from him.
Something was wrong with him.
Something was odd in the picture of him there.

Finally Colter saw me and says,
"What th' hell you lookin' at, Shannon?"

That's when it hit me.

"The gun," I said.

   York had a musket in the crook of his arm
   and a belt knife at his side.

"And the knife," I said. "I've never seen a Negro armed before."

All the men laughed out loud at that.
One of the Field brothers (I can't remember which)
slaps me on the back and says,

"Welcome to the wilderness, Tenderfoot!"

William Clark ◈ *the gentleman*

I have owned slaves
since the day I was born.

York's father belonged to *my* father
and it just makes sense that the son
of my father's body servant should belong to me.
All of us together, we are family.
It would be wrong to split up the family
for no good reason.
The Negroes are our children
and we have an obligation to take care of them.

Now, I understand that York
has got himself a woman and youngsters
across the river. God knows
when they might be sold away.
But York and I are family,
and family means forever.

Oolum ◇ *the newfoundland*

We left Clarksville behind after staying there for a week to gather up seven new humans. And to the man, these were a loud, rambunctious lot, but they knew the wilderness as only a man who is born and raised there can. Each human was steady as he stood. Strong. Muscular. And a sure shot. Where we were headed, there would be little room for softness. It was likely that not all who left on this voyage would return.

The Ohio's flow slowed with each passing day. The banks grew farther apart. Since the current was with us and the water was deep, our keelboat and pirogues made good time. After two weeks we came to at Fort Massac, just thirty miles upstream of where the Ohio empties into the Mississippi.

We were now a group of about twenty. We expected to pick up another small group of soldiers transferred to Lewis's command from a fort back East in Tennessee. But the soldiers had never arrived. Such was the way of the wilderness. The going was never easy and the way could take you days or weeks. Some folks simply started walking and were never seen again.

At Fort Massac, we met a woodsman, George Drouillard, who worked for the army as an interpreter and hunter, supplying fresh-killed meat for the men. He was a free spirit, dressed in Indian raiment, expressionless and silent as a stone. Unlike the white soldiers with their close-cropped heads, Drouillard let his long black hair hang loose down his back.

No man was the boss of him. When my master asked him to join the service and accompany us west, Drouillard flatly refused.

Meriwether Lewis ◇ *the explorer*

I have hired the half-breed Drouillard
to find the wayward Tennessee soldiers
and deliver them to our winter camp up in St. Louis.
He does not trust me.
He will not join our ranks permanently.
The fact is, though, we need his skills:
by all accounts he is an expert tracker and hunter,
and his role as interpreter is essential to our success.
The man speaks both French and English
as well as many of the native tongues.
And he is an expert in the art of hand signs
known by nearly all the different tribes.
I have offered to hire him as a civilian interpreter
at five times the monthly wages of the enlisted men.
He showed no response to any offer or entreaty.
I offered to advance him a couple months' pay.
He said simply,

> "The advance, then.
> And I will consider the permanent attachment.
> Give you an answer when I deliver your men to St. Louis."

I do not take his abruptness as any disrespect.
On the contrary, his unfriendly manner is quite honest.
I see in him a purity of purpose
and I see him looking for the same in me.

My purpose is simple.
I am going west.

York <> *the slave*

I was unloading supplies from the boat
when the half-breed tracker rides up
with a pack mule in tow, weighed down
with what looked to be bear meat
all dressed and bundled up
neat and tidy in its own black fur.

Just to make friendly I say,
"Afternoon, friend. I see you got a bear."
But he doesn't even look at me
on account o' he's staring and staring at Lewis's big dog,
who's standing by the water staring back
as if the two were long-lost cousins.
So I say, "That is Cap'n Lewis's dog.
He's what they call a Newfoundland.
He's a beaut, isn't he?"

Then without moving his eyes,
the tracker man says,
"Who is the girl?"
Now, I figure, this Indian has been in the sun too long
or else he's just having his fun
        'cause who cares about a damned ol'
        nigger man anyway, ain't that right?
I say, "Mister, I don't see anything but a big black dog."
He just looks down at me, like he's sizing me up,
and he looks at me for a good long minute.

Then he just says, "I see."
And trots up to the fort.

George Drouillard ◇ *the half-breed*

When I first saw the clumsy keelboat,
it was docked in the water by Fort Massac
as good as sinking up to its gunwales into the Ohio.
Only a white man would pack so much
to take on a trip upriver, against the current
and with winter coming on.

No Shawnee would be so stupid.

Even so, I have agreed to find Lewis's lost soldiers.
The money is good but it is not for the money that I do it.
     The land provides me all that I need.
And it is out of no great respect for the man Lewis.
     He is powerful, but there is a hole in his soul.
And it is not for the man Clark, who seems kind enough
     but is he not brother of George Rogers Clark,
       the man who drove the Shawnee from our homeland?

I have agreed to consider joining with them only
because of the vision down by the water:
the Indian girl standing by the bear dog.
She looked toward me with longing.

Then her name came to me on the breeze
from downstream. It was a distant whisper
as if it had traveled many miles
to reach my ears. It was a tongue unknown to me
but the sound was very clear:

sah-KAH-gah-WEE-yah.

Then, as if eating berries from the palm of her hand,
she brought her fingers to her lips again and again
and I recognized the movement as any Indian would,
a hand sign that means simply,

"My people."

Oolum ◇ *the newfoundland*

Our two days at Fort Massac seemed hardly worth the time. We left with only a couple new recruits, not counting the Indian interpreter, George Drouillard. And most of the soldiers were betting that Drouillard would simply keep the advance Lewis had paid him and disappear. But my master seemed sure of himself.

By then the Ohio was running fast and wide. There was relatively little hard labor to moving the boat downstream. Winter was on its way, so each night the men would set up tents on shore to protect themselves from the cold.

The two captains slept on board the boat mostly, where they were near their books and writing desks. Both slept on beds of rope woven into frames that folded down from the cabin walls. Most nights York and I slept outside on the boat's deck, under the stars.

In the night there was no human sound except for the occasional announcements of the men changing guard. There was wind off the river. The waves slapping against the keelboat's side. No intruder could possibly board the boat without waking me. I could produce a growl from deep inside that would sometimes frighten even myself. I was born with an instinct to fight, to defend . . . to kill. So are humans, although most will not admit it.

York ◇ *the slave*

Hey, Seaman,
you awake too, friend?
Just keeping watch like ol' York?
Heh, heh, heh.

I was just thinking on my wife and young'uns
back in ol' Kentuck.
There just isn't any contentment for the likes o' me, boy.
I can't allow my heart to settle
'cause before long I know
it'll be set down somewhere else.

I know it's best not to think on my young'uns
but I can't help it.
I can see 'em now, tearing around, kicking up dust.
You see, they're all young enough
so they don't know the whole truth o' things yet.

When Mister William and I were boys
growing up back in Virginia,
all the young'uns played together
black, white, slave, or free.
That was before we all got older
and learned which of us were the owners
and which of us were the owned.

We'd be out under God's blue sky for hours
playing tag, an' race, an' crack-the-whip.

Crack-the-whip. Heh, heh. Crack-the-whip.

Maybe eight or nine of us holding hands in a line.
We'd line up most times from biggest to smallest,
      sometimes from whitest to blackest.
On one end was the biggest boy standing in one spot
but turning slow like the hub of a wagon wheel
while the other little folks ran 'round 'n 'round 'n 'round
until the biggest young'un would start off running
then he'd cut a turn short and quick,
which would give the fellow at the other end
a flying tumble not soon forgotten.
Mister William, he was a bit older than me,
and at the time I wasn't so big as I am now,
so Mister William an' me made a good team:
Mister William was the flinger, an' York got flung.

Now, no child liked the getting flung part better than me.
Then one day Mister William was the whip handle
an' I was spinning 'round in a fury.
Mister William pulled up with a yank and I went flying
like a low-going turkey with a shot-off wing.
I was all legs an' arms an' laughing an' laughing
then *WHANG!* I run into the side of the outhouse
and get knocked out cold.

I came 'round but kept my eyes closed tight
and laid still just playing possum
like I was deader than a doornail.
And I could feel Mister William's hot tears dropping onto my face
an' I could hear him say,

"Oh, lovin' Jeezus! I've done gone an' killed my Negro.
And on a Sunday too!
Daddy'll take the switch to me and good!"

All the other young'uns had run off, an' there he was, kneeling
over top o' York wringing his hands, wishing I wasn't dead,
when suddenly I grin 'n bug my eyes open wide
an' Mister William lets out a squeal like a stepped-on piglet.
Then he smiles real big an' says, "York! You're not dead!"
Then he smacks me in the head.

An' without missing a breath, I say —
        "Pull me on up, Billy, and let's go again!"

An' he does.
An' we do.

Pierre Cruzatte ◇ *the fiddler*

Mes amis,
you see now how the one river
empties into the other?
For, of course, no river goes forever,
and where two rivers meet
is called a confluence.
A confluence is where two rivers
say *bonjour* one to the other.
A confluence is a rendezvous
and a sad adieu.
The rivers are no longer two,
but one.

Oolum ◇ *the newfoundland*

The Ohio had been flowing over nine hundred miles when it finally came to an end. Where it stopped, this pleasant river was consumed by the monstrous Mississippi, the power of which was more than we had counted on. Lewis and Clark commanded that the men set up camp for a week at the mouth of the Ohio to rest up for the next leg of the trip, sixty miles against the current upriver to Fort Kaskaskia. There they hoped more recruits would be available. Because of the missing Tennessee soldiers, the boats would all be undermanned.

During the day the captains would walk the land. Always in these early days of the expedition, York and I were with them. The four of us shared an odd camaraderie. One day, as we walked along the Mississippi shore, we were approached by a Shawnee Indian who offered my master three beaver skins in exchange for me. This was a shock. I was fully aware that Lewis had purchased me as any human might purchase a hat. But I had been with Lewis since I was a puppy, and I had never really felt "owned." I felt Lewis somehow needed me and so my station was secure. But here was a human who saw me as property.

Although I felt myself somewhat more enlightened than most humans I have met (my master included), I couldn't help but sense that there was something to be learned from Lewis. In fact, I was sure that there was something to learn from every man on the expedition. To be given to the Shawnee would have put an end to all of that. I was relieved when Lewis refused the offer.

I cut my eyes toward York, who was looking at me and grinning. White men couldn't read the black man's thoughts, but I could. And his thoughts were clear: That's right, Seaman, ol' boy. You jus' go on hoping like ol' York. You go on hoping that you're more 'n jus' a dog to your master. An' I'll go on hoping that I'm more 'n jus' a slave boy to mine. Switch rivers and you don't know what the new waters will bring.

Meriwether Lewis ◈ *the explorer*

November 16, 1803
Walking on shore with Clark, we met three friendly Indians of the Shawnee
nation. One of the Shawnees, a respectable looking Indian, offered me three
bever skins for my dog with which he appeared much pleased, the dog was
of the newfoundland breed, one that I prised much for his docility and quali-
fications generally for my journey.

Qualifications indeed.
There is something about the dog.
Something that I can't explain.
It makes no sense, but the dog
seems to understand what I say.
Even what I think.
Even though it is just an illusion,
the illusion is still a comfort to me.

So of course there was no bargan, I had given 20$ for this dogg myself.

William Clark ◈ *the gentleman*

Today we entered the hellish waters of the Mississippi!
And I fear we may not even make it alive to St. Louis.
Our pirogues and keelboat are drastically undermanned.
Our plan to keep our group to fifteen was a terrible miscalculation.
We'll need three *times* fifteen to muscle our way against this current.
The water spins and whirls and bats our boats about.
We try to keep close to the calmer waters near shore
but are then caught on sandbars and sunken logs,
which lay in wait for us like monstrous serpents.
The trees leaning over the banks threaten to snap our masts
and the banks themselves are not to be trusted—
they are there one instant and the next they have fallen
into the current, casting great clumps of earth
and whole trees toward us.

This great river is like a strange language
that I can neither read nor understand.
We row the boat to larboard and the river runs us starboard.
We attempt to wade in a shallow shoal
and sink past our heads into deep cold pools.
We hoist the sail to harness the wind
and the wind dies down to a whimper
or blows so hard it tears the sail.
For every mile the crow flies, this winding river meanders two!
Our average speed: one mile per hour.
Average miles traveled in a day: ten.
Miles left to go: 3,500.

Perhaps a planter's life was not so bad a thing.

Pierre Cruzatte ◇ *the fiddler*

Apply the oar and hoist the sail.
Roll on, roll on, roll on.
Hold tight the cord and catch the gale.
Roll on, roll on, roll on.

From morning fog to setting sun
Ye break yer back and when yer done
Ye come to where ye started from.
Roll on, roll on, roll on.

Roll on, roll on, my fair young maid.
Roll on, roll on, roll on.
Though ye be sad and sore afraid.
Roll on, roll on, roll on.

Though ye be sad and sore afraid.
Roll on, roll on, roll on.

Patrick Gass ◈ *the carpenter*

Welcome to Fort Kaskaskia, sirs.
I know that you've had a rough journey thus far,
and I know that you have plenty of soldiers to see,
so I thank you for taking the time to see me.
Now, Captain Bissell claims he can't spare me
but with all due respect, I'd like to plead my case.

Do I have any special skills?

Well, I'm a right handy carpenter.
With the proper tools and a few hands
I can clear you a field of trees in a week
and build you a cabin to boot.
Give me a broadax and a hewing dog
and I'll square the logs if you choose.
Give me a froe
and I'll build you a clapboard roof.
Give me a wedge and a maul
and I'll split a hundred rails in a day.
I can saddle-notch a log
or make a saddle for your horse.
Or a bed for to lay on or a bench for to sit on.
I know the ins and outs of raising a fort,
which I know you'll be needin' up north,
and with your permission, sirs, I've got an idea or two
to expand the capabilities of your keelboat.
I can row and push a setting pole.
I can shoot a gun and throw a hawk.
I can swim like a fish. I can run like the devil.
I'm strong and I'm fit.
I'm a soldier's soldier, sirs.

I never shirk and I do my work.
And I do the other feller's too.

What's that? *Why* do I want to join?

I mainly . . . Mainly, I want to see the trees.

William Clark ◇ *the gentleman*

And so we've added a carpenter to our crew
as well as a dozen other good men from Fort Kaskaskia.
These extra hands are most welcome.
Our winter camp near St. Louis
is still a difficult sixty miles up the Mississippi.

I've left Captain Lewis behind for a while
to make observations and watch the stars.
He'll catch up to us easily by riding on land.

Captain Lewis and Captain Clark,
how we share a destination
though we have our separate ways.

Captain Lewis has likened our party
to a flock of birds on a flight to the moon.
But to me we are just men,
without the gift of wings,
traveling by water without the gift of fins.
Were we birds, the way to St. Louis
would be an easy thing.
But this river has its own way,
winding as it will, here and there,
in no way straight,
and at every moment tossing obstacles
in our path.

I'm struck with how
like life the journey is.

George Drouillard ◈ *the half-breed*

I have discovered the lost soldiers from Tennessee.
It was not difficult.
White men move about the woods
like buffalo during the mating season.
Each white man makes the noise of ten Shawnee.
And so when I heard the sound of eighty,
I knew that the eight were close.

Except for one or two, this group is of no account.
Most of them stay drunk all through the day.
They jabber on about how fearless they are
and yet jump at the sound of a squirrel's chirp.

When I came upon their camp, I entered unchallenged.
No man was posted (or else he was asleep or drunk).
I could have slit their throats as they slept
and kept Lewis's cash advance.

Instead I woke them.
Their leader was happy to have the guide.
Most of the others were not—not an Indian.

The trip by land to St. Louis I'm guessing to be a month.
I have made up my mind: after I deliver these men,
I will tell Lewis and Clark that I want no part of their travels.
I have discovered all I need to discover about white men.

Let the spirit-girl named Sacagawea find another to help her.
Let the bear dog howl in my dreams.

I . . . will . . . not . . . go.

Oolum ◇ *the newfoundland*

As the December snows began to fall, we reached the mouth of a small river called Dubois, where it emptied its waters into the Mississippi on the Illinois shore. The captains had decided this would be the best place to set up camp and wait out the winter. Across the Mississippi, on the Louisiana side, the Missouri came to an end within view of the soldiers' camp.

There was much to be done. The first order of business would be the building of huts to protect the men from the cold. The keelboat and pirogues needed to undergo modifications. The backwoods Kentucky boys needed training in the ways of the army. There was hunting to be done and food supplies to be gathered. More presents for the Indians were needed.

My master, Lewis, spent most of his time down in St. Louis gathering supplies from the local merchants as well as information about the geography of the land we planned to journey through. St. Louis was a town made up mostly of French Canadians involved in the fur trade. These river people had grown up on the water and knew the Mississippi and the Missouri as well as they knew the sound of their own voices.

Our winter camp was to be home for the next five months. Our lively troupe was now faced with the first real challenge of the adventure: we were forced to sit still and wait. Waiting for Louisiana to officially be handed over to the United States. Waiting for the proper supplies to arrive. Waiting for the final crew to be selected. Waiting for the ice to break and the river to flow.

The waiting was torture enough without waking daily to see the Missouri River emptying itself into the current before us.

This was why they had come, to travel up this muddy, mysterious river. This was where the Missouri came to an end, yet no one knew where it began. The mouth of this river was, for them, a portal into the unknown.

But for now they had to wait, and wait, for spring.

Hugh Hall ◈ *the drinker*

Hello, friend, I didn't catch yer name. . . .
Good to meet ya, Collins. The name's Hugh Hall.
I see ya been to the local whiskey seller.
Mind if I sit a spell?
>　I been on the hoof for over a month now
>　following that damn half-breed Drouillard.

There was eight of us soldier boys from South West Point
making our way to Fort Massac.
We had stopped early to set up camp
>　and have a little tipple too
when all a sudden that crazy Indian just appears out of thin air.
And he's dressed a little like a white man
>　but mostly like an Indian.
And he tells Corp'ral Warfington that Lewis 'n Clark
had already moved on and done sent him to find us
and escort us up here to St. Louis.

"*Find* us?" I say. "I didn't know we were *lost*!"
Why, I told that half-breed then and there:
"Listen, chief, we don't need your kind to show us the way.
Captain John Campbell of the United States Army
chose me and these other fine boys for this mission
because we are expert woodsmen!"

Then that high 'n mighty Warfington
opens up his ugly mug and says, "Shut up, Hall!
The major chose you because yer a loud-mouth drunk
and he wanted to be shed of you!"

Now, I ask you, Collins, is that nice?

82

It was all I could do not to walk home to Pennsylvania
right then and there.
I may have a loud mouth, but I'm no drunk . . .
haw, haw, haw.
Not *yet,* anyway.

Hand me that bottle.

William Clark ◇ *the gentleman*

The interpreter Drouillard has agreed to stay on.
All men are busy about camp.
The ice flows in sheets down the river.
The huts are mostly built.
There are eggs, butter, and bread to be had
at Isaiah Joyner's farm nearby.
Today I write a letter to Julia's father,
and I think of her fair face the remainder of the day.
The memory of her warms me a bit
against this winter wind
as I make my home
in a makeshift mansion of rough-hewn logs,
an army camp in exchange for a plantation.
Ah, Julia.
I can almost see the image of her
standing down by the water,
standing next to Lewis's dog,
as if floating above the water.

Is she wearing a doeskin dress?
Did she blow me a kiss?

John Colter ◇ *the hunter*

I been huntin' my whole life
an' my whole life I ain't found
no single body who could do no better.
      Then along comes this half-breed Drouillard.
      George Drouillard is the Christian name his daddy give 'im.
      I hear tell his mama was Shawnee
      an' that he's scalped a white man or two.
      Hugh Hall even told me
      Drouillard scalped his own *daddy* alive!
Well, whether or not it's true,
I'll tell ya one thing certain—
that Indian can hunt.
That Indian can run.
That Indian can track.
That Indian can trap.
And he never cracks a smile
nor does he even hardly sweat.
Let Hugh Hall say what he says,
I'm gonna find out what makes that half-breed tick.
Even if'n I get scalped in the attempt.

York ◇ *the slave*

I spent most o' today breaking my back at the whipsaw,
cutting logs with Joe Whitehouse.

> That your real name? White House?
> 'Cause back East in Washington
> "The White House" is what the locals
> call the President's House
> on accounta it's all over whitewashed.
> I saw it once with Mister William,
> and you have *never* seen such a big fine house,
> set right in the middle of a field o' mud.
> President Jefferson lives there now
> on accounta he is the president, as you know.
> Now, President Jefferson has got himself
> a blackbird that does tricks
> like hopping up the stairs and such.

> I've seen it myself.

> After dark, Mr. Jefferson puts that blackbird away for the night
> in a iron cage hanging in the west window.
> Then he covers the cage with a cloth!
> Now, why do you suppose he does *that*?
> Why put a bird in a window
> then fix it so the bird can't see the view?

Yeah, Joe Whitehouse couldn't figure that one out either.
Whitehouse an' a lot o' the other boys
are already beginning to treat me just like one o' them.
Yessir, we talked an' talked an' talked
till that whipsaw nearly killed us.

William Clark ◈ *the gentleman*

These men are meant to be moving.
As winter wears on, the River Dubois has lowered to nearly nothing
and both the Missouri and the Mississippi are frozen over.

The camp huts are now built.
Other than target practice and hunting,
the men have no diversion but to drink and fight
and fight and drink.

It is as if all decorum and discipline
have stopped along with the flow of the river.

Reubin Field refuses to mount guard duty.
Hall and Collins, Reed and Newman, all drunk and out of order.
Even Colter is confined to camp for drunken misbehavior.

Behaving more like children than soldiers!

Spring is on its way, so the water will begin to move soon.
It can't be soon enough—this idleness is affecting even me.

And now what's *this*?
The farmer, Joyner, has come into camp
mad as a hornet,
shouting something about
his prize hog missing!

John Colter ◈ *the hunter*

I guess I've got a bit to learn about the army ways.
I have resolved to do better, though, 'n told the captains so.
My ten days' confinement to camp is finally done.
Cold 'n rain aside, it feels good to be back in the woods.

The squirrels are out,
'n I've been sent with Drouillard
to bag a few fer soup.

Huntin' squirrel is a delicate matter
which requires good aim 'n a little magic.
To shoot 'em straight on would mean
bone splinters in the meat fer certain.

So you aim your sights slightly off.
'N you fire jest an inch or two below.
It's the shock o' the lead ball hittin' the bark
that sends the fat fella tumblin'.

The carcass won't have a scratch,
as if that squirrel jest got tired
'n laid down 'n died right thar
to be scooped up and made into stew.

I guess aloud to Drouillard
that shootin' an Indian would be as easy as barkin' a squirrel
assumin' that Indian don't have a gun.

Drouillard don't smile nor frown.
He jest says,

"Yes,
but after you have killed that one Indian,
your gun will be empty
and the bows of that Indian's hundred brothers will be full.
On that day, the squirrels will make a stew of *you*."

I say, "I reckon I ought not shoot at that Indian
less'n he shoots at me first.
I don't even like the taste o' squirrel."

Drouillard says,
"Nor I. You're smart, Colter —
for a white man."

Then he smiles.

George Drouillard ◇ *the half-breed*

Today I told the white men that I will join in the journey,
although *not* as one of their soldiers.
I was surprised when both the captains welcomed me.
Perhaps they are better leaders than I thought.

Living among the Shawnee in the east
is a holy man called Tenskwatawa, the prophet.
He calls upon all native people
to band our spirits together as one spirit.
His vision is of all tribes uniting
from sea to sea, to live in peace as one tribe
or die in battle as one brave.

The spirit of the water—Sacagawea—says it over and over
and I see she means it. "My people. My people."
And yet she is plainly not Shawnee.
She is not of my people and I am not of hers.
And yet . . .

Perhaps it is these rivers. Perhaps it is the rivers
that carry the hopes of what might be and the dreams of what will be.
Just as these white chiefs, Lewis and Clark,
seek to unite the land from sea to sea,
so might the prophet do the same.

It seems that the rivers may be whispering secrets.
And if the water speaks to me,
who am I to close my ears?

Perhaps I have my own discoveries to make.

The winter finally broke and the rivers began to rise as the snows melted all around us. The warm winds came. The trees turned green and the birds arrived by the thousands. Every beautiful thing was in bloom. I followed my master Lewis about the mud-crusted streets of St. Louis as he gathered up last-minute provisions, wrote letters to the president, and tended to business with local government leaders.

Meanwhile, fifteen miles up the Mississippi, at the mouth of the River Dubois, Clark and the other men were ready to depart. By now the party consisted of about forty-five men. Some twenty-five of these men made up the Corps of Discovery, a special team that would attempt the actual trip all the way to the ocean and back. The other men, a mixture of soldiers and civilians hired temporarily as a support crew, were to go only partway. The keelboat would likely be too large to navigate the river as it neared the Missouri headwaters. The temporary crew would be needed to return the keelboat to St. Louis carrying letters, progress reports, and specimens bound for President Jefferson. The Corps of Discovery itself would continue on in smaller boats.

The keelboat was a large, cumbersome barge with decks on either end and a cabin at the stern. Mounted on the keelboat's bow was a small brass cannon. Two other guns, powerful blunderbusses, were mounted atop the cabin. Clark had had the guns mounted during the long winter wait. Patrick Gass had built large wooden locker-boxes along the inner length of each side of the boat. In the event of attack, the locker-boxes' lids could flip up, providing a defensive breastwork to hide behind.

The two other boats in the fleet, what the French call pirogues, were thirty-foot rowboats, both fitted, like the keelboat, with a mast and sail to take advantage of any helpful breeze. For defense a blunderbuss was mounted at the bow of each. In order to tell the pirogues apart from a distance, Clark had painted one red, the other white. The white pirogue held six soldiers. The red pirogue held a group of rowdy French river men who had been hired locally.

The captains determined that Clark would set out on Monday, May 14, and move the boats up the Missouri as far as nearby St. Charles. Master Lewis and I, after finishing our business in St. Louis, would travel overland to meet the expedition. From St. Charles we were to set off with the entire party intact.

But there was one final crew member yet to come aboard. He was a French Canadian, well known to the Frenchmen in the red pirogue as the best river pilot on the Missouri—despite the fact he had only one eye, and his one eye was nearsighted. His name to the captains would forever be Peter Cruzatte.

The other men just called him Pierre.

Pierre Cruzatte ◇ *the fiddler*

I can see, *mes amis,* I can see.
It is just that I have only the one good eye
and so I must be sure I know where to look.

Twenty miles upriver from St. Louis, for example,
the water is washing away the sandy bank. Do you see?
It may take a day or a week,
but once the sand under the bank is gone,
then *WHOOOSH!*—a mile-long stretch of the shore falls in!

Dirt, bushes, grass, rocks. All fall in.
Maybe even a buffalo or deer come to the river to drink.
But most of all, take note of the big oak tree.
He has been pulled into the river's flow.
The oak tree, he cannot swim, so he sinks.
His heavy roots, they stick fast in the river's muddy bottom,
but the tree's limbs, they are left to sweep back and forth
just under the surface—out of sight.
Can they be seen? *Non.*

What good is an extra eye when the dangers can't be seen?

My one eye is enough to see
the telltale swell of water that gives the hidden tree away.

And the day the soldiers pulled to at St. Charles
my one eye was all I needed
to see that their keelboat was loaded all wrong.

When going upriver, you must load the boat heavy up front,
so her bow will plow away floating logs.

The keelboat was packed heavy astern,
so the boat's nose rode up on top of whatever it happened to hit.

And it happened to hit the hidden oak tree.
No one died. But then there is another tree tomorrow.
And the next day there are two. The next day four.
So the captains were keen to have me aboard.
Even with just the one eye.

William Clark ❖ *the gentleman*

Orderly Book
St. Charles
May 16, 1804

Regarding tonight's celebration in town to which each member of
our party has been invited. Note the Commanding officer is full
assured that every man of his Detachment will have a true respect
for their own Dignity and not make it necessary for him to leave
St. Charles for a more retired situation. Any misconduct will be
subject to Court martial proceedings.

Signed Captain W. Clark, commanding.

Hugh Hall ◇ *the drinker*

Hey, Collins, lemme have a sip o' that coffee.
Whew, what a night!
I woke up this morning
covered in mud from head to toe
and propped up against a chestnut tree.
Haw, haw.
I was so lost,
I had to follow my own footprints
to find my way out o' the woods.
I had no idea where I was
nor how I got there.
But I'm guessin' by the looks o' my clothes
I must've had a roarin' good time!
Haw, haw.

What's wrong with *you*, Collins?
You look as bad as I feel.
What's that?
You're goin' to be court-martialed?
On account o' last night?
Absent without leave?
Sorry, Collins. That's rough.
You'll get the lash for certain.
What's that?
There's gonna be *two* men court-martialed?
Well, then,
who's the other poor fool?

Oh.

Oolum ◇ *the newfoundland*

Humans have a curious practice they call punishment.

It consists of either confinement, ritual beating, execution, or sometimes just a stern talking-to.

The human Hall did not come home. He said he was sorry and that he would do better. This seems unlikely, but the humans decided to give Hall only a stern talking-to.

The human Collins did not come home either, but he also acted rudely to many of the females at the dance. And later, he told Captain Clark exactly where to put his army regulations. Collins was given the ritual beating punishment.

Fifty lashes on his naked back.

With nine knotted leather straps.

Hugh Hall ◇ *the drinker*

Ouch, Collins.
I know that's gotta hurt somethin' awful.

Terrible doings, my friend.
Just terrible.
To whip a man like an uppity slave.
Still ya shouldn't o' said what you did about the captain.
Not out loud anyway.

I was just talkin' about it to Reed and Newman.
Sometimes it seems a soldier is treated
no better than a Negro field hand.

Just the same it *was* good of the captains
to allow us an extra gill
to celebrate us getting under way.
That crazy Frenchman, Pierre, has pulled out his fiddle,
and he's settin' it to life with a jig.

Why, Collins, you ain't even touched your cup.
Are you okay, friend?

Can *I* have it, then?

Meriwether Lewis ◇ *the explorer*

Yesterday, I *finally* completed my work in St. Louis.
Politics and paperwork, I tell you, will be the death of me.

I rode into St. Charles without further delay,
and today we turned our backs on the world.

Under three cheers from the gentlemen on the bank,
our little fleet cast off!

I feel the excitement of Columbus.
All my men are in good health and high spirits.

My dog runs about the boat licking each man's offered hand.
They expect to be gone two years—all of it together as a band.

From now until the time we return
these men and I will have no contact with civilization.

The wind picks up. The rain drenches us to the skin.
Darkness falls as we stop to encamp.

We have gone three miles.

Pierre Cruzatte ◇ *the fiddler*

Ye ring-tailed roarers, sing my song.
Roll on, roll on, roll on.
Step lively, lads—we'll soon be gone.
Roll on, roll on, roll on.

Farewell to all ye ladies fair.
Roll on, roll on, roll on.
Yon river rolls we know not where.
Roll on, roll on, roll on.

Roll on, roll on, roll on.

Part Two

St. Charles to the Teton Sioux

May 1804–September 1804

Arikara Villages
South Dakota
Reubin's Creek
Teton Sioux Council
Big Bend 30-mile detour
Teton River
Wyoming
Mountain of Little Devils
Yankton Sioux Council
Floyd
Rolote Creek
Floyd's Grave
Nebraska
Platte River
Oto & Missouri Council
Colorado
Kansas
Kansas River

Minnesota

Wisconsin

Iowa

MISSISSIPPI RIVER

Illinois

CREEK INDEPENDENCE

GOSLING LAKE

FOURTH OF JULY CREEK

St. Charles

RIVER DUBOIS

La Charette

Camp Dubois

CUPBOARD CREEK
NIGHTINGALE CREEK
MAST CREEK

St. Louis

OSAGE RIVER

Missouri

Oolum ◈ *the newfoundland*

We proceeded on. No one had forgotten the horrors of ascending the Mississippi last fall, so when the Missouri current showed itself to be more fierce and unpredictable than even the Mississippi, all hands knew the kind of hardships they were bound to endure.

The angry river was at flood level, so its main channels were too deep for setting poles to touch bottom. The crew mostly put their backs into rowing against the current. The current was fast and cluttered with debris. Entire trees crashed into the keelboat's hull with the force of a battering ram. Smaller limbs caught hold of the long oars and would not let go.

But slowly we made our way westward, past smaller and smaller towns along the way until finally passing La Charette, the last white settlement on the river. A breeze picked up. The sails were set.

In these first few weeks of the voyage, the humans were like rowdy, excited children, and yet to the man, all were frightened too. No one really knew what they would see. No one really knew what would become of them.

The wind died down. The sails were furled. The still air smelled of exhilaration and fear as the men took up their oars.

Hugh Hall ◇ *the drinker*

Push the oars forward. Pull the oars back.
Push the oars forward. Pull the oars back.

That was it. That was the last.
White settlement. On the river.

Push the oars forward. Pull the oars back.
Push the oars forward. Pull the oars back.

The trees along the banks. They're huge.
Limbs reaching out. Like arms. Over the water.

Push the oars forward. Pull the oars back.
Push the oars forward. Pull the oars back.

Now we're in Indian land.
The folks in La Charette said.
Upriver. Are numerous, warlike nations. Of savages.

Push the oars forward. Pull the oars back.
Push the oars forward. Pull the oars back.

Powerful. Gigantic. Treacherous and cruel.
And particularly. Hostile. To white men.

Push the oars forward. Pull the oars back.
Push the oars forward. Pull the oars back.

I need. A drink.

George Shannon ◆ *the kid*

Push the oars forward. Pull the oars back.
Push the oars forward. Pull the oars back.

Enough is enough! I thought we'd be. Seeing Indians.
All I see. Is Hugh Hall's back. In front of me.

Push the oars forward. Pull the oars back.

That's how you do it, you know. You watch the man's back.
And you match him. Stroke for stroke.

Push the oars forward. Pull the oars back.

Dig in, George Shannon. Dig in!
Don't give up. So soon.
You're just as good. As any man here.

Push the oars forward. Pull the oars back.

Oh, Lord. If I were to *crawl* to the Pacific.
On my hands and knees.
I would make better — *gasp* — time.

Push the oars forward. Pull the oars back.

No, George Shannon. This. Is what you're here for.
Success is never as you imagine. It.
Becoming. A man. Is not fast and flashy.
It is slow. Becoming a man. Is slow.
Now row!

Patrick Gass ◈ *the carpenter*

Push the oars forward. Pull the oars back.
Push the oars forward. Pull the oars back.

> The kid, Shannon. Isn't looking too good.
> I can tell he's hurting. 'Cause he stopped. Talking.

Push the oars forward. Pull the oars back.

> Hugh Hall is mouthing off. About gigantic Indians.
> The Field brothers aren't even. Breaking. A sweat.

Push the oars forward. Pull the oars back.

> We're running up. Near to the bank now.
> So I can see. The trees. Old growth.
> Oak. Ash. Walnut. Nice.

Push the oars forward. Pull the oars back.
Push the oars forward. Pull the oars back.

CRAAAACK!!

What the—
Sounded like an explosion. The keelboat is shuddering!
Pierre is cursing, part French, part Indian!
Somebody! Anybody, man the cannon!
A huge Indian is breaking through the trees.
Lifting our boat from the water like a twig!

God save us!

Pierre Cruzatte ◇ *the fiddler*

Facile? Non. Easy? No. There is no easy way to make a keelboat go *up* a river! You can sail, push, pull, or row. None is easy.

If the wind blows in the proper direction, run a sail up the mast. If the breeze is *too* strong, anchor to the bank, listen to the fiddle, and wait. Or else you will be killed.

When there is no breeze at all? Then use the setting poles. The men stay in place as they walk, while the boat, she moves upstream beneath their feet! Once each man reaches the back of the deck, he puts his pole back into the river and starts all over again. I have seen men walk a hundred miles this way, and never leave the boat!

If the water is swift, tie a strong rope to the bow. Grab the tow rope's other end and pull with all your might. And pull with all your life!

When ropes and setting poles won't do, then the crew has to take up the oars and row. And row. And row. And row. Ha!

The sergeant at the rudder steers close to shore. The shore-side crew can pull the boat along by grabbing the bushes while the river-side crew puts their backs into the oars. That, *mes amis,* is what we call bushwhacking.

And that, *mes amis,* is how we broke our mast. For when bush-whacking close to the bank, the trees on shore will lean over and . . . *CRACK!*

The boat, she will rock as if a cannonball struck her. You may think giant Indians are battering the bow.

Myself, I am half Omaha. Who am I to worry over Indians? Indians, they are smart. They will not rush to the river to kill us.

They will wait for the river to kill us first.

York ◇ *the slave*

I tend to Mister William as best I can,
with what the wilderness offers up.
An' it offers up plenty if you can just see it.
An' the farther I get from Kentucky, the more I see.
Like these sandbars that we all cuss so much:
they may block our passage but they're a good place to find greens to eat.
I swam out just this afternoon an' gathered up
wild cress an' tongue grass enough for whoever'd care.
That's what I do. I just jump overboard, swimming underwater
till I think my lungs might burst.
With my arms out an' my eyes closed I pretend that I'm flying,
an' imagine how far this river goes
an' feel a little bit o' myself being washed away
an' ending up somewhere warm an' free
from the sting of mosquitoes an' there's my Sally
in front of a house that belongs to us.
She's drying good fresh meat in the sun
an' she says, "Welcome home, Husband.
You've been gone from home too long."
An' my young'uns all gather 'round me
with fists full o' fresh-picked greens
an' those young'uns just singing away an' all smiles.
That's how I'm thinking as I climb back up
onto that big monster of a keelboat an' land
soft on my bare feet, dripping with river water.
I feel every scar on my back soothed and washed away.
I feel I've been baptized an' reborn.
Back onboard in time to make the supper an' see that late sun dim.
Then I hear Moses Reed, clear as a dinner bell:
"Clark's nigger sure can swim!"

Patrick Gass ◈ *the carpenter*

Push the oars forward. Pull the oars back.
Push the oars forward. Pull the oars back.

The woods here. Are so thick. It was not hard.
To find. A long, straight tree.

Push the oars forward. Pull the oars back.

They are so crowded. They can go. Nowhere.
But straight up. To reach. The sun.

Push the oars forward. Pull the oars back.

I fashioned a mast. Of ash.
By felling. And limbing. The tree.

Push the oars forward. Pull the oars back.

Nothing. More to it. Than that.
In the woods. Stand a hundred masts.
Waiting patiently. To be made.

Push the oars forward. Pull the oars back.
Push the oars forward. Pull the oars back.

This wilderness gives us.
Everything. We need.
Everything. But wind.
To fill the cursed sail!

William Clark ◈ *the gentleman*

Captain Lewis and I generally agree
that of all the Indian nations known to us
the Sioux will be the most dangerous.
And so it was with great joy that,
when Peter Cruzatte yelled out, "Rafts up ahead!"
we discovered, among the party of traders,
none other than old Pierre Dorion,
a Frenchman, and a friend of my brother George's
during the great War of Independence!

He has been living among the Sioux now
some twenty years and speaks the language fluently.
His skill as an interpreter may make the difference
between friendship and bloodshed.

He has agreed to proceed on with us
in exchange for a bottle of whiskey
and some gunpowder.

God is smiling down on us.

Joseph and Reubin Field ◈ *the brothers*

Push the oars forward. Pull the oars back.
Push the oars forward. Pull the oars back.

Reubin Joe?

Push the oars forward. Pull the oars back.

Joseph Yeah, Reub.

Push the oars forward. Pull the oars back.

Reubin When do ya s'pose we'll see some buffalo?

Push the oars forward. Pull the oars back.

Joseph I got no idea, Reub.

Push the oars forward. Pull the oars back.
Push the oars forward. Pull the oars back.

Reubin Hey, Joe?

Push the oars forward. Pull the oars back.

Joseph What, Reub?

Push the oars forward. Pull the oars back.

Reubin What if we row right past 'em?
If they show, do you s'pose we'll pull t' shore
an' take up our guns?

Push the oars forward. Pull the oars back.

Joseph   Heck no, Reubin. We're not even taking the time
to stop 'n cook a proper meal. Jest keep rowin'.

Push the oars forward. Pull the oars back.
Push the oars forward. Pull the oars back.

Reubin   Hey, Joe?

Push the oars forward. Pull the oars back.

Joseph   What?!

Push the oars forward. Pull the oars back.

Reubin   What if I sound out a loud roar like a buffalo cow in heat?
Then them buffalo bulls will swim right up t' the boat.

Push the oars forward. Pull the oars back.

Joseph   Shut up, Reub.

Meriwether Lewis ◇ *the explorer*

Now four hundred miles from St. Louis,
we reached the mouth of the Kansas River today
and so we'll camp here to make celestial observations
and thus fix our location on the map.
Captain Clark and I will also take time to doctor
the men's wounds and ailments as best we can.
At present many of the men are suffering
from inconvenient bouts of dysentery
as well as troublesome boils and tumors.
We've recommended them to drink
the cold clear deeper water of the river,
avoiding the scum that gathers at the surface.

Other than the poor quality of drinking water,
I cannot think of what the cause might be.
Each man is well exercised, of course,
and in excellent appetite — eating about ten pounds of meat daily,
and the meat has been abundant.
Some of the meat eaten is perhaps slightly spoiled
but not so that it smells rancid.
The mosquitoes swarm in clouds, enough to drive us mad.
Mosquitoes in themselves, of course, pose no threat to one's health.

Clark recently opened a boil on the chest of Hugh Hall
and drained an entire half-pint of fluid.
Hall, who likes his liquor,
commented that the liquid discharged
seemed to be equal in amount
to two full gills of whiskey.

Hugh Hall ◇ *the drinker*

Pssst. Collins. Don't shoot.
It's me, Hall.
I knew it was your turn at guard tonight
so I thought I'd stretch my legs and take a midnight walk.

I saw you looking at them whiskey kegs when I came up.
You must be thinkin' what I'm thinkin', eh?

Huh? We won't get into any trouble.
I'm tellin' you the reason you got your last lashing
is on accounta you got *caught*.
Then you pleaded "not guilty" like a fool.
Everyone knows if you plead "guilty" and promise you'll do better
you likely won't get lashed at all.
You gotta be smart, Collins.

Now, just look around.
That backwoods saint, Sergeant Floyd, is down by the boats.
Nobody here but you, me, and Lewis's dimwitted dog.
And the dog doesn't talk, so who's gonna know?

There now, that's the spirit.
And fill a cup up for yourself, too.
I'd like to make a toast:

> Here's to the great Misery River.
> May the fiery Whiskey River drown me first.

Fill 'er up again, Collins,
and this time pour me a double,

I feel another toast comin' on:

Here's to —

Sergeant Floyd!
I'm glad you're here, sir.
I just caught Collins, here, sneaking whiskey
under cover of darkness like a common rat.
Not only that,
he has also offended my honor
and tainted my good name
by tempting me to take a tiny tipple too!

Shame on you, Collins.

Shame on you.

William Clark ◇ *the gentleman*

Orderly Book
Camp Mouth of the Kanseis
June 29, 1804

A Court Martiall will Set this day at 11 oClock, consisting of five members, for the trial of John Collins and Hugh Hall, Confined on Charges exhibitied against them by Sergeant Floyd, agreeable to the articles of War.

John Collins charged with "getting drunk on his post this morning off of whiskey put under his charge as a Sentinal, and for Suffering Hugh Hall to draw whiskey out of the Said Barrel intended for the party."

> To this Charge the prisoner pleaded Not Guilty.
> The court are of oppionion that the prisoner is Guilty of the Charge and therefore sentence him to receive one hundred lashes on his bare Back.

Hugh Hall was brought before the court charged with "takeing whiskey out of the keg, intended for the party, Contrarry to all order, rule, or regulation."

> To this Charge the prisoner pleaded Guilty.
> The court find the prisoner Guilty and Sentence him to receive fifty Lashes on his bare Back.

The commanding Officers approve of the Sentence and order that the Punishment take place at half past three this evening.

Oolum ◈ *the newfoundland*

And so again the humans took to whipping their own kind. The strokes of the lash were applied well, and everyone took pleasure in the beating. Humans love their whiskey, though I cannot stand even the smell of it myself. The only clouded face in the crowd was that of York. He had seen and felt bloodied backs before. With every sharp slap of the strap, his face told how his own hard scars seemed to move beneath his shirt.

We set out an hour later, Hall and Collins groaning and weeping with every sweep of the oars.

A large wolf came to the bank and looked at the boats without fear. Three men took a shot at it but mysteriously missed. The wolf stood its ground, staring as if in a trance. All at once, the humans ceased their movement, as they realized the wild animal was looking at me.

Meriwether Lewis ◇ *the explorer*

Today is July the Fourth
and we welcomed the dawn with a blast from the cannon,
one shot that echoed up and down the Missouri for miles.

We proceeded on past a creek, thus far unnamed on the map
so I've named it Fourth of July 1804 Creek, and why not?

I walked on land with my dog
and together we climbed a high mound
where we were treated to an extensive view of the country.

The large clear lake I have named Gosling Lake
for the great number of geese floating there
tending their newborn broods.

The prairie is more vast than any I have ever seen,
the grass some four or five feet high.
It ripples and bends in the breeze
moving as if it were a green sea.
A beautiful sight to behold.

The hills and valleys are interspersed with trees
that cluster at the banks of yet another handsome creek.

This second creek I shall name Creek Independence
for today is a day of independence for me as well.
One year ago I was drinking a toast
to the president and bidding him adieu.
The next morning Seaman and I headed west,
and here we are still going.

We shall finish this day with a final cannon blast
and an extra gill of whiskey all around.

We deserve it.
For we lucky few shall discover
the new found lands of America.

Oolum ◈ *the newfoundland*

Cupboard Creek. Nightingale Creek. Mast Creek. Fourth of July Creek. Independence Creek. Gosling Lake. My master Lewis has a passion for naming things. All humans do. But few humans understand that any name is false unless it is embraced by that which is being named. For a name is not something that one person does to another; a name is who a person is.

I learned my true *name, as most dogs do, the very moment I was born. Then just before I was separated from my mother, she explained to me that I no longer belonged to her. From then on, she said, I was to be the property of humans who would never know my true name. They would give me a name of their own choice and* my future was to become their *future. That is the power of naming. Humans name a river because it makes them feel as if they own it. As if they can control it.*

Take Captain Clark's black man York, for example. Like me, York has a true name that is hidden deep inside. He probably does not even know it is there, because he is not listening for it. But it is there.

Everything in creation has a name that is true. The river knows its name. It whispers its name every day. York's name walks about inside his heart moaning, a forgotten ghost longing to be heard.

Mother warned me never to forget my name, for it would always be at the very center of my soul.

"Always remember your name, Oolum," she said to me. "For your true name is your compass needle's North. So long as you keep your true name in sight, you will never be completely lost."

York ◇ *the slave*

My name? My name's York.
I've got no last name —
that wouldn't be proper.
My daddy's name was York too.
An' my daddy belonged to Mister William's daddy.
You see,
we're all a family —
we've all got heritage.
Mister William isn't my daddy
an' he isn't my brother
but we're family just the same.
What am I gonna do with a last name?
Sign the Declaration o' Independence?
Ha, ha.
My name's York.
Plain
an'
simple.

Sacagawea ◇ *the bird woman*

The chief in the village of my captors
has named me Sacagawea.

In Hidatsa, my name means Bird Woman.

He does not call me this because of my childhood vision.
He calls me this because my eyes show no emotion
and my mouth never smiles nor frowns.
The line of my mouth is straight and hard
as a bird's beak, he says.

I like the name.
For the night after I became Sacagawea
a dream began to visit me in my sleep.

I began to dream of the birds.

Each time it visits, the dream is the same.
I am a snow white brant among a small motley flock
of eagles and sparrows and starlings,
of magpies and vultures and wrens.
And all of us are flying west
toward the Shining Mountains.

Toward my home.

Every night when I go to sleep
the birds bring hope in their beaks.

Oolum ◇ *the newfoundland*

Six hundred miles up the Missouri, more than two months since leaving our winter camp, we reached what the humans call the River Platte. As usual the men set up camp on a bank nearby in order to allow the captains to measure the movement of the moon, sun, and stars. To do so, they would stay up late into the night, Lewis holding a variety of odd brass contraptions close to his face and calling out numbers, Clark looking intently at a shiny ticking bauble that I could recognize as a timepiece. Clark would scratch writing on paper to note the numbers and measurements.

Over the winter, local voyagers and trappers in St. Louis told Lewis and Clark generally where many Indian nations might be settled along the Missouri. So they knew that, not one mile away, westward up the River Platte, there was a village of Oto and Missouri Indians.

As is their way, Lewis and Clark gave the encampment a name. Named for a very unusual creature one of the men had caught in a nearby pond, the spot was dubbed White Catfish Camp.

George Drouillard ◇ *the half-breed*

Today the men are tending to the boats
and drying out the goods and cleaning the guns.
But I am laying beaver traps in the still water of a pond,
up to my waist in the coolness it offers.
The sun is very hot, so this task is welcome.

Lewis and Clark are delaying here to meet with the Otos nearby.
But when Pierre and I made our way to the Indian village,
there was not a soul to be found — no doubt following the buffalo
and I hope they stay away. My heart is troubled.
The captains will tell these people that Thomas Jefferson
has purchased ancient Indian ancestral lands from Napoleon.
So the Indians are now to consider themselves
the children of the "Great White Father in the East."
Who is Jefferson? Who is Napoleon? This will make no sense.

I bait my traps with the scent of the animal I stalk.
I set my traps underwater to mask the smell of murder.
I drive a stake into the pond floor to keep the animal
from swimming away with the trap on its leg.
I submerge the trap deep so that the caught creature
will drown quickly before it has time to chew its way free.

I am lost in my task when a moccasined foot
appears at the bank of the pond.
I stand to see a beaded doeskin dress. A vision of Sacagawea?
No. This is no vision. And no woman. But no warrior either.
The young Missouri Indian smiles
and clasps his hands in front of his body, to signal friendship.
Then he holds out a basket and offers me grapes.

William Clark ◇ *the gentleman*

And so we have met with our first Indian,
a man of the Missouri tribe,
who appears to be more of a wood sprite
than a dangerous savage.

I have chosen one of the French *engagés*, La Liberty,
to follow the young Missouri man to the Otos' encampment
to invite the chiefs to our camp, upriver, for a council.

I fear that the absence of hostile natives
on this stretch of the lower Missouri is making the men careless.
I was compelled to punish one private for sleeping on guard duty.
Twenty-five lashes each day for four days.
It will not hurt the man much but will send a message to the others:
This is no pleasure trip.

    Unless you consider that many nations, hungry for guns,
    would take *pleasure* in killing us farther upstream.

Meanwhile all hands are ready to set out.
One man, Willard, dropped his rifle in the river.
Reubin Field jumped in and brought it back up.

Joseph and Reubin Field ◈ *the brothers*

Joseph   Hey, Reubin! We got t' get back t' camp and quick.
You won't believe what I jest shot out on the prairie!
Look at this thing, will ye?
Cap'n Lewis is goin' t' want t' see *this*.

Reubin   What in th' name of Sam *is* it?

Joseph   I got no idea, Brother,
but ain't it th' peculiarest-lookin' critter
you ever laid yer eyes on?
It's the shape 'n size of a beaver,
but it's got th' markin's of a skunk.

Reubin   An' a head like a dawg. An' a tail like a groundhog.

Joseph   And look at th' claws on its forelegs . . .

Reubin   Like a bear.

Joseph   And its hind legs is stumpy and pigeon-toed . . .

Reubin   like Mary Myrtle!

Joseph   Shut up, Reubin.

Meriwether Lewis ◇ *the explorer*

After observing and recording its measurements,
I skinned and stuffed the odd creature found by the Field brothers.

The animal life in this paradise
has provided me a few surprises—
I have been lucky to discover
many species of creatures unknown to science.

Although snakes have been scarce of late,
one specimen appeared to me as I walked on shore—
a rattler, enormous and pale, the likes of which I've never seen before:

    Five feet, two inches long,
    four and a half inches thick,
    Two hundred seventy-four scales
    on its belly and tail.

It moved with grace and surprising speed
before I killed it.

George Drouillard ◈ *the half-breed*

Before I gave up the ways of the white man for good,
I was taught, by the Black-Robes, about Noah.

Noah was a white man who built a large ship
to carry his family and every kind of creature on earth.

As I see it, Captain Lewis, in his big keelboat,
is a kind of Noah himself—
traveling toward the mountains
into a strange pure world untouched by sin,
and gathering up God's creatures as he goes.

Difference is
most of Lewis's creatures are dead

and stuffed.

Hugh Hall ◇ *the drinker*

Why, Moses Reed, your cup is already empty.
Here, friend, have half of mine.
Oh, don't you mention it —
what's a little whiskey among like-minded men?
The way I see it, you and I are cut from the same cloth —
the army jest isn't your style, is it?
Well, mine neither.

Now, I figure the time is about right
for me to take my leave of this grand adventure
before I lose my scalp.
These Otos and Missouris are friendly enough,
but even Captain Clark says we'll be whistlin' past the graveyard
when we pass through Sioux land upriver.

So I was thinkin', Reed.
The journey back to Pennsylvania would be
a mighty bit safer for a party of two.

      What? Collins?
      Ever since his little whippin', Collins has been actin'
      all responsible and trustworthy — like he's too good
      for the likes of us. Well, *forget* Collins.

What do you say, Reed?
We'll leave this miserable river behind.
      We can travel faster overland on foot.
We'll have guns, lead, and powder
      all compliments of the U.S. army.
We'll be a hundred miles away before they even *miss* us.

Why I bet Lewis and Clark won't even pause a moment,
they being so hell-bent on their suicidal trip
into the midst of murdering savages.

Here, Reed, have a bit more of my cup.

George Shannon ◇ *the kid*

Slowly
my muscles are growing
accustomed to the endless rowing
and pushing and pulling and poling.

> The rowing is the worst for me
> not because of the backbreaking work—
> > I'll pull my weight like the other men—
> but because I can't face forward.

> I don't like seeing where I've already been.
> I want to see where I'm headed!

Today I assisted the bowman, Pierre,
who stands at the nose of the boat
with a pole at the ready to push off driftwood
and watches upstream to calculate the most beneficial
approach to a bend or the least dangerous path around a sandbar.

> The things he does with his one good eye
> inspire me to do double duty with my own.

Pierre says,
"An extra eye, he does no good
if he's looking in the wrong direction."

> Now, that's more than any law school would teach me
> and the lesson was free!

I think my mother would be proud of me.

Pierre Cruzatte ◇ *the fiddler*

Rapidement.
Quickly.

To make decisions and make them quick.
That is the bowman's job.
And I figure that my having just the one good eye
works out in my favor.

The points of view, they are fewer for me,
so I make decisions quick,
the same way I play the fiddle at camp,
the notes coming out of the fiddle —
all follow the fellow who's got his hand on the bow.

The bow of a fiddle?
The bow of a boat?
They'll both get you somewhere
if you guide them in the proper way.

Rapidement.
Quickly.

Hugh Hall ◇ *the drinker*

Hey, Reed.
You hear what they're saying about La Liberty,
that half-breed Frenchman they sent to the Oto village?

They say he ran off!
Just as free as you please.

Now, isn't that just like a half-breed?
No loyalty. No honor. No respect.
La Liberty's done us a great disservice:

> Now that one man's already deserted,
> the captains will be on their guard.
> So it's goin' to be harder for us
> to slip off without causing suspicion.

Why, that Frenchman's not even a soldier.
What right does *he* have to desert?

George Shannon ◇ *the kid*

The sun was scorching us like eggs on a griddle.
Many of the men had stripped to nearly nothing as
we leaned into our setting poles to make the long slow walk
down the length of the keelboat's deck.
The deck is cleated with strips of wood to give us a better foothold.
At the end of the boat we walked back to the bow
and we started the leaning and walking again.

> Then that crazy Frenchman, Pierre, at the bow
> started yelling out, "*Plumes d'ange! Plumes d'ange!*
> The water, she is covered with angel feathers!"

> I thought at first that Pierre had been sun-struck,
> but then I looked and I saw he was telling the truth.

Upriver of us, floating on the water,
was a solid swath of white, some sixty yards wide.
From far away we thought it was a thin layer of dense fog.
Closer and we thought it was flowers.
When finally the boat was upon this sea of white,
Pierre cried out again, "Angel feathers!"

> And so it was.
> A stretch of brilliant white feathers adorned the river
> and it did so for three whole miles!

Now, *here* is a thing few men have done—
sailed a ship
through miles of feathers
cast off from angel wings!

Meriwether Lewis ◇ *the explorer*

The sight *was* beautiful
as if from heaven—

and yet this was *not* the work of angels.

The feathers were from pelicans,
hundreds of them nesting on an island upriver.

I had never seen a living specimen myself,
and so I killed one to examine it.

But the Frenchman's "angels"
turned out to be a miracle after all

> when upon experiment, I discovered
> the bird's amazing pouch was capable
> of holding five entire gallons
> of the Missouri River's

> "holy water."

George Drouillard ◇ *the half-breed*

I carry with me a medicine pouch,
which holds several items invested with power.
I cannot let you see
and I cannot tell you
exactly what it holds.
The contents are sacred to me alone.
The contents are meant for my eyes alone.

I will tell you only this:

Not too many sleeps ago, I gathered beaver traps
carelessly set by some of the other men.
One of the traps held only
the bones of a beaver's crushed foot.

> The trap had not been staked well.
> So the desperate animal swam, trap and all, to the bank.
> After failing in its attempts to gnaw the hard metal,
> it turned its attention to its own softer flesh.
> And after this grisly task was done
> it crawled away to live or to die as nature chose.
> The beaver's foot, left alone on the bank,
> was surrounded by hungry ravens
> that picked it clean of flesh and fur
> and left it to turn chalk white in the sun.

I was not there to see, but I know it happened.

As I freed the severed foot from the trap,
the small bones spoke and they asked me this:

> *How far will you travel*
> *to discover who you are?*

I will not tell you what I carry
in my sacred medicine pouch,
only this that I have said.

Hugh Hall ◈ *the drinker*

That good-fer-nothin', low-down Moses Reed!
He said two days ago that he was leaving to fetch
a knife that he left back at camp downriver.

And now it's looking like he's run off!
First La Liberty and now Reed.

And to think I shared my hard-earned whiskey
with that no-account, cowardly deserter . . .

    and he didn't even invite me along!

William Clark ❖ *the gentleman*

Tuesday, August 7, 1804

*Last night at 8 oClock a storm from the N.W. which lasted 3/4 of an hour.
Set out late this morning. Wind from the North.*

*At 1 oClock dispatched George Drewyer with 3 men to find the missing
engagé La Liberty, and go to Village of Ottoes & Missouries to invite their
cheifes to a council at our camp here near the Omaha village.*

*Also gave to Drewyer and men task to find the Deserter Reed with order
if he did not give up Peaceibly to put him to Death &c.*

Joseph and Reubin Field ◇ *the brothers*

Joseph Why the cap'ns are sending you off with Drouillard
without me goin' too, I'll never know.

Reubin They jest know that I'm th' better hunter's all.

Joseph Stop yer foolin', Reubin.
You jest remember that, this time,
yer huntin' a man with a gun,
an' he don't want t' be found.

Reubin We're goin' as a pack, Brother.
An' if he so much as looks at me wrong,
I'll shoot that lowlife deserter, Reed,
like th' sorry dog that he is!

Joseph You do what you got t' do, Reub,
but you come back alive, ya hear?
Remember you got t' stand as my best man
when me 'n Mary Myrtle hitch it up.

Reubin I reckon I can stay alive long enough t' be best man.
Although once Mary Myrtle sees us standin' side by side,
she may jest change 'er mind 'n marry me instead.

Joseph Well, then I'll shoot you dead myself
an' I'll feed yer carcass to Mary Myrtle's hogs.
But don't let that skunk Reed get a shot at you.

He ain't even kin.

Oolum ◇ *the newfoundland*

The men had been moving at a good pace, traveling sometimes up to twenty miles in a day. The river snaked in every direction and in places nearly circled back around upon itself. Sometimes it seemed as if this river were going nowhere at all.

It was easy for the wolves on land to keep up with us. Sometimes there would be just one. Sometimes there were many. It struck me how they looked so much like me, and yet they looked so different.

The wolves seemed to be the rough-hewn early idea of a dog, left unfinished by God. Their movements were wild and agitated, as if they never knew a moment of peace.

One evening, with the keelboat anchored near a sandbar in the middle of the river, a wolf that looked like no other came to the bank and barked. It seemed to be surveying the men, as if it were looking for a familiar face.

I could tell it was a fully grown male, and yet it was small, perhaps only half the size of the other wolves we have seen. Its muzzle was sharper and more delicate than that of a wolf. And its fur was lighter and a bit more fine.

Master Lewis, of course, tried to shoot the odd creature at once. It dodged and barked with angry indignity. Surprisingly its bark was just as ferocious as my own can be. More men tried to kill it, but it ran off.

"What a curious animal," Lewis said. "It looks so much like a wolf, and yet it looks so different. What on earth do you suppose that creature is?"

143

Sacagawea ◇ *the bird woman*

When the world was very young
it was Coyote, the Father,
who molded men from the land's red clay.

Coyote watches over his creations
and mostly hides his face from view.

But from time to time Coyote emerges
to take a soul away.

Away to the land of the Father.
He is the father of all fathers.
He is Coyote.

George Drouillard ◇ *the half-breed*

The track of a white man
is easy enough to follow.

The track of a white man
who is trying to run away
is easier still.

I found him by the afternoon of the second day
but we waited for Reed to settle in to sleep.

Forced confrontation would have been quicker,
but I am no white soldier. I had no mind to kill this man.
If the other three did so, so be it.

As Reed snored, we spread out and entered his camp at angles,
positioning ourselves to avoid being caught in the crossfire.
I picked up his rifle,
which was leaning against a tree out of his reach —
it was not even loaded.

Reubin Field, who is surprisingly silent when he needs to be,
tied Reed's hands without even waking him.
We all four feasted on the rabbit,
still warm, on the spit, above the orange embers
of his cooking fire,

speaking softly
so as not to wake him up
too soon.

John Colter ◇ *the hunter*

So George Drouillard was sent out
t' find the two deserters
an' bring on the Oto chiefs as well.

By now no one was surprised when, five days later,
he an' the others came into camp
with Moses Reed, tied to a lead rope, walkin' ahead
an' about ten Indians walkin' behind.
Reubin Field tells me Drouillard found La Liberty as well,
but the Frenchman somehow "slipped away."

"Slipped away, did he, George?" I asked 'im later.
Drouillard looked away an' said,

> "My gun was not loaded.
> He slipped away.
> He is a *métis* like me, half Oto.
> There was no finding him on Oto land."

I didn't press him for details,
an' since La Liberty wasn't an enlisted soldier,
I imagine Lewis 'n Clark didn't press him neither.

So th' Frenchman slipped away.
So th' gun wasn't loaded.

I've learned many things from Drouillard since startin' out.
Number one among 'em is
Never, never, never
leave your gun unloaded.

Meriwether Lewis ◈ *the explorer*

Today is my birthday
but any joy in it was nearly ruined by the punishment of Reed.
He confessed to deserting and stealing the rifle, the powder, and balls,
and he requested that we be kind—

    I feel it was a kindness not to have him put to death.

We sentenced him only to running the gauntlet
four times through the party

        walking between the men in two ranks
        each man holding nine switches.

He will no longer be considered a member of the party.
He will not be allowed to carry a gun.
We will send him back to St. Louis on the keelboat in the spring.

In my eyes he is a coward and no longer exists.

I will close the day with an extra gill for all.
Come now, come now, men. We have a new land to discover!
And I'm thirty years young today!
Peter Cruzatte, you old water dog,
grab your merry fiddle up,
and play!

York ◇ *the slave*

Seems to me the farther we get from civilization
the less of a slave ol' York becomes.
> Oh, I still work hard,
> but then *every* man here works hard.
> There's too much hardship on this trek
> to heap it all on the back o' just one black man.
No, I'm treated fair an' equal by the others — mostly.
> Equal as can be hoped, I guess.

'Course, the captains won't have me whip a white man.
> Much as I don't care for Reed.
Naw, I just stayed away from the badness
an' made like I was busy minding to this an' to that,
the way I always do when these white men commence whipping.

Then to celebrate Cap'n Lewis's birthday,
I danced in the firelight to the Frenchman's magic fiddle.
We were all of us dancing and spinning.
Even the Indian chiefs, Big Horse and Little Thief, joined in.
An' I linked arms with Charlie Floyd
an' we spun an' twirled an' whooped an' stomped.
> Charlie, he's always been kind to me,
> even back home in Kentucky.
It took me back to my boyhood, with all us young'uns,
black *and* white,
playing crack-the-whip an' horsing about.

Maybe it was the spinning,
or maybe it was the fiddling,
or maybe it was the extra whiskey gill,
but me an' Charlie both fell down.

148

Oh, I was laughing an' my spirit felt free
an' Charlie was doubled up too —
only Charlie was clawing at his gut,
an' screaming with some sudden pain,
only Charlie,
he didn't get up.

Oolum ❖ *the newfoundland*

Master Lewis diagnosed Sergeant Floyd's condition as bilious colic — a bad stomachache. York tended to his sick friend through the night and into the next day as Lewis and Clark held their council, on schedule, in the shade of an awning created from the keelboat's canvas sail.

The captains and their men were dressed in the uniforms of their various units. The men enlisted in Kentucky wore brown dress military coats of Lewis's own design.

The Indians wore nothing except breechcloths in the August heat. Two or three among them wore buffalo robes about their shoulders. As all men sat down to talk, a final Indian approached the circle wearing nothing at all.

With a white trader who lived among the Otos interpreting, the naked Indian declared that he wore nothing to symbolize his poverty. He made it clear that he expected gifts. The meeting began badly and grew worse with every word spoken.

Lewis began by delivering a speech informing the Indians that their land was now owned by the great chief Jefferson in the East, who was the leader of the seventeen great nation-states. He urged the Indians to live in peace with other Indian nations, to accept President Jefferson as their new father, and to be his children. If they did so, the white man would make them partners in the profitable network of trade that would soon cover all the land. If they did not cooperate, if they displeased their new father, they would be cut out.

Then the captains presented gifts, a handful of beads, eight carrots of tobacco, some face paint, and gilded paper certificates that declared the bearer's allegiance to the United States. Blank spaces among the incomprehensible lettering allowed Lewis to write in the recipient's name by hand.

Lewis hung medals from the necks of the Indians he considered chiefs. One side of these medals was stamped with the likeness of Jefferson; the other side bore the image of two hands clasped in friendship.

None of the Indians was pleased. The naked Indian complained that he was given less than the others. One brave wanted a medal rather than a certificate and threw the paper to the ground. The chief named Little Thief wondered aloud how their new great white father in Washington could protect his people from their enemies, the Omaha and the Sioux. What the remaining Indian braves wanted most was whiskey.

The council ended when Lewis produced a few trinkets designed to show the great power of modern civilization: a mirror, a magnet, a compass, a glass that magnified the sun, a corn grinder, a small stick tipped with sulfur and phosphorus that burst into flame when struck against a rock. And the grand finale of Lewis and Clark's magic show was an air rifle that could shoot a dozen lead balls noiselessly, without flint or powder, and without pausing to reload.

When Lewis demonstrated the air rifle, Little Thief and the others smiled for the first time all day.

They had been the children of the English, the French, the Spanish, and now the United States. This was nothing new. But a repeating rifle powered only by air? Now that was worthy of notice.

William Clark ◇ *the gentleman*

We said our goodbyes to the Missouris and the Otos
and made them a gift of a small canister of whiskey.

With Sergeant Floyd much weaker and no better
we sailed on under a gentle breeze from the southeast.

We made thirteen miles before York called out from the cabin
where he had been tending to Floyd's every need. The end was near.

We passed two islands and at the first bluff on the starboard side
Sergeant Floyd died with a great deal of composure.

We buried him on the top of the bluff,
half a mile below a small river to which we gave his name.

This man at all times gave us proofs of his firmness
and his determined resolution to do service to his country.

Our carpenter, Gass, placed the head post, on which he carved:
Sergeant C. Floyd, Died Here 20th of August 1804.

After the men fired a salute to our deceased brother,
we camped at the mouth of Floyd's River, about thirty yards wide.

A beautiful evening. Many curious wolves on the bank.
The smaller species of this animal, Lewis has named the prairie wolf.

Sacagawea ◇ *the bird woman*

When Coyote
calls a man home
the dead man's soul
is met halfway
by a spirit guide
that escorts the soul
to the home of
Coyote's brother, Wolf.

Wolf then washes the soul
and revives it
so that it might
live again.

Just as the river waters
never run dry
so too the spirit
flows forever to the sea.

Pierre Cruzatte ⬦ *the fiddler*

O weary sun, go down, go down
upon the soldier boy so brave
at rest beneath this sacred mound.
Sun, set upon his lonesome grave.

Then rise and light that sacred ground
and lead the soldier boy so brave
where war and woe are never found
beside his lonesome grave.

Hugh Hall ⟡ *the drinker*

Well, things are not happening as I planned them.
I've seen what happened
to poor Moses Reed when he tried to run off.
His whipping near killed him.
He lost all his pay
and now he's being put to work like a slave.

> Worse than all that,
> Reed won't be allowed to continue on
> with the rest of us
> to see the Pacific Ocean.
> And now, neither will that saint, Charlie Floyd.
> Not that I ever cared much for *him,* but still.

So I reckon I won't slip away to Pennsylvania just yet.

I'm thinking I'll do the right thing
and stay with the Corps of Discovery.

Least ways, until the whiskey runs out.

Patrick Gass ❖ *the carpenter*

Today I was promoted from private to sergeant
to take the place of poor Charles Floyd (God rest his soul).
All us soldiers voted
then the captains chose me from the top three men.
I'll have to keep a daily journal now as part of my various duties,
which is no concern since I keep one anyhow.
I'm flattered that I won the spot, and I feel I'm capable.

Still I'd rather not have won the promotion this way.
This Eden we've entered shelters many serpents:

>Floyd lying there dying and knowing he was going to die,
>both Lewis and Clark, who know so much,
>but helpless in the face of death,
>then Floyd breathing his final breath,
>the silent men digging the hole,
>strong York—who could like to break a man in half—
>strong York lingering awhile
>at the grave on the bluff, huffing and weeping,
>as the others returned to their labors,
>the cedar tree, already dead, which I engraved for Floyd's marker,
>and now every cedar tree I see reminds me
>that not all of us will make it home alive.

John Colter ◇ *the hunter*

To call this wilderness th' Garden o' Eden
ain't so far from th' truth
fer it seems like ever'where I turn
I see fruit, ripe an' juicy:
plums an' currants, an' raspberries,
an' more kinds o' grapes than I knew there even was!
There's greens that make good eatin' too,
though I don't hardly touch 'em.
But the tail o' the beaver,
now, *that* is a delicacy with no equal,
'cept perhaps fer the buffalo tongue 'n hump.
    Jest yesterday Joe Field killed hisself our first buffalo.
    It took dang near seven o' us t' haul th' thing t' shore.

I don't know nothin' about Eden,
but this here place is fer sure a hunter's paradise.
At this pace we may just *eat* our way
to th' Pacific Ocean!

Joseph and Reubin Field ◈ *the brothers*

Reubin   You did it, Brother!
Ya brought down a buffalo, an' a big one at that!
I tell you what, Joe, this here buffalo tongue
we're eatin' is some kind o' good!

Joseph   Thanks, Reubin.

Reubin   'Course, seein' as them buffalo are so big,
I guess thar ain't much skill in hittin' one.

Joseph   If killin' buffalo is such a lark, why haven't *you* got one, Reubin?

Reubin   On account o' I wanted you t' win our little competition
so's you could feel as if you rightly won th' hand o' Mary Myrtle.

Joseph   Brother, I done won Mary Myrtle's hand
with or *without* this here buffalo hide.
Now, you jest hush up or else I'll skin *you* too.

Reubin   You're right, Joe.
I suppose Mary Myrtle *would* prefer *my* hide t' a buffalo's.

Joseph   With both being so hairy, I don't imagine
she could tell th' one hide from th' other.

Reubin   I think you jest insulted me, Brother.

Joseph   Don't think same time as ya eat, Reubin;
you jest might ferget to swaller.

William Clark ◈ *the gentleman*

Last night I fell asleep
to the high whine of the cursed mosquitoes,
and in the midst of a fitful rest,
I fell into dreaming.

> I wake to the sound of bird wings, only to see an Indian woman
> standing at the campfire, holding an infant child in her arms. I
> walk toward her to speak, and she holds the child out to me,
> smiling as if she wants me to take it.
>   Suddenly the wind changes, hiding the woman and child
> behind a cloud of smoke. The smoke clears and both woman
> and child are gone. In their place stands Julia Hancock. Julia's
> arms are outstretched and empty. Her face speaks sadness to
> me. Then the smoke again rises and Julia vanishes into it. The
> wind continues to grow, whirling and whistling, and once more
> I hear the clapping of birds taking flight.

When I woke, I found myself standing at the campfire.
The great whistling wind was only the drone of mosquitoes
and the flapping of bird wings was just the sound of beavers
slapping their tails against the surface of a nearby pond.

Lewis's Newfoundland was standing beside me.
In silence we walked down to the river,
and as I looked westward, upstream,
a single word rang in my head.
Although the word was not one I had ever heard,
I somehow knew it was the name
for the longing that I felt inside.

The word was—Roloje.

Oolum ◇ the newfoundland

The next morning, Clark named the first stream he came to Roloje Creek.

Roloje. The language of longing spoken by all living things. You feel it in your heart. You see it when you sleep. It is the reason we wake up each day. It is everything that we ever want and hope for. Each human on the expedition held Roloje in his heart. Each human longed for discovery. Some, like Clark, knew what they were looking for. Some, like Master Lewis, did not.

The Missouri spoke Roloje well. The river longed to return to the sea, and it said so every day. And swept away in its current—along with the fallen timber, the cast-off sand, the mud, and the flood-claimed animal carcasses—was the unfulfilled wanting of a girl named Sacagawea, who lived so far upstream. The dream of Sacagawea was there in the river along with a thousand others.

The Great Plains and the Indians who lived there were at home with the whispering spirits, both good and bad. Magic was an accepted fact among all the native nations. Lewis and Clark sailed against the current, into these superstitious lands, on a keelboat powered by the winds of reason. These men of the Enlightenment did not believe in ghosts.

So when Lewis and Clark heard tell of a nearby mountain—just a day's walk away—said to be inhabited by evil spirits, they could not resist the chance to confront superstition head on.

William Clark ◇ *the gentleman*

Friday, August 24, 1804
In a northerly direction from the mouth of the White Stone River in an
imence Plain, a high Hill is Situated, and appears of a Conical form, and
by the different nations of Indians in this quarter is Suppose to be the resi-
dence of Deavels. These Deavels are said to be of human form but with
remarkable large heads, and they are but 18 Inches high and are very watch-
full and are arm'd with Sharp arrows with which they Can Kill at a great
distance; they are Said to kill all persons who are So hardy as to attempt to
approach the hill.
    Capt. Lewis & Myself have concluded to go and See the Mound which is
Viewed with Such terror by all the different Indian Nations.

A tiny devil
with an oversize head
and a deadly bow and arrow,
striking men down from a distance?

Did not the Romans call him Cupid?

Sacagawea ❖ *the bird woman*

Among my people there are many spirits.

Mugua is the spirit which resides inside the body.
The great spirit of spirits is Apo, the sun.

And there are the NunumBi — the Little People.
They are hideous dwarfs that roam the land
shooting their invisible arrows of misfortune
into anyone who displeases them.

The day that I was captured,
the day my parents were killed,
I could feel the arrows of the NunumBi
piercing my heart.

Yet I have pulled one arrow out
and now I keep it hidden.
Now it is mine.

And I will use it myself.

Next time.

Oolum ◇ *the newfoundland*

While the keelboat and pirogues proceeded on, the captains, with a crew of a half dozen men, began their hike up to the Mountain of Little Devils. We set out early before the fog was yet burned away by the sun, and we followed a creek a few hundred yards. Then we walked up a rise and onto the endless prairie. The large hill came into view immediately, even though it was several miles away, for it stood alone, the only rise in all the surrounding plain.

The sight of it made my fur stand on end, and every animal instinct I had told me to turn back. But I go or stay as my master Lewis wishes. So I went.

There was no wind on the prairie. The sun was relentless. I felt as if I would suffocate beneath my thick black fur. Finally, after four miles, we crossed a creek that was soothing and cool. I had no desire to go farther. York was short of breath. Captain Lewis was red-faced and faint, but he insisted that we all press on.

We walked yet another mile. The heat worsened, the wind picked up, and we began to hear the sound of birds. Thousands of birds. In the distance we could see them rise up as one enormous cloud and return to the mound. According to the Indians, this unnatural congregation of birds was evidence of the mountain's evil.

There was no water. There were no shade trees. I had no hat as the humans did, so I had no escape from the sun. My eyes suddenly blurred. My thoughts were becoming confused.

My head began to throb, and my shoulders tightened. One of the little spirits was riding on my back, its heels digging into my neck, its fists pounding against my temples. My legs buckled, and I fell to the ground. A great weight pushed me down. I could not move. I could not follow Lewis. I closed my eyes and waited to die.

George Drouillard ⬦ *the half-breed*

It was not my wish, at first, to follow
Lewis and Clark to the Mountain of Little Devils,
but something inside me told me to go.

> Perhaps my father's French blood
> goaded me to face the NunumBi spirits.
> Or perhaps my mother's Shawnee blood urged me on
> that I might approach the mound only close enough
> to destroy the weaker half of my self—my white half.

But then I saw the great cloud of birds.
It rose up against the glare of the sun
and formed itself into a man with a spear.
The sound of birds grew louder
and then became a single fearsome voice,
screeching at us to cease our approach.
And yet none of the others seemed to notice.
Could they possibly not have seen?

I heard the bones within my medicine pouch speaking:

> *How far will you travel*
> *to discover who you are?*

I saw a shadow descend upon Lewis's dog.
The huge dog dropped to the ground as if dead.
Only then did Lewis turn to look.
The captain was soaked with sweat, his face red.
He swayed on his feet and gasped for air.
And protruding from the center of his chest
was the shaft of a small arrow.

Meriwether Lewis ✦ *the explorer*

As surely as I am alive and well,
no spirits are in residence at Little Devil Mountain!

True, I was winded. And true, I was heated.
And yes, I'd a pain in my chest.
But all were due to my great thirst and the sun's fatiguing effect.
Nothing more. No arrows. No magic.
Only the magic of rational observation.

After Seaman collapsed from the heat,
Drouillard was only too eager to take the dog
back to the coolness of the creek.
The rest of us walked on.

What follow are the facts:

The mountain is really no more than a large mound
with a rectangular base of parallel sides, 300 yards by 60 yards.
The sides ascend steeply to a perfectly flat top, 12 feet wide, 90 feet long.
This flat area is some 70 feet above the plain
and afforded us a beautiful view of the landscape all around:
numerous herds of buffalo feeding on a flat grassy plain
that extends as far as the eye can see!

As for the birds, they are easily explained as so:
the plain around the mound lacks mountains or trees
of any kind to block the wind, which, as a result,
blows against the mound's windward side with great force
and blowing every airborne insect with it.
These insects, in great numbers, seek refuge on the mountain's quiet side,
only to become a feast for the lucky birds.

So, you see, the birds are not gathering for deviltry;
they are gathering for dinner.

> The birds, by the way,
> are mostly of the brown martin species.

George Shannon ◈ *the kid*

This morning I watched as a few of the men
made much-needed elk-hide tow ropes
tying and winding the strips of the skins—
one which I just shot yesterday.

>   Ha. Not only does George Shannon pull his own weight.
>   George Shannon helps make the rope to pull on!

Now I'm out on the upper plains
searching for a horse that walked off in the night.

>   Drouillard is with me
>   (that is, *I* am with *Drouillard*)
>   and it seems that the horse doesn't wish to be found.
>   So we split up to cover more ground.

Thirsty, I make my way
toward a line of trees (which indicates a creek).

>   Once there I lean to take a drink.
>   And I see my reflection in the water.
>   Even with a patchy growth of beard,
>   I still look like a kid.

I'm about to spit at my own likeness
when I hear the sudden snort of a horse over my shoulder.

>   I spin about.
>   I reach for my rifle.

I fall backward into the creek with a splash,
discharging my gun and shooting a nearby tree,

and I look up to see I have found the horse.

Or at least, the horse has found me.

Oolum ❖ *the newfoundland*

After my faint at the Mountain of Little Devils, the cool rains came to relieve me from the heat. Was I the victim of tiny spirits or sunstroke? I cannot be sure which. The effect was the same either way.

We left the evil mound downriver and proceeded on to happier times. Except for the relentless mosquitoes and the mysterious disappearance of Shannon, all was well. The supply of meat the men fed me was endless. I never went thirsty or lacked for a kind scratch behind the ears or under the chin.

Old Dorion, the Sioux interpreter, informed us that we may be seeing Indians soon. Master Lewis ordered the prairie grass set on fire as a signal to any nearby nations that a council was being called. To me these councils were all talk and bluster, a very drawn-out way of saying hello. Among dogs, meetings are simple. A bark. A growl. A sniff or two. And just like that, everyone has figured out what is what and who is who.

As Lewis set the signal fire, Clark oversaw the making of camp. The men set up their tents, cook fires, kettles, and drying racks. As always each man had a gun nearby, ready for anything.

And while the humans worked, I played. The river was a wonderland for a water dog. Everywhere I looked there were flustered geese and grumpy beaver. Both always offered a good challenging chase.

And so I set out into a deep channel of the river in search of mischief. My nose pushed across the surface of the river, when up from some hidden depth emerged a head of black hair followed by the grinning face of a boy. We said hello, simply, muzzle to muzzle.

Old Dorion was called for, and the boy informed him that we were in the territory of the Yankton Sioux nation.

Meriwether Lewis ◇ *the explorer*

Private Shannon is no deserter
but he is no first-rate tracker either.
He did not return to camp with Drouillard
nor has he turned up since.

It appears that the young man has found the missing horse
but lost himself in the plains.

Joe Field, after a day of searching,
informs me the tracks on the bank show
that Shannon and the horse are moving on ahead.

The timing is not good, however, as we must remain
camped to have council with the Sioux.
I have sent the Indian boy and Old Dorion to the Sioux encampment
with an invitation to visit us here and talk.

As for the wayward Shannon,
we have determined to send Colter
in pursuit, with provisions.

Private Shannon, that eager lad,
attempting to catch up to a boat that is not there.

George Shannon ◇ *the kid*

Here I lie in the Garden of Eden
watching the evening come.

I was pleased with myself when I found the horse.

Not even Drouillard had been able to find it.

So as I walked out onto the plain
with that horse on a rope,
I felt one step closer to being a man.

Drouillard didn't return my shouts
and the sun was going down.
I knew darkness would descend
before I could make my way back to the river.

By now the keelboat's probably far upstream.
I'll overtake it in the morning.

For now there's naught for me to do
but hobble the horse, keep near the water,
and count all the stars in the sky.

I can recognize that cluster there,
the one Captain Lewis calls Ursa Major,
shaped like a water dipper, so he says.
I guess if you're out here in the wilderness long enough
you begin to see almost anything.

No harm in my lying low
for just the one night.

I always have tomorrow

to catch up to the men.

Oolum ❖ *the newfoundland*

Today Old Dorion arrived with five chiefs from the nation of the Yankton Sioux. Following behind them were some seventy others of the tribe. Under the shade of a great oak tree, the chiefs, with their attendant warriors, sat in a line across from the captains and Dorion, who was to act as translator. Lewis, Clark, and the other soldiers were in their dress uniforms. An American flag flew on a tall makeshift pole.

As the flag snapped in the breeze, Lewis read off the usual speech, which let the Indians know of the white man's peaceful intentions and the desire to embrace the Sioux people as partners in trade and friendship. Lewis handed out gifts of peace medals, beads, and tobacco. And to the main chief, whose name was Weucha, or Shake Hand, Lewis presented a flag, a dress coat, and a fancy red-plumed hat.

The chief considered the red plume suspiciously, attempting to imagine the fanciful bird that had sacrificed such a startling feather. Then, with Dorion translating slowly, Shake Hand began to speak.

The needs of his people were simple, he said. He spoke of hunting and defense against the hostile Teton Sioux upriver. Guns, powder, and lead were needed to replace their bows and arrows. Regular contact with white traders was desirable. And, of course, his people were in want of what he called "the milk of the Great White Father."

In other words, whiskey.

William Clark ◇ *the gentleman*

The Yanktons are agreeable in every way
and as friendly as any citizen back in Louisville.
Perhaps more so.

They are dignified and handsome.
The warriors' frocks are greatly decorated
with painted porcupine quills and feathers.
All wear large leggings and moccasins
and beautiful buffalo robes of various colors.

The women all wear petticoats and elegant white buffalo skins
with the dark fur turned back over their necks and shoulders.

Here in this rough wilderness camp
is occurring a gathering of dignity and pomp
equal to any grand social affair in the East.

Chief Shake Hand has offered me a turn with the peace pipe.
Our eyes meet, and I realize this man is my same age.
I am sure of it.
Like me he wears the artillery officer's coat,
and should he exchange his black hair for my red,
we could just as well be the same man.

These men and women whom we call savages . . .
	how unsavage-like they are.

How human.

Meriwether Lewis ◇ *the explorer*

Into the night the Yankton Sioux danced around the fire.
      The rattles and drums and the wailing!
We tossed them gifts as they danced.
      Knives, tobacco, and bells.
A few of our men even joined them.
      Cruzatte, the Frenchman, brought out the fiddle
      and played us a reel or two.
All told, we raised a merry din.

But four warriors kept apart from the festivities,
dancing and singing around a private fire.
No others approached them.
They kept to themselves.

Old Dorion explained this to me:

      These four Indians were members of a society
      that had at one time many members.
      They had each taken a vow never to turn back or seek cover,
      no matter what the occasion or danger.
      One brother was lost to a hole in the ice.
      It was easily avoided, but the man
      would not be swayed from his course.
      In a recent battle, eighteen of twenty-two met their deaths.
      The remaining four had to be dragged off to safety.

And here they were, laughing around an honored fire
bought dearly with their blood.

Of all the men I've yet met, Indian or white,
I feel the most kinship with these four.
No matter what the destination.
No matter what the cost.
They will not be swayed.
They have vowed to keep moving

    or die.

George Shannon ◈ *the kid*

Keep moving, George Shannon.
You can handle this.

       The horse and I set out two days ago,
       and still I haven't seen the boat.

    The sail must have caught some mighty wind
    to be so far ahead.

         This morning I ate the last of my jerky.

And would you believe it,
my shot pouch contains no lead!
I used up so many balls hunting elk,
and I didn't take time to resupply myself.
So I've got a gun and plenty of powder and patches

but without lead they do me no good.

         There is fruit to be picked here and there
         but it'll take more than grapes to quiet my growling gut.

You can handle this, George Shannon.
Keep moving upriver.

         A man can't starve in the Garden of Eden.

And if worse comes to worst

    you can always eat the horse.

George Drouillard ◇ *the half-breed*

How many horses does each man have? What do you eat?
How do you treat sickness? Do you own slaves?
What are your dances? Your courtship rituals? Your games?
For hours the captains ask questions of the Indians.
They have filled many pages with their writing.
And yet Lewis and Clark have much to learn of tribal wishes and ways.

To hang a medal from the neck of a man does not make him a chief.

Shall Shake Hand travel to Washington
to braid a feather into Aaron Burr's hair
and thus appoint him president?
And when Thomas Jefferson protests,
will the "Great White Father" be quieted
with a gift of a tobacco twist?

The Otos, the Missouris, the Yankton Sioux — all have pledged peace,
but *peace* is a word with many meanings.
Will Jefferson pledge peace with the detested British
if Little Thief wishes it so?

During the nighttime celebrations
I was befriended by a Yankton chief, Aweawechache,
who told me, "This medal may mean something to some,
but it means nothing to me. I cannot hunt with it.
It will not kill the enemies of the Yankton.
It will not open the ears of the Tetons who rule the river above."

He showed me the society of warriors who never back down,
the ones that so impressed Captain Lewis.

Aweawechache smiled and confessed
that *he* belonged to a society of men
who hide behind a tree when there is a need.

"I am no warrior," he said. "I am only half a man."

Half a man indeed.
Perhaps the *better* half is all one needs to be.

Oolum ◇ *the newfoundland*

Thomas Jefferson expected Lewis and Clark to learn all they could of the native people, and the captains took their mission seriously.

Lewis spent many hours with the Yanktons asking questions about their lifestyle and living conditions. Questions included matters of love, war, hunting, trade practices, health, and spiritual beliefs. Clark wrote out a vocabulary of words in the Sioux language.

After two full days of meetings and speeches and dancing, the soldiers said farewell to their new Indian friends. Old Dorion stayed behind to escort a party of chiefs to visit President Jefferson in Washington. In return the captains gave him clothing, provisions, and a U.S. flag. The captains felt confident that, with Cruzatte's knowledge of the Sioux language and Drouillard's hand-signing skills, they would be able to communicate with the Teton Sioux who were yet to be encountered upstream.

For my part, I was happy to leave these humans behind. Unlike Master Lewis, I never felt comfortable in their presence. Chief Shake Hand would look at me intensely, expecting every minute to be offered a bowl of Newfoundland stew. These Yankton Sioux considered roasted dog a delicacy.

We proceeded on.

George Shannon ◇ *the kid*

I had to stop—

The little bear—told me to—

Of late I've been seeing a bear cub—in my dreams
and he told me—to stop for a while to eat grapes—

And so I have—eaten grapes.

I have—eaten more grapes—
than there are stars in heaven.

My gut feels small—and hard as a walnut—
from want of meat.

Every day I grow more—and more weak—
and I feel—like I'm losing my mind.

But at the moment—I am feasting—like a king on a rabbit that I killed—
by using—in place of a bullet—a straight, hard stick.

Oh—I fumbled and fumbled—for minutes—
I forgot—to load the priming powder—
I—dropped my powder horn—

But that rabbit just waited—and waited—
twitching its nose—like a gift—

a gift from the bear.

The rabbit's flesh is barely cooked.

Delicious.
Delicious.

I have never been so wretched in my life.

Meriwether Lewis ◇ *the explorer*

In all my life, I have never felt so completely alive.
Is it possible that the unspeakable beauty of the landscape downriver
has been surpassed by our present surroundings?

It is true!

The cottonwood, elm, red cedar, and willow
clustering in the bends of the river
and along the edges of the adjoining creeks.
The shy prairie wolves keeping constant watch.
The bold gray wolves shepherding the buffalo herds.
Buffalo herds, three thousand strong.
Elk and antelope as far as the eyes can see
grazing on the short prairie grass.
The grass covering mile after mile of plains
so flat as to be a bowling green to God.
The groves of plum trees, heavy with ripe fruit.
Whole vineyards of succulent grapes untouched by man.

Strange new species of every variety
never before described to science.

And the space. The empty space.
Enough to make you sure there is a God.
For who but God could create such a wonder?
Who but God could create such a paradise?

George Drouillard ❖ *the half-breed*

Before I gave up the ways of the white man for good,
I was taught, by the Black-Robes, about Adam and Eve.

Adam and Eve were a white man and woman
whom God made in his own image.
Then God put them in a garden paradise made just for them.
It was their job to name all the animals and trees.

As I see it, Lewis and Clark are a kind of Adam and Eve,
pointing at everything, christening this and christening that.

Trying to ease their endless hunger for knowledge.
Eating up all the abundant forbidden fruit.

And what of Satan, what of the serpent?

Lewis has killed it and counted its scales.
Cut open its belly to see what it eats.
Collected its skin in a specimen box.

Hugh Hall ◈ *the drinker*

Garden of Eden, my ass!
Do you think Adam and Eve
would stay around here
without a stitch of clothing on
in the midst of all these damned mosquitoes?

It ain't likely.

William Clark ◈ *the gentleman*

Are Captain Lewis and I,
in this beautiful paradise,
like Adam and Eve,
in the biblical Eden?

The very idea is more frightening than humorous,

for more unnerving than the thought of murderous Indians
is the thought of Lewis and myself
walking about the plains perfectly naked
except for the carefully placed fig leaves.

The buffalo would panic in fear.
I shudder to imagine the stampede
we would cause.

George Shannon ◈ *the kid*

Very sleepy.

I wonder, Is this how Sergeant Floyd felt
just before he died, clutching at his stomach in pain?

As near as I can tell I've been lost out here for over two weeks
with nothing but grapes and one rabbit to eat.

I have sat down at the riverbank for good
because the black bear suggested it.

Last night, in a dream, I saw the cub sitting by the river
facing downstream, and crying out for the longest time.
Until finally, its mother came lumbering up the bank.
The young bear knew its mother was coming
so he just waited on the bank and wailed.

And so I'm here now waiting myself.
Waiting for white traders to come along and save me.
Waiting for hostile Indians to come along and scalp me.
Waiting for my dear mother to come along and scold me.

I'm too feeble anyway to walk.
Very sleepy.
Afraid to eat the horse
as it is government property

and would be
deducted from
my pay . . .

Oolum ◇ *the newfoundland*

When I first saw the kid, Shannon, lying on the bank with his hand clutching tight to the rein of the horse, I thought he was dead. It was rare to get a glimpse of the young human when he wasn't speaking.

On closer inspection I was relieved to find he was still alive. I had been sorry to lose the human, Floyd, because he was particularly kind and wise. To lose Shannon next would have been a disappointment. There were others on board that I could have done without.

So I licked his lips to bring him around. He hugged me close and spoke as if I were a bear cub come to comfort him. Glassy-eyed, he talked calmly about rabbits and heaven and hunger. He was sun-struck, starved, and out of his mind.

After a few unsuccessful attempts, Captain Lewis finally talked the private out of his trance. When Shannon recognized me and his fellow soldiers, he stood to attention, and with a salute, he said, "Captain Lewis, sir, I've brought you back the missing horse as ordered, sir!"

Then he lost his legs and fell to the ground in a dead faint. As the keelboat proceeded on upstream with Shannon aboard, York brought him a tin plate of food. York knew enough not to bother with a knife or fork. With loud smacking and gulping, Shannon ate the dried deer meat and buffalo hump. He left the grapes on his plate untouched.

Sacagawea ◇ *the bird woman*

In order to become a man
a Hidatsa boy must take a sacred journey.

He leaves the comfort and safety of his village
to spend a number of days alone in the wilderness.

During this time, he does not hunt or eat.
He only prays.

He prays for a vision that will give him a clue to who he is.
If he is not ready, no vision will come.

If he is ready, he will see visions that remind him of his past
or warn him of his future.
He may not understand the vision fully
until many years later.

If the boy is lucky
he will be joined by his spirit guide—
a horse, a bear, the wind, a tree.
His spirit guide might be anything.

The spirit guide is a protector
and will lead a boy through the darkness into manhood.

Many women have spirit guides too.
Mine appeared to me when I was still a girl
the first day I lifted my face to see the sky.

Oolum ◇ *the newfoundland*

The late September sky turned dark with immense numbers of brant and plover. The days were still hot, but the nights became cool, the mosquitoes less troublesome. Fall had arrived.

The captains gave out new flannel shirts to those who needed them. All men, including the captains, wore moccasins of elk hide on their feet, their shoes and boots long worn out or rotted from the constant wet. Reubin Field discovered a stream that the captains named Reubin's Creek in his honor. Young George Shannon had been back aboard for two weeks, and to his constant chagrin, the name Reubin had given him—Tenderfoot—had caught on with nearly every member of the party, except for Drouillard and the captains.

The river meandered erratically, at one time flowing in a thirty-mile loop that returned to a point only two thousand feet from where it had started. Yet even with the river's maddening detours and switchbacks, the men made good time, sailing up to twenty and thirty miles each day.

By the end of September, we reached the mouth of the Teton River, which meant we had entered the territory of the Teton Sioux. Word of the warlike band had traveled all the way to the President's House in the East. Jefferson had warned Lewis about them. The Tetons had a reputation as bullies and pirates who would detain trappers and traders, demanding large tolls in exchange for safe passage.

When three young Indian boys swam out to the boat, Pierre Cruzatte told them that the white men wanted to council, and sent the boys back to the Sioux encampment with tobacco. The humans set up camp on a large sandbar, again erecting an awning from the keelboat's sail and preparing for meetings the next day.

As a precaution, the captains dropped anchor some seventy yards away from the shore. About thirty of the men slept aboard the keelboat. The rest were stationed as a guard on the riverbank. Every rifle was loaded and primed. The swivel cannon on the boat's bow gleamed.

Pierre Cruzatte & George Drouillard
the fiddler and the half-breed

Cruzatte Captain Lewis, this is the grand chief, Un-ton-gar Sar-bar,
which means *Buffle Noir*.

Drouillard In English, Black Buffalo.

Cruzatte And this chief calls himself Tor-to-hon-gar.

Drouillard The Partisan.
I think it wise to use French between the two of us, Pierre,
while together we attempt to translate from Sioux to English.

Cruzatte I agree, my friend.
With your knowledge of hand signs
and my small knowledge of Sioux,
we will act as one voice.

Drouillard Ha! Two half-breeds to speak as one voice —
it is simple math, eh?

Cruzatte No, George, perhaps not as simple as you say.
I may be *métis,* but I am not like you.
You shun your white blood.
I embrace mine.

Drouillard Then you embrace poison
while you shun your own heart.

Cruzatte No! My heart, he is so big
he can pump the blood of two men at once —

a Frenchman *and* an Omaha!
I am the better for it.

Drouillard I fear that with only one eye, Pierre,
you see only the white man's half of you.

Cruzatte You are wrong. I see only the safest passage up the river.
My people are those who row the boat—
whomever they may be.
You have two eyes, George,
but they are at war with each other.
Perhaps you should close them both
and open your heart.

Drouillard You look like a white man, Pierre,
and yet you talk like an Indian.

Cruzatte I may talk like an Indian
but I am afraid I do not talk like a Teton Sioux,
for I cannot make these chiefs understand
the meaning of Lewis's speech.

Drouillard Yes. I believe you just translated
"Great White Father in the East"
into "the sickly old fat man far away."

Oolum ♦ *the newfoundland*

The council with the Tetons was not going well. The main chief, Black Buffalo, seemed distant and reserved. A second chief, whom Drouillard and Cruzatte called the Partisan, held his face in a constant smirk, and acted impatient with all the talk. His eyes kept returning to the gift-laden keelboat anchored offshore.

Cruzatte discovered too late that his knowledge of the Sioux language was not complete enough to communicate anything but the most simple concepts. As well, Drouillard's hand signs were unable to do justice to the meaning of Lewis's words.

So the captains cut short the political talk and proceeded straight to the usual show of wondrous inventions. In all, three chiefs, along with their warrior attendants, were taken across the water to the keelboat.

As gifts were placed into the pirogue, each Indian was offered a small glass of whiskey. The chief named the Partisan gave a yell and acted as if he were drunk. He purposefully pushed against Lewis, who fell backward. Without thinking, I snapped at the Indian's hand. Master Lewis was not pleased; his face was turning red. But before Lewis could protest, Clark suggested they return to shore to distribute the gifts. Clark reasoned that Black Buffalo, who seemed annoyed by the actions of the Partisan, might still be won over.

With great difficulty, Clark talked the Indians back into the pirogue, and a small crew of soldiers, including Cruzatte and Drouillard, rowed the party back to shore. Lewis, who stayed on the keelboat, soothed his bruised pride and positioned himself behind the small brass cannon at the bow.

When Clark and the chiefs arrived at the shore, a group of warriors rushed the pirogue. One Indian grabbed the tow rope, and another wrapped his arms around the boat's mast. The Partisan again pretended to be drunk and complained that Clark had not given him enough presents. The Indian pretended to stagger, his body falling solidly against Clark's.

"No," the Partisan said, "you shall not go on." And he swung an open hand to slap the captain's chest. But Clark stepped backward and simultaneously drew his sword. The sound of the sword sliding from its scabbard was signal enough for Lewis, who said simply, "To arms!"

The lid of every locker on the boat's shore-facing side snapped up with a battery of loud cracks of wood against wood. The sound echoed up and down the river. Next followed the ratcheting click of metal and springs as forty flintlocks on forty rifles were full-cocked into firing position.

The Indian women and children on shore began to fall back, running up the slope of the bank. Hundreds of warriors strung their bows, notched their arrows, aimed, and stood waiting.

Lewis, still standing at the keelboat's bow, turned the cannon slightly on its swivel.

The cannon was loaded with a sixteen large lead musket balls that would, upon firing, scatter in a wide circular pattern. It was designed by humans to kill other humans—many humans all at once. Lewis had positioned the gaping hole of the muzzle directly at Black Buffalo and the Partisan. The warriors surrounding the two chiefs stepped away, with a movement similar to a fancy human dance I had seen back in St. Charles. Black Buffalo and the Partisan stood alone.

At some time during the commotion onshore, Lewis had subtly lighted a firing taper. The fuse hung from his hand and smoldered as he held it just above the cannon's touch hole. The two chiefs could not help but notice that Lewis's hand did not show the slightest tremor.

Overhead, a small flock of geese flew by in tight formation, honking. Then everything fell silent, except for the hissing of the Missouri River, which would not be stopped.

The Corps of Discovery

Meriwether Lewis   I will *not* be made the fool.

Patrick Gass   All hands await the command!

George Drouillard   Pierre?
If I am two men—
one white and one red—
which one do you suppose will die first?

Pierre Cruzatte   Oh, posh, *mon ami.* You both may live yet.
The odds, they are not so bad against us.

George Shannon   There looks to be about four hundred Indians
and there's about forty of us.
If *those* odds don't make a man of me
I don't suppose anything will.

York   I jus' may be gettin' all the freedom I want.

John Colter   I guess I mightn't get m' pay after all.

Joseph Field   I got aim on Black Buffalo.

Reubin Field   I got aim on the Partisan.

Hugh Hall   I got to have a drink.

PART THREE

———

THE TETON SIOUX TO FORT MANDAN

SEPTEMBER 1804–APRIL 1805

MISSOURI RIVER

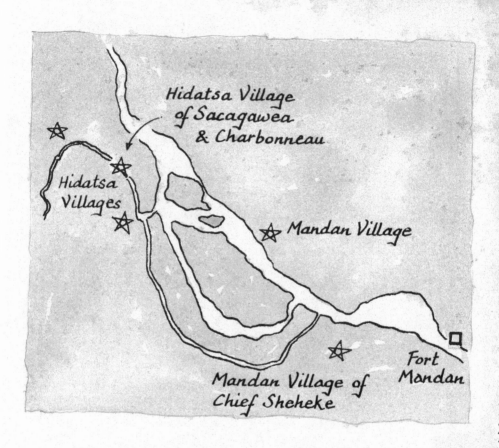

Hidatsa Village
of Sacagawea
& Charbonneau

Hidatsa
Villages

Mandan Village

Mandan Village of
Chief Sheheke

Fort
Mandan

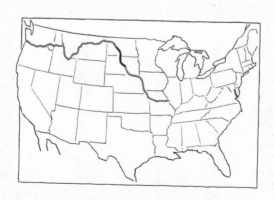

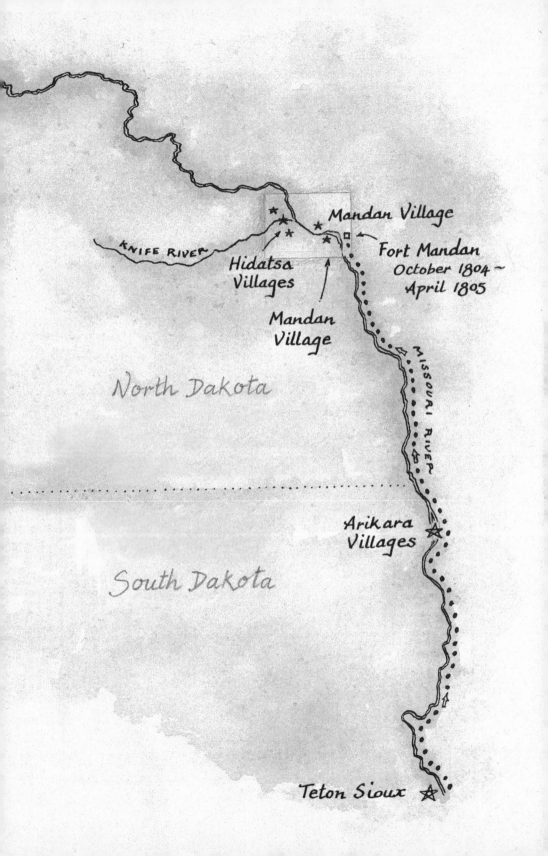

KNIFE RIVER

Mandan Village

Fort Mandan
October 1804 ~
April 1805

Hidatsa
Villages

Mandan
Village

North Dakota

MISSOURI RIVER

South Dakota

Arikara
Villages

Teton Sioux

William Clark ◈ *the gentleman*

I would be lying to say I did not feel a great bit of relief
when Black Buffalo ordered his men to release my boat.

I returned my sword to its sheath.
Hoping to salvage some possible friendship,
I held out my hand to the Partisan. He would not take it.
I offered it, then, to Black Buffalo. He would not take it.
So I turned on my heel and walked,
as calmly as possible, back to the pirogue.

Turning toward the keelboat for the first time
during this tense confrontation,
I found the lifted lids of the lockers to be an impressive sight.
      And I felt a tinge of disappointment
      that Gass and I had not been able to find
      more red paint back in St. Louis.
      The breastwork would have looked grand in red.

Then just before I reached the pirogue,
I heard the Indians approaching quickly from behind
wading into the shallows. I readied my grasp on the hilt of my sword
as I turned to see Black Buffalo's outstretched hand.
      I took it.

And with that, we all returned to the keelboat.
All chiefs (even the blackguard Partisan) appeared suddenly friendly
and declared that they wanted us to stay on another day.
Tomorrow night they would be holding a scalp dance, they said,

and they asked us to be their honored guests.

George Shannon ◇ *the kid*

It was not relief that I felt.

> God help me,
> but once it was clear that I wasn't going die a horrible death,
> well, I mainly felt pride —

> none of my brothers back home can boast
> *he* came so close to shaking hands with the grim reaper!
> O' course, I wouldn't want to experience it twice, mind you.

On this grand adventure I can hardly blink my eyes
without being treated to some fantastic happening.

For two nights running, we were the Tetons' honored guests.
And we watched 'round the fire at night
as the women danced and danced to the rhythmic beat
of drums and rattles and noisemakers of all sorts.

> Most women held up scalps —
>> human hair still attached to the skin,
>> cut from the head of some poor fallen foe.
>> The skin is stretched out like a small animal hide,
>> and then tied taut to a tiny hoop.
> The hoop was attached to the end of a long thin stick
> that each woman proudly waved about
> like a flag on the Fourth of July.

>> The warriors would jump up one after the other
>> singing out their brave deeds in battle.
>> I couldn't understand a word they said,
>> but words weren't necessary.

Yessir, I was sittin' pretty —
eating pemmican, potatoes, and even a taste o' dog.
I didn't much care for the flavor myself, mind you,
but I'll try anything once, just to say I did it.

But of all my experience with the Tetons
I must admit, there is one sight I had rather not seen.
And I suspect the memory of it will stay with me forever.

The Sioux were celebrating their latest raid against the Omahas.
Pierre, who had talked to the prisoners brought back to the camp,
learned that the Tetons had destroyed forty Omaha lodges,
killed seventy-five men, plus some of the children as well.
And they made prisoners of forty-eight women and children.

Well, idiot me,

while I was whoopin' it up and makin' merry,
my eye caught hold of one of the Omaha women
with a boy child on her hip.
The woman and boy looked drained of hope
and I could tell they were watching one scalp in particular.
They followed it all through the night,
as if they expected it to grow back

into a man.

Meriwether Lewis ◈ *the explorer*

I was carried into the Teton village upon a fine buffalo robe
supported on the backs of six warriors.
Captain Clark received the same honorary escort.

Their lodges are finely made tepees of buffalo hide
and each warrior decorates his tepee's outer face in his own way
so that each home is a testament to the courageous deeds of its occupant.

Clark and I were taken to a large semicircular council lodge,
        a framework of poles covered over in skins,
and we sat on the ground with the tribe's most important men.

We circled around a long ceremonial pipe resting upon two forked sticks.
With much pomp and show, Black Buffalo held up the pipe
as he said prayers toward the east, west, north, and south.

The pipe was filled with kinnikinnick,
the usual mixture of tobacco and bark.
With these people, no discussion commences until the pipe goes 'round.
I suspect the standoff at the river was designed to test our mettle,

for Black Buffalo and the others seem friendly enough now.
As I sit before them I regret
leaving our Sioux interpreter, Dorion, with the Yanktons below.
Cruzatte and Drouillard cannot make my mind known to these people.

Still, Black Buffalo has agreed to free the Omaha slaves — in time.
Although the Teton Sioux are known as the pirates of the Missouri,
(a name well earned) I feel these noble savages may just prove
to be loyal friends of the white man.

Pierre Cruzatte ◇ *the fiddler*

Black Buffalo has ordered the Teton warriors
to plunder the keelboat and slit our throats
once we have moved farther upriver.

This I was told while I gave gifts to the Omaha prisoners.

The river I understand, *mes amis.*
I cannot tell you why, but I do.

The fiddle, too, I understand, *mes amis.*
I cannot tell you how, but I do.

And easily from my mouth
flow the sounds of many Indian voices.
But this Teton tongue is a puzzle.
It is a thing I can make no sense of.

Omaha is my mother's tongue
and *this* I can speak nearly as well as I can fiddle.

That is why tonight I have no music in me.
For tonight the Omaha women pleaded for their freedom.

Save us now. And save yourselves, they wept.
Slay the Tetons as they sleep and take their murderous scalps

before they have a chance to kill us all!

William Clark ◈ *the gentleman*

Cruzatte has warned Captain Lewis and me
of the possible mischief to come.

We think it may be a lie on the part of the Omaha slaves
in order to orchestrate their own freedom.

I do not care for this band of ruffians called the Teton Sioux,
for they have crossed the line from pride to arrogance.

They feel they have the right to bully any man
who dares to use these waters for trade.
They are at war with nearly every other tribe.
They are severe even with their own people.
> A select group of braves act as constables,
> walking through the villages policing the people.
> I have witnessed them inflicting harsh discipline,
> severely beating two women who had erred.
They treat their women poorly, as little more than slaves.

The Tetons, constantly at war, take on many prisoners—
> although I must say, nearly *every* Indian nation
> seems constantly at war with some other,
> and slavery is common among them *all*.

Lewis and I have let it be known to Black Buffalo and the others:

In order to ensure peace on the Missouri—
in order for the red man to embrace his civilized white brother—
the Indian must discontinue the practice of slavery.

York <small>◇</small> *the slave*

I must admit, it *had* crossed my mind,
to just up an' disappear one day soon.
Take up with most any Indian tribe that'll have me.
An' I know most any of them would make me welcome.
Why, even these ornery Teton Sioux
seem to judge a man by his courage an' deeds
rather than the color of his skin.

But *then* I saw those wretched Omahas
an' it about broke my heart.
Even red savages have slaves!
Seems like everybody's got himself a slave.
Everybody but the slave himself!

Wait till I tell the missus back home:
There are even slaves in the Garden o' Eden.

Oolum ◇ *the newfoundland*

Among dogs and wolves, the alphas are the ones in charge. Alphas are chosen based on health, wisdom, strength, and courage. Indian chiefs are chosen much the same way. No human may appoint another to be chief. A chief must earn the respect of his people through leadership and courage in peace and war—but mostly war.

The remainder of our visit with the Teton Sioux was a days-long display of heel nipping, shoulder shoving, and teeth baring, all with an aim to establish who would become the alpha leader. But at the contest's end, all the humans, both white and red, refused to tuck their tails.

Having agreed to treat the chief known as the Partisan to a final night's sleep aboard the keelboat, Clark and a small group of men rowed toward the center of the river, where the keelboat waited, anchored at a safe distance. A clumsy bit of steering, though, caused them to break the anchor's rope, the rope that held the keelboat in place.

The collision jolted the keelboat. The anchor jumped and sank. The taut rope snapped like the crack of a rifle. From my position onboard, I thought we were under attack and barked to wake the others. Captain Clark, seeing the boat begin to drift downstream, shouted, "All hands, man your oars!" The Partisan began calling out in his own language that the Omahas were launching a counterattack to take back the prisoners. Within minutes the shore was lined with two hundred warriors, muskets aimed and arrows drawn. Every human present was talking excitedly. Every man was looking for an enemy.

Eventually it became clear what had happened. No Omahas. No treachery. Just a broken rope and a boat cut free. Most of the Indians turned and went back to their lodges to sleep. The white men tied up the keelboat to a tree near the shore. Too near to shore to be safe.

A group of sixty Tetons stayed all night on the bank and watched the boat. The guards aboard the boat watched the shore. And so on and so on until the morning light came. No man slept for a minute.

Such is life among the alpha dogs.

George Drouillard ⬦ *the half-breed*

Flying from the keelboat's mast are two cloth flags.
One red. The other white.
A message to the Teton Sioux:
If you are for peace, stay home and let us be.
If you are for war, prepare to bleed.

I do not have to look up
to see the flags flying—the red flag just below the white.
I do not have to look up
for I feel them both inside my chest.

They are hoisted there within my heart.

Until this confrontation with the Teton Sioux
it had never occurred to me
that I might take the life of a brother Indian.
Perhaps it is the white man's blood in me,
but I felt myself ready to die
in defense of Lewis and Clark and the others.

Is it possible to be both Indian and white?
Can a stranger in another man's land
be for war and peace at once?

Oolum ◇ *the newfoundland*

In time we made our slow, tedious escape from the land of the Teton Sioux. The ambush the Omaha prisoners had warned us of never came. Still, Lewis's duties as ambassador of peace to these new children of the "Great White Father" had failed. Even my master had to admit that there was little hope of embracing these people as allies. He simply consoled himself that no one had been killed.

At first Lewis was overcome with gloom. He barely spoke. He would not write. Then without warning Master Lewis became full of laughter and life. He turned his eyes upriver, with a mind to cover as many miles as possible before making winter camp.

It was now early October, and signs of the coming winter were everywhere. The leaves were changing colors and dropping from the trees. Geese, swans, brants, and ducks were in the sky and covering the river's numerous sandbars. The bars became an increasing problem as the river level dropped. Pierre and the others kept busy searching between the shifting islands of sand for deep navigable channels. My summer fur thickened against the increasing cold.

George Shannon ◇ *the kid*

I'm beginning to wonder
if maybe we'll never see another living Indian.
For days all we have seen are large abandoned villages
along the river's edge.
Each village contains enormous lodges
of circular earth mounds.
As many as sixty lodges in a ring.

I'm told not long ago a sickness killed nearly every soul.
It's a mystery how they contracted it.

More and more villages lay abandoned on the bluffs.
Some have been emptied only recently.
Some have been empty for many years.

Sitting down to dinner one night with our dog, Seaman,
I looked across the Missouri at an empty Mandan village
encircled by abandoned corn and tobacco fields,
dappled now with patches of grass.

A forsaken field of corn is an awful lonely thing.

Suddenly Seaman perks up his ears,
and across the river, I can make out a wounded wolf
running for its life through the corn stubble.

The men were all in merry mood
chattering more loudly than the magpies
and feasting on their fresh-killed meat.

Across the river a group of healthy wolves chased down
the lone, lame beast and killed it.
It was horrible and brutal.
Seaman growled a deep, low growl.

Lewis took out his field book.
He made a note.

Meriwether Lewis ◇ *the explorer*

We discovered a village of Arikara Indians
situated on a three-mile-long island in the middle of the river,
their mound-shaped houses like those in the abandoned villages.
But here there is much life and much laughter.
Smoke pours forth from the tops of the lodges.
The fields beyond the village are brimming with an abundant harvest
of corn, tobacco, sunflowers, beans, and squash.
Hundreds of curious faces — male, female, old, and young —
lined the riverbanks to glimpse the strange spectacle we, no doubt, are.
Women and children, in curious round canoes, paddled out to welcome us.

And we are in luck, for living among these people
is a French trader, Joseph Gravelines, who speaks the language fluently.
This is just one of three villages of Arikara
but with Gravelines's help we will be able to conduct
our usual councils with every important chief.

We have paraded the men and demonstrated the air gun.
We have given out gifts of tobacco, sugar, salt, flags, and medals.
We have been met with much respect and wonder.

Oddly enough, the possession which causes the greatest delight —
even more than the iron corn mill —
is Clark's black man, York!

York ◇ *the slave*

These Arikara are the oddest lot:
soon as we make our way to shore
those Indians just about knock us down with touching us
an' chattering on an' on an' on,
as if we were Jesus an' his pack o' disciples,
showing up at a Sunday camp meeting.

And they're mostly looking at ol' York! Me!
Rubbing at my skin, feeling of my hair,
like they've never seen a black man.
And I come to find out later that they *haven't*!

After a while I figure I'll have my fun,
so I act like a wild animal, jumping an' growling,
an' I tell them I'm half black bear, half man—
a wild animal captured 'n tamed by my master.

Didn't that send them women 'n young'uns running!
How they did laugh 'n squeal 'n clap.

So now it's dark 'n quiet as can be,
an' here lays ol' York, honored guest,
between fine soft buffalo robes.
An' it occurs to me that, in the eyes o' these Indians,
I can be whoever I say I am.

The thought keeps me awake all night long.

Patrick Gass ◇ *the carpenter*

To build an Indian earth lodge is no easy feat.

First you've got to dig a hole some four feet deep
and some forty feet around.
You then set into the ground four thick supporting pillars.
Then lay on smaller cut trees for a roof.
Then add dirt on top of that and maybe sod.

The Indians can climb on top to take in the view.
That's how sturdy the roofs are.

And an earth lodge sleeps forty or so Indians
and their horses too!

Still an earth lodge is inferior to a sturdy-built log cabin
or a frame and plank house if you've got the mill.

And me,
I'd rather fell a tree than dig a ditch
any day of the week.

George Shannon ◇ *the kid*

The Arikara are very friendly

        Perhaps *too* friendly.

They have a curious habit . . . of . . . of . . .
        of, well, *offering* a squaw to their guests.

            The Arikara women are treated little better
            than those among the Teton Sioux.

    I tried to give a hand to a woman who was toting wood
    and she looked at me in confusion, as if I was a mad man.
    "I just want to help," I say.

Just then a brave came up to me quick with a smile and says,
"You like her? She's mine. You take."
The squaw seemed content enough and apparently felt no disgrace.
Among these people it is impolite to refuse such an invitation.

Other men among the crew
were not the gentleman I was.

        Just let the others call me Tenderfoot if they will
        but *I* declined the brave's invitation
        as graciously as possible.

That would be *one* adventure on my journey to manhood
that Mother would surely frown upon.

Hugh Hall ◇ *the drinker*

I think perhaps I may be sick.

Tomorrow we move on upriver.
And I've got to admit I'm rather sad to go.
Them Arikara women are friendly as can be,
and the men think I'm some kind o' hero.
I been called a lot of things in my life,
but "hero" ain't one of 'em.

One brave was so friendly,
I was moved to offer him to partake of my tin cup,
but, "No!" he says. He doesn't drink a drop.
He says liquor makes him act the fool!
Imagine that.
I've been acting the fool my whole life
and it never hurt *me*! Haw. Haw.

Seriously though,
all nonsense aside,
I feel a little strange inside.

Tonight, my good friend Newman started talking nonsense.
He says, "Reed's punishment is unfair!"
He says, "The captains are treating us all like dogs."
He says, "We ought to stay the winter where we are,
and take up arms to make it so."

He asked if he could count on me.

I told him no.

217

Oolum ◈ *the newfoundland*

Although the Arikara were gracious hosts, the captains were anxious to move on. They wanted to reach the Mandans in time to construct lodgings before the river iced over. The Arikara and the Mandans had long been at war. In order to make peace, an Arikara chief came aboard, along with Joseph Gravelines as interpreter. This pleased Lewis, especially in the wake of his failure to broker peace with the Tetons.

Private John Newman, unhappy with the captains' treatment of the deserter, Moses Reed, urged the other humans to mutiny. Not one soldier joined him, and the day after setting out from the Arikara villages, Newman was treated to seventy-five lashes and discharged from the party. He was moved from the keelboat to man an oar alongside Reed and the French engagés in the red pirogue. Neither Reed nor Newman was allowed to carry a gun. In the eyes of Captains Lewis and Clark, Reed and Newman ceased to exist.

Life among the rest of the crew continued as usual. The captains, sergeants, and a few privates wrote in their journals and compared notes. Captain Clark caught an unusual species of whippoorwill, which Captain Lewis examined carefully. Game was plentiful and men took turns walking out to hunt.

For two weeks, Drouillard, Colter, and the other hunters saw signs of the grizzly bear. Many Indians had warned the white men about this massive, deadly creature that could "kill a buffalo with one blow." No one took the warnings seriously. That is until Pierre Cruzatte came upon one while hunting. He looked down the rifle sight with his one good eye and shot the bear through the lungs. The bear reared up, nine feet high on its hind legs—and charged. Pierre dropped his rifle and tomahawk and ran for his life.

John Colter ◇ *the hunter*

Me 'n Drouillard set out t' track th' wounded grizzly.
We expected t' find it jest a few yards away
from th' clearing where Pierre shot it.

There we are, trampin' along, until at last
we see Pierre's gun 'n hatchet on th' ground.
Th' ground's tore up, an' we can see where somethin'—
somethin' *big*—
had chased th' crazy Frenchman.

Across from th' clearin' is a hole in th' thicket
th' width of about four men.

"It went through there," says Drouillard. "You go first."

I hesitate fer jest a second an' Drouillard cracks that dang smile.
"I'm goin'!" I says, an' I crouch down low,
an' I move through th' thorny shrub,
with Drouillard followin' jest behind.

We come upon droppings, too small for bear.
"Wolf," says Drouillard. He's whisperin' now.

A few feet from the scat, we see the drops of blood,
an' the clear track of a wolf in th' dirt.

"Maybe we're onto a wounded wolf," I says.

"No. The wolves are stalking the wounded bear," he says.
"See there. Two wolves. One male. One female."

"Female? How can you tell?" I says.

"See there how the toes of the hind feet angle out? Female," he says.

A few more feet an' we come t' a spring with mud all 'round,
an' in the mud is *the* largest bear track
we have ever, ever, *ever* seen in all our lives.

"Holy Lord in heaven!" I says.

"Some big bear," he says.

Then we hear the buzzin' o' th' blue-tail flies,
an' we see the two wolves,
both of 'em dead,
with their backs broke
an' their tongues jest hangin' out.

"Some big bear," I says.

"Some big bear," he says.

"Let's head on back," I says.

"I'll go first," he says.

Oolum ◇ *the newfoundland*

Leaves were falling fast. The beaver worked feverishly in the streams and ponds we passed. Autumn berries of every kind presented themselves in the chill air. One cold morning we awoke to find a light snow had turned the plains and river bottom white. The cold brought on rheumatism in the necks of Captain Clark and Reubin Field, as well as in the legs of Pierre, who was still recovering from his escape from the grizzly.

Finally, toward the end of October, we began to see members of the Mandan Indian nation lining the banks to watch us. Coming ashore, we met with a group of Mandan hunters. One among them, the son of a recently killed Mandan chief, in order to mourn his father's death, had cut off the two small fingers of his left hand at the first knuckle.

One year and four months after leaving Washington, Master Lewis and I had at last arrived at the Mandan villages.

Meriwether Lewis ◇ *the explorer*

Now, sixteen hundred miles up the Missouri from St. Louis,
we have discovered a suitable location to make our winter camp
just six miles below the most southern of the two Mandan villages.

This place is easily traveled to from all neighboring Indian towns.
Convenient access is essential in order to allow us to counsel the natives
regarding the wishes of the United States, and to gather information
pertaining to the unknown lands that lie ahead.

Living among the Mandans is a Canadian Frenchman,
a free-trader named René Jessaume, who speaks the Mandan language.
With his help I have met with the main chiefs of the Mandan nation.

The grand chief of the lower village, Sheheke, we call Big White
due to his light skin and very wide girth. He is jolly and talkative.
He may prove a useful ally.

Three villages of Hidatsa Indians lie across the river, twenty miles north.
Though the Hidatsa live in relative peace here, they make frequent raids
against the Shoshone Indians who, I'm told, reside at the foot
of the Rocky Mountains — with many fine horses.

Imagine my delight, then, to discover another French Canadian trader
living among the Hidatsa with equal fluency in their tongue.
He came alone to our encampment with the desire to hire on as interpreter.
He mentioned as well that he has a Shoshone wife. Which has me thinking.

His name is Toussaint Charbonneau. He seems a braggart.
And he is useful to us only while we are near the Hidatsa.
But it crosses my mind that it would be to our advantage,
upon meeting the Shoshone, to have his *woman* along.

Charbonneau's wife can act as interpretress.
The horses will be ours, and we will be on our way—
over the hills and on to the sea.

William Clark ◈ *the gentleman*

This spot is well situated for our winter quarters:
water, game, clay, timber, and pasture are all very near.

I have set Sergeant Gass and the others to work
laying the foundation of a fort that will protect us from the cold
and whatever other dangers this wilderness might present.

The Indians are constantly about the camp,
which makes it difficult for my men to go about their business.
The native men are forever asking questions
and some of the women are openly affectionate toward the soldiers.

This afternoon I myself was approached by a squaw
(small and dark-complected) who was not much more than a girl,
yet her mouth was set firm and hard.
She held a large buffalo robe folded in front of her,
which she attempted to hand to me.
I assumed that she had been sent by her husband or brother
to do trade in her affections.
I declined, of course, as graciously as possible.
The young squaw was confused, and again attempted to press herself
    on me.

Just then Drouillard came near with the new interpreter,
    Charbonneau.
"George, tell this woman that I am *not* interested in her — eh —
    attentions."
Both Drouillard and Charbonneau smiled. The squaw still looked
    confused.

"Captain," Drouillard said, "this woman is not offering her—
   attentions.
She is offering you a buffalo skin. It is a gift from Charbonneau.
This woman is his wife."

The young squaw again presented the robe to me,
and when I took it, I saw for the first time
that she was with child (some six months along, by the look of her).

I apologized for the misunderstanding and asked the girl's name.
"Sacagawea," Drouillard said. "She is of the Shoshone tribe."
"Sar-kah-gar—" Her name tripped my tongue.

"Sah-*kah*-gah-*wee*-yah, Captain. It means Bird Woman."
I looked at her fully for the first time,
and I gave her a small knife as a gift.

All through the day I have been searching my mind:
I cannot shake the feeling
that I have seen this young woman's face before.

Sacagawea ◇ *the bird woman*

I passed four winters with the warrior on the white horse.
He adopted me as his own daughter, though he never loved me well.

At harvest time the corn was placed in a pile
over hidden strips of buffalo meat.
The boys would circle around and tear the outer husks from the corn,
racing to uncover the prize beneath.
The girls circled the boys and made necklaces
of the inner husks to give to the boys as a gift.

There was a Hidatsa boy in the village
who always smiled and talked nonsense.
He was not right in the head.
He would hand me husks and I would weave them into links,
but I never gave him the necklaces.

The boy who smiled and talked nonsense
always came to my lodge with gifts,
but I would not take them.

Then one day the warrior on the white horse sold me away
to the white man of the village with hair on his face.
So I became the wife of Toussaint Charbonneau.

There is no ceremony in this.
Just the selling makes it so.
Charbonneau smells.
But he treats me well—mostly.

He has another Shoshone wife, who is jealous and silly.
She is mad because I have a baby inside me while she does not.
She is mad because we live in a tepee instead of an earth lodge.

She has forgotten that she is Shoshone.
I have *not* forgotten.

This tepee reminds me of my home.
If the buffalo were plentiful, we would cover our lodges with skins.
If we had no skins, we wove lodges of grass.

Home.

I have prayed to the white brant.
Send me home, I have prayed. Send me home.
Send me home. Send me home.

Now I am going.

George Drouillard ◆ *the half-breed*

I knew at once that Charbonneau's wife
was the woman from my visions
even though she did not know me.
There was no telling the captains this.
They would have called me a superstitious Indian.

This woman was the spirit of the water
repeating the sign for "my people."
Finally I understood why I had come on this journey.

I helped convince the captains
that a woman and infant would be no trouble.
In fact they might be seen as a symbol of peace
to many Indian nations we encountered.
War parties usually do not bring along their women and children.

The next day, as Colter and I set out for a days-long hunt,
we saw Sacagawea (six months with child)
in the freezing cold, carrying mud to the men building the fort
while Charbonneau slept by the fire, snoring loudly.

Ice had begun to form at the river's edge.
A flock of brant flew overhead, heading south.

Colter spoke: "Look thar, George. Thar's one white brant
amongst that whole flock o' black. Am I seein' thangs?"

"No, Colter," I answered. "I can see it too."

Patrick Gass ◈ *the carpenter*

The cottonwood tree.
In summer it fills the air with white fluff
so that you'd think it was snowing in June.
It resembles the Lombardy poplar.
It's a light, soft wood.
Not my first choice to build a fort,
but it's about all the land has to offer.
Oh, there's elm and there's ash, but all too small to be of use.
I've finally been set to work doing the work I do best.

First we had to fell trees for logs.
I would have squared every log with a broadax and hewing dog
if I had the time and the tools.
But since I lacked both, I opted to stack the logs
in the usual way and leave 'em rough.

A crew of ten or twelve rolled the logs up inclined poles
while the corner men sat atop the end of each wall
to saddle-notch the logs as they came.
And so on and so on, we stacked them to a height of eighteen feet.
That's enough to accommodate a sleeping loft inside
and to discourage an Indian attack outside!

The fort's layout consists of two sides in the shape of a horseshoe.
The open end of the horseshoe will be protected
by a wall of tall pointed logs set on end.
Once finished, our fortress will be virtually cannonball-proof.
Inside there will be shared rooms for all the men,
a cabin for Charbonneau and his wives,
quarters for the captains, a smokehouse, and a blacksmith forge.
Not unlike a small village.

Winter is upon us and we are in a rush
to commence with the building of chimneys.
Every day the Mandans come to watch us work.
The Indians call our hubbub of construction *great medicine.*
At first I laughed at that and said, "No, sir!
This is just a good old backwoods log raisin',
only without the jugs of liquor and the home cookin'."

But now a fort has taken shape
where no fort stood before.
And I think about all those cottonwood trees
left by God as a gift—*great medicine.*

Then I think
maybe the Indians are right after all.

Oolum ◇ *the newfoundland*

For days every human hand was applied to the work of making a fortress from the trees. They swung axes. They rolled logs. They split the soft wood into puncheons. They daubed every crack and gap with mud and grass. The structure was christened Fort Mandan.

One room in the fort was reserved for the captains. This is where they worked at their desks and slept. I slept there too on a floor spot between Lewis's bed and the fireplace. Some evenings I slept outside his door. I would watch the night guard shiver as he walked.

Large chunks of ice had begun to flow down the Missouri. Cold as it was, I found the weather welcome. I could still remember the heat that overcame me on my hike to Little Devil Mountain. This frigid air was comfortable to me, as if the cold was something I was born to. It seemed that when the icy winds blew, they howled out my name.

The humans got by as best they could. They wore animal fur against their skin. They wore hats on their heads and gloves on their hands. But mostly they kept moving. Indians came by every day to talk and trade and watch. White traders from the North West Company and the Hudson's Bay Company stopped by to talk politics and share what knowledge they had of the Indians and the land. Master Lewis did little to mask his contempt for these particular visitors. They were British. And Lewis hated anything British. Captain Clark, always the gentleman and diplomat, was much more accommodating.

Clark knew it was not wise to hold a grudge sixteen hundred miles from civilization. Captain Clark, more than Lewis, understood that the expedition's success would be measured in part by the friendships that were made along the way. And among the Mandans there was no greater friend than Sheheke, Big White. Sheheke knew that the white humans were the only hope his people had of defending themselves against the Sioux and preserving their way of life.

It was on a cold day early in December, with the smokehouse nearly empty of meat, that Sheheke entered through the unfinished pickets of Fort Mandan's forward wall. He shouted to all that could hear, "Pti! Pti! Our prayers have been answered. Mount your horses. Bring your guns. There will be meat enough for all!"

Big White was inviting his new white friends to join the Mandans in a buffalo hunt.

John Colter ◇ *the hunter*

I set out in comp'ny of Cap'n Lewis 'n ten other hunters,
all of us with a mind t' gather in a heap o' buffalo hump 'n hides.
For some o' th' men this was their first chance t' fetch a buffalo robe.
Me, I was in it fer the adventure o' the hunt.

By th' time we arrived, th' Mandan hunters had formed a surround —
by circling 'round th' buffalo an' movin' in close, bit by bit
them Indians had corralled an entire herd o' bellowin' animals,
all runnin' in circles lookin' for a chance t' break free.

In all my life I never seen no better ridin'.
Them crazy braves would charge in close (breakneck speed)
on th' buffalo's right side, an' shoot an arrow
jest behind th' creature's right shoulder.
Then they'd cut back hard 'n fast
in case th' buffalo charged.
An' all o' this mounted bareback, both hands on their bows,
controllin' th' horses with their legs 'n feet alone.
They carried in their quivers an endless number o' arrows.

Us hunters from th' fort, with our Kentucky rifles,
on foot or saddle mounts, could do no better.
In the time it took me t' reload my gun,
they'd let fly six or so well-shot shafts.
All in all we claimed eleven buffalo; the Indians, forty.

That's when th' women 'n children ran out into th' field
t' skin 'n slaughter th' kills. Them Indians use ever' inch o' th' animals.
Nothin' goes t' waste:
The skin becomes a tepee cover, moccasins, or boat.
The hooves become a rattle. The fur becomes a robe.

The shoulder blade becomes a hoe blade.
The brains 're used fer tanning. The bladder's used t' tote water.
The sinews 're used fer bowstrings 'n threads.
What little is left, th' wolves 'n birds will get.

These Indians 're superstitious, it's true.
But I reckon you cain't blame 'em
fer worshipin' an animal
that provides 'em so much
in th' way o' food, tools, clothing, 'n shelter.

By the end o' th' hunt, we were all nearly froze,
but even after Cap'n Lewis 'n the others turned back fer the fort,
I lingered a little fer one last look.

Drouillard tells me th' buffalo have souls.
An' I half believe it's true.
As it was a few degrees below zero, th' steam rose up
from them butchered carcasses

like ghosts on their way t' paradise.

William Clark ◇ *the gentleman*

It has been nearly a week since we last saw the buffalo.
There is little game and much cold weather.
The mighty Missouri has finally frozen over.
The river oddly silent.
Snow and sand blow across the ice
and collect themselves into drifts
while I pass the day tending to my maps
alone in the captains' quarters.
I am forced to recall last winter near St. Louis.
I was lonely for Kentucky then.
Today that loneliness is tenfold.
I calculate we have some two thousand miles yet to go.

When it comes to great Herculean deeds,
I much prefer having done them to *doing* them.
> To be sure, my friend Lewis thinks the opposite.

I've collected information from the Indians and traders
and I have filled in the map as well as I am able.
But from here forward, most of the landscape is unknown.
Like life.

Our hunters have suffered frostbite in their faces,
ears, hands, and feet.
> A soldier who does not relieve himself quickly
> will find himself frosted.

The young Shoshone wife of Charbonneau
seems not to feel the effects of the cold.
I find her rather . . . remarkable.

The thermometer this morning read forty-five degrees below zero.
I have lined my gloves and hat with lynx.
And I keep my writing desk close to the fire

to ensure that the ink won't freeze.

Oolum ◇ *the newfoundland*

Even in the midst of winter's bitter cold, the warm friendship between the red and the white humans continued to grow. Then one day an unfortunate event happened. Five Mandan hunters were attacked by a party of Sioux and Pawnee. Nine horses were taken. Two men were wounded. One man was killed.

Within an hour of hearing this, Captain Clark organized twenty-three volunteers to help avenge the attack on our neighbors. But when the white men arrived at the Mandan village, they could not rally the Indians. "It is too cold," they said. "The snow is too deep. By now the Sioux are gone." There was nothing for Clark to do but return to the fort.

In order to defend the Mandans, Clark and the others had been willing to risk their lives and the expedition's success. I thought about the wolves I had seen attacking one of their own wounded brothers. What wild animal would do what Clark had done?

As December came to a close, Clark and Lewis were visited by the father of the dead Mandan. He brought presents of pumpkins and pemmican. Sacagawea, who was tending a kettle, added the pumpkin to a soup of beans, corn, and chokecherries.

As the dead Mandan's father stared into the kettle, he spoke. Jessaume translated the Mandan words into French; Drouillard translated the French into English. And through the murky layers of language, the fallen brave's father opened his heart.

"I have come to thank you for attempting to avenge the death of my son," he said. "I come to you with gifts from the earth and the buffalo. But it is because of you that my son is dead. You told us if we lived in peace, the Great White Father would protect us. So we sent out small hunting parties, unprotected. And now my son is dead."

The man had said what he came to say. He bent over the kettle and dipped a spoon into the broth for a taste.

"Shusu." He smiled. "Good."

George Shannon ◇ *the kid*

Finally, the ground thawed just enough
for us to finish placing the thick log pickets
that completed our fort's defensive wall.
      We were at it all of Christmas Eve.

          Next morning we were much fatigued.
          Still, all us men rose early to wake the captains
          with a discharge of our guns!
          Christmas had arrived, and we were ready for it.

After an early-morning ration of brandy,
we raised the flag and fired the cannon three times.
This was the first time the United States flag
had been hoisted over what we had dubbed Fort Mandan.
"A toast to the United States!" called out Captain Lewis.
And he issued another round of libation.

      At one o'clock the gun fired to signal all hands to dinner.
      We feasted on elk and apple tarts.

At half past two the gun fired to gather us together, the whole lot of us
crowding into a room that we had cleared for the purpose.
And we danced to Pierre's fiddle.
The only women there, the Indian wives of our interpreters,
stood along the wall and watched.
So we men just danced among ourselves.

          We were at it until near nine o'clock.
          Then our daylong frolic ended.

You couldn't have found a more happy group of fellows
amongst the civilized cities in the Atlantic states.
In fact, I think it was perhaps our general lacking
that made the magic happen—we had only one another.
Would there be another Christmas? No one knew.

So we had determined to make the present one count.

York ◈ *the slave*

Happy birthday, 1805!

We welcomed in the new year properly —
with two blasts of the cannon an' a whoop an' a holler!

Big White invited us to his village to dance an' sing an' carry on.
Nearly fifteen of us went.
Pierre sawed on the fiddle.
Sergeant Gass fashioned a pair o' fiddlesticks
an' he tapped out a rhythm on the strings
while the Frenchman's fingers were all a blur.
Tenderfoot blew the tin horn. Reubin twanged a jaw harp.
The Indians joined with their rattles an' drums.
One o' the other Frenchmen even danced on his *hands*
with his feet up in the air — topsy-turvy!

I twirled an' I shuffled. I jumped an' I spun.
I circled an' kicked till I was dizzy.
An' oh how the Indians stared to see a man my size so agile.
To these Mandans ol' York is *great medicine*.

The Mandan children laughed an' ran whenever I came near,
all the time pointing an' calling out, "Ohkinhedhe! Ohkinhedhe!"

I later came to learn that Ohkinhedhe is the name of an Indian spirit
acted out in their summer solstice sun dance.
In order to dance the part o' Ohkinhedhe, an Indian paints himself
with crushed coal 'n bear grease, so that he is all over black as night.
Then he runs though the village causing mischief.

Now, just look what gift the new year's brung, I thought.
I'm a powerful Indian spirit come to life
with the strength to strike fear into the heart o' any man.
Then it commenced to snow.
Then Mister William said it was time to go,

so I followed him home.

William Clark ◇ *the gentleman*

I find much to despise about the Indian ways.
They treat their women badly.
They are superstitious and moody to a fault.
They are generally immoral and promiscuous.
And yet I have been witness to all these same vices
among my own more civilized white race.
> Some of these natives are afflicted with the venereal
> and yet our soldiers waste no time
> in contracting the affliction for themselves.

The Mandans, despite their faults, are also caring and courageous.
A man and a thirteen-year-old boy were recently lost
on the plains overnight with only buffalo robes for warmth.
Though the man was of no tribal prominence,
yet the entire village wept for his safe return.
> The next morning he arrived home in complete health.
Though the boy was a prisoner from another tribe,
yet his adopted Mandan father worried over him
as if the child was his own blood.
> This boy came to our fort with badly frozen feet but quite alive.
Mandan hunters gladly feed whomever among them is in need of meat.
No one goes hungry, unless they *all* go hungry.
These people do not possess corn grinders.
They do not go to church, nor dine on china and crystal.
And yet, as a people, they possess
some of the best qualities of a healthy society.

Lewis and I are of one mind with President Jefferson: Indians are savages.
But in time they *can* become civilized neighbors
who peacefully coexist with the white man.

Oolum ⬥ *the newfoundland*

The feet of the Mandan boy were badly frostbitten. Lewis placed them in cold water and did whatever else he could. Ultimately, the boy's toes had to be amputated, and it fell to Lewis to remove them. The youngster was allowed to stay at the fort as he healed.

Lewis spent the remainder of January administering to the winter ills of the soldiers as well as the Indians. York often acted as doctor's assistant. George Drouillard, complaining of chest pains, fever, and breathing difficulty, was diagnosed with pleurisy. Lewis's treatment included bloodletting, sweat baths, and hot sage tea. Sacagawea, who was well into the eighth month of pregnancy, became ill twice, and was given stewed fruit and tea.

Nearly all the men at the fort suffered from venereal disease, which was treated with a dose of mercury, taken as a pill, applied as a cream, or administered into the affected area with a gleaming pewter syringe. The treatment was painful and unpleasant, but effective—mostly.

Lewis's favorite medication was a laxative of extraordinary potency called Rush's Pills after the inventor, Dr. Benjamin Rush. Because of the pills' explosive power, the men called them Rush's Thunder Clappers.

As Lewis went about the work of doctoring, I stayed outside in the open air. I watched the humans struggle with axes to break up the ice around the keelboat and pirogues. The men broke through eight inches of ice, only to discover a second layer, three feet thick, beneath the first.

The river continued to flow in small channels inside the ice, so that every hole created filled instantly with water. As January came to an end, the men gave up and left the boats alone. Lewis determined that he would try again when the weather turned. For now the river had won.

All Lewis had to do was wait. And keep himself busy.

Meriwether Lewis ◇ *the explorer*

The ice has slowly enclosed the boats.
The buffalo have not been near for some weeks now.
And our supply of meat is nearly gone.

Clark has taken a number of hunters down the frozen river
to discover game, even if it takes him a week.
And I fear it might.

As Fort Mandan's security has become too lax,
I take advantage of Clark's absence to tighten a rule or two.
> I spied one of the privates scaling the wall after dark
> as well as an Indian who followed the soldier's bad example.
> I've ordered the private court-martialed.
> I've ordered the Indian to leave.
> From now on there will be no Indians within the fort's walls
> from sundown to sunup.
We cannot allow our friendly relations with the natives
to cloud our judgment and compromise our security.

I also occupy myself and our blacksmiths
at a forge and bellows we have constructed
for the purpose of manufacturing and repairing battle-axes,
which the local natives prize and pay dearly for.

I write and I write until I can scarcely hold the pen.
There is no shortage of Indians in need of a doctor.
And the Shoshone woman should deliver any day.

Without these diversions
I would certainly go mad.

Oolum ◇ *the newfoundland*

On the eleventh day of February, the Bird Woman began her labor. Her husband, Charbonneau, was no use, pacing outside, wringing his hands, and muttering to himself in French. Charbonneau's other wife, jealous of the attention paid to Sacagawea, was a reluctant and sullen assistant. Lewis checked in every thirty minutes or so to note his patient's progress.

It was the interpreter Jessaume, along with his wife and me, who stayed by Sacagawea's side. The Bird Woman looked to be about sixteen years old. She had not known womanhood long. She moved about the room like an agitated animal waiting to escape. With each contraction she stopped and moaned, and in the tone I heard my name. The name I thought no human knew.

Sacagawea began to bear down, but the baby would not come. Some hours passed. And the baby would not come. The young female's eyes were glassy. She had no more strength to push. And the baby would not come.

Then Jessaume returned to Sacagawea's side. Had he left the room? He was crumbling the rings of a rattlesnake's tail into a cup of water.

Bois ceci, mignonne, he said. Drink this, darling. And she drank the magic potion as she had been told.

Sacagawea ❖ *the bird woman*

The waters have broken. My baby is coming.
In the time of the Snow Blind Moon.

Riding hills of pain like a white horse.
The white brant is flying above me.

Even as a small girl I rode horses.
My thin legs latched on. I would not let go.
Shoshone horses are the finest. Better than Hidatsa.
The warrior on the white horse
rode a stolen Shoshone animal
and so it seemed my right to ride her.
That same day, the blood of my womanhood
began to flow from me.
Its darkness smeared across the horse's white back
and it was something I could not hide.
The warrior beat me and beat me
and he never again rode the horse to make war.

Hills of pain like a white horse.
White brant flying above.

Whenever the birthing pains come,
I ride the horse in my mind.
Whenever the birthing pains come,
my spirit guide flies over me.
The horse will give me strength to push.
The brant will help me not to tire.
Time after time the pain comes over me.
Time after time until I can no longer be in my body.

Pain like a white horse.
White brant flying.

I ride the horse higher and higher into the sky
until the voices of the men all around me fall away.
Then the horse and the brant become one thing—
a horse with soft white down and wings.
I am on it. Then inside it.
Then the animal is in me and pushing to get out.
I fall to earth fast. The voices of men, now very loud.
I am pierced by the sounding of a rattlesnake.
The winged horse pushes and pushes to get out.
The animal splits me open.

Pain.
Flying.
A baby crying.

He is slick.
Wet. Warm. Red.
The cord still pulsing.
This is my own beating heart that I hold.

I bring my son to me.
Close to my chest.
He latches on.
He won't let go.
My baby.
Born
in the Snow Blind Moon.

Oolum ◇ *the newfoundland*

It seems to me that the memories of human children begin as snippets of sight. Little living pictures in the mind. Maybe it is Mother's face. Or Grandpa's wrinkled hands. Perhaps it is a piece of scarlet cloth. Or a sweet lump of sugar. Or a trip to the ocean.

Dogs, however, are born with eyes closed. My first memory is of something that I heard—the howling of hounds. Everything was dark. And the howling, low and distant, was the only sound I could hear. The noise grew louder and louder until it became a roaring forceful wind. Then everything was lightning, thunder, and explosions. It was planets forming and stardust clouds the size of oceans hissing through nothingness. The blowing heat and crackling wind-flare of a new-made sun. A beautiful, horrible roar.

But as quickly as it had begun, the great howling stopped, and my mother pushed me out into the cold air. My eyes would not open. I felt as if I were barely more than a bean. Mother's tongue was licking my slick fur. I could still hear the wind, though this time it whispered so, so softly. It was scarcely there, and it was telling me my name. Ooooolum. Oooooolum. Oolum. My first memory was the sound of my name. To this day it lingers in my head like the distant tone of a bell.

William Clark ◇ *the gentleman*

For the past eight days, my men and I
have been hunting game, dressing kills,
and packing the meat out of reach of the wolves,
as well as the magpies and ravens.
The cold has been bitter.
The buffalo, deer, and elk have all been thin and meager.
The winter has been hard on man and beast alike.
By the hunt's end we had gathered more meat
than was possible to carry upstream.
Horses and sleds were needed from the fort.
So we braced ourselves for the sixty-mile trip back home.

The uneven river ice bruised and cut my feet
even through the double soles of my fur-lined moccasins.
Land travel was difficult as well, the snow well past our knees.
We pulled our caps close over our eyes
to guard against the glare of the sun on the snow.
        I thought of Julia in Virginia,
        a fair young girl in a handsome gown,
        by the warm hearth in the sitting room—
        busy at her needlepoint.
The contrast to my present situation made me laugh,
but the image *did* warm me some.

We finally arrived at Fort Mandan
and found that, in our absence, Charbonneau's wife
had increased our numbers by one!
I was allowed in the room long enough to see
Sacagawea sitting up by the fire of Charbonneau's hut.
Steam rose from my wet clothing.

The baby was swaddled and at his mother's breast.
The slightest sight of the child's tiny ear—
how it humbled me.
It was delicate and strong all at once.
A single crocus bloom in the snow.
A miracle.

Meriwether Lewis ◇ *the explorer*

This being the Indian woman's first child,
it is typical that her labor was long and difficult.

Mr. Jessaume is convinced it was the potion of rattlesnake
that induced her to finally bring forth.

Whether this medicine was truly the cause or not
I shall not undertake to determine.

Perhaps this remedy may be worthy of future experiments.
I must confess that I lack faith as to its efficacy.

George Drouillard ❖ *the half-breed*

Even though my horse was newly shod,
he struggled to find a foothold on the frozen river,
so I kept as well as I could to the rougher ice.
The three men with me talked and talked
the way that white men do.
All, including me, were in happy mood
despite the harsh cold and want of food,
for we each carried in our thoughts the infant
that the Bird Woman recently brought into our family.
Family. That is what we had become,
and despite the Shawnee side of me,
I had come to trust many of the men.

We were traveling south with two ice sleds,
each one drawn by a single horse.
Robert Frazer, who was always writing, drove one horse.
Silas Goodrich, who was always fishing, drove the other.
I was mounted on the third horse in front of them both.
John Newman, holding a broken musket,
sat on back of Frazer's sleigh.
Newman had been working hard to win reinstatement to the party.
Even so, he was not allowed to carry a weapon.
His gun was just for show.

It was Newman who saw them first. "We've got comp'ny, men."
I turned around in my saddle and looked upriver.
"Not good," I said.
Frazer shifted in his seat. "Oh, Lord."
Goodrich shaded his eyes and leaned forward.
"Damn," he said. "What in hell *are* they?"
I said, "Stay put. Let them come to us."

We squinted as a large party of mounted warriors
emerged from the sun-glare riding toward us.
I counted to assess our odds: just over one hundred painted braves.
From what nation I could not tell.
Their manner told me they had not come to smoke the pipe.

"Not good," I said.

The Indians circled tightly around us.
A handful of braves busied themselves about the two sleds,
cutting each horse free of its harness.
The man I took to be the leader rode up close to me
and spoke in a tongue I did not know,
though the sound of it was distantly familiar.
Using hand signs, I asked him his nation.
He signed back that they were Arikara. He was lying.
That's good, I thought.
No sense in lying to a man you are about to kill.
There was no escaping this now.
My horse could not run on the ice.
And anyway, to run would be to leave the other three men
to their certain death.
I thought of Newman — with his worthless gun.

The Indian leader asked me why
I was in the company of white men,
while my face and demeanor told I was an Indian.
I could think of no response. I offered none.
He tried to take the reins from my hands,
but I would not let go. He did not press the issue,
choosing not to risk a contest of strength in front of his men.

Then he said he would give me a choice:
I could keep the horse and ride away free
or else I could die with the whites.

I turned to the three soldiers and spoke to them a moment in English.
Then I faced the Indian leader
and explained myself as well as my hands would allow.
     "You will not take my horse from me.
     Now *I* will give *you* a choice.
     I keep the horse and we *all* ride away free,
     or else *you* can die with these white men."
     I nodded slightly downward at my gun
       which lay across my lap, its muzzle pointed upward at the Indian.
       Frazer, Goodrich, and Newman as well, held their guns
       casually in the crooks of their arms, fingers on the triggers,
       all muzzles pointed in the same direction as mine.
     "Perhaps one of your braves will take my horse," I continued.
     "But *you* will not, for *you* will be very dead."

The Indian was not afraid to die.
I did not doubt his courage.
But, as I had hoped, he did not wish to die
over an old packhorse and a half-breed.

"Question," the Indian signed. "Are these white men your people?"

"No," I signed back. "These people are my friends."

The Indian waved a hand in the air. He shouted some orders,
and the whole group turned away, continuing on downriver.
Their laughter, jeers, and whooping finally fading
as they disappeared from sight.

Frazer, Goodrich, Newman, and me,
we all commenced, at once, to breathe.
I dismounted to ease my horse's burden
as the others harnessed her to one of the sleighs.

Then we turned north, and pulled our caps down
to blinder our eyes for the cold walk home.

Oolum ◇ *the newfoundland*

When they finally arrived at the fort in the dark, Drouillard, Newman, Frazer, and Goodrich seemed more dead than alive. Lewis was enraged when he heard what had happened. By the next afternoon he was at the head of a twenty-four-man posse, hell-bent on revenge. A handful of Mandans joined the chase.

I stayed behind at the fort, as Lewis requested, and watched the men march off. I could in no way see the sense in this pursuit. No men had been hurt, and two stolen horses hardly seemed cause to jeopardize the expedition. Overnight, rising water had pushed its way up through holes and cracks in the Missouri's ice, only to spread out and refreeze. As a result, the rough ice that had so plagued Clark and Drouillard was smooth as glass for Lewis.

But by sundown the next day, the Indians and soldiers began to trickle back. They informed us that their feet were frozen and the horse thieves were too far gone. They also said that Lewis had determined to continue on with a smaller party until he found whatever was left of the meat that Drouillard and the others had failed to retrieve. Meanwhile the fort's store of food had run out.

Then, six days after he had set out, Lewis returned with two sleighs fully loaded. One sleigh, drawn by the sole remaining horse, held six hundred pounds of meat. The second sleigh was estimated to be holding twenty-four hundred pounds. It had taken sixteen men to pull it up the ice some forty miles or more.

"Seaman," he said, kneeling close, "you're looking as thin as a prairie wolf." My heart was glad to see Lewis laugh.

We all ate well that night.

Oolum ◈ *the newfoundland*

The energy these humans exert in order to survive is astounding. The next day, Lewis and Clark turned their attention back to the keelboat and pirogues. After four full days and numerous broken ax handles, the boats were freed and pulled up onto the shore for repairs. The pirogues would do, but the large keelboat would sit too deep in the water to safely navigate the more shallow waters upriver. Other arrangements had to be made.

Patrick Gass went in search of trees large enough to be carved into dugout canoes. These were the craft that would carry the men westward. Gass and his crew would have to make six in all—each one made from a single tree. Hollowed out and shaped with only muscle, adz, and ax.

About six miles north of the fort, Sergeant Gass finally found what he was looking for. He gazed upward at a stand of old cottonwood trees. He squinted. His mind's eye saw six dugouts standing on end waiting to be won.

Gass calculated in his head. Even considering the soft wood, *he thought,* the job will take about three weeks of hard labor.

He picked up his ax, and he took the first swing.

Patrick Gass ◇ *the carpenter*

Lift. Swing. Chunk!

Drouillard offers tobacco.
To the animals. He kills.

Lift. Swing. Chunk!

He says. It is a way.
Of thanking. The animal.

Lift. Swing. Chunk!

For giving up its life.

Lift. Swing. Chunk!

Before cutting down. This cottonwood tree.
I looked at it. And I said, Thank you. Mr. Cottonwood.

Lift. Swing. Chunk!

Then before I started. Chopping.
I pinch a bit. Of tobacco from a twist.
I pop it in my cheek. For to chew.
Then I spit a bit o' juice. On the roots.

Oh, I *do* appreciate the tree. For making the sacrifice.

Lift. Swing. Chunk!

But why sacrifice. Good chewin' tobacco too?

Hugh Hall ◈ *the drinker*

Lift. Swing. Chunk!

Sergeant Gass. Says.
That.

Lift. Swing. Chunk!

The good. Thing. About cotton. Wood.
Is that. It's so soft.

Lift. Swing. Chunk!

Which makes. The job.
Of carving out.

Lift. Swing. Chunk!

A canoe. So easy. That.

Lift. Swing. Chunk!

A child can do. It.
Well, I wish I. Was a child. Right now.

Lift. Swing. Chunk!

'Cause seein'. As I *ain't*. A child.

Lift. Swing. Chunk!

This work. Is killin' me!

Joseph and Reubin Field   ◇   *the brothers*

Lift. Swing. Chunk!

                                  Lift. Swing. Chunk!

Reubin   Joe?   *Lift. Swing. Chunk!*

Joseph   *Lift. Swing. Chunk!*   What, Reubin.

Reubin   Cap'n Clark says we can send along   *Lift. Swing. Chunk!*
gifts t' th' family back home.   *Lift. Swing. Chunk!*
Reckon we ought t' send Pap that nice   *Lift. Swing. Chunk!*
ram's-horn dipper spoon?   *Lift. Swing. Chunk!*

Joseph   *Lift. Swing. Chunk!*   Pap'd like that.

Reubin   I s'pose you'll be sendin' Mary Myrtle a buffalo robe.

Joseph   *Lift. Swing. Chunk!*   Nope. She told me
Lift. Swing. Chunk!   I had to hand it over
Lift. Swing. Chunk!   in person.

Reubin   We still gonna hunt t'gether?   *Lift. Swing. Chunk!*
After you 'n Mary hitch it up?   *Lift. Swing. Chunk!*

Joseph   Who's the better shot, Brother?   You?   Or Mary Myrtle?

Reubin   I reckon we'll be huntin' t'gether all our lives.

Joseph   I reckon yer right, Reub.   *Lift. Swing. Chunk!*
Now, get choppin'.

George Shannon ◈ *the kid*

Lift. Swing. Chunk!

It seems. This tree. Is. Reluctant.
To become. A canoe.

Lift. Swing. Chunk!

Come on. George. Shannon.
If you can. Carve a canoe.
From a. Cottonwood.

Lift. Swing. Chunk!

Then you can carve. A man. From. A boy.

Lift. Swing. Chunk!

All you. Have to do. Is keep.

Lift. Swing.

Oh, my God!
My foot.
Sergeant Gass!
I've cut off my foot!

Oolum ◇ *the newfoundland*

I was concerned for Shannon when I first saw the deep cut left by the blade of the adz. But Lewis simply dressed the wound and set the private to shelling corn. Shannon had nearly shaken himself of the nickname Tenderfoot, but because of his bandages and wincing walk, the other men took up the comic moniker with renewed vigor.

The young human healed quickly and never stopped talking.

Finally the canoes were completed, and all available hands carried the heavy boats nearly two miles to the water. Each canoe was then paddled downstream to Fort Mandan. It was now near the end of March, and the river's ice was reduced to an endless procession of fast-moving sheets. Once he brought the canoes safely to the bank, Patrick Gass plugged and patched any cracks he found with pitch pine tar.

Indians came to the shore in force to retrieve the carcasses of dead buffalo that had fallen through the ice as it melted upstream. Mandan and Hidatsa boys jumped from one sheet of ice to the next, some no more than two feet square. Swans and wild geese filled the sky, flying northward. Beyond the stench of the rotting meat and wet buffalo wool, I could smell the coming spring.

The river swelled and swirled and rose up high against its banks. During the day the men dried meat and corn for the pending journey. They gathered and packed provisions. Important papers and specimens were loaded onto the keelboat for its trip back East. Captain Clark packed a special bundle to be sent directly to his brothers at the Falls of the Ohio.

At night the captains continued to write by candlelight, while the men danced and sang. Some, reflecting on the untold dangers to come, turned their thoughts to home and family.

York ◇ *the slave*

I shot this buffalo myself.

I skinned it, too, an' gutted it.
An' I hung the strips o' meat to dry.

I dressed the hide as carefully as I could.

I slept on it some thirty nights.
One night I dreamed that the skin
had grown around me.
I had become a buffalo bull,
roaming the open plains
with Sally sitting high up on my back
an' she's laughing an' crying all at once.

Mister William says I can send the skin
in the box bound for Kentucky.

I figure maybe I'll just send it along.
Maybe that way Sally
can dream about *me*.

Oolum ◆ *the newfoundland*

*Finally it was time to go. We had lived among the Mandans and Hid-
atsa for nearly six months. The shores were lined with Indians from
every village come down to see us off. Before setting out ourselves, we
launched the keelboat on its own journey back downriver.*

*Joseph Gravelines, the Frenchman who had served as our Arikara
interpreter, was now to act as the keelboat's pilot. Corporal Warfington
was in charge of the crew. Warfington had orders to shoot his way
through the Teton Sioux if need be. Onboard the keelboat was a small
crew of soldiers and French engagés. Also onboard, John Newman and
the deserter, Moses Reed, shouted their farewells as loudly as any. Smile
as they did, both men would be forever haunted by the sight of their
comrades paddling away upstream.*

*With the keelboat safely on its way, the thirty-three humans bound
for the ocean set their backs into their paddles and oars. Six newly
crafted canoes. Two well-traveled pirogues. Indian gifts, food provisions,
celestial instruments. Guns, gunpowder, and lead. Pens, ink powder,
and paper. Twenty-three privates. Three sergeants. Two captains. One
black man. A half-breed tracker. A French Canadian interpreter. A
Shoshone Indian girl. And strapped to the Shoshone Indian's back — a
baby, two months old.*

*That first day out — April 7, 1805 — Lewis and I walked. My mas-
ter was stiff from days of endless writing at his desk. He was filled with
joy to be on the move again. He gave the appearance of a man returning
home from a long journey. Yet here he was, setting out to make the long
journey longer. We walked up onto the prairie and on past the slow-
going boats as if Lewis meant to complete the expedition on foot. Master
Lewis walked quickly. And as he walked, he talked.*

Meriwether Lewis ◇ *the explorer*

There they are, Seaman! See them there!
Our boats are on the water and headed west.
>Two large pirogues and six small canoes
>their holes patched up with pitch
>and their holds loaded down with supplies.
Every man merry and singing as he works.
And among them all, not a single voice of dissension.

Our little fleet is not so unlike those of Columbus or Cook:
though our boats are not nearly so big,
our sailors are as fine a crew as any that has ever sailed.

Nearly one year and nine months ago
we set off from Washington, walking just as we are now.
>Only then I wasn't clad in skins
>and your fur wasn't covered with burrs.
But you and I go back even further than *that,* don't we?

I remember well when I first met you, friend.
Even before I could make my pick of the litter,
you came over to me and smelled my hand,
and you would not leave my side.

And now, Seaman, old traveler, you and I have reached
the edge of the civilized world—just as we planned.
Nothing left now but to jump off with one loud halloo!
Come, boy, let's not tarry. We cannot rest

until we smell the salt air of the sea.

Part Four

Fort Mandan to Maria's River

April 1805–June 1805

MARIA'S RIVER

MILK RIVER

White Cliffs

ROCKY MOUNTAINS

JUDITH'S RIVER

MISSOURI RIVER

Newfoundland
bitten by beaver
5·19·1805

MUSSELSHELL RIVER

YELLOWSTONE RIVER

BIGHORN RIVER

Indian dog killed
5·2·1805

Newfoundland disappears
overnight 4·24·1805

MISSOURI RIVER

Indian dog joins
corps 4·14·1805

Fort Mandan

YELLOWSTONE RIVER

KNIFE RIVER

North Dakota

Montana

Arikara
Villages

South Dakota

Wyoming

Oolum ◈ *the newfoundland*

The French engagés *were gone. Corporal Warfington and his soldiers were gone. The discharged civilians, Reed and Newman, were gone. Although their numbers had been reduced, this smaller band of men seemed somehow stronger and more able. The group Captain Clark called the Corps of Discovery had been pared down to include only the best and the most essential.*

The Corps' manner of navigating the Missouri had changed considerably from the previous year. The crew of twenty-six who had manned the large keelboat were now in charge of eight smaller boats. Each of the six dugout canoes was paddled by three soldiers. The remaining men were divided among the two pirogues. The white pirogue was the smaller and more stable of the two. And because it was considered the safest craft, the white pirogue held the most precious possessions: the navigational and celestial instruments, the medicines, the journals, the books, the maps, and the three men of the group who could not swim, including Toussaint Charbonneau and Hugh Hall.

Generally the white pirogue sailed at the lead, for either Captain Clark or Lewis was nearly always onboard. Pierre Cruzatte was at the bow. And Drouillard was often at the helm manning the rudder. Sacagawea and her son, Jean Baptiste, were also members of the crew.

The current was rapid. The water cold and clear. On good days the wind would blow in the proper direction to catch the humans' makeshift sails. On bad days the wind would blow violently and in the wrong direction. On such days the soldiers pulled up onto the riverbank to dry out their wet possessions and wait for the wind to change its mind.

No longer held back by the lumbering keelboat, the soldiers were able to average about twenty miles each day. The sandbars and falling banks that had so plagued them downriver were now rare.

During the first few days of our spring journey, Clark and Lewis took turns hunting onshore, leaving Drouillard and the other hunters to help the boats along. On these excursions I could detect the scents of many familiar animals. The elk, the deer, the buffalo, the bear. Badger, beaver, antelope. Even skunk. But the scents were all there was. The animals themselves were nowhere to be seen. Lewis would look down at me and throw out his hands saying, "Look at it, Seaman. Our Garden of Eden is empty." My master was a hunter with nothing to hunt.

Sacagawea ◇ *the bird woman*

These white men will walk many miles
in search of game that is not there,
all the while stepping over edible roots and herbs.

Once I have sought out Gopher's burrow,
I need only a sharp stick for digging.
Gopher worked hard to gather this harvest,
so I give him thanks and offer my apology.
And always I leave a bit behind.
I know what it is like to have everything taken away.

These white men think they own the land.
A beaver is caught at once, one leg each,
in two separate traps, each trap owned by a different man.
The two men who set the traps, each one
thinks the prize is his own.
But the beaver belongs to no one.

My feet, too, are in two separate traps.
I am promised to Sitting Hawk and Charbonneau both.
In truth I belong to no one.
White Brant is my Great Father.
And baby Baptiste is my Pa-Ump ("Pomp" to the white men)—
he is my leader, my firstborn son.

As for my two husbands, that is a simple matter.
It would not be right that Charbonneau be left with nothing.
Sitting Hawk will offer Charbonneau a fine horse.
Or better yet, a mule.

That should be a fair exchange.

Oolum ◇ *the newfoundland*

Gradually the plains began to turn green. Unseen Indians had set fire to the grass in order to bring on the spring's new growth, in hopes that the tender shoots would attract the buffalo. Though the fires were gone, the lingering scent of smoke stung my muzzle. Large white cranes added variety to the usual birds — the brants, the ducks, the geese — that flew overhead out of reach of the hunters' guns.

Leaves began to appear on the cottonwood trees. Plum bushes bloomed. Gooseberries, serviceberries, and currants were greening. The smell of hyssop, sage, and other aromatic herbs seasoned the air.

Aside from the shift into spring, life on the river was much the same. The humans would stop around noon to sup. When game was scarce, they ate boiled corn. When game was abundant, they ate fresh meat. The captains kept writing in their journals each day. Every creek and river that met the Missouri had to be explored, and recorded, and given a name. Camps were created. The fiddle was played. The guns were inspected. The lonely guards marched at night searching the darkness for friend or foe. And they tended to their every precious possession, the way humans do.

On just such one of these typical days, a ragged Indian dog entered our camp. I ran to him to establish the proper order of things. He was smaller than me, but stocky. Although he was thin from hunger, he looked to be strong while in prime. The brown fur on his shoulders was worn — most likely from the rubbing of some heavy travois. This was a pack dog, somehow separated from his Indian masters. Perhaps he had run away.

I had occasionally fallen in with other dogs on this trip, yet I had no true companion beyond Lewis and the other humans. I chose not to chase him away.

He could not — would not — speak to me except in the usual canine ways. He tucked his tail. He bowed low. He offered me his pulsing throat. "Fine, then," I said. "You may stay. For a while."

Meriwether Lewis ◈ *the explorer*

The game is scarce of late,
owing, I suspect, to Indians
in this area not long ago.

The Shoshone woman has provided for us well
during these days of little meat.
We have seen many signs of the grizzly,
mostly in the form of tracks in the mud of the riverbanks
where these monsters come to drink
and to feed off the rotting buffalo floating
down the river in great numbers.

The Indians fear this beast and never attack it
except in the company of many hunters.
They prepare to hunt the grizzly
as carefully as they prepare for war.
The Indians, though, use only bow, arrow, and lance.
And the muskets they obtain from the British
are useless beyond fifty yards.

When we finally *do* meet the grizzly,
the grizzly will have met his better.

Oolum ◇ *the newfoundland*

Indian Dog proved to be good, if silent, company. He attached himself to me and the humans, who threw him raw scraps from time to time. It embarrassed me how he begged and whined and constantly kept under-foot. He was not allowed on the boats, so he kept to the shore, like a stalking wolf. Indian Dog was tolerated. He was not loved. Still it was good having one of my own nearby. I had begun to think too much like a man.

Indian Dog was familiar with the land through which we trav-eled, and silently he guided me to abandoned huts and cold forgotten campfires. We chased squirrels, barked at prairie dogs, ran after ante-lope. Gradually game became more abundant, and one day a buffalo calf mistook me for a brother, following me wherever I went. I pre-tended to be a bull, while Indian Dog played the part of a wolf. He played the part well and the calf ran away, bawling.

A week after Indian Dog had first joined the expedition, the humans, halted by strong winds, set up camp near an area crowded with trees. Indian Dog seemed to recognize the site. He whined and walked in slow circles as he stamped his feet. He wanted me to follow.

He led me to a clearing among a stand of trees where a high scaf-fold had been erected. I took it to be a storage place used by hunters to keep fresh meat out of reach of the wolves. Indian Dog began to tug at the scaffold. With his teeth clamped solidly on the wood, the dog pushed and pulled and shook the structure until something fell to the ground with a heavy thud. The carcass had been bound tightly in buffalo skins. I could tell by the smell that it was human.

This was no hunter's cache. This was a grave. I remembered see-ing many of these behind the Mandan villages, high platforms where the Indians placed their dead. As Indian Dog watched, I examined the scene more closely. The corpse was that of a female. Looking up from beneath the scaffold, I could see the outlines of two dogsleds that had been placed there. On the ground nearby, I found the decayed body of a dog that looked similar to Indian Dog. So similar, I thought, they could be from the same litter.

It dawned on me now why Indian Dog had led me here. When Indians die, their relatives often sacrifice a favorite dog or a horse, so the animal can accompany its master into the afterlife. The spirit of the woman before me had been sent away with one dog too few. While the first dog fell sacrifice to a well-meant hatchet, Indian Dog had selfishly slipped away, leaving his dead mistress to fend for herself.

I looked into Indian Dog's panting face. This dog is not as dumb as he looks, I thought.

Indian Dog barked and began to chase his tail.

Oolum ◇ *the newfoundland*

Indian Dog continued to follow our group, becoming more and more of an annoyance to the humans. He had become progressively bolder, stealing bits of choice meat from the fire, knocking over kettles and drying racks with his constant motion. More than one of the cooks had threatened to shoot him.

One day toward the end of April, a sandstorm struck our camp. The wind would not allow the boats to go. The sand stung our eyes and covered everything. We ate the sand. We drank the sand. We breathed it in, and it coated our throats.

As evening set in, I again left camp and followed Indian Dog, who led me across the high plains to the base of a low hill. The side of the hill was perforated with many mouths of dark caves dug into the earth. Wolves, I thought, and I turned to ask Indian Dog why he had led me here. Indian Dog was gone.

I heard a chorus of high yips and low growls grow from every direction. Dark shapes began to appear. I was suddenly encircled. I felt helpless and human. The wolves had all come closer now, showing themselves. I counted eight. They watched me and smelled me and sized me up. I supposed they were trying to guess what I was. A buffalo? A bear? An odd breed of wolf?

I was tensed and ready to defend myself, but the next move was not my own. I had been watching wolves work now for months. I knew I could not outrun them.

One of the largest among them emerged from the group and approached me slowly, taking his time. The alpha wolf. He circled me and pushed his shoulder hard against my side.

He circled once more and turned to face me. I felt as if a mosquito was trapped in my brain, the whining itch of its wings growing louder and louder until the noise began to shape itself into a language I had heard as a puppy — when my mother would speak to me. Alpha Wolf's eyes held me in place. I realized now that the voice inside my head was his.

"Hello, Cousin. It's good of you to visit."

I tried to speak but couldn't.

Alpha Wolf continued: "No, no. There's no need to speak to me. You've lived so long among the humans, I doubt that you remember how.

"What do you remember, Cousin? Do you remember how to wear your victims down? Do you remember how to weed out the sick? The wounded? The weak?

"Do you remember how to wait till your prey attempts to swim the river? That's when they are most defenseless. They cannot run. They cannot fight. Their superior speed is — equalized. A land beast in water makes a fine fat feast.

"But no, you don't remember that, do you?

"Well, we remember you, Cousin. We know who you are, Newfoundland. We've been watching you. We know where you come from. We know your true name.

"Why live as a slave to humans? You belong here. With us. We've come to take you back!"

Alpha Wolf sprang forward and sunk his teeth into the back of my neck. Up until that instant, any death I had caused was the result of some mysterious murky instinct — an impulse that seemed separate from myself. But the pain and fear of Alpha Wolf's vicious bite released in me the deeply rooted need to survive at any cost. And with that need came the long forgotten knowledge of killing.

I dropped low and rolled onto my back, freeing myself from Alpha Wolf's jaws, clawing upward at his exposed throat to force him backward. As I had expected, all members of the pack had closed in. I picked out what looked like the weakest one of the lot, and I sprung upon it. My intention was not to kill them all — just as many as I could.

I knocked the weakest wolf off balance and bit down on his throat until he stopped moving, until I had bitten clear through. I turned to choose my next kill, but the other wolves had backed away, disappearing into the shadows. Alpha Wolf alone remained.

In my brain I felt him speak again. "You remember well, Cousin. You see, you are not so different from us after all." Then the huge animal turned and slowly walked after the others.

I stood alone, over my kill. Then I threw back my head and howled into the violent wind.

Meriwether Lewis ◇ *the explorer*

Thursday, April 25, 1805
The wind was more moderate this morning, tho' still hard; we set out at an
early hour. The water friezed on the oars this morning as the men rowed.
About 10 oclock A.M. the wind began to blow so violently that we were obliged
to lye too.

My dog had been absent during the last night, and I was fearfull we
had lost him altogether, however, much to my satisfaction he joined us at
8 Oclock this morning.

Oolum ◇ *the newfoundland*

I woke that morning in the hollow of a fallen tree. The events of the previous night seemed distant, and they faded more with each waking minute.

Outside my sleeping quarters I saw a raccoon lying dead on its back. Its stubby legs jutted out straight from its corpulent body. Its throat was ripped open and bloody. Gradually I recalled the fight to claim this shelter from the blowing winds. Where had Indian Dog gone?

Returning to camp, I found the men had already moved on. When I caught up, they were fighting to pull their boats upstream against the relentless wind. Finally they gave up and brought the boats ashore to set up a forced encampment. Master Lewis greeted me with a smile.

"Hello, Seaman, ol' boy! It's good of you to visit. We all feared you had been eaten by the wolves."

The wind and sand picked up and blew against my fur. Beyond the wind I heard the mournful howling of the wolves. And it struck me how they were calling my name.

"Ooolum. Ooolum."

They had been calling my name all along.

Meriwether Lewis ◇ *the explorer*

Monday, April 29, 1805

Game is still very abundant. We can scarcely cast our eyes in any direction without percieving deer, elk, Buffaloe or Antelopes. The quantity of wolves appear to increase in the same proportion; they generally hunt in parties of six, eight, or ten; they kill a great number of the Antelopes at this season.

The wolves take the Antelopes most generally in attempting to swim the river; in this manner my dog caught one, drowned it, and brought it onshore.

Oolum ◈ *the newfoundland*

I had in my mouth a bone from the antelope, caught just two days earlier. I wondered, for a moment, where Indian Dog might be. The smell of the humans' cooking fires brought my nose the answer. The soldiers were camping below the bluff. They were out of view, but the aromas and sounds in the air told all.

Since killing the antelope, it had occurred to me that I might be able to survive alone without the aid of humans. It would be easy enough to hang back and never catch up. I was not the beggar that Indian Dog was.

The thought was crazy.

I felt as if I was two different conflicting creatures. I was wild and domesticated all at once. I was Oolum, and yet I was Seaman. I thought of York. Was he wild or domesticated? He had told the Arikara children that he was a bit of both—a wild animal tamed by Captain Clark. What of Drouillard? What of Sacagawea? What of Master Lewis himself? Is every living thing a bit of both?

My thoughts turned to Indian Dog just as a rifle was fired below. The gun blast traveled across the river along with Indian Dog's startled yelp.

From below the bluff, laughter reached my ears. "That thievin' dawg jest stole his last piece o' meat!" More laughter.

Snow had begun to fall. It covered the new grass and clung to the fragile spring leaves. It dusted the wild roses white.

I bit hard into the antelope bone. I broke it in half. I splintered its hard shell. I exposed the soft red marrow inside.

George Drouillard ◇ *the half-breed*

This evening I walked with Captain Clark on the shore
and I was happy to be off the boat for a while.
My hands, it seems, were meant to hold a rifle
more than a riverboat's rudder.

This far west the grizzly bear has completely replaced the black bear,
so we were not surprised to discover one of them
wading at the river's edge—very large, say, six hundred pounds,
a feast for the entire crew and a week's supply of grease.

Clark and I separated and approached slowly at opposite angles
to catch the bear in a crossfire. We kept close
to the trees, should we have to run and hide in time to reload.

At Clark's signal we both fired at once, aiming for the lungs.
I was not prepared for what happened next.
The bear, when hit, began to scream and roar
as if it held ten other bears inside its skin.
The bear's wailing was so terrible and strange,
both Clark and I forgot, for a second, to reload
and ready ourselves for the angered animal's charge.
But the bear simply sat and cried out.

Clark signaled again, and we both let fly another round.
Again the bear sat. It did not charge. It did not flee.
> I recalled then that I had not offered thanks to the bear
> before I had pulled the trigger. Idiot.
> I had been hunting with white men much too long.
Both Clark and I began to fire and reload, fire and reload,
walking without cover onto the open sand beach, closer and closer.
Damn you, Grizzly Bear! Fight back!

Finally the bear took to the water.
It swam near half the width of the river
to a small island of sand. Then it sat down and bellowed—
not so much in pain but in sorrow
as if it had been betrayed.
It roared for twenty minutes more before it finally died.
I felt as if I had murdered a man.

Most Indians hold that the bear is in some part human.
It may be the way it stands upon its hind legs.
It may be the tender way it cares for its young.
Perhaps it is the way the bear fights back.
Perhaps it is the way it dies so hard.

Perhaps it is his heart.

I scattered some tobacco in the air—a gift
to the soul of the bear—a gift
for its long journey home.

In all, Clark and I had shot the grizzly ten times.
After cutting the beast open, to examine its inner works,
Captain Lewis discovered the largest heart he had ever seen.
"Larger than the heart of an ox," he said.

We removed the skin. We rendered the oil.
We divided the meat among the men for soup.

Meriwether Lewis ❖ *the explorer*

This country is no place
for the delicate sensibilities of refined society.
In this wilderness there is no one to feed you.
There is no one to clothe you.
There is no one to lend you a book of poetry
or pour you a glass of fine French wine.
In this land you must kill your own game,
slaughter your own meat, make your own clothes,
and dress your own wounds.
There is nothing to read here but stars in the sky by night
and tracks in the sand by day.

I wonder, when I return to proper society
(and I have no doubt but that I *will* return),
I wonder . . .

      what possible life can I find
      that will equal, in intensity,
      the life I am living at this moment?

Pierre Cruzatte ◈ *the fiddler*

The men, they call Pierre crazy!
But I say, Captain Lewis, he is the crazy one.
Fou!
The more the wilderness tries to kill him, the more full of life he becomes!
Not so with Pierre, *mes amis.*
A gentle breeze and a straight easy river.
That is the life for me.

But not so today!
Today, the captains, they were both onshore.
And neither was Drouillard, my helmsman, onboard.
Who should be at the rudder, then?
Of course it was Toussaint Charbonneau,
the most timid of all water men in the world!
And what bad luck! To be hit by a sudden wind!
And what else does Charbonneau do but turn *into* the wind!
"Tournes de l'autre côté!" cried I. "Turn the other way!"
But too late.
The wind, he had tipped us, sail and all!

A full minute, the pirogue, she lay on her side
taking on water, taking on water, taking on water.
I thought we would surely sink any second.
"Cut the halyard!" cried I.
"Haul in the sail!" cried I.

And Charbonneau? He cried to his god,
        "Pitié! Pitié! This terrible river will kill us all!"
He would *not* take up the rudder
until I raised my gun to shoot him should he not.
"Imbécile! Take the helm and steer,

or I will kill you myself right now.
This is no jest.
                    You men, grab those kettles!
Now bail this water and save yourselves!"
It is true, more water was inside the boat than out!

Charbonneau, he finally took the rudder!
Mon Dieu! If only he had half the courage of his Indian wife —
calm in the chaos she sat, plucking up one package and then another.
Sacagawea, she saved our cargo from floating away.

Now all is quiet and we have laid out the items to dry.
The captains have served us all a dram to ease this day's alarm.
I say, keep the whiskey, Captain.
Just keep that Charbonneau away from the rudder!

Sacagawea ◇ *the bird woman*

I cannot speak the white man's words
but I know what they are wondering:
Would I be sad if Charbonneau had drowned?
I say I would not will it to be,
for if he drowned, his blood would be on me.

Charbonneau is not a bad man.
Charbonneau is sometimes a weak man.
Charbonneau is not always kind to me.
I think sometimes he hates to look at me
because I have more courage than he.

Today, because of my courage,
Captain Lewis named a river after me.
But the river with my name
will not lead me to the place our people live.
Look, firstborn son.
That is our river.
Not the one with my name,
but the one the Hidatsa call Amahte Arz-zha,
the one the white men call Missouri.
See Mother Elk and her fawn as they swim the water?
That is you and me, little one.
Bull Elk is not with them.
Bull Elk could not swim.
See that water coming from the sunset?
That is the only river for us.

Oolum ◇ *the newfoundland*

On the plains game was plentiful, so the hunting was good. The river, too, was crowded with life. Standing onshore or waist-deep in water, the humans shot many swimming beavers. One evening in mid-May, young Shannon wounded one and called me into action.

"Go get 'im, Sea! Bring me back some supper!"

I had gradually become fond of the wild animal inside me. I felt strong as a grizzly and cunning as a wolf. I could pluck the largest antelope or deer from the river. A half-dead beaver would be a lark.

I swam the river and caught the creature easily. I opened my mouth and, in my usual way, clamped my jaws against the back of the animal's neck. What happened next was a blur. The beaver rolled and broke my grip. Facing me now, he bit and clawed my muzzle, then he went underwater, where I could not gain the advantage of a foothold.

I felt a sharp tug inside my back leg. Felt the beaver's teeth puncture my skin. A stabbing pain. I let loose a high-pitched yelp, and in panic finally found the safety of a sandbar. The wounded beaver surfaced and swam awkwardly away. I saw blood on its sharp orange teeth. My blood.

I recalled watching these creatures gnaw through hard wood. A single beaver could bring down a cottonwood tree as thick around as a man's waist.

Flashes of light floated in front of my eyes. I sat. With every heartbeat, warm blood pulsed out of the wound on my inner thigh. I licked at it, but the blood would not stop. The sandbar around me turned dark as the blood continued spilling out.

"Seaman! Captain Lewis, Seaman's hurt bad!" It was Shannon, his hand on my head. "Seaman! Where'd it get you, boy?" Tired. I lay on my side. So tired. I could not see. "Captain, come quick!" Must sleep. My legs shaking from the cold. "Seaman!" So tired. So cold.

Meriwether Lewis ◇ *the explorer*

Sunday, May 19, 1805

*The last night was disagreeably cold; we were unable to set out untill 8 oclock
A.M. in consquence of a heavy fogg, which obscured the river in such a manner that we could not see our way. Captain Clark walked on shore with two
of the hunters and killed a brown bear; notwithstanding that it was shot
through the heart it ran at it's usual pace near quarter of a mile before it fell.*

    *One of the party wounded a beaver, and my dog as usual swam in to
catch it; the beaver bit him through the hind leg and cut the artery; it was
with great difficulty that I could stop the blood.*

    I fear it will yet prove fatal to him.

George Shannon ⬦ *the kid*

Even though my cut foot had healed,
it was still sore to walk on.
Of course that wouldn't keep George Shannon
from walking guard duty. No, sir.

      We figured Indians were near
      on account of the many abandoned camps we found.
      As well, Indian items had been appearing in the river—
      a tossed tepee pole, a lost skin football stuffed with buffalo hair.
      So I was on my mettle and ready for anything.
      At least that's what I thought.

There I was, facing the river, with my back to the fires,
when I make out the form of a buffalo
swimming toward the boats tied down on the shore.
Seeing a buffalo swim was nothing new
but this one kept on coming, huffing and puffing,
directly at our boats! Like he meant to hop in and row away!

        Instead, though, he reaches the side of the white pirogue
        and he leaps up into it free as you please
        with the greatest clatter and rattle you've ever heard.

Now, *that* was a sight that few men have lived to see:
a huge old bull buffalo standing at the bow of a boat.
He turned and leaped from the pirogue to the shore,
shattering the pivot and stock of the boat's mounted blunderbuss.
The buffalo was crazy with fright! And just like that
he charged up the bank and into our camp.

Finally I thought to holler out to the others
but by then the beast was running through the camp,
its hooves tramping not eighteen inches from the heads of the men,
and most of them still sleeping.

As the men woke and shouted, the bull turned quick
and charged head on toward the tepee—where the captains slept
along with Charbonneau, Sacagawea, and baby Pomp.
Every man in camp woke up and hollered out at once to the tepee.
Even had the captains heard, there would have been no escape
with the buffalo going straight at the tepee's only exit.

Not one eye blinked. No one could turn away.
The bull was big, at least a thousand pounds.
The tepee would be entirely crushed!

My heart sank as I thought of the baby sleeping inside.

Then all of a sudden, the flap of the tepee flew open
and out came good old Seaman, barking and charging
straight back at the angry old bull!

Luckily for everyone, the buffalo turned again
just like a lamb at a sheep dog's command
and it disappeared onto the plain quick as it had come.
Oh, we all gave our dog three cheers
and about a hundred pats on the head.

A scant week earlier, we had given Seaman up for dead.
It's almost as if that dog is not of this world.
I find myself talking to him as if he was human.
'Course my mother always told me,

> *George,* she'd say,
> *you'd talk to a tree*
> *if it would give you the time o' day!*

Well, I don't know if *that's* true
but I sure do like to talk to the dog.
That dog is likely my best friend of our whole group.

Meriwether Lewis ◇ *the explorer*

Sunday, May 26, 1805

In the after part of the day I walked out and ascended the river hills. On arriving to the summit of one of the highest points in the neighbourhood I thought myself well repaid for my labour; as from this point I beheld the Rocky Mountains for the first time.

The points of the Rocky Mountains were covered with snow and the sun shone on it in such manner as to give me the most plain and satisfactory view.

While I viewed these mountains I felt a secret pleasure in finding myself so near the head of the heretofore conceived boundless Missouri; but when I reflected on the difficulties which this snowey barrier would most probably throw in my way to the Pacific, and the sufferings and hardships of myself and party in them, it in some measure counterballanced the joy I had felt in the first moments in which I gazed on them.

But as I have always held it a crime to anticipate evils I will believe it a good comfortable road untill I am compelled to believe differently.

William Clark ✦ *the gentleman*

The discomforts and difficulties of our journey
are now the most plentiful since leaving the Mandans.
The current is very swift, which compels us to pull our boats by cords.
Yet the steep muddy banks offer no footholds.
The wet and mud have rendered moccasins too slick to be of use.
The men's feet are cut and bruised from sharp river rocks.
The elk hide ropes threaten to break every minute.
These ropes, like the skin clothing we now wear,
are rotting away from constantly being wet.
Much of the time the men are forced to wade
waist-deep in the ice-cold water
while the open air is miserably hot.
The plague of mosquitoes torments us without mercy.
Generally the landscape is like that of a desert
with scarcely a tree to be seen.
The air is so dry, my inkwell dries up if I don't close it tight.
And so the gentle river we passed today was a welcome oasis indeed.
It was a handsome thing, surrounded as it was
by box elder and cottonwood trees,
the undergrowth thick with full-blooming roses and fragrant honeysuckle.
I've named it Judith's River
after the Christian name of my own beloved Julia.
Like this river, Julia is an oasis in the desert.
To me she is the current of beauty and hope that runs through
a lonely, barren landscape.

It seems so . . . so . . . contrary to the nature of things
to push a boat against the desires of the river.
Tonight I shall issue a dram to every contrary man.
Tonight we shall toast to Judith's River
and the beauty and hope that she holds.

Hugh Hall ◈ *the drinker*

I am nearly beat to death
with the hard labor of pulling these boats!
But I guess there's a little life left in me yet.
Captain Clark issued us a gill all around.
There was a time not long ago
when a little sip of whiskey just wasn't enough for me.
Now I make do just fine
with one little tipple every day.
But, boy, does that little tipple ever deliver a big wallop!
As a result, I'm a bit tipsy right now.
Nevertheless, I've been doing some calculations.
I've been thinking about our company's whiskey supply
as a mathematical problem.

If a gill of whiskey is about a quarter of a pint.
And each man, of thirty, is drinking one each night.
That makes seven or eight pints each night,
or just over two hundred pints every thirty days.
I figure we got about one and a half kegs left,
each keg holding five gallons.
Now, by dividing the number of pints drunk each day
by the quantity of whiskey we've got left,
I can pretty much determine how long the spirits will last.

I've scratched it out on this piece of paper here.
And by my calculations, the number of whiskey days
we have left is . . .

well, not nearly enough.

Patrick Gass ◇ *the carpenter*

Honestly, I thought I was seeing things.
It was the end of May and was it ever hot!
And not a single tree stood to offer shade.
I figured I was sun-struck when I looked up
and saw the rocky bluffs transforming themselves
into stone walls, like in the bigger cities back East.

But it was true.

For two days of hard travel we sailed through an enchanted world.
All about us were sandstone bluffs
interlaced with slabs of black rock
that stood sometimes a hundred feet high!
Stood straight up like walls of a house built by giants or gods.

The angles were straighter,
the surfaces smoother than anything crafted by man.
And the sandstone itself was formed into spires
and turrets and statues and pyramids.
Great boulders balanced upon thin rock columns
as if God Himself placed them there on a dare.

The place was quiet except for the many martins and swallows.
A few of the men were spooked by these cliffs.
But me, I thought they were a thing of beauty.

What carpenter wouldn't admire such skillful craftsmanship?

York ❖ *the slave*

Something about these odd-shaped cliffs makes me uneasy.
Looks to me like all these stones were shaped by witches,
an' what man here can prove that's not true?
I can't think with these rock walls closing in around me,
with the birds screeching day an' night.
Last night I woke up in a sweat from a dream.

Birds are everywhere, flying all around. It is a gorgeous day. A big yellow sun is beginning to rise, an' I've got my free papers in my pocket. The reins of a six-horse team are in my hands. I'm bumping along, perched up high at the front of a noisy freight wagon hauling what looks to be kegs o' corn. Then the road starts getting more 'n more rough till my teeth are nearly shaking out o' my head. An' all around me the poplar trees are squeezing in. The birds are getting louder 'n louder when my wagon wheels finally bog down to a halt in the undergrowth.

Then all that bird noise seems to disappear inside me. Everything is silent except for the creaking o' the wagon's iron seat spring. The poplars start turning into iron bars. My heart quickens. My arms become wings. My skin turns into black feathers. The wagon's bench becomes a swinging bird perch. I can't keep it still with my big claw feet. An' that big yellow sun has turned into the huge face of a man familiar to me. It is the face o' President Thomas Jefferson.

I've turned into Mister Jefferson's pet bird! The one that he keeps in a window o' the President's House. Mister Jefferson reaches in and places a handful o' feed on the papers lining the cage floor. The top o' the paper reads Instrument of Manumission. The bottom o' the paper is signed, *William Clark*.

George Drouillard ◇ *the half-breed*

I was glad when the whispering white cliffs came to an end.
To me they seemed to be left there intentionally.
They were a warning that I could not decipher.
The air was filled with flocks of birds that lived
in their nests of clay among the rocks.
The sight of them reminded me of the frightful
swarm of wings at the Mountain of Little Devils.

One night as we passed through the cliffs,
I dreamed of the grizzly that would not fight.
Though nearly a month had passed,
I was still haunted by the sound of its dying wail.

But as we left the cliffs behind, game became more plentiful
and I was happy to be hunting again.
I was in the company of Toussaint Charbonneau,
who tramped about and talked loudly,
frightening off any near animals.
With such men it is always best
to let them walk behind, chasing deer and elk my way,
where I would wait atop a rise to fire my gun.

I had been waiting silently for half an hour.
It crossed my mind that Charbonneau may have fallen asleep.
Then I heard him screaming.
Breathing hard, he crested the rise before me,
his eyes red and wide with alarm.
Behind him, running at full gallop,
was a very angry grizzly bear.

Seeing me, Charbonneau ran in my direction.
I called out in French, "Your gun, Charbonneau. Fire your gun!"
Without looking back, the frightened man fired—into the air.
Not good, I thought.
That left only my one lead ball
to stop the bear from killing Charbonneau.
The grizzly a month ago had required *ten*.
Now time seemed to stop and offer me salvation:

Let Grizzly Bear have Charbonneau as a peace offering.
Grizzly Bear would smile and forgive me.
And Sacagawea would surely be better off.
I need only drop my gun and step aside.
In the time necessary for Grizzly Bear to eat the Frenchman,
I could make an easy retreat.

Then time resumed at its frantic pace.
I had made up my mind.
I called out, "Quickly, Charbonneau, take to the bushes!"
Without looking up, Charbonneau dove out of sight
into a thicket of wild roses.
The bear continued on its straight course,
past Charbonneau's hiding place,
toward the spot where I stood with my gun raised.

The bear came on fast, climbing the small incline
that separated the two of us.
By now I could see the white of the bear's teeth,
its mouth hung open as it roared.
Its jaws sprayed spittle and foam.

I aimed toward a spot, about two inches square,
where its eyes and the bridge of its nose came together.
He looked to be six hundred pounds or so.
If I missed, there would be no running away.

A minute later

I gave my thanks over the dead bear.
Charbonneau emerged from his rosebush,
cursing the thorns that tore at his clothing and skin.
As I scattered more tobacco to the animal's spirit,
Charbonneau spat. "Don't waste it, George," he said.
"I could *use* a smoke about now. More so than him!"

Charbonneau looked down at the massive creature.
The man's knees buckled under him.
He fainted dead away.

Meriwether Lewis ◈ *the explorer*

Saturday, June 8, 1805
Came to at a bend in the Missouri where an unanticipated river entered
from the west. Being fully of the opinion that the mysterious stream was not
the main branch of the Missouri, I determined to name it Maria's River in
honour of Miss Maria W—d. It is true that the hue of the waters of this tur-
bulent and troubled stream but illy comport with the pure celestial virtues
and amiable qualifications of that lovely fair one; but on the other hand it is
a noble river which passes through one of the most fertile and beatifully
picteresque countries that I ever beheld. The Maria's River runs past innu-
merable herds of living anamals, it's borders garnished with one continued
garden of roses, while it's lofty and open forests are the habitation of miriads
of the feathered tribes who salute the ear of the passing traveler with their
wild and simple, yet sweet and cheerfull melody.

And what is more,
according to specifications of the Louisiana Purchase,
the farther north Maria's River flows
the farther north the boundary of our nation grows.
North or south?
Which way will she turn?
Which suitor will Maria choose?

Oolum ◇ *the newfoundland*

Any journey, long or short, is simply a series of decisions that must be made. You gather your facts. You search your heart. You choose between your options. Decisions can be wrong or right or somewhere in the middle. Whichever they are, they must be made. Stop making decisions and you stop making progress.

As May gave way to June, the soldiers came to a place where the water divided equally into two streams. Clark and Lewis consulted their maps. The next major landmark should have been a great waterfall. The Indians had never mentioned a fork in the river.

The question then became which fork to take.

To make the wrong choice could cost them weeks, months, maybe even their lives. The captains sought the opinion of every man there. Both Clark and Lewis felt that the left-hand fork, flowing from the southwest, was the proper choice. All the soldiers, including Pierre, thought the right-hand fork, flowing from due west, was correct.

After some thought, the captains determined to explore both forks before making a final decision. Clark, with York, Gass, Shannon, and the Field brothers, headed down the left-hand fork. Lewis took Drouillard, Pierre, and some others to discover where the right-hand fork went. The rest of the men organized temporary camp on the point formed by the two streams. I went with my master about sixty miles up this river that was not supposed to exist. The journey was wet, cold, and exhausting. When we finally returned five days later, Lewis was convinced the right fork was not the Missouri. Pierre Cruzatte, however, was convinced that it was the Missouri. Clark and his crew were still unsure.

In the end, Lewis decided to explore the left fork until he reached the Great Falls—the landmark, learned from the Indians, that would prove the river was beyond doubt the Missouri. Meanwhile, so no more time would be lost, Clark would follow behind in the canoes with the party of soldiers.

The river had become more shallow and difficult to navigate. The captains lightened the men's burden by leaving behind many possessions and supplies. Guns, gunpowder, and lead. Tools, furs, axes, and augers. Chisels, files, tin cups, and traps. All of it was carefully buried in caches to be dug up upon the men's return. Cruzatte supervised the caches' construction.

The red pirogue was hidden under brush on an island in the middle of the river. From then on, its crew was to ride in the canoes, offering the fleet greater paddling power.

Master Lewis, who wanted to prove that his hunch was correct, was anxious to find the Missouri falls. He would set off in the morning in the company of a small party of men. As usual George Drouillard would be among them. Lewis thought Drouillard one of the most valuable members of the Corps. Also joining Lewis's party, one Joseph Field and one large Newfoundland dog.

So, right or wrong, the decisions had been made. The left fork would be the gateway to our next adventure. Even though every soldier thought the captains were mistaken, not one man voiced an objection to their leaders' final determination. These soldiers would go wherever the captains commanded.

We were to set out in the morning. Lewis issued a drink all around. And Pierre, that one-eyed wonder, who it seemed could do most anything, rosined up the fiddle bow, and did what he did best.

Pierre Cruzatte ◇ *the fiddler*

The sun's meridian altitude,
it fixes on our latitude.
Our longitude's a mystery
unless you've got the time.

Don't ask me what the time is, lads.
My watch, she has run down.
Just listen to the fiddle play,
you'll soon be homeward bound.

Oh, latitude and longitude,
our boats have traveled far.
Although we know that we're not lost,
we don't know where we are.

We travel north, then east, then south,
then west, and when we're done,
we chase our tails and end up
in the place we started from!

Oh, latitude and longitude,
our boats have traveled far.
Although we know that we're not lost,
we don't know where we are.

PART FIVE

MARIA'S RIVER TO THE ROCKY MOUNTAINS

JUNE 1805–OCTOBER 1805

Idaho

Nez Percé
Villages

Lolo Trail

Lolo Pass

HUNGRY
CREEK

KOOSKOOSKEE RIVER

BITTERROOT

Cameahwait's
Shoshone Villag

MARIA'S RIVER

White Cliffs

Great Falls
(Falls of the Missouri)

Portage Route

MISSOURI RIVER

JUDITH'S RIVER

Gates of the Rocky Mountains

BIRTH
CREEK

Three Forks

3000-Mile
Island

JEFFERSON'S RIVER

MADISON'S RIVER

GALLATIN'S RIVER

Montana

CONTINENTAL DIVIDE

emhi
Pass

Beaver's Head
Rock

Rattlesnake
Cliffs

Wyoming

UNTAINS

Meriwether Lewis ◇ *the explorer*

I set out in the morning determined to reach the falls.

My departure was delayed a day because the Shoshone woman
had suddenly fallen ill. Her condition was serious,
a situation that caused me much alarm, to be sure.
Her death would lessen our chances for Shoshone horses.

And of course to lose her would sadden us all.
Captain Clark, I know, is quite fond of her.
Until I return, I have given her into his capable hands.
But I had to move on and attempt to discover the falls,
for the falls would let me know with certainty
that we were still, indeed, following the correct river.

My first day out I was sick myself, with an attack of dysentery.
My stomach was cramping and my fever raged,
but still my party made nine miles.
I ordered Joe Field to brew chokecherry twigs into a strong tea,
of which I took one pint—first at sunset, again at ten—
something I learned from my mother.
By this morning the potion had worked its magic
and I walked twenty-seven miles over rolling hills
with a fifty- or sixty-mile view of the plains
which contained the largest herd of buffalo I've yet seen
grazing by the thousands in one continual pasture.

We kept to the river, which bent sharply south.
Thunder rumbled far off. A storm was coming.
My dog barked at a column of smoke rising up from the plain.
No. Not smoke, but water spray.
Not thunder, but the roar of falling water.

Nearer and nearer. We were running now.
Louder and louder, as we came close to the river's edge.
Water vapor filled the air. We breathed it in. It coated our skin.
I descended the huge bluff to take in the sight:
> A cataract of eighty feet or more. Three hundred yards across.
> The entire flow of the Missouri River cascading
> in one smooth sheet over a razor-straight edge of rock.
> Then broken by jutting boulders, exploding as it fell.
> Spraying upward. Dancing. Sparkling jets of foam.
> Water smoke rising two hundred yards in the air.
For all time this sublimely grand spectacle
has been hidden from the view of civilized man,
with only a dumb audience of cedar and cottonwood trees.

Tonight we are dining on buffalo hump and tongues,
marrow bones and fine trout, all seasoned with salt and pepper.
I began this trip unable to keep a bite on my stomach;
tonight my appetite has returned.

John Colter ◇ *the hunter*

Well, Cap'n Lewis, he proved us *all* wrong.
Th' big falls proves this river is none other than th' muddy Missouri.
An' not only that, beyond th' big falls is another 'n another 'n another!
All in all twelve miles o' rapids 'n cataracts.
It's th' most fearsome grand sight a Kentucky boy like me
could ever hope t' see.

So th' next order o' business is th' "portage,"
which is fancy river talk for "walking around rough water overland
so as not t' break yer necks in th' boats."
Me 'n George Shannon jest got back
from scoutin' out th' land fer th' portage.

> Tenderfoot is quick turnin' into a crack backwoods hunter.
> When that boy stops talkin' long enough t' squeeze a trigger,
> he hits what he's aimin' at more 'n not.

It had taken us more 'n half th' day, round trip,
across a rapid creek, down 'n up two steep ravines,
and an eight-mile stretch without a lick o' water.
Why, we crossed up 'n down ditches that we could scarcely climb.
An' us with only our packs 'n guns.
There jest ain't no way t' haul six heavy dugouts 'n all our belongin's
fer eighteen miles over setch land as this.
Me 'n Shannon told th' same to Cap'n Clark soon as we returned.
I said, "Cap'n Clark, with all due respect, sir.
But thar ain't no way we can carry them heavy canoes all that way!"
The Cap'n jest looks up from his writin', 'n he says,
"Very well, then. We shall begin first thing in the morning.
If we can't *carry* the canoes, we shall fashion wheels, and *roll* them."

Cap'n Clark says he aims to sail on *land*!

Patrick Gass ◇ *the carpenter*

Today I saw a bona fide miracle.

I set out with a crew of five to oversee
the transformation of our dugouts into freight wagons.
All in all we required four sets
of axletrees with couplings, tongues, and bodies.
The resulting wagon can be used either with*out*
the bodies for to transport the canoes
or *with* the bodies for to transport the baggage.
We took down the mast of the white pirogue
and cut it into lengths for to make axles.
The mast was a bit too thin for the purpose
but seeing as it is the hardest wood we've got
the mast will have to suit.
At the top of the creek where our portage is to begin,
I found a large cottonwood tree,
near perfectly straight and some twenty-two inches around.
We felled the tree, and after a rigorous session with the whipsaw,
we produced sixteen round wheels and a couple to spare.

That solitary cottonwood tree was perfectly suited
for to become four sets of wagon wheels.
That tree growing on the very spot
where we were to begin our journey by land.
And there being no other such tree for twenty miles in any direction.
(I know, 'cause I looked.)

Now *that's* a miracle.
I thought about George Drouillard.
I spat another bit of tobacco juice
and I gave that tree my thanks.

Meriwether Lewis ◇ *the explorer*

Happily, it seems assured
our Shoshone interpretress will recover.
Her husband, Charbonneau, is much gratified
and calls me a worker of miracles.

But there is no miracle in this.
The woman's pulse was very weak
and she had a twitching of the fingers and arms.
Her pelvic area was inflamed and painful,
      some sort of obstruction of the menses.

We first bled her.
But bleeding seemed to make her worse.
So I gave her sulfur water to drink from a nearby spring.
      I'd say by its look, it contains also iron.
A poultice for the infected area.
Doses of bark and opium.
Vitriol when she regains her legs.
She is nursing now and able to attend the child.

So Charbonneau calls me a worker of miracles.
But I am better than a worker of miracles.

I am a practitioner of medicine.

Oolum ⬥ *the newfoundland*

As the Bird Woman grew stronger, the humans prepared for the over-land journey that they called *portage*. Over the winter the Hidatsa had warned Lewis and Clark about the "Great Waterfall," but they had said nothing about five waterfalls and miles of impassible rapids. The Indians had assured the captains that the portage would amount to two or three strenuous miles. After Captain Clark had finished placing marker stakes to show the way, the portage was eighteen miles long over steep inclines and waterless flatland strewn with prickly pear cactus and no shelter from the burning sun.

The men set up two camps on either end of the trail. At the lower camp, located at the foot of the falls, Charbonneau and Sacagawea tended to the fires and fed the hungry men. This arrangement pleased the soldiers as Charbonneau was an excellent cook. This arrangement also pleased Charbonneau as it excused him from hard labor.

Here at the lower camp, Captain Clark had all the baggage divided into three groups, one for each of three planned trips. Among the first items to go was the disassembled iron framework for a boat that was to be reassembled at the upper camp and covered with skins. The boat, nicknamed the Experiment by the men, had been designed and built by Lewis himself back East. It was to replace the white pirogue, which Clark now left behind, carefully hidden beneath some brush.

The upper camp was situated above the falls, where the boats would eventually be placed back into the river. Lewis was camped there, acting as cook in order to free up every available man. Patrick Gass and John Shields were there as well to assemble and cover the Experiment. Joe Field and George Drouillard hunted and helped about camp as they could.

Lewis dubbed this upper camp White Bear Island, because of the numbers of grizzlies that hung about. The grizzly, called the white bear by the Indians because of the long silver-tipped hairs in its fur, lurked around the falls to feast on the buffalo carcasses that lined the shores of

318

the rapids. Buffalo who lost their footing were washed away by the current and dashed to pieces downstream as they plummeted over the high falls. The stink of flesh with its promise of easy meat was more than the bears could resist. They were hungry and aggressive, coming within an inch of killing Joe Field and chasing George Drouillard up a tree.

I rarely rested at night because of them. While Lewis slept, I barked and barked to keep the beasts at bay.

Earlier in the week, I had entered Lewis's camp to find wolves all about. They had eaten much of the meat that my master had prepared for the soldiers. When they saw Lewis with me, they ran. A female lingered defiantly at the edge of camp. I understood by her look that she knew who I was. Cross over the loss of the men's supper, Lewis raised his rifle to shoot. But the female had vanished.

What followed for the humans was a week of long exhausting days. The dugouts were heavy even when empty. When the ground was firm and the wind was good, the sails were hoisted on the wheeled dugouts to "sail" across the prairie. But at its worst, the plain was too muddy to allow the wheels to turn. Or else the mud, churned up by buffalo, dried in the sun into sharp points that cut the men's feet. And even the doubled soles of the soldiers' moccasins were not thick enough to stop the needle-like spines of the prickly pear cactus that blanketed the ground.

Axles broke. Men fainted. The sun overheated them. Rain and wind chilled them. Sudden hailstorms showered down, with no trees near to hide beneath. More times than not, the soldiers crept across the plain, making the eighteen-mile journey one slow step at a time.

Joseph and Reubin Field ◇ *the brothers*

step — HEAVE — step   *step — HEAVE — step*   *step — HEAVE — step*

Hey, Joe?   *step — HEAVE — step*

I don't know about you, Brother.
But I'm done tuckered out.

step — HEAVE — step

Oh, but that's right.
You ain't tuckered out.
'Cause *you* ain't here.

step — HEAVE — step   *step — HEAVE — step*

Oh, Gawd, no. You're workin' hard.
Huntin' under some shady tree.
Liftin' your big, heavy gun.

There *you* are huntin'. An' here *I* am pullin' on this boat.

step — HEAVE — step   And me being the better shot!

step — HEAVE — step   *step — HEAVE — step*   *step — HEAVE — step*

You know, Joe.
We ought t' talk like this more of'en,
me an' you.

step — HEAVE — step   *step — HEAVE — step*   *step — HEAVE — step*

George Shannon ◇ *the kid*

step—HEAVE—step   *step—HEAVE—step*   *step—HEAVE—step*

Inch by inch.   Mile.   By mile.

step—HEAVE—step   *step—HEAVE—step*   *step—HEAVE—step*

I'm making.   My way.   Into man.   Hood.

step—HEAVE—step   Went hunting.   *step—HEAVE—step*

Brought in.   Six hundred pounds.   Of meat.   *step—HEAVE—step*

Feel strong.   *step—HEAVE—step*   Like I could.   Go on.

step—HEAVE—step   Forever.   *step—HEAVE—step*

When I get.   Back home.   I'll tell my.   Brothers.   I've done something.

Something not one of them.   *step—HEAVE—step*   Has done.

I'll say.   We hoisted.   We hoisted a sail.   *step—HEAVE—step*

On a ship.   With wheels.   *step—HEAVE—step*   *step—HEAVE—step*

I'll say.   George Shannon.   Can.   Sail.

Without.   Water.

I'll.

Say—

Pierre Cruzatte ◇ *the fiddler*

step — HEAVE — step   *Mon Dieu!*   *step — HEAVE — step*

I think young Shannon.   *step — HEAVE — step*   He has fainted up ahead.

Even me.   Pierre.   *step — HEAVE — step*   I had grown tired.

Of the hard work.   *step — HEAVE — step*   On the winding.   River.

Even Pierre.   Longed to go.   To go by land.

But I had hoped.

step — HEAVE — step

To leave the boat.

step — HEAVE — step

Behind!

step — HEAVE — step

And now.   *Mon Dieu!*   It is raining yet again!

William Clark ◇ *the gentleman*

This rain may yet prove the death of me.

The men have been halted by mud on the plains
and so I have chosen to walk along the river.
My goal is to replace some notations recently blown away
by this cursed wind. I'm in the company
of Charbonneau, Janey, and little Pomp.
     To keep my tongue from tripping on her name,
     I've taken to calling the Indian girl Janey.
My man York is off searching for game.
We've arrived at the largest of the Missouri falls,
a drop of over eighty feet and a beautiful thing to see.

But a cloud overhead warns us of a coming storm,
and I've seen this kind of cloud enough to know
that this will be no light summer shower.
The wind picks up and threatens to throw us into the water,
so we leave the river's edge and walk upstream
to a deep ravine above the roaring falls.

As usual, I place under a ledge the guns, powder horns,
my compass, and circumferentor—anything we hope to keep dry.
I add to this my umbrella, a handy invention
     but useless in this wind.
And so we settle in to wait out the coming storm.

Janey has removed Pomp's clothes
to arrange him a diaper of rabbit skin and grass.
     Little Pomp, just four months old
     and the most courageous voyager of us all.

I wonder if the most observant and perceptive explorers
are also the most innocent?
I've just begun to ponder this question when
a low resonant rumbling noise interrupts my thoughts.
I can hear the sound and feel it all at once.

FLASH FLOOD!

What a fool I was.
This ravine is a spillway.
"Move! Move!" I yell.
Charbonneau cries out and begins to scramble up the rocks.
Janey, with the naked child in one arm,
is attempting to gather Pompy's clothes.
"There's no time for that!" I say,
and I push her upward after her husband.
I then scramble up too, as best I can,
grabbing my gun and shot pouch in my left hand,
climbing the steep ravine with my right hand.

By now rain and hail is falling in torrents from the sky
and the gully has filled almost instantly to five feet,
the coming flood forcing rocks, trees, and mud before it.
Charbonneau is frozen in fear and won't move.
"Lend her your hand, man. Pull her up!"
The water reaches to my waist now.
        It has wet my pocket watch.
Finally Charbonneau extends his wife a trembling hand
as I push from behind when I can.

At last we reach safety at the top of the ravine.
The rock shelter where we had huddled just minutes before
is now submerged under a terrible current
more than fifteen feet deep.
The red-brown clay washing down the gully
gives to the water
an appearance of blood.

Oolum ◇ *the newfoundland*

The storm that nearly killed Captain Clark's party was typical for the plains. Storms would begin without warning, dropping hailstones, rain, or both. The hail that fell that day assaulted the soldiers exposed on the open ground of the portage route. Hailstones the size of musket balls knocked some of the men off their feet. When Clark returned to camp, he found the men bruised and bloodied, as if he had come upon a field hospital near some recent battle.

Clark had lost his compass and umbrella. Charbonneau had lost his tomahawk and gun. Little Pomp's clothes and mosquito netting had been washed away as well. The naked child was wet, cold, and inconsolable. Sacagawea, who only last week had recovered from near-fatal infection, whispered to her baby and wrapped him in a dry blanket.

As July began, the humans finished transporting the last of the baggage and boats around the falls. But Lewis's experimental boat was not yet finished. The many skins had to be sewn together and attached to the metal frame. Some substance had to be found to seal the many seams. The season was growing late. If Lewis's boat did not work, many days would be lost. My master was pensive. The Indians had not given him proper information about the Missouri falls. What other surprises would he come upon in the days ahead?

The Fourth of July was reason to celebrate, and as usual the men rejoiced with rifle fire and fiddle. A mysterious boom, like the discharge of a cannon, was frequently heard in the mountains. Even Lewis was at a loss to explain its source. The men simply reasoned that it was the wilderness's way of celebrating Independence Day.

The last drops of whiskey were handed around. No more would the soldiers drink merriment from canteen or cask. The only spirits, from then on, would come from each man's heart. They feasted on bacon, beans, buffalo, and sweet suet dumplings. They joked and sang and ate. My master Lewis, retiring to a secluded fire, opened his journal to write.

Meriwether Lewis ◇ *the explorer*

Thursday, July 4, 1805
We all believe that we are now about to enter on the most perilous and diffi-
cult part of our voyage, yet I see no one repining. All appear ready to meet
those difficulties which await us with resolution and becoming fortitude. And
all appear perfectly to have made up their minds to suceed in the expedition
or purish in the attempt.

Hugh Hall ◇ *the drinker*

I've never been one to lay down my life for anyone or anything.
Oh, I've been dying for a spot of liquor before
but that's about it.
Now here I sit,
a soldier for the U.S. government
in the middle of God knows where!
My feet are bloody from prickly pears.
My head is bruised from hailstones.
I've got untold aches in my muscles and bones.
Captain Lewis has rigged up a boat
that I *swear* won't float.
We're fixing to cross monstrous, freezing mountains.
We're looking for Indians who don't want to be found.
And *now* the whiskey's run out.

All of this in order of increasing calamity.

When I joined the army back in Pennsylvania,
I intended on being a snowbird.
> You know, a man who joins the army in the winter to keep warm,
> but then deserts at the first whiff of spring.
Well, here I sit and I take my last sip.
And I guess after all I'm no snowbird.
I've passed enough springs without flying away
that I *must* be an honorable man.

Meriwether Lewis ◇ *the explorer*

I had no pitch to pay her seams.

In Washington, I spent many hours designing and planning
my unique boat. The boat Sergeant Gass calls the *Experiment.*
At Harper's Ferry I delayed my journey for weeks
to oversee the boat frame's proper construction.
I transported it overland to Pittsburgh.
I brought its metal skeleton along the entire Ohio River
and up the Mississippi.
I kept it dry through the St. Louis winter
and the Mandan winter as well.
I hauled it carefully against the current
2,857 miles up the Missouri River,
so I might assemble her and cover her hull with the skins
of thirty-eight elk and four buffalo.
I've had Gass and Shields and Joseph Field
working nonstop, putting in her woodwork
and lining her inner walls with bark.
But I had no pitch to pay her seams.

You see, there are seams where the skins were joined
which can be easily made watertight with generous application
of sticky pitch pine tar, extracted readily from the sap of the tree.
But here there are no pines.
So I made do
and fashioned a cement of tallow and crushed coal.
She was beautiful, her hull as smooth as glass.
She was thirty-six feet, four and a half inches long,
light as a feather, and as few as five men could carry her,
yet she would hold eight thousand pounds.
When we placed her on the water, she floated like a perfect cork.

And then it rained.
And the tallow and coal slid away.
Then she took on water and sank.
Not like a stone, but slowly.
For I had no pitch to pay her seams.

There was nothing to do at that moment
but
go fishing.

So here we are, Seaman my friend,
at the bank with a meager hook and line,
    even though I *know,* by earlier observation,
        that this area of river above the falls contains no fish at all.
    I theorize the reason why is —

But wait.
A tug at my hook.
A bite.
It's a chub.
A bit of light on a dark day.
Look here, you beautiful Newfoundland.
Watch it shine.
A silver fish to scoop up in my net.
It seems our luck is turning yet.

George Drouillard ◈ *the half-breed*

I will be happy to leave this place.

The spirit of the bear is very strong here.
I feel as if the bears have gathered above the falls
to guard the gateway to the rest of the river.

The day the soldiers finally finished their portage
Captain Lewis organized the men into a war party.
Our aim was to enter the large island nearby
where the bears had been frequently sighted.
Just this morning I had seen one,
       a male, maybe four hundred pounds, not fully grown.
He stood in full view by the water
and he seemed as if he was urging me to follow.
But I had no desire to meet him.
Days ago, one of his tribe had been stalking me.
He had hunted Joe Field and me,
following our tracks to the base of a tree,
where I got in a lucky shot from above.

The captains treated our assault of the island
as a decisive counterattack.
About fifteen of us, including the captains,
split up into smaller groups of three and four.
But the thick willow made it impossible to stay together,
and I soon found myself alone.
I saw the young male bear just as he saw me.

He came on fast.
I raised my gun in reflex,
       checking the flint to be sure it hadn't slipped.

I aimed for the spot right between his eyes,
but he suddenly halted and raised himself up.
Just twenty paces in front of me, he stood on his hind legs.
And as the tall bear roared, I shot him in the chest,
which toppled him onto his back.
Before he could get to his feet,
I jumped headfirst into the thicket.
In the time it took to reload my gun, the other men joined me,
and we followed the bear's trail of blood
one hundred yards to where he lay dead
with the lead ball from my gun in his heart.

Strangely there were no other bears on the whole island,
this place where they had been numerous and troublesome for days.
There was just this one that I had killed.

I scattered tobacco into the hard cold wind
blowing from the snow-covered mountains.
Perhaps this bear was trying to kill me.
Or perhaps this bear was warning me to abandon my journey.
Or perhaps he was showing me the way.

Sacagawea ◈ *the bird woman*

It is wise to fear Grizzly Bear, little Pomp.
But you must also give him thanks.
For when the time comes for you to leave this world,
Grizzly Bear will show you the way.

See up there? Those seven stars?
The white men call them the Dipper.
But really those stars are Grizzly waiting patiently.
I will tell you the story as it was told to me
when I was very small.
The story of how the Great Bear came to be in the sky.

One day Black Bear, with her cubs,
was eating berries from a bush.
Grizzly Bear walked up to Black Bear
and he said to her, "I want those berries for myself."
And selfishly, he pushed away Black Bear.
And he pushed away Black Bear's children.

Black Bear was much smaller than Grizzly
but she had courage and fought him.
She avoided Grizzly's powerful blows
and each time Grizzly missed, Black Bear would strike him
with her own sharp claws
until Grizzly Bear fell to the ground—defeated.
Black Bear then banished the greedy Grizzly Bear.
She told him, "Leave this place and never return."

Grizzly Bear left in disgrace.
He felt ashamed because all his life
he had placed his own needs before the needs of his brothers.

He wished now to make up for his selfish ways.
He wished to do something good for his brothers.
Alone, he walked into the Shining Mountains.
For miles and miles he walked up the steep slopes.
Day turned to night, but he kept climbing higher.
He reached the deep snow on the mountaintops,
and the snow turned his brown fur white.
Yet he kept on walking higher and higher.

And when he reached the highest mountain peak,
Grizzly Bear stepped into the air
and he continued walking upward into the sky.
And as he climbed, a dust of snow fell from his fur,
leaving a milky white trail as he went.

Finally Grizzly Bear found his place
and he became a cluster of stars.
To this day, the Great Bear lives in the night sky,
guiding the souls of his people
to their proper place in heaven.

Oolum ◇ *the newfoundland*

After the portage was complete, the humans kept busy stockpiling meat against the lean days ahead. They knew that game would become increasingly scarce as they traveled closer to the Rocky Mountains. The failure of Lewis's frame boat meant that two more canoes had to be made. Five days (and countless broken ax handles) later, the men added two very large canoes to the fleet. Finally, now with a total of eight boats, the Lewis and Clark expedition proceeded on. The half-day portage promised by the Indians had taken us, in total, twelve days.

The captains knew from the Hidatsa that the Shoshone would not be far, and Sacagawea gradually began to recognize familiar landmarks. So that the rifle shots of the party's hunters would not cause the Shoshone to go into hiding, Clark, with a small group, walked ahead to meet the Indians. But he was forced to return. His feet were so badly punctured by thorns, infection had set in. A sore angry boil rose up from his ankle.

Meanwhile Lewis and the remaining men continued to navigate the Missouri current, which grew stronger with each passing day. Walking on shore, Master Lewis caught sight of the first pine tree and thought about his cherished metal boat, buried at the head of the Great Falls. He consoled himself by foraging through the ripe currant bushes of red, yellow, purple, and black. The yellow one he proclaimed the best.

Eventually the river reached an area of high cliffs, which hemmed the river in to a narrow channel without embankments. For three miles the river ran between rock walls that rose straight upward more than a thousand feet. Master Lewis called this the Gates of the Rocky Mountains.

After leaving behind this narrow pass through the mountains, we entered a fertile prairie. The river began to meander. The way became choked with islands. The landscape had opened into an extensive plain, where the Missouri split itself into three rivers at the center of a beautiful flat meadow.

My master recognized this area from Indian descriptions. "Finally," he shouted. "The three forks of the Missouri."

Meriwether Lewis ◈ *the explorer*

Sunday, July 28, 1805

Both Captain C. and myself were of the same opinon with rispect to the impropriety of calling either of these three streams the Missouri and accordingly agreed to call the Middle fork Madison's River in honor of James Madison, U.S. Secretary of State. The South East fork we called Gallatin's River for Albert Gallatin, the Secretary of the Treasury.

The South West fork, that which we meant to ascend, we called Jefferson's River in honor of that illustrious personage Thomas Jefferson, the author of our enterprise.

Our present camp is precisely on the spot that the Shoshone Indians were encamped at the time the Hidatsa first came in sight of them five years since. From hence they retreated about three miles up Jeffersons river and concealed themselves in the woods. The Hidatsa pursued, attacked them, killed 4 men, 4 women, a number of boys, and made prisoners of all the females and four boys.

Sah-cah-gar-we-ah, our Indian woman, was one of the female prisoners taken at that time; tho' I cannot discover that she shews any immotion of sorrow in recollecting this event, or of joy in being again restored to her native country. If she has enough to eat and a few trinkets to wear I believe she would be perfectly content anywhere.

Sacagawea ◇ *the bird woman*

Captain Lewis does not understand why
I do not show my heart to him.
He does not understand why
the line of my lips remains hard as a bird's beak.
And it is not my place to help him understand.

Many days now I have seen signs of my people:

The creek of the white clay.
We make paint from the white earth
that we gather from its banks.
I see the creek of the white clay.
This tells me my people are near.

The bark peeled from the trees.
We do this to obtain the sap
and the soft inner bark for food.
I see the bark peeled from the trees.
This tells me my people are near.

The empty grass and willow lodges.
We weave the grass
when we have no skins.
I see the grass and willow lodges.
This tells me my people are near.

Smoke rising over the mountains.
The meadows set ablaze.
The smoke is a signal to all Shoshone bands
to gather together and leave their mountain hideouts
to hunt the buffalo.

I see the smoke rising.
This tells me my people are near.

And now we have come to the place
where the three rivers become one.
The place where we saw the *Pah-kees*, the enemy,
and we tried to run.
The place that I was taken from.
I vowed when I was captured never to smile
until I had returned to my people.

How am I to show these white men how I feel?

I left this place as a slave;
what am I now that I have returned?
Who is Bird Woman now?

Today Captain Lewis caught a young crane.
The crane was helpless, newly feathered, unable to fly.
I thought he would surely kill it,
and yet he set it free.

The crane was full of joy at being returned
to its home in the meadow.
But the sight brought sadness to me:
> there is no joy in freedom
> when freedom is granted only
> at the whim of another.

William Clark ◇ *the gentleman*

We encamped at the three forks for two nights,
resting the men, drying our baggage, and hunting for meat.
Without Shoshone horses we shall find ourselves
in an—unfortunate state.
Accordingly Captain Lewis has now set out by land
to find these shy Indians if it takes him a month.

The rest of the men and I will continue to struggle up the Jefferson.
The current is rapid and can only be run with cord and pole.
The soldiers spend three-fourths of their day in the water.
Every three hundred yards or so we hit another riffle
obliging us to pull the heavy boats across the rocks.

The days are very hot. The nights are very cold.
The men wish much to leave the water
and resume their journey on land.
I cheer their spirits as best I can.
I even push a pole myself from time to time.

On the plains above us there are but few deer and antelope.
The only signs of the buffalo are droppings and dried bones.
The prickly pear is now in full bloom,
      a beautiful plant that I very much loathe.

Today we met a small stream, which I've named Birth Creek
for my thirty-fifth birthday is today.
My only gift? A painful boil rising on my ankle.
I console myself that, assuming I'm not killed,
it will be just a year before I return to polite society.
Sufficient time, I should hope,
to recover my feet for dancing.

Oolum ◈ *the newfoundland*

I joined Master Lewis as he set off by land to search out the Shoshone. George Drouillard, too, was with us, as well as privates Shields and McNeal. Sacagawea had recognized a large rock and declared that her people could probably be found camped on a river over the ridge to the west. She called the rock the Beaver's Head, so named for its resemblance to a swimming beaver. It was huge, and the sight of it made the tender scar on my inner thigh throb.

The first day out, our little party found and followed an Indian road over rugged mountains that confined the river below to a narrow chute. Lewis named this area Rattlesnake Cliffs. The serpents were basking on every rock. I took care to avoid them. So did the men. The river below the cliffs was rapid, rocky, and crooked. Clark and his men were in for a difficult time along this stretch of water.

Once over the Rattlesnake Cliffs, we followed the water's edge for miles to a handsome level prairie where the river divided into two branches. Both streams were shallow and rocky. Lewis declared that, past this point, the boats would be able to go no farther. He wrote Clark a note, urging the main party to camp at these forks until he could return with Shoshone or horses or both. Then we followed the right-hand branch, which bent to the west.

The small creek led us along a narrow corridor between steep cliffs, which eventually spread apart to form a vast open area surrounded by a perfectly circular ring of high mountains. At the center of this mountain bowl was a beautiful grassy prairie, itself encircled by rolling hills with rivulets running through them. Each rivulet cut a small valley through the base of the surrounding mountains. There were perhaps only four small trees as far as the eye could see.

"This is one of the handsomest coves I have ever seen," Lewis declared. The privates built a fire of willow brush. Drouillard hunted. Lewis scratched ink into his leather-bound book. And we camped.

The next day we entered the cove in search of an Indian road that might take us over the mountains. Any trails were hidden from view amidst the prickly pear and grass that covered the ground. So Drouillard walked far to the right. Shields walked far to the left. Lewis, McNeal, and I took the center. Whoever came upon a path was to hold his hat up high on the muzzle of his gun as a signal to the others.

After some five miles of searching, an Indian on horseback appeared, riding slowly toward us. Lewis quickly lifted his spyglass and shouted, "He's Shoshone. I know it!"

My master was beside himself and rushed to drop his glass and gun. He told McNeal and me to stay, and he walked toward the Indian slow and easy. A mile from Lewis, the Indian halted. The captain pulled a blanket from his pack and flung it high, spreading it out as it fell to the ground. He repeated this motion two more times. This, Lewis knew, was an invitation to talk.

Drouillard and Shields continued walking toward the Indian, who eyed them with suspicion. Lewis cried out, "Tab-ba-bone! Tab-ba-bone!" He understood from Sacagawea that this was the Shoshone word for white man. Drouillard and Shields continued walking. The Indian shifted his attention from left to right to left. Before Lewis could stop his men from advancing farther, the jittery Indian tugged on his rein and vanished over the low rolling hills.

Lewis watched as what may have been his only hope for horses disappeared. This had been the first Indian seen in 1,400 miles of travel. It may have been the last. That night it rained and rained until my master was soaked to the skin.

In the morning Drouillard discovered that the prairie grass had raised itself up to drink in the last night's rain, completely erasing the Indian's tracks. So we resumed our search for signs of a recently traveled path that would lead us to any Indian villages hidden in the mountains. We passed small conic lodges of willow brush at the mouth of a clear, cold creek. The Indians had been there. The ground was torn up from a recent search for edible roots. I felt small gravel stones crunch beneath my paws. I looked down. There near the abandoned huts of brush was a wide plain road that a blind man could have found.

Not even the evening's cleansing rain could erase the strong scents from this road's yellow dirt. I detected the smell of tanned leather, grease-paint, roots, horses, dogs, and humans. This was the well-traveled path of an entire nation. The open road beckoned, so we followed. The creek followed too, growing more narrow with every mile. This stream was all that was left of the Missouri. Now it was a creek. Now it was a rivulet. Now it was a trickling rill. McNeal stood with a foot on either side of the running water and yelled aloud with great ceremony, "Thank God, that I lived to bestride the mighty and heretofore deemed endless Missouri River!"

I sprang to the opposite bank and back. My master bent to take a drink.

Meriwether Lewis ◈ *the explorer*

I had followed the road to the most distant fountain
of the waters of the mighty Missouri
in search of which we had spent so many toilsome days
and restless nights.

Thus far, I had accomplished one of those great objects
on which my mind had been unalterably fixed for many years.
Judge then of the pleasure I felt in allaying
my thirst with this pure and ice-cold water.

I urged the others on. I was impatient to get to the top of the ridge.
We had finally reached the Great Divide,
the long high spine of land that separates the continent's waters.
On the eastern side, all rivers flow east
to the Atlantic and the Mexican Gulf.
On the western side, all rivers flow west to the Pacific.

I was fully prepared to stand on that ridge and face west
to behold open land similar to that I had just passed through,
with the Columbia, like the Missouri, meandering
through flat or waving prairies on its way to the sea.
Instead, what I saw was mountains.

And not a single simple chain as the Appalachians were.
The Rockies were a sea of high peaks, all covered with snow,
a jumble of immense ranges that folded and collided, one into the other,
spreading out across the land for miles and miles to the west
as far as the eye could see.
My heart sank at the thought of the terrible task
my men would be forced to endure.

We proceeded on down the steep western slope
and in less than one mile we came to a handsome bold running creek
of cold clear water. My dog lapped at its surface.
I knelt. I cupped my hands.
I looked up at Drouillard, Shields, and McNeal.
"Drink up, men—you've certainly earned it.
This is the distant water of the great Columbia River.
From this point on we shall travel *with* the current!"

George Shannon ◇ *the kid*

Captain Lewis has been gone now nearly six days.
He seems to be nearly four days ahead of us now.
Every now and then we happen on a dead deer in a tree,
a welcome gift from Drouillard.

We recently passed a large island
that we called Three-Thousand-Mile Island
as it sits three thousand miles upstream from St. Louis.
It seems that this river will never end.

Captain Clark tries his best to raise our spirits
but the men are nearly spent.
We're forever in the water, pulling the boats over rocks
and our feet are in constant pain.
We exert ourselves to the verge of collapse
to progress only four miles in a day.
And all the while those terrible mountains loom to the west
with their snows that never melt.

The men all want to proceed by land:
winter is nearly here and may make those mountains impossible to cross.
And anyway, how can we hope to cross the Rockies,
even carrying only the most essential supplies,
without the aid of horses?

The men fall more and more silent as each day passes.
I'm not even certain what to say myself.

Every soldier ponders but one thought:
if Captain Lewis doesn't find the Indians soon,
we will all surely die.

Oolum ◇ *the newfoundland*

I cannot speak as the humans do, and yet as a seer, I may understand what they say even better than they. Weeks ago Lewis asked Sacagawea to sound out the Shoshone word for "white man." Specifically, Lewis asked Drouillard. Drouillard asked Charbonneau. Then Charbonneau asked Sacagawea. It seemed a simple enough request to the men. But I could see the confusion on Sacagawea's face as she searched for a word that did not exist. At last she said with satisfied certainty the only word that fit. She said, "Tab-ba-bone." It was the Shoshone word for stranger.

"Tab-ba-bone! Tab-ba-bone!" *Lewis was approaching two seated female Indians and a male who sat atop a horse. A pack of a dozen Indian dogs swarmed nervously at the horse's feet. Lewis held beads and trinkets in his hand. With the other he attempted to roll up his sleeve to expose his white skin.*

The Indians watched from the top of a rise a safe half mile away. As usual Drouillard, the two privates, and I hung back as Lewis performed his awkward dance of friendship.

"Tab-ba-bone! Tab-ba-bone!" *Lewis held the gifts up. He lifted his sleeve. He smiled. He kept walking.*

The women vanished behind the rise. The man held his ground for a while, observing Lewis as one observes an unusual animal. Then the Indian disappeared as well. The dogs were the only ones left.

Finally reaching the top of the hill, Lewis approached the mongrel pack. He tied trinkets to ribbons and ribbons to a handkerchief. He reasoned that a gift around a dog's neck might reach its master's hands. But try as he might, the skittish dogs would not be caught.

"Tab-ba-bone! Tab-ba-bone!" *Lewis cried to the animals without thinking. And he fell backward as a dog got tangled in his legs. The pack rushed off all at once, leaving Lewis alone, sitting in the grass at the top of the hill. Without standing, he returned the gifts to his bag and removed a plant specimen he had gathered by the river. An unusual*

346

variety of honeysuckle, he thought. And he held it upward to the light to get a better look.

"Tab-ba-bone! Tab-ba-bone!" *We had taken the three Indian females by surprise when we crested the top of a steep ravine just thirty paces from them.*

One of the three, a young grown woman, ran away. A girl child and an old woman stayed behind. They saw they could not escape. They knelt and bowed their heads and wept. They expected any moment to be killed by this crazy man who shook his fist full of beads, yelling "Stranger! Stranger!" and clawing at his arms.

Lewis helped the Indians to their feet, placed the trinkets in their hands, and smudged their cheeks with vermilion paint, a bright red swath under each eye. It was a Shoshone sign of peace he had learned from Sacagawea. He urged the child to bring the other woman back before she could alarm her tribe. A few minutes later the young woman returned, and the three Indians, together, began happily to escort the friendly, if somewhat strange, white men to the Shoshone camp.

No more than two miles down the road, a party of about sixty warriors mounted on excellent horses came on at full speed. Lewis left his gun with his men and advanced with the Indian women, who spoke excitedly and showed the head chief the gifts they had been given.

The chief of this small band was called Cameahwait, or He Who Never Walks. Lewis was delighted with the name because an Indian who never walks must own many horses. After speaking to the Indian woman, Cameahwait, with two braves at his side, approached Lewis and, for a moment, met the captain with a fierce, piercing gaze. Then he laughed and embraced my master with startling affection. The chief swung his left arm over Lewis's right shoulder, clasping the captain's back as both men's left cheeks met. In the midst of the hug, Cameahwait said repeatedly, "Ah-hi-ee. Ah-hi-ee." *I am much pleased. I am much rejoiced.*

347

What happened next was a minutes-long dance of embracing. Arms entwined. Backs slapped. Cheeks besmeared with grease and paint. The men's voices were a jarring chorus of ah-hi-ees as all sixty warriors felt obliged to individually greet Lewis and his three human companions. Long before the greetings were complete, the soldiers had had their fill of the Shoshone traditional hug.

After arriving at Cameahwait's village, the men sat down to smoke the pipe as usual. As was their custom, the Shoshone removed their moccasins, an oath that they would speak the truth. Any Shoshone who lied at such a council was obliged to forever walk the prairie barefoot, a horrible fate, since the prairies were blanketed with cactus. Lewis took off his moccasins as well. His boots had long since fallen apart.

Lewis regretted, now, his decision to leave Sacagawea behind with the boats. Through Drouillard's hand signs, my master did what he could to explain himself. It had been many months since he last gave his speech about Jefferson and the United States. There would be time enough for that later. Besides, by crossing the Great Divide, we had also crossed the new boundary established by the Louisiana Purchase. We were no longer on U.S. soil. What Lewis wanted now was horses and help moving his baggage to the nearest river that flowed into the Columbia.

Lewis explained that there was a second white chief waiting at the Jefferson River forks. Lewis asked Cameahwait to come and meet Clark. From there he would need horses to carry any trade goods to the Shoshone camp. And if no water route was near, he would purchase the horses necessary to cross the Rockies by land.

Cameahwait's eyes narrowed.

"The river near my village is too rough for water travel," he warned. "My people have lost many horses in the latest raid. I fear there may not be enough horses to spare.

"Some among us do not trust you. They fear you are working with our enemies. If a man wishes to sell his horse, it is his own business. Help to carry your possessions must be each man's own choice. Every man here is his own chief. But I will tell them my mind."

Cameahwait stood to address his people. Shells adorned the chief's hair. Seashells. As the chief began to speak with great ceremony, the ocean seemed closer than ever before.

"I shall go to the place where the strangers are camped," he said. "I wish to meet the white man, and I wish to know his mind. I am told that among the white men is a woman of our own nation, who is now returned from afar. Among them they tell me is much big medicine. Among them they tell me is a white man who is black with great strength and hair that curls.

"Stay or go as you will. But this black man, I must see."

York ◇ *the slave*

This Missouri River is longer than a Sunday sermon
an' just as full o' hell, sweat, an' discomfort.
An' still no sign o' Cap'n Lewis, nor Indians, nor horses.

I am plumb wore down to a nub,
but every time I tug a rope
an' every time I push a pole . . .
For every hard-won mile I go,
I just may be closer to earning my freedom.
It's not my place to bargain, o' course,
but I can't help having my secret hopes.

I've been listening to the white folks moan.
They say they want to go on land.
Their feet are sore.
Their muscles are tuckered.

Now, don't get me wrong.
It's not my place to criticize.
An' most all these boys possess goodness an' courage to spare.
I'm not saying they've got no right to complain.

But at least Mister William isn't driving them with a whip.
At least they get a monthly wage.
At least if they live to make it back,
they can walk on home free men.

Yessir.
This Missouri River is mighty long.
But life is a lot longer.

George Drouillard ◇ *the half-breed*

We rode with the Shoshone slowly
toward the forks of the Jefferson.
Clark, with the other soldiers and boats,
was due to meet us there.
Cameahwait was strong and wise.
His eyes held the intensity of a true chief,
but his face was thin and sunken.
He was a starving warrior.
His people were goodhearted but very poor.
Among the sixty men,
I counted only three indifferent muskets.

Captain Lewis offered four braves payment
to carry himself, McNeal, Shields, and me.
Thus I found myself riding double behind an Indian
who wore a headdress of wolf skin.
Like myself this Indian was a hunter and a scout.
Later he shadowed me when I left the group to hunt.
He was suspicious. I respected that.

All men with us, white and Indian, were suffering from hunger.
Luckily I brought down a large buck
and before I could properly butcher the deer,
the Indians set upon the carcass,
devouring the organs I had cast away.
I kept a hindquarter for myself and the soldiers
and gave the balance of the meal to the Shoshone.

The next day as we neared the forks area
the Indians slowed the horses.
Cameahwait placed his robe upon Lewis's shoulders.

The robe was an ornate tippet of otter fur
adorned with hundreds of weasel skins
and accented with shells.
But Cameahwait was not offering a gift.
He wanted Lewis to look like a Shoshone
in case of any ambush ahead.

The scout who shared his horse with me
bid me to wear his own headdress as well.
I fitted the wolf skin over my head and shoulders,
and following Lewis's example, I gave the Indian
my army-issue hat—and my gun, too.
We took each other in and laughed.

Later, the scout told me, through hand signs,
"You and I are much alike. I consider you my friend.
It is Shoshone custom among friends to exchange names."
And so I took to calling him George
and he called me by his own name,

Sitting Hawk.

Soon after, Sitting Hawk and I saw,
up ahead, a woman and two men.
The woman began to jump and point toward us,
and she touched her fingers excitedly to her lips.
My people. My people. My people.

It was Clark. It was Charbonneau.
It was Sacagawea coming home.

Sacagawea ◇ *the bird woman*

Today I am filled with much joy.
Today I can smile again.
Today I can cry again.
Today what was missing has been returned.

I walked up the river ahead of the boats.
I walked ahead of Captain Clark.
I walked ahead of Charbonneau.
I heard the blowing of horses and I knew.
And then I saw the otter fur and ermine skin and abalone shells.
The bear claw necklaces and calumet feathers.
Leggings and moccasins. Baskets of tight-woven willow.
I saw the dresses of antelope.
Porcupine quills dyed red, dyed yellow, blue, and black.
I saw poggamoggans, bows, lances, and shields.
I saw tight-skinned starvation. Weary hunted eyes.
Hair cropped close to mourn the dead.

These people were Shoshone and the very band that I was born into.
My cousin was among them.
My cousin who was with me the day that I was taken.
They call her Leaping Fish now because of how
she skipped across the water to escape.
Even the man I was promised to, Sitting Hawk, was there.
He looked much older. The past five winters had been hard.

Later I sat down at the council to transfer the men's words.
I looked at the chief whom my people called Cameahwait.
And I stared at and studied his face.
I realized this man was my brother!
My older brother.

The very brother I thought was dead.
He was here and alive.
I ran to him and threw my blanket over both our heads.

I cannot say what Captain Lewis was thinking
as he waited impatiently for my weeping to cease.
But there was a smaller, more important, council to be made
beneath a blanket, hidden from view.

Lewis heard, I suppose, the urgent embracing.
My brother's startled cry of recognition.
The whispered sorrows over our murdered mother.
The laughter over memories of better days.
The quiet flutter of the white brant's wings.

Oolum ◈ *the newfoundland*

It was my master's way to come alive to meet a challenge, only to withdraw as soon as the challenge was met. He had followed the Missouri River more than three thousand miles to its headwaters. He had crossed the Continental Divide. And he had found and created a friendship with the Shoshone Indians. He had thus ensured us the horses we needed to seek out a water route to the ocean. He had accomplished all of this, yet he was still visited by a familiar gloom that had haunted him from childhood.

Within my master's heart, joy and sadness were constantly at war. Perhaps after all there had been evil at the Mountain of Little Devils. Perhaps the spirits' arrows had poisoned him somehow.

Meriwether Lewis ◈ *the explorer*

Sunday, August 18, 1805
This day I completed my thirty-first year, and conceived that I had in all
human probability now existed about half the period which I am to remain
in this Sublunary world.

I reflected that I had as yet done but little, very little indeed, to further
the hapiness of the human race, or to advance the information of the succeed-
ing generation. I viewed with regret the many hours I have spent in indolence,
and now soarly feel the want of that information which those hours would
have given me had they been judiciously expended.

But since they are past and cannot be recalled, I dash from me the
gloomy thought and resolved in future, to redouble my exertions and at least
indeavour to promote those two primary objects of human existence, by giving
them the aid of that portion of talents which nature and fortune have bestoed
on me; or in future, to live for *mankind, as I have heretofore lived* for *myself.*

Oolum ◇ *the newfoundland*

Master Lewis soon cleared his mind for the tasks at hand, and the tasks at hand were many. Clark left with eleven men to explore the river that flowed by Cameahwait's village. In honor of his friend and co-captain, Clark named the stream Lewis's River. Both the Shoshone and Clark were certain that the waters of Lewis's River eventually drained into the Columbia, but all Indians insisted that neither the wild river nor the rugged land through which it flowed could be traveled. Clark wanted to judge the route for himself. Indian information had been wrong in the past. And so he set out.

Lewis, meanwhile, stayed behind to oversee the portage of the baggage from his camp where the canoes had halted to the Shoshone village. He dug another cache for unessential items. He ordered that the canoes be sunk to protect them from flood or prairie fire. Drouillard trapped beaver and brought in what game could be found. Many were occupied with the usual tedious packing, sorting, and arranging. Still other hands were busy building pack saddles from dismantled wooden boxes and the blades of canoe paddles.

Sacagawea ◇ *the bird woman*

Sweet Baptiste.
Firstborn son.
I fear that we may be a tribe of two.
Although I hoped it would be so
Sitting Hawk will not have me.
He says I have been ruined.

I did not abandon my starving people.
I did not ask that my mother would be murdered.
I did not choose to leave the Shining Mountains.
I did not choose to be Charbonneau's wife.
All these things were put upon me.
Yet Sitting Hawk will not have me.

He says I have been ruined
because I birthed the child of another man.
Yet how can that possibly be
since you are the only pure thing in my life?
How can you have ruined me?

I will not give you up, Baptiste.
We have many mountains to cross.
You cannot yet even walk.
I shall be your legs.
You shall be my heart.

If having you has ruined me,
then ruined I shall be.

Oolum ◇ *the newfoundland*

After many days' exploration, Clark was forced to admit that Cameah-wait had been correct about Lewis's River. Continual violent rapids and waterfalls snaked through high cliffs and deep ravines that would not allow even a safe path by land. But Clark had heard of a trail to the north that the Nez Percé Indians used to cross the mountains in search of buffalo. A Shoshone Indian named Swooping Eagle told Clark that he had once accompanied the Nez Percé and learned the way. Swooping Eagle, whom Clark and the men nicknamed Old Toby, warned the captain that it was a long, difficult hike over high ridges and down steep slopes. There would be little game for the men and scarce water and pastures for the horses. But Clark reasoned that if an entire band of the Nez Percé could cross with their women and children, his seasoned soldiers should be able to manage, whatever the obstacles.

When Lewis learned from Old Toby that the Nez Percé Indians lived along a river that eventually led to "a great pond of ill-tasting water," my master was convinced. While Clark was exploring Lewis's River, Lewis himself had successfully transported all his possessions to Cameahwait's camp. Now the two captains had reunited and were busily trading whatever they could to purchase Shoshone horses.

Sacagawea ◇ *the bird woman*

At first the prices had been good.
One horse in exchange for an old checkered shirt,
a used pair of leather leggings, and a knife.
Three horses in exchange for a few handkerchiefs,
three knives, and a uniform coat.

But my people are preparing for a trip themselves.
They are gathering with other Shoshone bands
to hunt the buffalo east of the Shining Mountains.
My people's own need for packhorses is driving the prices up.

My task is to translate between two worlds,
assisting the barter:
my people's horses for the white man's wonders.

The women of my village, even Leaping Fish,
say that I have changed.
They say I trade in favor of the white men.
Because I can speak the Hidatsa tongue
they feel I cannot be trusted.
They criticize the way I dress.
They feel that I look down on them.

Perhaps they speak the truth.
The Shoshone are a poor people.
I do not want to be hungry and poor,
and at times I miss all I had among the Hidatsa,
the abundant harvests and the grand celebrations.
The blankets and glass beads of the British traders.

I am ashamed of the feelings at war in my heart.

Oolum ◇ *the newfoundland*

Finally Lewis and Clark had acquired twenty-nine horses. The last of our provisions and Indian gifts were lashed to the saddles with strong leather thongs. Each man had a hundred rounds of ammunition in his pouch. Each soldier carried a set of winter clothes. With Old Toby and his son showing us the way, we set out on our route, past Cameahwait's encampment and along the river's edge.

We said farewell to the Shoshone, and we went our separate ways. Cameahwait and his people were headed east to the land of the buffalo. The Corps of Discovery was headed west to the land of the Nez Percé.

William Clark ◇ *the gentleman*

I will miss these Shoshone Indians.
They are polite and respectable people.
The other day a brave offered me
the use of his mule so that I might ride.
I gave the honorable fellow a fine waistcoat in return.
Even among savages, and in the rough wilderness,
it is always important to be, above all else, a gentleman.
No gentleman, for example, would strike his wife,
as Charbonneau did at supper just a fortnight ago,
the evening before we met the Shoshone.
Struck young Janey over a dish.
Failed to fetch it quick enough, he said.

Truth is, Charbonneau was jealous of her:
He knew that *her* job as interpreter
was far more important than *his*.
He knew that without her help,
we might not make it over the mountains alive.
He knew she was smarter and stronger than him.
He knew she did not fear him.

I took him aside and I gave him my mind.
This puppy! This coward!
My blood was up, I promise you.
And I'll promise you one thing more.
Now that Janey is to continue on our western tour,
I promise you this: Toussaint Charbonneau
will *never* raise his hand to her again.

Sacagawea ◇ *the bird woman*

My heart is heavy.
I could not stay with Cameahwait. So much has changed between us.
I overheard him speaking to the men of the band.
The tribe was to set out in search of the buffalo
before giving the soldiers the horses they needed.
He was going to break his promise to Lewis
because his own people were starving.
My brother did not want the captains to know.
But Captain Lewis *did* find out. He spoke sharply to Cameahwait.
He shamed my brother into postponing the hunt.
And Cameahwait knows it was I who told.
He knows his own sister betrayed him to the whites.
I have reunited with my people, yet I still feel far from home.
I may as well continue flying west.

Not long ago Captain Clark spoke sternly to Charbonneau.
Would any Shoshone man do the same?
And now Charbonneau has brought me a horse.
A horse that is white like the snow.
　　　"Here," he said. "I got this for you.
　　　She is gentle and healthy and in good order.
　　　The horse, it may help ease your burden,
　　　what with Jean Baptiste and all.
　　　I know your hands they are very full."
So with Charbonneau and the others I will go.
I once left this place as a girl,
walking behind a warrior on a white horse.
I now leave this place as a woman,
riding on the horse's back.

Oolum ◇ *the newfoundland*

And so we set out over the Rocky Mountains. We left before daylight. The day was warm. Our trip had an easy beginning. But as we climbed higher into the mountains, the temperature dropped. It snowed many days. Some mornings we were forced to wait for wet frozen baggage to thaw. The horses initially gave us trouble. It became clear that many of the Shoshone had bartered away only the worst of their herds, old, sore-backed, and tired, or young and not accustomed to the pack.

On our fifth day out, we had the luck to meet a band of Indians who called themselves the Ootlashoots. Their manner was friendly and their clothing was simple. They appeared to be generally as poor as the Shoshone. The Ootlashoots were rich, however, in horses. They had with them a herd of five hundred or more, some of which they readily sold and exchanged for our own. After two days of trading, smoking, and talk, we resumed our journey, eleven horses richer.

We made over twenty miles each day. It frequently rained. The September chill reminded us that winter was nearing. We ran out of flour. The horses habitually walked off in the night in search of food and had to be retrieved in the morning. At the end of the first week of September, our trip had been relatively gentle as we encountered a creek running through a grassy prairie at the end of a wide valley. Old Toby told us this would be the last abundant grass for a while, so the captains decided to make camp for a couple of days in order to rest and water the horses. Meanwhile Colter and Drouillard hunted. Lewis urged the men to conserve their rations for the hard times he knew were ahead. We called this area Traveler's Rest.

After two days, we resumed following Traveler's Rest Creek, which led us along a valley that cut into the Rockies. The trail became steep and stony. We arrived at a natural spring of extremely hot water. Many of the humans stripped off their clothes and swam. I dipped a paw into the water and would have nothing more to do with it. It was as hot as soup.

364

The next day I longed to return to the hot springs, as the trek over the mountains quickly became a nightmare. It snowed. The snow turned to rain. The rain turned to sleet. Old Toby lost the road. In consequence he led the entire party of humans and horses down into a steep valley to the bank of a cold, rapid river.

"This is not right. This is not right," he said. "The snows must have covered the road. The road is there." And he looked behind him, pointing up the steep ridge that we had just descended. To turn back would have taken far too many miles, so we followed the river for a while until we turned sharply to the right and began to scale the mountain. Horses and men slipped and fell along the steep incline. Clark's packhorse lost its footing and rolled forty yards down until it was halted by a tree. The impact smashed the captain's small writing desk into sticks.

Thus began the most difficult challenge we had yet faced. It rained or snowed every day and night without fail. The mountains were covered in knee-deep drifts, which in turn concealed the treacherous fallen timber that tripped both human and horse. I bounded and leaped for miles over logs and deep snow. No game showed itself, except for an occasional thin pheasant. Even the portable soup, which the humans declared repulsive, had been consumed. And to the west, the mountains continued on to the horizon. It seemed there was no end to them.

No one in the world, civilized or otherwise, knew where we were. Among these massive, unforgiving mountains there would be no one to watch us die but the tall, uncaring pines. The ravens, come spring, would pick our bones clean. In time the bones and the specimens, the journal entries and the celestial observations, the guns and powder, and Indian trinkets would all quietly return to the dirt.

William Clark ◇ *the gentleman*

I have been as wet and as cold
in every part as I ever was in my life.
My writing desk has been crushed.
My umbrella was washed down a ravine.
And now we have broken the last thermometer.
It seems that this new found land of ours
does not care for the inventiveness
of civilized man.

Patrick Gass ◇ *the carpenter*

I am chilled to the marrow
and empty as a hollow tree.
I don't know what to die of first:
cold or starvation.

Much of the timber about us is fallen or standing dead,
but even these dismal, horrible mountains
have a certain beauty.
Why, I've counted at least eight different species
of pine on this one mountainside alone.
Not a bad place to die.

Plenty o' wood for coffins.

John Colter ◇ *the hunter*

Thar ain't nothin' more cold than a hungry cold.

I cain't recollect ever bein' so cold.
An' I cain't recollect my trusty gun
ever bein' so damned useless.
  'Ceptin' fer the snow-covered path
  thar's nothin' here t' hunt.
I ain't seen but a pheasant an' a couple o' squirrels
in near th' past five days.
Totin' a gun in these woods is foolish.
I may's well be totin' a fishin' pole to th' outhouse.

It's almost like we been killin' too *many* critters
an' cuttin' too *many* trees,
an' now the land is dishin' out a vengeful comeuppance!
  Us men's the hunted now.
  An' these here mountains is th' hunter.

Oh, listen t' me carry on.
I'm soundin' like George Drouillard talkin' setch nonsense.
Jest let these damned mountains hunt me down like a goat!
Let 'em freeze me 'n starve me 'n swallow me whole.
Jest let 'em!

'Cause once I'm in their belly, I'll thaw out good
'n I'll shoot these blasted mountains from th' inside out!
An' when they're dead, I'll cook 'em
over a flamin' mound of fallen timber
an' I'll *eat* the Rocky Mountains,
wind, boulders, rivers, ice 'n snow 'n all.

Then I'll lean back an' pick my teeth
with th' whittled-down point of a pine tree.

Lord.
Thar ain't *nothin'* more cold
than a hungry cold.

George Drouillard ◇ *the half-breed*

I am nearly frozen.

I can no longer feel my feet.
I can no longer feel my hands.
I have suggested to the captains
that we send a hunting party ahead,
where, if we are lucky, we will find game.

Just ten days ago I was checking beaver traps
and found one trap had been poorly staked.
It was missing.
But I found that trap clamped tight to a beaver's foot.
The beaver had drowned
but only after swimming two miles downstream.
I cannot stop imagining that animal's final journey.
I wonder,
did it think that there was no escape?
I wonder,
did it ever give up hoping?

This mountain cold is like a spirit,
an evil thing that wraps itself around you.
I place my hand upon my medicine bag.

How far will you travel
to discover who you are?

Sacagawea ◇ *the bird woman*

I am cold and hungry
and, little Pomp, I know you are as well.
I fear I have but little milk for you.
You who were born in the Snow Blind Moon,
I will do my best to keep you warm.
This robe has room enough for us both.

When I set out walking to the West
my people walked to the East.
I feel as Grizzly Bear must have felt,
banished into the freezing mountains.
This snow that clings to our robe
we will shake into the sky
as we paint the way to heaven.

But up until we die, my son,
you must do your best to eat.
I will melt small handfuls
of snow in my mouth,
let the warm water drip
from my lips to my breast,
let it mix with what little milk is left.
I feel I'm growing very weak,
but you may have what remains of me.

Come, little one.
Do not cry.
I will be your tepee now.

Meriwether Lewis ◇ *the explorer*

The terrible cold and wet I feel is little discomfort
compared to the possibility of failure
that speaks to me through the hungry moans of the men
and the listless whinnies of the sore, stiff horses.
Our only provisions left are bear's oil and candles.
The men suffer much from dysentery and eruptions of the skin.

Clark and I have decided that he will ride on
to discover whatever flatlands may lay
on the other side of these infernal mountains.
He and a few hunters will kill what meat they can
and hang it up for us to collect.

The men have nearly reached the limits of their mettle.
Even young Shannon, the talker, has fallen silent.
If nothing else, Clark's going ahead
may give these soldiers hope.

William Clark ❖ *the gentleman*

With a mind to revive the party's spirits,
I set out ahead of the rest in the company of six other men.
For two days we ascended and descended several steep mountains
over the usual crisscross of fallen timber.
The first night we encamped on a bold running stream
we named Hungry Creek as we had nothing to eat.
The second day Hungry Creek led us to a small glade
where we found a horse as if placed there as a gift —

> we made a meal of it
>
> such was our urgent want of food,
>
> and we hung up the balance for Lewis to find.

The road ahead grew worse and worse
as we were forced by the terrain
to switch back on ourselves time and again
so that one mile's advance required two miles' walking.

But eventually, at the end of a very high ridge, we began to descend.
And as we descended, the air grew warm.
And as we grew warmer and warmer still,
we entered a beautiful flat plain, well timbered with pine.
Three miles more brought us to what was the most delightful
prairie I had ever beheld. Scattered throughout the prairie
were many tepees, their bottoms rolled up against the afternoon heat.
My men began to peel off gloves, scarves, buffalo robes, and blanket coats.

Three Indian boys ran in fear and hid themselves.
I dismounted, gave my gun and horse to one of the men,
and plucked up two of the boys from the tall grass.
I gave them both small pieces of ribbon.
I was giddy with fatigue, heat, and hunger.

I didn't bother with signs. I knew the startled children understood.
"Go, boys," I said. "Go now with all speed to your warriors and chiefs.
Tell them to come on with open hands or arrows drawn.
Tell them the men with hats and hairy faces
have crossed the terrible, cursed Shining Mountains.
Tell them we are alive!"

PART SIX

THE MOUNTAINS TO THE SEA

OCTOBER 1805–NOVEMBER 1805

Washington

Pacific Ocean

RANGE

COLUMBIA RIVER

YAKIMA RIVER

Ft. Clatsop
Nov. 1805 –
March 1806

Salt Camp

Great Chute
(The Cascades)

Short & Long Narrows
(The Dalles)

Great Falls of the Columb
(Celilo Falls)

Beacon
Rock

COLUMBIA RIV

COLUMBIA RIVER GORGE

SANDY
RIVER

WILLAMETTE RIVER

CASCADE

DESCHUTES RIVER

Oregon

Montana

Idaho

Lolo Pass

Nez Percé
Villages

Lolo Trail

O Traveler's
Rest

SNAKE RIVER

SNAKE RIVER

KOOSKOOSKIE RIVER

SALMON RIVER

Oolum ◈ *the newfoundland*

The easy hike from the navigable waters of the East to the navigable waters of the West, the journey Thomas Jefferson guessed might take two days, had taken the captains and their men a total of twenty-seven days. To survive they resorted to eating game birds, three colts, and a wolf.

Clark had discovered one of many villages of the mighty Nez Percé Indian nation. The Nez Percé lived variously in skin tepees and mat-covered lodges. At times they would cross the Rockies to hunt buffalo on the plains, but they mostly subsisted on fish, small game, berries, and a versatile and nutritious root they called quamash. By the time Lewis and the main party arrived from their hellish trek over the Rockies, Clark had already met one of the main chiefs. His people called him Twisted Hair.

Twisted Hair's village was situated on the shore of a river called the Kooskooskie. The Indians assured Clark that, to reach the ocean, the soldiers needed only to travel down this river to another called the Snake. The Snake River in turn would empty into the Columbia. It seemed that Lewis and Clark were closer than they had ever been. They needed only to make canoes for the journey. There was ample timber to carve into boats. But there was yet one more setback to endure before reaching the Columbia.

The soldiers climbed down from the mountains in a state of starvation, so when offered a feast of dried salmon and berries, quamash roots and bread, the men gorged themselves. Their digestive systems, used to an all-meat diet of buffalo, deer, elk, and beaver, were at a loss to process the sudden change of menu.

As a result, the humans became sick as the fibrous roots and bacteria-rich fish caused chaos in their stomachs and bowels. Captain Lewis was unable to ride a horse because of the intense pain of his intestinal cramps. The soldiers frequently fell over and lay down in the grass, unable to move.

It was not a pleasant sight.

The men prepared to continue their journey as best they could. Recovery was slow, but their systems grew somewhat used to the quamash. These strong-willed humans who had endured so much to conquer the impossible Rocky Mountains had been brought to their knees by a tiny round root that tasted of pumpkin and filled its victims so full of wind they could scarcely breathe.

Patrick Gass ◈ *the carpenter*

I have always had an iron constitution.
I figure I may just outlive every man in our company
as long as the good Lord is willing.
Oh, I got sick on the roots along with the rest,
but the rigorous effects of Rush's Thunder Clappers
returned me to my usual health.

Men, unlike trees, fall down when they're sick,
and a couple of the soldiers are still lying about the camp
moaning, wincing, and making for the bushes every now and then.
Us men with the strength to manage an ax
are busy carving canoes from trees.
To save hard labor I've adopted the Indian method
of burning the tree slow and careful.
You chop it away as it burns down.

At this rate we'll be back on the water in about ten days.
That's two days for each canoe.

Five tall, thick pines,
transformed as if by magic into five dugout canoes.
The pine has proved a better wood
for making boats than cottonwood.
And unlike Captain Lewis's *Experiment,*
these boats of pine provide their own tar
for to patch any cracks or seams.

Although I wouldn't say so in front of Captain L.,
I don't hold out much hope for the future of metal boats.

Sacagawea ♦ *the bird woman*

Today as Pomp crawled about the grass
I helped a woman of the Nez Percé nation
grind her *pah-see-goo* roots for bread.
She is a very old woman and much respected
by even the men.
She tells me that many men of the village
wanted, at first, to kill us and take the soldiers' guns.

    "But I spoke to the chiefs," she said.
    "I reminded them how I was taken far away by the Blackfeet.
    I told them how white men allowed me to return to my homeland.
    The white man protected me and showed me kindness.
    To kill these soldiers in return
    will surely bring bad luck to all our tribe.
    These men come here in peace.
    There would only be dishonor in their deaths."

The old woman offered me a piece of salmon,
then she continued to speak.

    "Every year, when the air turns cold, the salmon swims to the ocean.
    Many die. Still he tries. This is a thing that cannot be stopped.
    But when the air warms, the salmon returns.
    Even against the strong current, he returns.
    Over falls, rapids, and rocks, he returns.
    I am like the salmon.
    I am Watkuweis. I am Returned From Afar."

"I am Sa-*kah*-gah-*wee*-yah," I said. "Bird Woman."

    "Ah yes, the bird, like the salmon, has its own journey to make."

"I too returned from afar," I confided.
"But when I did, I found I was not home."

> "Then you must have farther still to go.
> Home is not a tepee.
> Home is who you are.
> Who are you, girl?"

"I am Sacagawea. I am Bird Woman."

> "Then fly!
> Sacagawea and Watkuweis are sisters forever.
> You will fly above, while I swim below.
> But we have made too much talk, and too little bread.
>
> Now we must work."

George Shannon ◇ *the kid*

Nearly every man working was as sick as a dog.
It was a miracle that we got our canoes built at all.
But miracles happen, and in about twelve days
we set five big dugouts into the water
and launched off—whooping and hollering—down the Kooskooskee.

Three days later one of the canoes cracked herself against a rock,
and of course, everything in her got wet.
We came to and camped
so Sergeant Gass could patch the cracks
and the rest of us could lay out the baggage to dry.
There were Nez Percé fishing camps all along the river,
and Indians were always about.

The near miss in the canoe was nothing new to us men
who had survived the gauntlet of the Missouri River.
But Old Toby, our guide, must have thought otherwise.

He seemed nearly scared to death
and the next morning he and his son
had up and left without a goodbye.
They didn't even collect their pay.

Twisted Hair and another chief named Tetoharsky
joined the expedition as our new guides.
Our camp was just above the junction
of the Snake River and the Kooskooskie.
We were getting closer and we all knew it.
Were we *ever* merry!

We sang all day and danced into night.
Pierre played the fiddle by the fire.
Even Captain Lewis joined us,
though he looked a bit green, still,
from that unsettling combination
of quamash roots and rapids.

Not long after dark
a Nez Percé woman commenced to dance
and she did so around the fire,
stopping to face every white man she encountered.
She smiled and handed each man a trinket of some sort:
a brass bracelet, a pearl-shell earbob,
a blue beaded necklace, a ring.

But when she stood in front of Captain Lewis,
she had nothing left to give him,
and she commenced to wail and cry.

She wept tears and seemed in pain,
and from nowhere she produced a sharp flint,
knapped to a razor-sharp edge.
She slashed at her skin
and cut herself from wrists to shoulders
before some of the other Indians finally stopped her.

We were all at a loss to make sense
of the woman's actions.
It was as if she wanted nothing more
than to give us everything she had.

And when she had no more to give
she tried to give her own blood.

Twisted Hair explained.
"She wants you to take all she has
as an offering so you will go away.
She said she saw you in a dream.
She said your coming here would cause the Nez Percé
to vanish from the land. Pay her no attention."

Whatever the woman's meaning was,
her fit put an end to the evening's merrymaking,
and we all settled in for the night.

By seven the next morning
we were loaded and ready.
And we set out west down the Snake River
toward the Columbia.

Oolum ◇ *the newfoundland*

The humans were sick to death of fish and roots. Horseflesh was palatable in times of need, but they had left all their horses with the Nez Percé for the winter. Game was scarce, and anyway, hunting took up valuable time from river travel. The men were in need of an easily accessed source of hearty meat. At this point in the journey they began to purchase dogs.

The situation was uncomfortable for me. Mind you, I was not concerned that the soldiers might make a meal of me. But how was I to interact with those of my own kind, knowing what their fate was to be. There is no way I could have warned them. They lacked the capacity to understand. Still I could not help but grow fond of them as I had grown to like Indian Dog so many months ago. I decided it was best to keep my distance from them. And as a rule, I would not eat the meat. Clark, to his credit, did not care for the taste and did what he could to avoid it.

There was no avoiding the rapids and rough water ahead, and the humans seemed to welcome it. Finally the river current was working for them and not against. Most had become skilled river men. They shot every rapid they met as they sped down the Snake River past encampments of Nez Percé and Palouse Indians. As they came to the end of a striking canyon, the landscape became barren and treeless. The many varieties of pine that covered the western slopes of the Rockies had suddenly vanished. We had entered a desertlike land.

Then, in the middle of October, the boats passed down the mouth of the Snake where it emptied its waters into a very wide, handsome river. Without warning or fanfare, the humans at last found themselves on the grand Columbia River. Here we met the Yakama, and the Wanapum, and the Walla Wallas. And as usual, Twisted Hair and Tetoharsky were able to introduce us as friends who were not to be feared. The Nez Percé chiefs acted as interpreters for these and many other meetings.

We camped at the junction of the Snake and Columbia for two nights to take celestial observations to determine the confluence's latitude and longitude. The water of the Columbia was as clear as any I had seen. No matter how deep it was, I could see the fish as they swam. And the numbers of fish were astonishing. In places the river seemed to run more with salmon than water. By the time we arrived, fall was coming to a close, so the fish were mostly dead or dying. The salmon had spawned. Their journey was over.

Meriwether Lewis ◇ *the explorer*

What the buffalo is to the Indians of the plains,
the salmon is to the Indians of the Columbia.
Scaffolds stand in every village holding immense quantities
of this fish—fresh, dried, pounded into powder, pressed into cakes.

It is a noble fish and a mystery.
Every spring and autumn, the salmon arrives
from its ocean home miles and miles away.
It lays its eggs.
Then the eggs hatch and new fish swim
downstream to the sea.
Spring arrives again, and each new salmon
makes its way back to the river where its life began,
battling currents, leaping over rapids, jumping steep waterfalls—
all of this struggle to reach the waters of its birth.

There is much to admire in the salmon's fortitude.
Are we not like the salmon, my men and I?
With our labor against the Missouri currents
over terrible rapids and around tall falls?

But the mystery is this:
once this fish has reached the ocean,
how then does it find its way back home?
Does it navigate the oceans by watching the heavens?
The sun? The moon? The stars?
Does it see familiar sights? Smell familiar smells?
Does it know it will likely die after its task is done?
After it has contributed to the next generation, is it then satisfied?

Oolum ◈ *the newfoundland*

The chief of the Walla Wallas urged us to stay for an extended visit, but the captains were anxious to make the coast before winter. After promising a longer visit on the return trip, we proceeded on with great speed until we heard the distinct roar of waterfalls.

Clark called it the Great Falls of the Columbia. The river snaked between rock cliffs, two and three thousand feet high, and descended a total of thirty-eight feet, including one drop of twenty feet. With the help of local Indians, the soldiers carried their baggage around the falls by land. They carried the canoes only around the twenty-foot cascade. Otherwise the men lowered the boats over ledges, rocks, and rapids using their elk-hide ropes.

William Clark ◈ *the gentleman*

Given the height of the Rockies
and the short distance left to the sea,
Captain Lewis and I had calculated that our little flotilla
would encounter more than a few falls and rapids.

Unfortunately, we were correct.
We seem to have entered a large gorge
through which the river descends from the mountains.

Now just three miles below the Great Falls,
we have discovered a four-mile run of very bad rapids.
To make matters worse, our Nez Percé chiefs
have informed me these rapids indicate we have entered
the land of the Chinook Indians,
longtime enemies of the Nez Percé.
Twisted Hair claims to know, from his relations,
that the Chinooks are awaiting our arrival.
They are anxious to see if we arrive without drowning.

Twisted Hair says that if we arrive safely,
the Chinooks are planning to kill us all.

Oolum ◇ *the newfoundland*

Master Lewis persuaded the two Nez Percé chiefs to stay on in hopes of bringing about peace between their nation and the Chinooks. Twisted Hair and Tetoharsky reluctantly agreed. Pierre Cruzatte examined the next river obstacle, a pair of rapids that squeezed between high cliffs of dark volcanic rock. Clark determined the first rapid was a quarter mile long. The second rapid was three miles long. He named them, respectively, the Short and Long Narrows.

The Short Narrows was first. Attempting to ride out the churning, rock-strewn white water was not the safest way to proceed, but it was certainly the fastest. Somehow, cheered on by Pierre's manic chanting and whooping, the canoes made it through.

Later in the day, two Chinook chiefs from a village downstream came to pay a visit. Lewis was eager to arrange peace between all of his Indian guests, so he set up a council at once. The Chinook and Nez Percé languages were very different, so Drouillard was on hand to translate using signs.

George Drouillard ◇ *the half-breed*

He smiled and nodded
and he said, "Yes, I understand."
But I knew that he did not.

I was attempting to interpret
the words of the Chinook chief.
Lewis and I were sitting between the Chinooks
and the two Nez Percé.

"The Nez Percé and the Chinook
should be at peace," Lewis said.
The Chinook smiled and nodded
and he said, "Yes, I understand."
Clearly my hand signs were confusing
to these people of the coast.

Still, the Nez Percé chiefs and Chinooks
all shook hands, and Captain Lewis seemed pleased.
But I am not so certain.
Simply because an Indian *says* he will not make war
does not make it so.
Today the friendly handshake
between these two longtime enemies meant,
"We will be at peace from now on,
until next we meet."

Captain Lewis does not understand how Indians think.
As our council today came to an end,
Twisted Hair indicated to me, through signs,
that he needed to think.
He did so by touching his hand to his heart.

He did not point to his head,
for the heart is where all Indian decisions are made.

I attempted to explain this to Lewis.
He smiled and nodded
and he said, "Yes, I understand."

Oolum ◇ *the newfoundland*

After the captains concluded peace talks with the Nez Percé and Chinooks, they turned their attention back to the river. The Long Narrows was as dangerous as the Short Narrows had been. The water swelled and sloshed between more dark rock walls that constricted the churning current into a channel that, at one point, narrowed to only fifty yards.

Again the humans emptied the canoes of anything valuable: journals and papers, instruments, guns and powder. The heaviest and least essential baggage was left to chance. The best paddlers then turned the bows of the canoes into the raging foam.

By now word had spread up and down the river that the crazy white men were recklessly running the deadly rapids in tree trunk boats. Indians lined the cliffs to watch the strangers drown. Others waited downstream to fish out whatever cargo would float by from the inevitable wreck.

The canoes themselves could be chopped up for much-needed firewood.

Oolum ◇ *the newfoundland*

We camped for three days at the base of the Long Narrows and played host to the Indians who constantly crowded us. Twisted Hair and Teto-harsky left to join their people hunting buffalo. Local Indians arrived with delicious trout and venison to eat. Everyone feasted and danced to the fiddle. There was no interpreter left among the Corps of Discovery who could speak the Indians' native tongue. But when Pierre Cruzatte began to play, the music was understood by all.

In camp, small items began to disappear. A knife. A tomahawk. A spoon. It was obvious that white men had been here before. One Indian man wore a sailor's jacket. When the Chinook Indians cursed, they cursed in English. Keeping an eye on their belongings, the soldiers set out to portage around one final rapid the captains called the Great Chute.

The Great Chute was four miles of large boulders and churning waves hemmed in by sharp embankments. Its current ran faster than any the men had yet encountered. The canoes were emptied completely and lowered down by ropes over ledges up to ten feet high. The humans pronounced this the most fatiguing portage of the journey, excepting for the hellish trek around the falls of the Missouri.

To save time, the soldiers placed the canoes back into the river with just over a mile of white water left to go. Pierre Cruzatte gave a high-pitched yell of defiance as he led the canoes through this final stretch of danger and velocity. One by one the other humans joined in, from onboard the canoes and then from along the banks. White men and Indians created a chorus of shrieking that came together as one monstrous exhilarated scream of joy. For a moment the humans' voices nearly drowned out the river's roar.

One canoe had split a little against a rock. Three canoes had taken in water. But in the end, every boat and man was in good order.

"Très bien, mes amis!" said Pierre, catching his breath. "Très bien."

Meriwether Lewis ◇ *the explorer*

We've encamped at the foot of the Great Chute
to give the men a much-needed rest
and to patch the cracked canoe.

Off the river's starboard bank
a monolith of black stone stands.
Clark and I estimate its height at eight hundred feet.
Because of its resemblance to a towering lighthouse,
we've named it Beacon Rock.

As the men have set about their work,
I've been keeping busy measuring the water's depth.

My dog has trotted over to stand at my side.
> My dog who has endured every hardship
> of our journey with perseverance
> equal to that of any man here.

"Seaman, my friend. Look here, boy.
The level has risen nine inches or more.
It can mean only one thing.
The ebb tide.
This rise in the river is the ocean's doing!"

Oolum <> *the newfoundland*

It had taken almost two weeks to pass through the eighty-five miles of the Columbia Gorge. With the last of the dangerous water behind us, we set out past Beacon Rock into a land as humid and lush as the land upriver had been arid and barren. Fir, spruce, ash, and alder clung to the cliffs, promising logs for lodging, wood for fires, and game to hunt. Migrating birds flew over—cranes, ducks, geese, swans. Sacagawea clapped her hands at the sight of a flock of white brants.

We saw many Indians as well, navigating the river in finely crafted cedar canoes. One magnificent boat passed by with the image of a bear carved into its bow. The Indians who so skillfully paddled the river were an odd sight to us all. Local custom was to fit newborn infants with special cradleboards that pressed upon the babies' skulls as they grew. As a result, the Chinooks' foreheads sloped backward to form a rounded point at the crown of their heads. The captains and men felt these Indians were unattractive, ill shaped, and badly dressed. The Chinooks felt the same about the white visitors. The humans were in high spirits, though their annoyance grew daily at the Indians, who continued to steal whatever the soldiers left unattended.

The men longed for the company of the friendly Mandans, the respectful Yanktons, the noble Shoshone. The local Indians were used to driving hard bargains with rich traders and sailors from visiting merchant ships. The Chinooks had developed a tightfisted style of bartering, and theft was a common practice. The white men had very few trade items left to last them through the coming winter, not to mention the return trip. Every trinket, then, was precious and worth defending. The soldiers were weary and running short of patience. It seemed that a confrontation was inevitable.

George Shannon ❖ *the kid*

It all started off innocent enough.

> We were camped and resting easy
> after a hard day on the water
> when a sizable group of Chinooks came to visit.

They got out of their fancy boat
all dressed up in gaudy colorful costumes,
bits and pieces of white man's clothes and such.
And they were armed with every weapon
known to man, Indian or otherwise:
spears, knives, shields, quivers, bows, clubs,
pistols, rifles, and even a sword.
These were by far the most rude and disagreeable Indians
we've encountered since the Teton Sioux.

All of a sudden Drouillard's wool blanket coat was missing
and then the shouting began.
Drouillard begins yelling in English,
then French, and eventually what I took to be Shawnee.
Drouillard doesn't talk much,
but he's not a man you want to cross.
He's not one of us soldier boys,
and he has his own way of doing things.
Let's just say that I'm glad he's on our side.

> Now we don't understand a word these Chinooks say
> and they don't understand us any better.
> Of course Drouillard was so angry
> you didn't need to know hand signs *or* Shawnee
> to understand his meaning.

Luckily Captain Clark intervened
and gave a good search of everyone present.
Eventually the coat was brought forth.

No sooner had Captain Clark warned all us soldiers
not to lose our tempers in the face of Indian insolence,
when the captain reaches down for his tomahawk pipe
only to find it's not there!

A few of the Chinooks are snickering
like boys who just raided the watermelon patch.
And now it's Captain Clark's turn to yell.
He goes into a rip-roaring tirade,
searching every Indian once more.
The tension was even thicker than the fog.

I kept my hand near my gun.
The thought of getting killed
so close to the ocean
was painful to me.

Clark's tomahawk pipe never did turn up,
so the captain fumed and the rest of us offered
one unified cold shoulder to our unwelcome guests.
Eventually, the Chinooks grumbled away.

They got into their canoe,
shouting at us and laughing.
I don't know what they said,
and I don't care.

We didn't struggle all this way
to be bullied by a pack of obnoxious
pointy-headed savages.

We're all keeping our guns loaded
and ready for action.

Oolum ◇ *the newfoundland*

We proceeded on. One morning, a couple of days after the theft of Captain Clark's tomahawk pipe, we awoke to the usual fog. Most men had risen early, for the ground was hard, sloped, and rocky. The larger boulders had been cleared away to make space to lie down upon the smaller stones. All was wet and damp. It had been a restless sleep.

As usual young Shannon woke up talking. "I have never passed such a miserable night in all my life! That is except for maybe nine or ten miserable nights in the Rocky Mountains."

Shannon directed his chatter toward Hugh Hall, who was busy tending to his bedroll, half listening. Hall said, "That right?"

"Yes. And now come to think of it, one or two of those nights I spent lost on the Missouri were miserable indeed. Well, anyway, last night may not be the worst miserable night of them all, but it ranks high."

Hugh Hall stood up straight, staring downriver over Shannon's shoulder. Taken aback by what he saw, Hall dropped his bedding on the rocks.

Shannon kept talking. "Why, I barely slept a wink. And I'm all over bruised black and blue. Why, it wouldn't surprise me if—"

Shannon stopped. Hugh Hall's eyes had opened wide. His jaw dropped. He stood, unable to move, his stare fixed upon something downstream.

Shannon turned around to look. Every voice in camp fell silent. The thick fog was dispersing. It slowly lifted to unveil the hidden water ahead.

One tense moment of quiet.

One instant of recognition.

One long unison shout.

William Clark ◈ *the gentleman*

November 7, 1805
Great joy in camp. In the morning the fog cleared off just below the last vil-
lage. We are in View *of the* Ocian, *this great Pacific Ocian which we have*
been So long anxious to See. And the roreing or noise made by the waves
brakeing on the rockey Shores may be heard distinctly.

Ocian in view! *O! the joy.*

Field Note: Ocian 4142 Miles from the Mouth of Missouri *River.*

The Corps of Discovery

step — HEAVE — step
step — HEAVE — step
Push the oars forward.
Pull the oars back.

Reubin Field
Yeeeeeee! Haaaaw!
It's th' ocean, Joe!

Joseph Field
I see it, Reub!
I see it big as day!
Yeeeeeee! Haaaw!

Sacagawea
The Lake of the Bad-Tasting Waters.
This completes the vision I began as a child.
I have found, gathered here, the many tears
that I have so long refused to cry.
The weeping water throws itself against the land.
It moans in sorrow. Over and over
it tries to escape, but it can't.
It must be true, Pomp, what Swooping Eagle said:
certainly this is the end of the world.

Lift. Swing. Chunk!
Lift. Swing. Chunk!
Push the oars forward.
Pull the oars back.

George Drouillard

Just look at it.

This ocean is who I am.

All that I feel inside

is here before me.

Pierre Cruzatte

The ocean.

The heaven

where all rivers

finally rest.

Mon Dieu.

York

At long last there it is. The Western Sea.

Though why it's called the Pacific is beyond me.

There is nothing peaceful

'bout those crashing waves.

George Drouillard

This ocean is who I am.

The peaceful solid rock.

The restless watery sea.

They mingle and part.

They merge, then flee.

York

No, there is nothing peaceful

in those crashing waves.

Still, it's an impressive work o' God.

How can it be that the God who made

this wonderous ocean is the same God
who made me?

step — HEAVE — step
Lift. Swing. Chunk!
Push the oars forward.
Pull the oars back.

Sacagawea

Certainly this is the end of the world.
And yet see above the waves?
See how the white brant flies higher and higher?
The earth may come to an end,
but the sky continues on.
Now whenever I look into the sky
I will know there is a part of me there
that no sorrow can reach.

John Colter

I've done reached the ocean.
And I'm all undone.
Now that I look at this here water
I figure I cain't *never* go back home.

Patrick Gass

Yeee! Haw!

Push the oars forward.
Pull the oars back.

Reubin Field
Yeee! Haw!
Have you ever in yer life
seen so much water all at once?

Joseph Field
Why, it jest goes on ferever!

John Colter
I cain't *never* go back home.
Ain't *no one* back in Limestone
who'd believe me when I told them
what a wondrous sight this ocean is.

Push the oars forward.

York
Why, in God's name, am I weeping?

George Drouillard
This is who I am.
The endless advancing waves.
The roar, the spray, the rising swells.
Is it a battle I am watching?
Or a dance?

George Shannon
It's ... It's ... I ...

Sacagawea
I have seen the white brant fly

407

above the Lake of the Bad-Tasting Water.
No one can take this away from me.

Push forward.

Hugh Hall
We did it.
We actually made it through.

           Pierre Cruzatte
           Très bien, mes amis!
           We did it! Yeee! Haw!

Joseph Field
Yeeee! Haw!
We did it, boys!

           Reubin Field
           We did it, boys!
           We kept our scalps
           an' we beat th' devil!
           Yeeee! Haw!

Meriwether Lewis
Captain Clark?

William Clark
Captain Lewis?

Lewis and Clark
Yeeeeeeeeeeeee! Haaawwww!

PART SEVEN

HOME

NOVEMBER 1805-JULY 1819

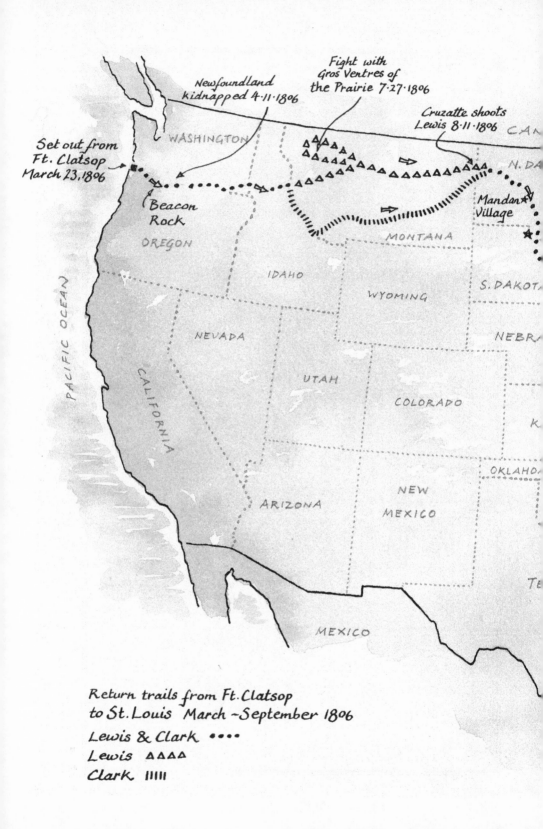

Fight with
Gros Ventres of
the Prairie 7·27·1806

Newfoundland
kidnapped 4·11·1806

Cruzatte shoots
Lewis 8·11·1806

CAN

Set out from
Ft. Clatsop
March 23, 1806

WASHINGTON

N. DA

Beacon
Rock

Mandan
Village

OREGON

MONTANA

IDAHO

S. DAKOTA

PACIFIC OCEAN

WYOMING

NEVADA

NEBR

CALIFORNIA

UTAH

COLORADO

K

ARIZONA

NEW
MEXICO

OKLAHO

TE

MEXICO

Return trails from Ft. Clatsop
to St. Louis March~September 1806
Lewis & Clark ••••
Lewis ∆∆∆∆
Clark |||||

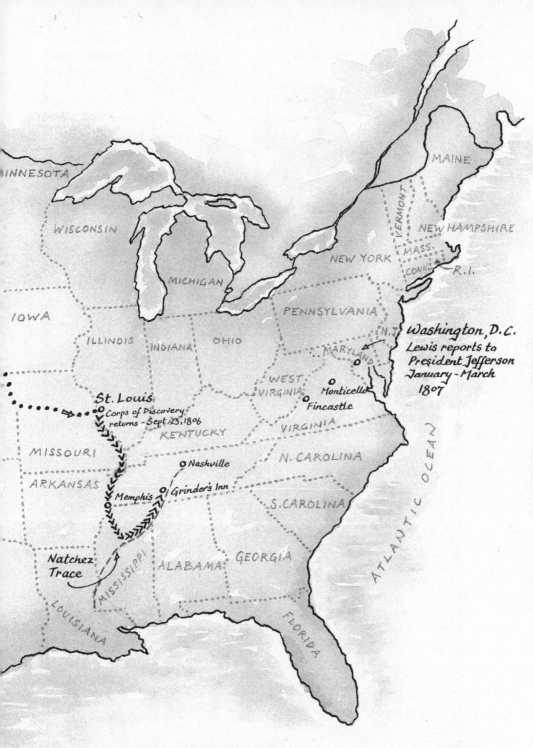

MINNESOTA

WISCONSIN

MICHIGAN

IOWA

ILLINOIS INDIANA OHIO

PENNSYLVANIA

MAINE

VERMONT NEW HAMPSHIRE

NEW YORK MASS.

CONN. R.I.

N.J.

MARYLAND

Washington, D.C.
Lewis reports to
President Jefferson
January - March
1807

WEST
VIRGINIA

Monticello

Fincastle

VIRGINIA

St. Louis
Corps of Discovery
returns - Sept 23, 1806

KENTUCKY

MISSOURI

Nashville

N. CAROLINA

Grinder's Inn

ATLANTIC OCEAN

ARKANSAS

Memphis

S. CAROLINA

Natchez
Trace

MISSISSIPPI ALABAMA GEORGIA

LOUISIANA

FLORIDA

>>>> Lewis and the Newfoundland's
final journey - October 1809

Meriwether Lewis ◇ *the explorer*

To be precise,
we had arrived at an estuary of the Columbia,
where the river opened into a very wide channel
in which the fresh waters met with the ocean tide.

It was not until today, several days later
that I first gazed upon the true Pacific Ocean.

Just think where we are, Seaman!
We are the salmon who fought our way to the sea.
I feel as if I'm finally home,
standing as I am on Cape Disappointment
gazing at last, upon the landscape of Cook,
and Vancouver, and Grey, and Meares —
Meares who named this place so well.
Cape Disappointment — how apt.
For in my joy
I cannot help but dwell over certain failures.

I had guessed the Rocky Mountains were as tame and tidy
as the regular ranks of the Appalachians.
Instead the Rockies are a continual tangle of irregular ranges
that crisscross endlessly and haphazardly — a tumultuous sea
of high stony peaks, ravines, and crooked creeks.

I had guessed that the portage over the Rocky Mountains
would involve perhaps two days' labor through a low mountain pass
from the headwaters of the Missouri to those of the Columbia.

Instead the path is a 240-mile trek
over virtually impassable mountains with little grass for horses

and little game for men. And one-fourth of the journey
is covered with snow all year round.

I may have discovered the most practicable
all-water route across the Rockies, but I also proved
that for all practical purposes,
the Northwest Passage does not exist.

Still I am somewhat gratified to be standing
on the very point of land where so many great men must have stood.
To mark this occasion, I carve my name into a nearby tree.

M. Lewis

Nothing more.

Now I turn my attention back to the ocean.
What an astounding amount of salt water all gathered into one—
salt!
We've no salt left.

I'll set up a salt works on the beach.
If we begin now, we should have sufficient stock
to last us throughout the return trip.

I've seen the ocean
but there is still much to be done.
So let us begin, Seaman.
Even the salmon must make good its return.

Joseph and Reubin Field ◇ *the brothers*

Reubin   Hey, Joe?

Joseph   Yeah, Reub.

Reubin   Can you believe we left off makin' salt in Kentuck
and traveled more 'n four thousand miles
only to commence makin' it again at th' ocean?

Joseph   Actually, Brother, our labors here are givin' me some comfort.
Workin' this salt reminds me o' th' easy times back home.
'Ceptin' for the cold, it feels good to be back pursuin' an honest trade.
Salt makin' is a noble perfession, Reub.

Reubin   Noble per—? What nonsense are you talkin', Brother?
What's so noble 'bout watchin' water boil?

Joseph   Thar's more to it 'n that, Reubin. An' you know it.
"A tongue can taste th' differ'nce when th' salt's made right."
"Take yer time."

Reubin   "Make it fine."
"Boil it strong 'n white."

Joseph   Ha. Ha. That's right. Jest like brother Ezekial always said.
Fact is I was thinkin'
once we get back t' Kentuck
I might use my land grant t' set up my own works,
across the river, north, on the Indiana side.

Reubin   Salt!
Use yer head! We've been makin' five dollars a month on this trip,

415

and land is worth some two dollars an acre.
We ought t' collect our back pay, sell off our land,
an' see th' world.

Joseph See th' world?
What do ya think we been seein', Reubin?
I've done enough seein' t' last me a lifetime.
The only thing I want t' see after I get home
is Mary Myrtle's open arms.
You think Mary Myrtle's gonna wait forever?
No, sir. I'm goin' t' settle on a spot well situated fer farmin',
salt works, maybe a mill, chickens, hogs,
an' the biggest log cabin in all o' Kentucky.
We can put our lots together, Reub, an' be partners.

Reubin Well I hate t' remind you, partner,
but them land grants we're due are nowhar *near* Mary Myrtle.
All them parcels are located west of the Mississippi.
You think Mary Myrtle's goin' t' follow you t' Louisiana?

Joseph I done thought o' that.
Us Kentucky men can sign a pertition to th' gover'ment
askin' that our grants be local.
Cap'n Clark tol' me so.

Reubin An' I s'pose, once yer all settled in,
you and Mary Myrtle are goin' t' raise
more children than chickens.

Joseph Oh, maybe forty. Fifty.
I'll need plenty o' hands to do all the chores
that you'll be too lazy t' do yerse'f.

Reubin That hurts me, Joe. I carry my own weight, an' you know it.

Joseph Well, then, why don't you carry this here empty bucket
to that big ocean over thar,
an' bring me back some seawater?

William Clark ❖ *the gentleman*

I ascended this high point of land
to allow our party of twelve
the opportunity to take in the sublime view
of the Pacific Ocean from Cape Disappointment.

I know I speak for each man with me
when I say I am transformed by this sight
that I have toiled so long to see.
Each man here has discovered something new in himself.
Now, God willing, we shall return
within a year to our families and homes.

I discover Captain Lewis's name on a tree and I begin to carve my own.
One after the other, my companions set upon the tree with their knives.
Even York inscribes the only four letters of his alphabet.
We pass a mad moment of flying bark and silence
as each man slices his own name into the tree's white flesh.
Those men who cannot write are helped by those who can.

As the waves of this magnificent ocean
roar and crash against the rocks below,
we stand back with pride to admire our handiwork.

Nathaniel Pryor	George Shannon	T. Charbonneau
William Bratton	John Ordway	York
John Colter	François Labiche	Reubin Field
Peter Weiser	William Clark	Joseph Field

By Land from the U.States in 1804 & 1805

Oolum ◆ *the newfoundland*

In order to determine where to pass the winter, the captains put the decision to a vote of sorts. Should we stay north of the Columbia, south of the Columbia, or travel east back up the river a distance? Captain Clark diligently recorded each human's wish, writing the results in his journal. Even the opinions of York and Sacagawea were given equal weight. York, like the majority of the men, was in favor of examining the south shore first before making a decision. "Janey," Clark recorded, "in favour of a place where there is plenty of roots to dig." Then he wrote, "Captain Lewis & Friend, in favor of examining south shore."

Lewis and "friend."

All that time with Lewis, and I had never really thought of us as friends. Can you be friends with the man who owns you? Would York think so? I'm sure Alpha Wolf would not. Just the thought of him makes my fur stand on end. As for my own vote, I wished only to camp as far away as possible from the fleas that infested the villages by the river.

In the end we determined to make camp south of the river, where there was plenty of elk to hunt and timber to chop into fuel and cabin logs. The location was also far away from the troublesome Chinooks and closer to the more accommodating Clatsop Indians. Patrick Gass again organized the construction of a sturdy fort, which was dubbed Fort Clatsop in honor of the friendly tribe. We were to live there for four months, forced to endure a winter of boredom and perpetually overcast skies. Christmas and New Year's Day came and went. At the end of March 1806, we started back east at the first slight signs of spring.

Oolum ◇ *the newfoundland*

The return trip home was toilsome work, but since we knew what to expect of the land, we were able to make excellent time. The Columbia River was high due to the spring runoff. Because of this the rapids were much worse than they had been on our westward journey the previous fall. The men were obliged to pull the canoes over many of these rapids, which was exhausting.

Meanwhile, local Indians crowded into our camps, and once again the humans' articles began to disappear. My master was in a foul mood during much of this early leg of our return journey. He knew the adventure would soon be over. Thoughts of returning to life as it was made him melancholy and irritable. He disliked the local natives. Except for a few individuals, Lewis thought they were unpleasant to be around or even to look at.

By the second week in April, Lewis had run out of patience. He sprang upon an Indian thief, slapping the man repeatedly and chasing him away. My master gave orders that, from that day on, any thieves were to be shot.

We were camped, later, near a village of Indians called the Wah-clel-lars, who seemed to be a friendly sort. I met three of these fellows when they offered me bits of biscuit. The biscuits had come from a trading vessel. They were well baked and very good. The taste reminded me of my comfortable life back East.

The Wah-clel-lars wore their hair in braids, interwoven with strips of otter skin. Unlike Lewis, I found these Indians no more unattractive than any other humans. They were friendly, and they were free with their biscuits. It did not occur to me until we had walked nearly half a mile that I was alone with my new friends, no Corps of Discovery soldiers in sight.

I stopped. I sat down. I declined the latest biscuit.

The three friendly Wah-clel-lars stopped smiling.

It occurred to me that I had just been kidnapped.

Meriwether Lewis ◇ *the explorer*

My dog.

   My dog.

      And now they have stolen my dog.

         Good people of the village!
            Hear me out.
               Gather 'round, please.
                  For I wish to let my mind be known to you.

We have entered this land with hands extended in friendship. Yet you have pestered us for weeks with your beggarliness and thievery! You take a spoon, a hatchet, a coat. And now I am told you have taken my dog? An act equal in villainy to the theft of my very soul! *Colter! Take two men and go with all speed before our dog can come to harm. Arm yourselves and when the thieves are found, put them to death if the dog's not released at once. Go now. Fly. They've taken our dog!* As for the rest of you savages—listen well. For what I say, I swear upon my father's grave: If one thing more is stolen—a sugar lump, a bead, a button—if even the tiniest trinket should disappear, I shall suffer my men to set fire to your every last heathen hut and burn this pathetic flea-infested village to the ground!

Oolum ◈ *the newfoundland*

The three friendly Wah-clel-lars were frowning now. They gathered all the biscuits into a large seductive mound. I refused to move. The largest one attempted to pull me forward, but I had made up my mind. There was no budging me. Two of the Indians attempted to pick me up but I stiffened and growled deeply. I had been perfecting this frightening pre-emptive growl for months now. The Indians backed away.

I had made up my mind to run on back to the boats when two of the Indians notched arrows onto their bows and the third pulled out a large knife. The knife belonged to one of the soldiers. It dawned on me then that the Indian with the knife was the same one Lewis had slapped earlier.

I was standing too far away to attack and too close to make good an escape. Think. Think.

The Indians lifted their arrows and aimed. I could tell they were calculating the best shot, the one that would least damage my fur.

"Lower them pig stickers!"

The command was sudden, angry, and loud. It was John Colter, with George Shannon and Hugh Hall. They ran up fast and out of breath.

Hall spat out, "Would you steal our dog, you damned savages? Have you got no decency? Get going before we shoot you where you stand and feed your bones to Seaman!"

I finished eating the pile of biscuits as the Wah-clel-lars ran off. My kidnappers did not wish to die over a dog. My rescuers, on the other hand, had come prepared to do exactly that. Colter, Shannon, and Hall had rushed in without a moment's hesitation in order to save . . . a dog. "Our dog," Hall had said. The men owned me. Not only Lewis, but all of them. I was grateful to the humans for owning me.

I was ashamed with myself for being grateful.

Oolum ❖ *the newfoundland*

With great difficulty, the soldiers managed to trade with a band of Eneeshur Indians for enough horses to portage around the Columbia River falls and continue the journey by land. Once back at Traveler's Rest, the Rocky Mountain camp of the previous fall, our party split up. Master Lewis, with Drouillard and the Field brothers, set out to explore Maria's River, that mysterious river that had been the object of so much disagreement during our trip west. Captain Clark traveled south with York, Sacagawea, Pomp, Charbonneau, and five other men. Their object was to explore and map out the Yellowstone River. Another party was to reclaim the cached supplies and hidden boats and float them as far as the mouth of Maria's River. Lewis and his crew would meet the boats there. Lewis would continue on with the boats to rendezvous with Clark's party at the mouth of the Yellowstone.

All parties went their separate ways. I traveled with Lewis as far as the Missouri falls. It was here that Lewis told me to stay with the boats. My master would be on horseback a far distance and wanted to make good time.

By the time I finally reached the mouth of Maria's River, I had not seen my master for eleven days. The men and I expected to wait there a day or two longer and busy ourselves by digging up more buried supplies. But before we could even pull the boats ashore, Lewis rode up with Drouillard and the Field brothers. Their horses were lathered and exhausted. The men looked as if they hadn't slept. They climbed down, set their horses loose, and boarded our boats with urgency.

"Sail on, men," Lewis ordered. "There's no telling how many of them may be in pursuit of us!"

"What's happened, Cap'n?" asked Pierre.

Before Lewis could formulate an answer, Reubin Field looked up, his face ashen, his eyes red-rimmed and glassy.

"I done kilt a man," he said.

Meriwether Lewis ◇ *the explorer*

When I first saw the herd of thirty horses or more,
I thought we may be in for a fight.
But as we came closer I realized
they were only eight young braves.
And only two had muskets.
I calculated that Drouillard, the Field brothers, and myself
were an easy match in case of hostilities.

They turned out to be a tribe of Indians
called the Minnetaree of the North,
a nation with a warlike reputation.
Even so, the evening passed with friendly smoking and talk.
We camped together in a flat open spot ornamented
with a solitary congregation of three cottonwood trees.
The Indians built a lodge of willow poles and buffalo skins
and invited us to partake of its shelter.
Drouillard and I accepted and talked with them late into the night.
Outside, the Field brothers waited on watch.

As morning broke
our council became bloody.

Joe Field had carelessly laid his gun down by his sleeping brother.
All at once an Indian snatched up both Fields' guns,
while another grabbed the gun of Drouillard.
"Damn you. Let go my gun!" he cried.
I woke up at the sound of Drouillard's struggling
and I reached for my own rifle.
It too was gone.

Drawing my pistol, I set off in pursuit of the Indian with my rifle.
"Drop the gun or I'll fire," I said.
The Indian halted, set down the gun, and slowly backed away.
Drouillard wrestled his own gun
from one of the other thieves, who then ran.
Meanwhile the Field brothers chased the Indian stealing their rifles,
caught the thief, and in the struggle,
Reubin plunged his knife into the Indian's heart.
The poor soul shrieked,
ran about fifteen feet,
and then fell dead.

As the four of us regrouped,
the remaining Indians began to drive off our horses in all directions.
I chased two braves in possession of my own horse,
but at some distance they fled up a steep niche.
I was too much out of breath to pursue.
I called to them again, warning that I would shoot.
One Indian jumped behind a rock.
The other, with a gun, turned toward me,
and I shot him through the belly.
He fell to the ground.
He lifted himself on his elbow.
With his free hand he fired his musket
and then crawled off behind the rock with his comrade.
I had seen such wounds before.
I was certain he would not survive.

The wounded Indian had discharged his gun slightly high
and as I had on no hat,
I felt the wind of his bullet very distinctly
as it missed my head.

The previous night the Indians had informed us
that there was a large party of their people nearby.
It was only a matter of time before they came after *us,*
or worse,
the soldiers waiting for us by the boats at the mouth of the Maria's.

We retreated at a trot, stopping only to allow
the horses to graze and drink for short periods.
We passed many numbers of buffalo on the high plain.
We rode on through the night and into morning.
We rode over one hundred miles,
stopping only three hours to sleep.

I had shot a man
and I could not shake his pain-filled face from my mind.
I had felt the wind of the Indian's bullet
and I felt as if the bullet was still coming.
As if it would pursue me wherever I went,
over mountains and prairies and rivers and time,
until it finally met its mark.

Joseph and Reubin Field ♦ *the brothers*

Reubin   I been thinkin' and thinkin'
            and it jest don't set right.

Joseph   Reub, you got t' set it aside.

Reubin   I cain't. That Indian wasn't much more 'n a kid.

Joseph   A kid who nearly shot you with yer own gun.

Reubin   If they were goin' t' kill us,
            why not jest slit our throats as we slept?

Joseph   Because one o' our boys was always awake on watch.
            They prob'ly planned t' shoot us as they rode away.
            I'm tellin' you, Little Brother.
            It was a fair fight.
            You did what you had t' do.

Reubin   I guess. Did you see him shudder
            as I pulled out the knife?
            It was like I pulled out his soul.

Joseph   Reubin, yer tryin' to undo a knot tangled by another man.
            Did *you* try t' steal that Indian's gun?
            Did you wake up that mornin' an' say,
            "I'm goin' t' kill me an Indian today!"

Reubin   No.

Joseph   That Indian, he made a choice.
            He forced you into a fix

an' you did what you had to do.
Reub, if you was celebratin' havin' jest kilt a man,
I would smack yer head.
But you ain't celebratin'—
yer hurtin',
'cause yer human is all.

Reubin   It seems no matter how I twist it,
it jest don't set right.

Joseph   You didn't kill a squirrel, Brother.
You kilt a man.
I reckon that fact
mightn't *never* set right.
But before you start lyin' awake at night,
I'll tell you the fact thet matters more:
> yer a good man, Reubin.
> Brother or not, yer the best man I know.

Pierre Cruzatte ◈ *the fiddler*

Shhhh.
We must whisper, *mes amis.*
The butt end of my musket,
she is set against my shoulder,
and the elk in the thicket I have drawn into my sights.
Pierre's best thing is not hunting
and so I am taking my time.
Taking my time.
Waiting for just the right time.

Ah, *Monsieur* Elk, you present your shoulder to Pierre.
Bonjour, Monsieur Elk. *Comment allez-vous?*
Pardonnez-moi, but I am going to shoot you now.

I squeeze the trigger and await the delay.
The hammer pecks. The flint scratches.
The powder catches. The chamber explodes.
The bullet flies. And down goes the bull with a thud.

Ha, ha! *Merci, Monsieur* Elk.
This will show the other men that—

But the wounded elk,
he cries out like a man.

> He says, "Damn you!
> Damn you, Cruzatte!
> You *shot* me!"

Mon Dieu!

Oolum ◇ *the newfoundland*

My master, clad in elk skin and creeping through the willows, was as close to being an elk as a man could be. The resemblance was enough to convince Pierre's overworked nearsighted eye. It was lucky for Lewis that Cruzatte did not shoot a gun as well as he played the fiddle. The badly aimed ball of lead struck the captain's left hip, passing through both buttocks to emerge out the right hip. The ball hit no bones and finally came to rest, slightly misshapen, inside Lewis's leather britches. Lewis inserted gauze into the wound, allowing it to drain.

The next day Lewis and his crew of sixteen men finally caught up to Clark, who had been first to arrive at the rendezvous point at the mouth of the Yellowstone. The mosquitoes had been so bad that Clark was forced to move on, leaving Lewis a note to inform us of the change. Now the entire Corps of Discovery was reunited once again. Two trappers, named Dickson and Hancock, joined the party as well. These were the first white men we had seen in almost ten months.

Lewis was forced to lie on his belly on a stretcher in the white pirogue. He applied poultices of Peruvian bark and called out orders as he could. Writing in his journal became impossible in this position. He decided to leave the daily entries to Clark alone—that is, after just one more description of an unusual type of cherry tree.

In the middle of August, we finally reached the Mandan and Hidatsa villages, where we had spent our long friendly winter in relative harmony. Chief Sheheke, Big White, agreed to go with us to St. Louis in order to meet with President Jefferson. But before we continued, we lingered for three days of feasting, trading, and talk. It was time to say hello to old friends. It was time as well to say goodbye to Charbonneau, Sacagawea, and little Pomp.

Sacagawea ◇ *the bird woman*

You are a smart one, Jean Baptiste Charbonneau,
my firstborn son. My Little Chief.
Already you talk. Already you walk.
Already you know the hand sign for 'day.'
Place both hands in front, palms down.
Turn them over and out
as if releasing a bird into the air.
Day. Day. Day.

Captain Clark has grown very fond of you, Pomp.
He has offered to raise you as his own.
To take you to St. Louis and give you a white man's education.

I think this would be a good thing.
Your father and I will take you to him
when you are old enough to leave me.
Perhaps in four more winters.

It is good to have a protector.
The white brant has been mine.
I thought the brant was taking me home.
But I found out the only home I have is who I am.
Inside of me is a place that is strong.
That strength is who I am.

Strangely, my heart is glad to be back
among the Mandans and Hidatsa.
My life is here now
at least until another day,
at least until the white brant flies away.

John Colter ◇ *the hunter*

The thought o' goin' home a hero
don't appeal to me a'tall.
I'd rather be a hunter than a hero.
And I'd rather be fishin' than famous.

Hancock 'n Dickson have offered t' make me partner
in their upriver trappin' crew.
Seein' as they've so far caught nothin'
but a lickin' from the Teton Sioux,
I guess they figure I'd be an asset to their venture.

My army enlistment ain't up fer another two months,
but I asked the captains anyway.
They said I could go so long as I was crazy enough to want it
and long as all the other boys promised not to follow my example.
All the fellers promised as much.

So tonight I had me a word with my friend Drouillard—

"Tell me, George. Tell me *now* 'cause
we may both be dead when next we meet.
Tell me what makes you the best hunter
I ever set my blue eyes on?"

So he commences to givin' me advice.

"Keep your gun loaded always."

"I *know* that, George."

"Approach your kill from a rise if you can."

"I *know* that, George."

And so on and so on.
Finally he stops and he looks down at his medicine pouch.
The one that no one's 'llowed to see into.
He thinks a bit and he says,

> "Only Indians know this, John.
> But since you already hunt like an Indian,
> I will tell you the secret."

He leans over close so no one else can hear.
I lean over close so as to listen.
He gets that serious Indian look in his eye and says,

> "Take a bath, Colter. You smell very bad."

And then he cracks that damned smile.
An' I smile too.
I slap him on the back an' say,
"I promise, George, I'll never tell a soul."

All the men think I'm crazy,
(except for Cap'n Lewis, who seems t' see my point)
'cause tomorrow I'm headin' back west
before I even make it home from th' *first* adventure!

I'll be a ring-tailed roarer
an' a mountain explorer.
I'm goin' t' see the sights.

I'm goin' t' win the fights.
I'm goin' t' be a trappin' man!

I may even take me
a bath or two.

Maybe.

Hugh Hall ◇ *the drinker*

Since leaving the Mandans
we've been making fifty, sixty, seventy miles each day.
Hunting slows us down
so we've been skipping meals to make better time.
Everyone wants to get on home.

Today I whooped and hollered at the beautiful sight of a cow.
She was standing on the riverbank
just watching us paddle on by.
That cow meant that at last we had returned to civilization.

Funny, I had never really looked at a cow before.
Seems like since I stopped drinking liquor
my vision has gotten a good bit more clear.

Earlier this month we met a trading boat on its way to the Mandans,
which gave the captains a chance to buy whiskey for the men.
The first we've had since over a year ago!
The captains passed around a dram for every man.

"To discovery," says Clark.

"To discovery," we all shout.

But when I brought the whiskey to my lips
I could not drink it down.
The smell alone near made me retch.
It stank of what I used to be.

This past Christmas Day, under the clouds of Fort Clatsop,
I had nothing with which to celebrate but cold, clear water.

It was likely my best Christmas ever.
I have drunk the waters of the East.
I have drunk the waters of the West.
I have drunk from the most pure springs
of the distant Rocky Mountain ridges.

I've been drinking whiskey all my life
but it never made a cow look pretty as the one I saw today.

I'm not saying I'll never touch another drop.
I'm simply saying,
if a plain old cow looks good to me now,
what about hogs, chickens, children, trees?

There's a whole homely world for my new eyes to see.

William Clark ◈ *the gentleman*

Tuesday, September 23, 1806
We rose early. Took Big White to the publick store in St. Charles & furnished him with Some clothes &c.

   Took an early breckfast and Set out.

   Descended to the Mississippi and down that river to St. Louis at which place we arived about 12 oClock. We suffered the party to fire off their pieces as a Salute to the Town.

   We were met by all the village and received a harty welcom from its inhabitants.

Oolum ◈ *the newfoundland*

"I'm afraid you'll not be going this time, Seaman, old friend. Sergeant Pryor will need you more than I. Shannon will see that you are taken care of. I shan't be gone long. And meanwhile, look. I've gotten you a gift."

The Corps of Discovery had traveled eight thousand miles. We had been gone from St. Louis two years, four months, and nine days. To me the numbers meant nothing. What mattered most were the banquets and the balls. The people, the excitement, and the abundant table scraps. But Lewis was anxious to report to President Jefferson with all speed. And although my master and I had been separated many times before, I was disappointed to hear I would not be going to Washington too.

"I'm afraid you'll not be going this time."

Master Lewis and Captain Clark set out from St. Louis to share their discoveries with the president. Very few people had expected to ever again see Lewis and Clark alive. The chain of newspaper stories telling of the expedition's triumphant return would give the country a valuable lesson in hope.

By the end of December, Lewis was in Washington. He would stay at the President's House from January through March. Eventually the dinners, the toasts, the honorary balls all came to an end. President Jefferson appointed Lewis governor of the new Louisiana Territory. My master promised the president he would return to St. Louis by July. That gave him three more months. He made his way to Philadelphia, where he called upon the men needed to prepare his precious journals. He needed sketches made. He needed numbers calculated. He needed a publisher. And there was that other matter now weighing on his restless mind. He needed a wife.

"Sergeant Pryor will need you more than I."

*The president appointed Captain Clark the territory's superin-
tendent of Indian Affairs. After reporting to Washington, Clark rode to
Fincastle with York, and there he became officially engaged to Miss Judith
(Julia) Hancock. A wedding date was set for the following January. But
first there was work to be done. By July, Clark had arrived in St. Louis
to take up his duties. By that time, Big White was back in St. Louis as
well. Lewis was not. My master had promised the president he would be
in St. Louis by July. And here it was July.*

"I shan't be gone long."

*Clark's first task was to return Big White to the Mandan villages.
He organized a small group of soldiers as an escort. The group included
a few Corps of Discovery veterans: George Shannon, the Field brothers,
and Nathaniel Pryor, who was to command the mission.*

"Sergeant Pryor will need you more than I."

*I was glad for the chance to be on the move again. The streets of St.
Louis offered little excitement. There were no wolves skulking about. No
elk to chase. No bears to fret over. Even a dog can have his fill of mud
and horse manure. St. Louis had gotten old. I had gotten old.*

"I've gotten you a gift."

*Late in the summer, with still no sign of my master, I followed
Shannon down to the river. With Big White and his family safely
onboard, we set out, a little fleet of pirogues and keelboats, back up the
Missouri. It felt right to be on the water once again. Lewis would have to
fend for himself.*

My master had gotten me a gift. Indeed.

George Shannon ◈ *the kid*

You should've heard the whooping
as we pushed off from St. Louis.
Big White was sitting in the government boat like a king.
Was that Indian *ever* proud. He had been to see
the wondrous white man's world in the East.
And now he was making his triumphant return
to the land of savages.

It was something like launching off with the Corps of Discovery
only this time we knew what to expect.
I was manning an oar of Sheheke's boat.
Seaman was onboard with me like old times.
A little way ahead was another couple of pirogues
with men from Pierre Chouteau's trading company.
I could see the Field brothers there,
Joe 'n Reubin cracking jokes as usual, making it all look easy.
Just downstream from us was a keelboat
filled with trade goods with its own crew of men.
Every boat was armed to the teeth
with rifles, swivel cannons, blunderbusses, and pistols.

All of this over a single Indian
along with his wife and son.
The chief's son had cried all the way to Washington,
"I don't want to go! I don't want to go!"
Now he was crying all the way back,
"I want to stay! I want to stay!"

You'd think with so many men and guns
that this would be a routine trip:

440

sweat and strain our way upriver,
speed like the devil back down.

We'd been on the river about a month
when we reached the Arikara villages.
Our last visit with these folks was a friendly one.
But since that time, as I understood it,
their attitudes toward whites had changed.
The Arikara chief, convinced by Lewis to visit Washington,
got the fever and died. The Indians, understandably,
were none too pleased.

Pryor, now an ensign, was in command of our
combined military and civilian forces.
He'd been a member of the expedition,
so he knew as well as I did
that something was wrong.
When we had arrived in the past
the women and children had lined the banks
to say hello and gawk.

But now the banks were empty.

I saw the Field brothers glance my way.
They sensed it too.
Ensign Pryor stood up to commence organizing the men.

Suddenly I hear a loud *ping* at my side
like a hammer striking an anvil.
No. Not a hammer, but a bullet.

A bullet has struck the metal gunwale nearest me.
Seaman begins to bark.
We're under attack!

The bow cannon of the keelboat behind us roars,
but before he can reload, the cannoneer falls back
with an arrow in his neck.

I see the Field brothers up ahead
firing their guns as their boat is paddled downriver
to reinforce the escort.
Now we can barely lift our heads
for all the arrows and lead in the air.

"How is it that these Arikara
have so many guns?" Sergeant Pryor shouts.
Suddenly Big White stands up screaming,

"I am Sheheke, the twenty-second keeper
of the sacred turtle drum!
I am Sheheke, the Coyote.
I am the father of all fathers.
You cannot kill me!"

"Take that man to the cabin," commands Pryor.
Jessaume, the Mandan interpreter, forces Big White to sit.
But Jessaume is hit by two balls at once,
which spin him around and toss him,
unconscious, onto Big White's lap.

"Pull back! Pull back!" shouts Pryor.

The man at the helm of our boat cries out
and falls into the river, wounded.
He comes up gasping and clings to the side of the boat.
"Oh, Gawd. Oh, dear Gawd," he says.
I spring forward to take hold of the rudder
as the oarsmen turn us around.
By now all our boats are falling back,
letting the current sweep us away in retreat.

Slowly. Too slowly.

My knee explodes, and the leg gives way beneath me,
tossing me into the river.
I'm blinded by the pain of the bullet that has struck me.
Unable to swim.
Choking.
Swallowing water.

Then Seaman is swimming beside me
first biting at my collar, then circling me,
offering his neck, his tail,
anything to keep me afloat as he swims us to the boat.
The men pull me to safety.

"The dog!" I say. "We mustn't leave the dog."

Another man from the civilian force falls dead,
and another in quick succession.
Seaman swims to help another
who is hurt and floundering.

The Indians are standing in plain view of us now
to better aim their final shots.
A few more yards, we'll be out of range.

But Seaman has fallen far behind.
I see him watching us go
as he paddles in an indecisive circle.

Now finally out of the range of guns
I can just make out the dog's figure
emerging from the water
and scrambling, with some difficulty, up an
embankment.

He's been shot.

He disappears, limping
into the cover of the high grass.

Joseph and Reubin Field ◈ *the brothers*

Reubin   Hey, Joe?

Joseph   Yeah, Reub.

Reubin   It feels good to be back on the river, don't it?

Joseph   Yep. I reckon. It *is* right purty.

Reubin   Maybe we ought t' set out fer good, like John Colter.
Make our fortune trappin' furs.

Joseph   I ain't goin' t' be no trapper.
I jest hired on with Chouteau fer this one time
to add a bit to me and Mary Myrtle's nest egg.

Reubin   So yer *really* goin' t' do it?
Yer goin' t' grow up on me?

Joseph   I'm tired, Reub.
After this last trick's over,
I jest want t' go on home —

CRACK!

Did you hear *that?*

Reubin   I heard you fine, Brother.

Joseph   No, not me. *That.*
Gunshots. We're bein' fired upon!

445

Look to yer primin', boys. It's the Arikara
and someone's gave 'em guns!

CRACK! CRACK!

Reubin   They've hit the keelboat's bowman.

CRACK!

Turn this boat 'round boys.
Let's go help 'em out.

Joseph   Damn. They got Jessaume.
An' right in front o' his young'uns.
That ain't right. Killin' a man whilst his children watch!

CRACK! CRACK!

Reubin   Joe. I'm certain I spy a few Teton Sioux in this bunch.

CRACK!

Joseph   I know. I see 'em too.
Oh, Gawd! Now Shannon's down!

CRACK! CRACK!

Will you look at that dawg.
Why, he's helpin' Tenderfoot get back onboard!

Reubin Yeeeeeeeee! Atta boy, Seaman!
That dog has been to the ocean and back!
There ain't no stoppin' the Corps o' Discovery.
Ain't that right, Joe?

CRACK!

Ain't that right, Joe?

Joe?

William Clark ◇ *the gentleman*

I've begun my new life in St. Louis,
Julia at my side, finally my bride.
Our firstborn child — a boy of four months.

Lately when I look upon my wife and son,
I can't help but remember another
young woman and child from my past.
Janey and Pomp — more and more they seem
like characters from a fanciful dream.
A life so different from the life I'm living now.

My position as superintendent of Indian affairs
has proven a good match for me.
Already St. Louis is known to the Indians
as the Red-Headed Chief's town.

The grounds of my estate are in fine order.
I've hired out Priscilla, Nancy, Alek, Tenar, and Juba.
Ben is making hay.
York is employed at pruning, and at tending the garden and horses.
Venos the cook is a very good wench
since I gave her about fifty.

Since moving to St. Louis,
these servants threaten to turn my red hair gray.
Indeed I have been obliged to whip almost all my people.
And they are now beginning to think
that it is best to do better and not cry hard
when I am compelled to use the whip.

I fear you may think I have become a severe master.
It is not the case,
but I find it absolutely necessary
to have business done.

My slaves steal a little, take a little, lie a little,
scowl a little, pout a little,
deceive a little, quarrel a little,
and attempt to smile.
I almost wish my old stock of Negroes
were with good masters and I had money
to put into trade.

But of course, there is no selling them.
They *are* family, after all.
For now I make do,
applying the strap or switch when I feel there's a need.

Since arriving in St. Louis,
York has been but of very little service to me.
He is insolent and sulky
and he will not give over that Kentucky wife of his.
I gave him a severe trouncing the other day
and he has since mended his manner.

He has it in his head that I should free him,
but I can't see what good would come of it.
> And to free a servant
> you must first set him up with a trade.
> *That* takes money.

York has an easy life here with us.
I don't see that he has any need to sulk.
But perhaps I *could* send him to work
at a place near his wife in Kentucky.

Perhaps if he was hired out in Louisville awhile
to a *truly* severe master, he would see the difference
and do better.

York ◇ *the slave*

Not two years ago,
Mister William was asking my opinion
about where to winter over at the ocean.
I put in my vote, same as any man there.
Seems like the wilderness shows no preference
between white man, black man, Indian, or animal.
I could o' stayed there easy.

But I came back for Sally —
when me 'n her hitched
we jumped the broom backwards
an' we vowed our devotion
till death, or distance, do us part.
Now, I've been about as far a distance
as any black man in this world.
An' I took my Sally with me the whole way in my heart.

I can't stop asking for my freedom.
I can't.
Oh, I can stop the *saying*.
I just can't stop the *asking*.
Me 'n Mister William have been together all our lives.
He knows what I'm thinking just by lookin' in my eyes.

He beat me good the other day.
Slapped me with his open hands,
whipped me with his hickory switch.
     Mister William is one frustrated man
     who has plumb run out o' ideas.
Funny thing is, I feel bad for him.

I wish I could help him.
I very much wish it.

After he trounced me,
Mister William was breathing harder than me.
He looked me in the eye, an' he saw me still asking.
An' he saw what the wilderness had done to me.
It made me a worse servant,
but it made me a better man.

I looked Mister William in his eyes back
and we stood there a spell
thinking, *Well, there's* that —
now what?
He just shrugs his shoulders
and lets out a big breath.
For a second that big ol' man
was just little Billy again.
Then he saw me seein' it
so I turned my gaze away.

That night was fitful for me.
I tossed an' turned an' dreamed.
I dreamed o' Sally so far away
and the young'uns running an' shouting.
I dreamed I was a blackbird in a cage.

I dreamed I saw two boys playing crack-the-whip,
cutting up an' loving each other,
one o' them smacking against the outhouse
an' playing dead but never waking up.

George Shannon ◈ *the kid*

Dreaming
by Mr. George Shannon

As to the question 'whether there be anything prophetic, in dreams, or not' I must if I give my opinion, answer in the affirmitive. It is however no more than an opinion, for I believe I cannot support it by any arguments.

 To begin I must first . . .

Thus began my first assignment: Are dreams prophetic or not?
I was required to write a defense of my opinion.

 What was I to say?
 That I had dreamed my way to the West and back?
 That when I was lost and starving
 a young phantom bear comforted me in my dreams?
 Do I say that when I was freezing in the Rockies
 the little bear guided me over the snow-covered path?

Ha.

It is difficult to write about dreams
when you have lived your dreams every day.

 This fall I set out to accomplish something
 I had never before attempted. And it was a thing
 of which I could certainly boast to Mother.
 I enrolled at Transylvania University in Lexington, Kentucky.
 I commenced to pursue a proper education.

What Mother does not know is that
I am here engaged in classical study
rather than law. But it's a start.

It has been nearly two years since the Arikara attack.
I now walk with a bit of a limp.
My wound was rather extensive,
but it has since stopped affording me much discomfort.

I read in the paper that Governor Lewis
was finally able to arrange Sheheke's safe return.
I wish I could have been there.
The wilderness is always imposing itself into my thoughts.
I'm afraid I am not much of a scholar.
My mind is often filled to distraction
with remembrances of the expedition days.

Between my memories, dreams, and occasional leg pains,
I find it difficult to concentrate on my studies.
So I was doubly relieved and pleased
when none other than William Clark came to call.
He is now General Clark of the Louisiana Militia
as well as the territory's top Indian agent.

General Clark was passing through on his way east
on business and to visit family.
His wife, Julia, was there with him
as well as their brand-new baby son.
I looked for York among the slaves,
but he wasn't there.

We shook hands and embraced.
He introduced me to his wife.
I began my social pleasantries.

"Hello, Mrs. Clark. It is an honor
to at last meet the woman who inspired
the naming of Judith's River."
Mrs. Clark did not smile.
As well, Mr. Clark's face was serious and worried.

        Without ceremony, Clark handed me
        a two-day-old edition of the *Argus of Western America,*
        and he pointed to an article.

"It's Lewis," Clark said.
"Lewis is dead.
He's killed himself."

George Drouillard ◈ *the half-breed*

I am back at the place where the three rivers become one,
near where we met the Shoshone so long ago.
My medicine pouch still whispers to me.
I have heeded its message and traveled far,
setting my traps, giving thanks to the grizzly,
helping the white men and Indians talk.

The man I have been working for, Manuel Lisa,
is not the diplomat that Clark and Lewis were.
Lisa offers the Indians threats instead of peace medals.

One of those peace medals hung around the neck of Sheheke
when our fur-trapping expedition returned the chief to his people.
Big White was full of self-importance
and he showed the medal to all who would look.
On one side was the image of two hands clasped in friendship.
On the other side was the image of Jefferson.
One side was peace. One side was politics.

I feel that the truth lies somewhere in between.
Set the medal on its edge. Flick it with a finger. Start it spinning.
And the two sides become one — a third thing altogether.
I once thought I was only half a man.
Now I see that I am two halves.
I am a medal with one side white, one side Shawnee.
I can translate between both worlds,
for I speak both languages equally well.
And as more and more white men enter the Indian's world,
there will be much need for interpreters
who can place the peace medal on its edge,
give it a flick, and set it to spin.

Sacagawea ◆ *the bird woman*

You have grown much, Baptiste.
Still, you are but five winters old.
You do not yet understand
how the heart is the home
of two fighting wolves:
>One good. The other evil.
>One filled with calm and joy.
>The other filled with rage and sorrow.
>One wishes peace. The other wishes war.

In the heart of Captain Lewis, I fear the evil wolf has won.
I know these wolves well,
for they also live in the heart of Sacagawea.
It is not easy for me to give you up,
but you will have education here in St. Louis.
Captain Clark is an honest man.
In the past he took good care of me.
Now he will take good care of *you.*
I know your clothes and store-bought shoes
will take some getting accustomed to.

Come now, Pomp. No more tears.
I shall visit you as often as I can.
And when you are older you may come see me.
Since you traveled to the ocean even before you could walk,
I am certain you will find your way wherever I may be.
I pray you never lose your way,
as Captain Lewis did.
Never let this happen.
Never let this happen!

Remember this, Jean Baptiste Charbonneau:
You are yet very young,
but as you grow to manhood
your own heart will become home
to many fighting wolves.

Which wolf will one day rule them all?

The one you feed.

Patrick Gass ◈ *the carpenter*

I'm happy to answer any questions you have
to the best of my abilities.
You picked a good time of year to visit.
The leaves are truly a sight to behold here in the fall.
I'm happy to be back home in Wellsburg for a while.
I was sent home from the war, to recover from my wound, o' course.

How'd it happen? Oh, we was fightin' the British on the Mississippi.
Well, to be precise, I was choppin' wood
and I lost my eye to a sliver of hickory.
I don't hold a grudge against the tree, though.
That's why God gave me two perfectly good eyes.
I fair fine with just the one.
Though I've had to learn all over how to properly swing an ax.

How did the expedition change my life?
Well, as you can see, sir, it hasn't made me rich.
You might say, though, that my time in the wilderness
has changed the way I look at things.
See that big pine tree over there?
I look at that pine tree and I see a dugout canoe.
Those smaller trees? Those are the walls of a fort.
That cedar there is the grave marker of a goodhearted soldier.
A length of mast is an axle. A slice of a log is a wagon wheel.
A boat sail makes a handy awning shade.
A buffalo is a quick-built round boat.
An elk is one half of a hunting frock.
A deer is a pair of women's leggings.

Why did Meriwether Lewis kill himself?
I don't know that he did. But if he did
maybe it was the fact he never got 'round
to publishing his book on the expedition.
I published my own journal in 1807,
only a year after we returned.
That made Lewis madder than a hornet, I know.
I heard he had trouble finding a wife.
I heard he owed money. I heard he'd been drinking.
Heck. I heard a lot of things. Same as you.
But I can't believe any of it.

I heard a big black dog, lame in one leg,
was with him when he died.
That would be Seaman, I suppose.
I hear they buried Lewis in the woods
and could not persuade the dog to leave the grave.
Just lay there on the spot and died.

Do I think Lewis was murdered?
I don't know. I wasn't there.
But I'll tell you this:
　　　　Killing Meriwether Lewis would be about as easy
　　　　as sawing down a full-grown oak with a hunting knife.
I can't see it at all.

Pierre Cruzatte ◇ *the fiddler*

The fiddle I cannot see so well.
It is my left eye that is blind.
The bow I hold in my right hand.
The fiddle I hold in my left.
I play in the blind spot.
I play songs not by sight but feel.
Losing this one eye has made me play the fiddle better.
If ever I lost the other eye
I would play the best fiddle on the river.

To a river man, a steady boat is important
as well as a smooth paddle and stout setting pole,
strong hemp rope and strong rye whiskey.

But the thing that matters most is the music.
For it charms the river; it soothes her anger.
She thinks it is a part of her.
For what is a river if not one long song of many verses?

Boatmen, too, need the fiddle — to survive.
The Corps of Discovery would not have stayed
long afloat without it.
These men are more music and mirth than muscle.

Forget the fiddle?
Mon Dieu!
You may as well forget the food!

What happened to Captain Lewis?
Was it murder or suicide?

Pierre, he will tell you
the answer to this riddle.
I'd wager he stopped listening
to the music of the fiddle.

Joseph and Reubin Field ◇ *the brothers*

Reubin   Hey, Joe.
How are ya, Brother?
I know. I know. It's been a long time
since I come by t' visit. I know!
Ever'thin's goin' good. I done partnered up
with brother Zeek at th' salt works.
An' me 'n Mary Myrtle been lookin' at fifty acres
o' farmland on Little Bee Lick.
I mean—
well, I guess I'll jest come out with it, Joe.
Me 'n Mary Myrtle done hitched it up.
Yep, I know. I know. She's *yer* girl.
But you bein' dead 'n all . . . well.
So it's Mary Field now.

I did give 'er the buffalo robe.
We been usin' it on top th' bed quilt
on two-dog nights.
I tell you honest, Joe.
I think she married me t' be close t' *you.*
Close to the memory o' you anyways.
Maybe that's why *I* married *her* too.
It's jest that, well . . .
I miss you, Joe. That's all.

I got t' go now, Joe.
Mary Myrtle's waitin'.

York <small>◇</small> *the slave*

Gee up there, Reubin! Haw there, Joe!

I've named the horses after some o' the Kentucky boys
who went to the ocean an' back.
That's Joe'nReubin Field in th' lead as usual.
Charlie Floyd an' John Shields in the middle there.
The tongue horse to my right. That's Johnny Colter.
An' the wheel horse here,
the one I sit atop to guide them all,
this one's Billy Clark.

I kept asking for my freedom for more than ten years.
An' one day Mister William gave in.
He bought me this wagon 'n six-horse hitch
an' he handed me my papers.

The man who owns my Sally
moved to Nashville, Tennessee,
so I've been running freight between Lexington an' Nashville
with a spur trip over to Richmond, Kentucky.

I'm not claiming it's an easy life.
Being free in these parts can be more trouble
than being owned.
But it's *my* trouble an' no one else's.
An' the hard labor isn't *anything*
compared to lugging those dugouts 'round the Missouri falls.

I've even got my own Corps o' Discovery:
    six big black horses—each one stronger then ten men.
    Each one under the command o' Captain York's jerk line.

Oh, I've got a blacksnake whip
that I hardly ever touch.
An' if I feel the need to crack it—

well, I don't.

Oolum ◇ *the newfoundland*

CRACK! CRACK! CRACK!

I regained consciousness just as the Indian guns had begun to die out. I kept low and listened. By now Shannon and the other white men were floating downstream with the current, out of musket range. The Arikara and Sioux were whooping and boasting. I examined my wound.

The ball had entered the upper half of my left front leg. The white fur was soaked red with blood. I lost consciousness a second time.

I came to after dark. A bright half-moon lit the ground. Still dark enough to allow me to limp from shadow to shadow. After a painful climb I was out on the open plain.

With luck I could make my way to Shannon's boat below. No good. They were traveling fast, with the current. I could hardly walk. I decided I would follow the river anyway, making whatever progress I could. Eventually a trading vessel would pass by. I licked my wound. I rolled dirt onto it. Anything to stop the blood. My cloak of darkness would do nothing to mask the smell of the blood.

I limped forward, placing my functional front foot one painful step at a time. Each lurch jolted my shattered leg, which hung from my shoulder like a broken branch. No use.

I stopped. I was more thirsty than I had ever been. Water. Find water. River. I turned to go to the river. But the bank was steep. I would never make that slope. Think. Where to now? What next?

"Hello, Cousin. You don't look so good."

Alpha Wolf. And seven others. No, eight. They appeared as if from air. Alpha Wolf's words forced a path through the cluttered thicket of my head.

"Welcome home, Oolum. It appears that you have bloodied your pretty white foot. Ah, but I see you are wearing a handsome collar now."

Lewis's gift.

The day he left me, he read the inscription aloud, deliberately and slowly, with the same ceremonial voice he had used to award peace medals to the Indians, explaining how the white men now owned the land.

The greatest traveller of my species.
My name is SEAMAN, the dog of Captain Meriwether Lewis,
whom I accompanied to the Pacifick Ocean through
the interior of the continent of North America.

Lewis had fastened the collar around my neck. Then he left me.

"I see he certainly owns you now. And what has become of your master, the explorer?"

I did not know where Lewis was. For years I had carried his spirit upon my back, whenever it had become too heavy a burden. On the journey to the ocean, he would leave his spirit lying on the plains like a forgotten hunting frock. He left it everywhere and often. In the rapids. By the falls. On the spines of a prickly pear. Beside the rain-drenched failure of his iron frame boat. Each time I found it and restored it to its sad, uncertain home. What will become of Lewis now? I bared my teeth and growled from deep in my throat. Alpha Wolf continued to speak undisturbed.

"How brave you are. Obedient and loyal to the end." Alpha Wolf was seated upon a rise. Even in the summer his coat was full and magnificent. "That loyalty will prove the death of you."

The other wolves circled me casually. Think. Think. I began to scan the pack, seeking out the weakest one. I felt a tug from behind. I turned to find a wolf biting down on my tail. I sank my teeth deep into its muzzle. It shrieked and withdrew.

Another tug at my back foot. I turned again, forgetting I had but one front limb. I fell, my full weight collapsing onto my useless leg. The pain was sublime. I rolled onto my back, frantically kicking upward.

One of the wolves grabbed my dead leg and pulled. I gasped for air and found none. I was blinded by fur. Smothered under snarls and snapping jaws. Growling and scratching claws.

Meriwether Lewis ◇ *the explorer*

Smothering! I tell you I'm smothering!
This heat will drive me mad.
No. No. I must stay calm. It is the fever.
The servants are not far behind.

My master was traveling through Tennessee, on his way to Washington.

Madam! I beg of you.
I assume the jug hanging from your sign—
do you have whiskey? I'd like a room.
My servants are not far behind.

He did not drink his whiskey.

No, madam. Don't make up a bed.
I only sleep on the floor.
My servants will bring bear skins and buffalo robes.
This fever. This fever.
Excuse me, please. It is the ocean inside me.

He stopped at a small cabin called Grinder's Inn.
Two servants were not far behind, coming on.

Thank you, madam. This looks delicious.
Now William Eustis says I'm a cheat?
Is my word no good?

He did not eat his dinner. His servants arrived.

Here, man. Lay out my bear and buffalo.
Bring me my powder and pistols.
I think there's an Indian not far behind!

William Eustis, the secretary of war, refused to refund the expenses
Lewis had incurred to send Big White back to the Mandan villages.

I am ruined! I am ruined, sir.
And this fever will not leave me.
Nor the Indian, sir. I wore no hat.
I felt his bullet distinctly!

The servants retired to the barn to sleep.

The secretary of Eustis! Scoundrel. Puppy!
Will this sensation ever subside? The ocean is in my head.
The Pacific Ocean. The Indian is not far behind.
I felt his bullet distinctly.

He was on his way to Washington to explain his expenses. He was in debt.

The Indian is crossing Maria's River.

Miss W. would not have him.

Maria's River goes nowhere.

Miss C., Miss R., Miss B. would not have him.

Maria's River goes NOWHERE. Lewis's River
is too rocky. TOO ROCKY!

The secretary of war is behind me.
I felt his bullet distinctly.

Madam, this *is* a pleasant evening.

He had not prepared a single word for publication.

Patrick Gass is coming up behind me.
He is on Lewis's River, but it is too rocky.
I feel this ocean in my head. In my chest.
Yes, Maria, of course you may retire.
Captain Clark will be here soon.

He had been delirious, off and on, for weeks.

Good night, madam. It is a pleasant evening.

The innkeeper went to bed for the night. She locked her door.

Big White must go home.
Do you hear me, Mr. William Eustis?
William Clark is coming up behind me.
He knows I am in trouble. I must drive
this ocean from my head. These waves.
We must make salt. We must load the boats.

He loaded his pistols.

I felt the bullet distinctly. I AM NO CHEAT, SIR!
I am no coward. The president knows this. The Indian

is coming. His bullet. MARIA. Clark. The ocean
waves are in my skull.

He discharged one pistol. He fell.

Oh, LORD! Oh, Lord.
The waves — are in my chest — now still. The ocean
will not leave — my chest.
This fever — will drive me — mad.

He stood. He discharged his second pistol. He fell.

OH, MADAM! GIVE ME SOME WATER
AND HEAL MY WOUNDS!

He crawled into the yard. He crawled to the water bucket.

Oh, Lord. I am thirsty.

*He scraped the dipper against the sides of the empty bucket.
I licked his face hello.*

Seaman, my friend! It *is* a pleasant evening.
See in the sky. Ursa Major — the dipper.
That's what I need to quench my thirst.
It is a pleasant evening. Come inside, boy.

He stood and returned to his room.

The ocean is everywhere under my skin. Like an itch.

He found his razor.

Just shallow cuts, you see. Just enough
to let out the ocean. Seaman, go fetch
me a squirrel. I feel my appetite is returning.

His servants arrived.

I've done the business, my good servant.
Give me some water. I am no coward,
but I am so strong, so hard to die.

We had traveled to the ocean.

Come on, Seaman. I am thirsty
and much in need of exercise.

We walked past the servants.

I know of an excellent spring of clear, cold, pure water.

We faced to the west. And we walked

But first we'll need that dipper.

down the road. Along the river. Across the plains. Over the mountains.
Into the sky.

And we followed the Milky Way home.

William Clark ◇ *the gentleman*

My friend Lewis has been gone now ten years
and I dearly wish he could see the changes.
St. Louis is not so rough as it was.
Louisiana Territory has been divided in half.
I am now the governor of the Territory of Missouri.
And if the population growth continues at this rate
Missouri will surely earn her statehood soon.

Lewis would be proud to know
that our adventure was finally published
in the form of a book for all the world to see.
Although in nearly five long years,
I have yet to see a copy for myself.

Just last month a paddleboat that runs on steam
went 250 miles up the Missouri River
to the village of Chariton, carrying flour, sugar, whiskey, and iron.
It was nothing less then a miracle.
What was its name?
Why, the *Independence* of course.
Lewis would have liked that.

We both took such pleasure in the naming of things.
I still find pleasure in it myself.
Just ask my ten-year-old firstborn son,
Meriwether Lewis Clark,
who walks about and beats his drum
through the streets of St. Louis.

That child is forever into something.
He won't sit still for a minute.

George Shannon ⬦ *the kid*

When I was a young man
I wanted nothing more than to accomplish
a task no other man could.
Now I'm a good bit older, and I think
maybe staying alive is accomplishment enough.
And let me assure you, I have lived through a lot.

> I finally did open up a law practice
> much to Mother's gratification.
> My natural gift of oratory makes politics and law
> two of my three inevitable avocations.
> I was practicing my *third* avocation at the tavern not so long ago
> when a fellow lawyer foolishly challenged me to a contest of sorts.

He proposed that if either of us would do a particular act,
and the other should fail to follow suit,
the delinquent should treat the crowd to a drink.
I had been waiting all my life for just such a challenge.
I accepted the fellow's proposal.
A crowd gathered near the fire where we were seated.
And with great ceremony I stood.

> I reached down, rolled up my pant leg,
> and I fumbled at the straps around my stump.
> > You see, that Arikara gunshot wound
> > never did heal correctly.
> I yanked at the hickory wood shaft
> and held up the peg and harness for all to see.

Then balancing on my sound leg,
I threw my other leg onto the fire.

475

"Ladies and gentlemen," I said. "If I might have your attention.
My companion would very much like to buy you a drink."
In what may have been my finest moment,
the crowd erupted with cheers and applause.

And as my companion was not disposed
to thus jeopardize a sound limb,

he was forced to foot the bill.

Thomas Jefferson ◈ *the president*

For months, here in my garden at Monticello,
I have been tending this handsome little shrub
of snowberries brought to me
so long ago by Meriwether Lewis
who first discovered its small neat flower
by the River Columbia at the far side of the continent.

As a boy he was *constantly* bringing me things:
A mushroom. A frog. A raccoon skin.
Why, Meriwether Lewis was born in a house
within sight of where I'm standing now.
Close enough that on a sunny day
I could signal to him by means of a mirror.
With three quick flashes I could tell the boy
to stop by and visit me here in the garden.
Three quick flashes, repeated until at last
I would see him signal me back.
Then later that day, I would see him
coming toward Monticello up that very hill there
with his musket and panting dogs.

I remember the morning, many years later,
when he set out for the Pacific.
The day before, it seemed as if every citizen in Washington
had been celebrating Independence Day
on the Commons in front of the President's House.
But by that next morning everything was calm
as Lewis and his dog quietly made their way
across the empty Commons. Off they went.
And although, years later, he did return as a hero,
in some way you might say Lewis never came back.

As I stand here tending this snowberry bush,
I am struck with a fanciful thought:
What if I were to lean out
the highest window of the house
and just once more flash my small mirror
in the direction of young Meriwether's home?
Or better still, face the western skies
and signal for him there?

I wonder, would Lewis signal back?
Three quick flashes.

And a short while later, just at sunset,
would I see him come into view,
walking up the hill toward Monticello?
A full-grown man,
a rifle in one hand,
a quill pen in the other,
a huge Newfoundland at his heel?
Anxious to report all he's learned about heaven.
Eager to show me the map
and rough sketches he's made
of the wonders
he has discovered
in paradise.

NOTES

AUTHOR'S NOTE

All but two of the characters in this novel really existed. Seaman's alter ego, Oolum, is fictional, as is Split Feather, the slain Shoshone brave. Where historical characters' names remain a mystery, I created them: Sacagawea's would-be husband, Sitting Hawk; Lewis's drunken boat builder, Noah Johnson; and York's wife, Sally.

For the captains' journal entries, I excerpted actual passages from the most recent edition of the Lewis and Clark journals, *The Journals of the Lewis and Clark Expedition,* edited by Gary Moulton. Letters are excerpted from *Letters of the Lewis and Clark Expedition, with Related Documents: 1783–1854,* edited by Donald Jackson. I have preserved most of the unique spelling and style of the originals, while condensing for clarity.

At times I strayed slightly from the straight and narrow path of fact. For example, no evidence exists to verify the family legend that Thomas Jefferson would signal to his young neighbor Meriwether Lewis by means of a mirror. And when a fiction writer transforms a real person into a character, the result is interpretation. Joseph and Reubin Field were almost certainly not so comical. Meriwether Lewis was not so obsessive. William Clark was not such a gentleman. Sacagawea was not so wise. And George Shannon was not so naive. Dog lovers might argue, however, that the Newfoundland was *indeed* more empathetic than any human of the expedition.

What became of our story's players after they returned from the West? In the 1820s, William Clark attempted to account for many of the members of the expedition. By then, just twenty years after their return, only three of the fourteen speakers in this book were still living: George Shannon, Patrick Gass, and Clark himself. Hugh Hall could not be accounted for. The remaining ten were dead.

WHAT BECAME OF THEM?
SOME POST-EXPEDITION HISTORY

Meriwether Lewis (1774-1809)

As governor of the new Louisiana Territory, Meriwether Lewis helped finance a second attempt to return Chief Sheheke to the Mandans. This time the trip was a success, but the War Department and newly elected President Madison refused to reimburse Lewis's expenses. This was a severe blow to Lewis's honor and financial standing. On October 11, 1809, while en route to Washington, D.C., to plead his case, Meriwether Lewis died, apparently from two self-inflicted gunshot wounds.

Why would a man struggle to the Pacific and back only to take his own life after safely returning? There are many possibilities. One theory is that Lewis suffered from bipolar disorder or depression. Some theorize that he had syphilis; others that he had an advanced case of malaria. He could have been addicted to laudanum, used as a treatment for either disease. Lewis's inability to find a wife, financial troubles, pressures of political office, and excessive drinking have all been suggested as possible catalysts to his mental collapse. Add to this a colossal case of writer's block. Early in 1807, he had made preliminary arrangements to publish the narrative of his amazing journey, but in the three years following his triumphant return to St. Louis, there is no evidence that he had prepared a single word for publication.

William Clark (1770-1838)

After the expedition, Clark settled in St. Louis. During most of the remainder of his life, he worked for the government, in charge of Indian relations west of the Mississippi. Most Indians, in fact, called St. Louis "Redhead's Town." He attempted to treat the Indians fairly, even as government policies toward them became increasingly unfair.

After twelve years of marriage, Julia Hancock died in 1820, the same year in which Clark was defeated in a race for governor of Missouri. The following year, he married Harriet Kennerly Radford, Julia's cousin. True to his word, he arranged for and financed the education of Sacagawea's son, Jean Baptiste. Pomp lived in a nearby boarding school.

I took many of Clark's comments regarding the treatment of slaves directly from letters he wrote to his brother, Jonathan, as found in *Dear Brother: Letters of William Clark to Jonathan Clark,* edited by James J. Holmberg. In them Clark matter-of-factly describes beating nearly all of his servants, including York. Two hundred years later, these letters are as chilling to read as they are illuminating.

With our twenty-first-century views on slavery, it is easy to condemn William Clark or Meriwether Lewis or Thomas Jefferson. In order to justify slavery, otherwise rational men had to convince themselves that their dark-skinned servants were somehow less than human. William Clark inherited this way of thinking from his father. Clark's father had inherited it from *his* father. In this way William Clark, as a slave owner, was born into slavery along with York.

After a long, successful career, Clark died at the age of sixty-eight. At his side was his thirty-year-old firstborn son, Meriwether Lewis Clark.

Seaman (ca. 1802–?)

Where and when did Meriwether Lewis first lay eyes on the industrious Newfoundland who would accompany him to the Pacific? No one knows for sure. We *do* know that on September 11, 1803, dog and master were together. This is Lewis's first written mention of the dog, catching squirrels on the Ohio River.

Most written references call our canine adventurer simply "our dog," "my dog," or some variation of "Capt. Lewises dog." The men's journals tell us that Seaman chased wounded game, barked at stalking grizzlies, faced down a charging buffalo, and nearly died from a beaver's bite. The dog struggled every mile of the way alongside the humans. On July 15, 1806, Lewis wrote: "My dog even howls with the torture he experiences from them," referring to the maddening swarms of mosquitoes. With this final mention, the dog disappears from history.

I feel strongly that the dog *did* successfully complete the journey. The sudden loss or death of the dog, "our dog" to the men, surely would have been worthy of note. A recent discovery by historian James Holmberg seems to suggest that the story of Seaman starving himself to death on his dead master's grave has some truth to it. Since a Newfoundland's life expectancy is eight to ten years, Seaman was probably dead by 1812 or so.

The Oolum of our story is fictional, yet a real Oolum *did* exist about eight hundred years before Seaman was born. You might even say that the real Oolum still exists today. Around 1000 A.D., Norse explorer Leif Ericson crossed the Atlantic from Greenland to the island of Newfoundland off the coast of Canada, just north of today's state of Maine. At Ericson's side, they say, was a large black "bear dog" named Oolum.

North American Indian tribes had been living on Newfoundland Island since 6500 B.C. Some theorize the Viking bear dogs bred with the local Indian dogs, themselves large and accustomed to hard work and cold water. Eight centuries and many litters later, the hero of our book was born. Humans named the dog Seaman, yet according to some experts, locked deep within its DNA were traces of Oolum the Viking dog. Look into the eyes of any Newfoundland today, and you may well see Oolum staring back.

Sacagawea (ca. 1788–1812)

Sacagawea is one of the most famous American Indians in United States history, yet very little is known of her life. Even today, scholars disagree about the proper place and date of her death, and the meaning, spelling, and pronunciation of her name.

In the fall of 1809, Sacagawea and Charbonneau brought the nearly five-year-old Jean Baptiste to St. Louis, where he was baptized. Charbonneau signed his "X" in the church records, which listed Sacagawea only as "_____, savage of the Snake Nation." After a short-lived attempt at farming, Charbonneau and Sacagawea joined Manuel Lisa's expedition up the Missouri River to establish Fort Manuel, in what is now South Dakota. They left Jean Baptiste in Clark's care.

While at Fort Manuel, Sacagawea gave birth to a girl named Lisette. Four months later, on December 20, 1812, Sacagawea died of a fever. The fort's clerk wrote that "she was a good and best woman in the fort, age about twenty-five." An alternate story holds that Sacagawea lived to be nearly one hundred years old and died on the Wind River Reservation in Wyoming.

William Clark became the official guardian to both of Sacagawea's children. Lisette apparently died very young. Jean Baptiste lived to become a trader, guide, and adventurer whose travels took him as far as Europe and Africa. Like his famous mother, he was also an interpreter. When he died in Oregon at the age of sixty-one, Jean Baptiste "Pomp" Charbonneau spoke English, German, French, and Spanish, as well as many American Indian languages.

York (ca. 1770–?)

As is the case with most slaves, York's history is known only through the written words of the white man who owned him. Clark's post-expedition letters document a progressively sour relationship between master and slave. Initially Clark refused to free York. Instead he hired York out in the Louisville, Kentucky, area at various jobs. By the summer of 1811, York had been in Louisville for about two years and was miserable.

Between five and nine years after returning from the Pacific Ocean, Clark finally freed York, providing him with a wagon and team. According to Clark, York's freight-hauling business was unsuccessful, and while en route back to St. Louis, the man who had been such "great medicine" to the Indians in the West, died of cholera. Sadly, it seems that York never permanently reunited with his wife.

George Shannon (1785–1836)

In 1810, when editor Nicholas Biddle agreed to prepare the expedition journals for publication, George Shannon traveled to Philadelphia to assist him. The loss of a leg, amputated above the knee, did not prevent him from becoming a prominent lawyer and politician. Sources say he gambled and drank and generally led a colorful life. To help Shannon describe the scene in which he throws his leg into the fire, I have borrowed some words directly from W. V. N. Bay's *Reminiscences of the Bench and Bar of Missouri,* published in 1878.

On August 30, 1836 (thirty years to the day after he had set out with Lewis from Pittsburgh), George "Peg-Leg" Shannon died in court at the age of fifty-one while defending an alleged murderer.

I like to think he died talking.

George Drouillard (ca. 1775–1810)

After the expedition's completion, Drouillard became a full-time fur trapper with the volatile and shrewd trader Manuel Lisa, whom Meriwether Lewis detested. Under Lisa's command, Drouillard was sent to capture a man who, much like the soldier Moses Reed, had deserted one of Lisa's trapping expeditions. This time, however, the deserter wound up dead, and Drouillard found himself on trial for murder.

Happily, George Shannon was a member of the jury, which found the defendant not guilty. Although Drouillard was acquitted, lawyers' fees and other debts left him broke. He returned to trapping at the Three Forks. There, on the bank of the Jefferson River, Drouillard was killed, reportedly by Blackfeet Indians. Eyewitnesses who found his corpse saw evidence of Drouillard's tenacious defense. In the end, this man, who had been such an important bridge of peace, died a violent death—disemboweled, dismembered, decapitated, his heart cut out.

John Colter (ca. 1775-1813)

Choosing not to return to St. Louis with the others, John Colter became the first white man to describe the geysers and steaming sulfur springs of what would become Yellowstone National Park. Not long after, he found himself in the middle of a full-blown battle between the Crow and Blackfeet Indians. He was wounded in the leg.

While trapping in the early fall of 1808, his leg barely healed, Colter was captured by a large group of Blackfeet Indians near the Three Forks area. The Indians forced Colter to strip naked. Then they told him to run for his life. So he ran. Colter ran nearly six miles, chased by one hundred or more Indians, across an open prairie that was blanketed with the sharp spines of prickly pear cactus. Amazingly, he outdistanced all but one of the Indians. With blood gushing from his nose, his bare feet numb and bleeding, Colter suddenly turned to face his lone pursuer. The startled Indian fell to the ground, breaking his spear in half. Colter quickly ran the Indian through with the spear point, grabbed the brave's blanket, and continued running to the nearest river. At nightfall, he slipped away downstream and eventually took to the land. Then, with only a blanket to protect him against the cold autumn air, Colter walked almost three hundred miles in eleven days back to Fort Raymond on the Yellowstone River.

Unbelievably, Colter returned to the Three Forks the next spring to retrieve his traps. He was attacked again, and again he escaped. Eventually Colter had enough and returned to St. Louis for the first time in six years. He married and settled down on a farm in Dundee, Missouri, where he died of jaundice at the age of thirty-eight.

Pierre Cruzatte (?–?)

How is it that Lewis and Clark chose as a river pilot a man with only one eye, and a nearsighted eye at that? Perhaps it was Pierre Cruzatte's previous experience as an Indian trader and boatman on the Missouri River. Perhaps it was his supernatural empathy with the ways of the water. Although he contributed to the expedition's success in many different ways, Cruzatte is known best for skillfully playing the fiddle and accidentally shooting Lewis. No solid evidence tells us what happened to Cruzatte after the expedition. William Clark's 1820s accounting simply lists him as "killed."

Hugh Hall (ca. 1777–?)

While making an early assessment of the soldiers who would come to form the Corps of Discovery, William Clark observed in his notes that Hugh Hall was a drinker. Since *all* the men likely drank, Clark's comment implies that Hall drank whiskey with remarkable zeal.

He was court-martialed in June 1804, when he and John Collins tapped the company's whiskey keg contrary to orders. In 1809, Hall was in St. Louis and on terms friendly enough with Lewis that his old commander lent him money. After that, Hugh Hall disappears from history.

Patrick Gass (1771–1870)

Family lore claims that the mouth of carpenter Patrick Gass was always full of chewing tobacco and profanity. Rough manners or not, we can conclude from his popular "election" to sergeant that he was respected by his fellow soldiers and trusted by his superior officers.

As a sergeant, he was required to keep a daily journal, which he published in 1807, only a year after the expedition's return. Meriwether Lewis was not pleased. By the time Lewis and Clark's "official" account was published, Patrick Gass's version had already been printed in the United States, England, France, and Germany.

Gass re-enlisted to fight in the War of 1812. Ironically he was discharged when he lost his left eye chopping down a tree. At the age of sixty, he married sixteen-year-old Maria Hamilton and fathered seven children. Incredibly, he outlived his young wife. He was the last surviving member of the expedition when he finally died, just before his ninety-ninth birthday.

Joseph Field (ca. 1780–1807)
Reubin Field (ca. 1781–ca. 1823)

Sources provide conflicting stories of the Field brothers' births and deaths. The most current information argues convincingly that Joseph was the older of the two by a year. At the expedition's conclusion, Lewis described them as "two of the most active and enterprising young men who accompanied us. It was their peculiar fate to have been engaged in all the most dangerous and difficult scenes of the voyage, in which they acquitted themselves with much honor." William Clark thought enough of Reubin to recommend him for a lieutenancy in the army.

Joseph Field was dead by October 1807, and it is plausible (though by no means certain) that he met his demise during the same Arikara battle in which George Shannon received his leg wound.

Mary Myrtle's eventual marriage to Reubin is a fact, but Joseph's romantic designs on her are my own wicked fabrication.

Thomas Jefferson (1743–1826)

Thomas Jefferson was the primary architect of the Lewis and Clark expedition. He had been planning it for years and had made three failed attempts. Finally the presidency gave him the power to see his dream come true.

Jefferson's interest in establishing a coast-to-coast route for trade and his subsequent purchase of Louisiana from France gave the United States the loudest voice in the clamor of countries claiming rights over the New World.

Jefferson's political opponents, the Federalists, criticized the Lewis and Clark expedition as costing too much money and producing too little information. Unfortunately the first publication of the Lewis and Clark journals was too little, too late. The story of the expedition would not find its way into print until 1814, five years after Jefferson had left office. The 1814 publication was a narrative paraphrase only and did not include the detailed scientific notes describing the various previously unknown Indian nations and chronicling the discovery of some three hundred plant and animal species. These would not be published for nearly one hundred years.

When Jefferson retired to Monticello, among many other pursuits, he tended to his garden. Growing there in the Virginia soil were plants sprung from the seeds and cuttings collected on the far side of the Rocky Mountains by his loyal apprentice Meriwether Lewis. Did Jefferson think of Lewis when noting how Mandan corn was a thing of beauty and utility, or how the wood of the Osage orange tree bends but will not break? Did the flowers of the snowberry bush remind Jefferson how people and history come and go?

Exactly fifty years after he wrote the Declaration of Independence, Thomas Jefferson died at Monticello, on the Fourth of July, 1826. That same day, twenty-two years before, Jefferson had watched Lewis leave Washington, D.C., bound for the Pacific Ocean.

THE CORPS OF DISCOVERY

By the time the expedition left St. Charles, Missouri, in May 1804, the crew had swelled to around forty-five members. A few others, such as Toussaint Charbonneau and Sacagawea, joined along the way. Only thirty-three of these people (and one dog) would actually travel from Fort Mandan to the Pacific Ocean and back. Their names are listed below.

Military Personnel

Captains: Meriwether Lewis, William Clark
Sergeants: Patrick Gass, John Ordway, Nathaniel Pryor
Privates: William E. Bratton, John Collins, John Colter, Pierre Cruzatte, Joseph Field, Reubin Field, Robert Frazer, George Gibson, Silas Goodrich, Hugh Hall, Thomas P. Howard, François Labiche, John Baptiste Lepage, Hugh McNeal, John Potts, George Shannon, John Shields, John B. Thompson, Peter Weiser, William Werner, Joseph Whitehouse, Alexander Hamilton Willard, Richard Windsor

Nonmilitary Personnel

Jean Baptiste Charbonneau, Toussaint Charbonneau, George Drouillard, Sacagawea, York, Seaman

AMERICAN INDIAN NATIONS ENCOUNTERED

From an American Indian viewpoint, Lewis and Clark discovered nothing; they merely arrived. The members of the Corps of Discovery would likely have died without the assistance of the many American Indian people they encountered. Most of these nations were well organized, with complex social orders, organized religion, and systems of government. Some were agrarian and lived in thriving villages much larger than most cities in the United States. It is challenging to accurately list every Indian nation that came into contact with the expedition. Particularly west of the Rockies, translation became increasingly difficult and the journal references are inconsistent. Even today, proper names and pronunciations vary. The list that follows is by no means complete.

Arikara (uh-RICK-uh-ruh)

Assiniboin (uh-SIN-uh-boyn)

Atsina (at-SEE-nuh), also called Gros Ventres (groh VAHNT) of the Prairie; also called Fall, or Falls, Indians

Blackfeet: actually a confederacy of three tribes: Blackfeet, Blood, and Piegan (pee-GAN)

Chinook (tch-NOOK — as in *book*)

Clatsop (KLAT-sop)

Delaware (DELL-uh-wair)

Fox

Hidatsa (hee-DAHT-sah), also called Gros Ventres (groh VAHNT) of the Missouri; usually called Minnetaree (min-uh-TAHR-ee) by the Americans and the Mandans

Kansa (KAN-zuh)

Kickapoo

Mandan (MAN-dan)

Missouri

Nez Percé (nez PERZ), also called Chopunnish (choh-POON-ish)

Omaha

Ootlashoot, sometimes called Flathead

Osage (OH-saje)

Oto (OH-toh)

Palouse (puh-LOOSE)

Pawnee (paw-NEE)

Salish (SAY-lish)

Sauk (sawk)

Shawnee (shaw-NEE)

Shoshone (shoh-SHOH-nee), often called Snake

Skilloot (skil-OOT)

Tenino (teh-NEE-noh), also called Eneeshur (eh-NEE-shoor)

Teton Sioux (TEE-tawn SOO), also called Lakota (luh-KOH-tuh)

Tillamook (TIL-uh-mook — as in *book*)

Umatilla (yoo-muh-TIL-uh)

Wahkiakum (WAH-ky-AH-kum)

Walla Walla (WAH-luh WAH-luh) or Walula (wuh-LOO-luh)

Wanapum (WAH-nuh-pum)

Watlata (waht-LAH-tuh)

Wishram (WISH-rum)

Yakama (YAH-kuh-mah)

Yankton Sioux (YANK-tun SOO)

EXPEDITION MISCELLANY

Dates of expedition: May 14, 1804–September 23, 1806

Total time: Two years, four months, nine days

Miles traveled: Around 8,000

Percentage of travel by water: 80

Total number of vessels used: 25

Number of present-day states traveled through: 11

New species recorded: 178 plants, 122 animals

Pounds of meat consumed: Approximately 300 pounds a day

Number of deaths: 3 (1 soldier, 2 Native Americans)

Oldest member of the expedition: Toussaint Charbonneau (45 years)

Youngest member of expedition: Jean Baptiste Charbonneau (2 months)

Number of captains: 1 (Although his men called him captain, William Clark
was actually a second lieutenant. This was Lewis and Clark's little
secret. The other soldiers never knew.)

Number of different ways William Clark spelled *mosquito*: 20

Number of times he spelled it correctly: 0

Most popular trade item on Northwest Coast: Blue glass beads

Supplies that did not run out: Guns, powder, lead, paper, and ink

Projected cost of the expedition: $2,500

Actual cost of the expedition: $38,722.25

Amount Lewis paid for his Newfoundland dog: $20

York's 1804 market value as a slave: $450–$500

Corps of Discovery earnings totals:

Meriwether Lewis: $2,776.22 plus 1,600 acres of land

William Clark: $2,113.74 plus 1,600 acres of land

Privates: $333.32 plus 320 acres of land

George Drouillard: $1,666.66

Toussaint Charbonneau: $818.32

York: Nothing

Sacagawea: Nothing

FURTHER READING

Many good books on various aspects of the Lewis and Clark expedition are available. The titles below are essential reading for any serious Lewis and Clark scholar. If your time is limited (or your scholarly intentions less lofty), you can cut to the chase by reading the two books marked with an *.

*Ambrose, Stephen E. *Undaunted Courage: Meriwether Lewis, Thomas Jefferson, and the Opening of the American West.* New York: Simon & Schuster, 1996.

Betts, Robert B. *In Search of York: The Slave Who Went to the Pacific with Lewis and Clark.* rev. ed. Boulder: University Press of Colorado, 2000.

Chuinard, Eldon G. *Only One Man Died: The Medical Aspects of the Lewis and Clark Expedition.* Glendale, Calif.: Arthur H. Clark, 1979.

Clarke, Charles G. *The Men of the Lewis & Clark Expedition: A Biographical Roster of the Fifty-One Members and a Composite Diary of Their Activities from All Known Sources.* Lincoln: University of Nebraska Press, 1970. Bison Books Edition, with an Introduction by Dayton Duncan, 2002.

Cutright, Paul Russell. *Lewis & Clark: Pioneering Naturalists.* Urbana: University of Illinois Press, 1969 (reprinted by University of Nebraska, 1989).

Holmberg, James J. *Dear Brother: Letters of William Clark to Jonathan Clark.* New Haven: Yale University Press, 2002.

Jackson, Donald, ed. *Letters of the Lewis and Clark Expedition with Related Documents, 1783–1854.* 2nd ed. 2 vols. Urbana: University of Illinois Press, 1978.

Moore, Robert J., and Michael Haynes. *Tailor Made, Trail Worn: Army Life, Clothing, and Weapons of the Corps of Discovery.* Helena, Montana: Farcountry Press, 2003.

Moulton, Gary, ed. *The Journals of the Lewis & Clark Expedition*. 13 vols. Lincoln: University of Nebraska Press, 1988–2001.

*——, ed. *The Lewis and Clark Journals: An American Epic of Discovery*. Lincoln: University of Nebraska Press, 2003.

Rhonda, James P. *Lewis and Clark among the Indians*. Lincoln: University of Nebraska Press, 1988.

Saindon, Robert A., ed. *Explorations Into the World of Lewis & Clark: Essays from the Pages of* We Proceeded On, *the Quarterly Journal of the Lewis and Clark Trail Heritage Foundation*. 3 vols. Scituate, Mass.: Digital Scanning, Inc., 2003.

Trenholm, Virgina Cole, and Maurine Carley. *The Shoshonis: Sentinels of the Rockies*. Norman: University of Oklahoma Press, 1964.

INTERNET RESOURCES

http://www.lcarchive.org
Lewis & Clark on the Information Superhighway
A comprehensive list of links to websites on the expedition

http://lewisandclark.org
Lewis & Clark Trail Heritage Foundation
Includes a history of the expedition, as well as information about the
     Lewis and Clark National Historic Trail

http://www.lewisandclark.net
Discovery Expedition of St. Charles, Missouri
Website of a nonprofit organization that annually reenacts a portion
     of Lewis and Clark's river journey

GLOSSARY

French and French-Derived Terms

bois ceci (bwah suh-SEE): drink this

bonjour (bohn-ZHOOR): hello

Buffle Noir (BUH-fluh nwahr): Black Buffalo

cache (kash): from the French *caché* (kah-SHAY), hidden; a large hole dug into the ground to store supplies for long periods

Comment allez-vous? (KOH-mahn TAH-lay VOO): How are you?

engagé (on-gah-ZHAY): hired boatman

facile (fah-SEEL): easy, simple

fou (FOO): crazy (masculine form)

imbécile (em-bay-SEEL): imbecile or idiot

merci (mehr-SEE): thank you

mes amis (may zah-MEE): my friends

métis (may-TEE): of mixed French and Indian descent

mignonne (mee-NYUN): darling (feminine form)

Mon Dieu! (mohn DYUH): Good heavens!

monsieur (muh-SYUH): mister, sir

non (nohn): no

pardonnez-moi (pahr-DON-ay mwah): excuse me

pitié (pee-TYAY): mercy

plumes d'ange (ploom dahnj): angel feathers

rapidement (rah-peed-MOHN): quickly

rendezvous (RON-day-voo): a meeting

rivière (ree-VYAIR): river

Tournes de l'autre côté (toorn duh LOH-truh koh-TAY): Turn the other way

très bien (tray byen): very good

travois (trah-VWAH): a frame slung between two long poles, used to carry people or goods, pulled by dogs and horses

American Indian Names and Terms

Ah-hi-ee (Shoshone): I am much pleased. A greeting.

Amahte Arz-zha (Hidatsa): the Missouri River

kinnikinnick: a mixture of tobacco, bark shavings, or leaves; used for smoking

medicine: a general term for anything mysterious, wondrous, or inexplicable

pah-see-goo (Shoshone): camas root, or the bread made from it

pa-ump (Shoshone): possibly firstborn or leader. There is disagreement about whether this is truly the source of the nickname "Pomp," and indeed if this word existed at all.

pemmican: dried, pounded meat mixed with fat and, sometimes, berries

poggamoggan (Chippewa): a war club consisting of a leather-covered stone attached to a wooden handle by means of a short leather strap

pti (puh-TEE) (Mandan): buffalo

quamash (Nez Percé): camas root

shusu (Mandan): good

Snow Blind Moon (Mandan): refers roughly to the month of February. The Mandan and Hidatsa also called it the Moon of the Rut of Wolves.

Tenskwatawa (Shawnee): literally, the open door. Religious leader who lived from approximately 1775 to 1837 and began preaching in 1805.

Watkuweis (Nez Percé): literally, returned from afar. Tradition says that a woman with this name urged her people not to kill Lewis and Clark.

River Terms

cascade: a waterfall or steep rapid

confluence: the junction of two or more rivers

estuary: a wide body of water, such as a bay, located at the mouth of a river as it pours its waters into an ocean

riffle (or ripple): a swift, shallow current, usually over rocks; a rapid

sandbar: a rise, ridge, or small island of sand formed by water currents; can obstruct river travel

shoal: a shallow place in water

tributary: a river, stream, or creek that flows into a larger river, stream, or creek

Nautical Terms

bow: the front end of a water craft

cordelling rope, cordelle: a rope or line, attached to the mast or some other part of a boat, which allows the craft to be pulled from shore by humans or animals

dugout: a canoe carved from one solid tree trunk

gunwale (GUN-uhl): the edge of a boat's deck

helm: the steering mechanism of a boat or ship; the wheel or rudder

keelboat: a bargelike river craft, used primarily for transporting trade goods; so called because of the long wooden beam, or keel, that runs the length of the boat's bottom

larboard: the left, or port, side of a water craft

pirogue: a river craft, larger than a canoe, made of wood planks and typically fitted with a mast and oars

rudder: a wooden plate mounted at the stern of a boat that directs its course

setting pole: a long wooden pole, usually fitted with an iron tip; when pushed against the river bottom, it propels a boat forward

starboard: the right side of a water craft

stern: the back of a water craft

Other Terms

dram: a very small serving (less than an ounce), usually of liquor

gill: a unit of measure equivalent to four fluid ounces; a gill of whiskey contains the alcoholic content of about four beers

ACKNOWLEDGMENTS

Thanks to the following for valuable information and inspiration: everyone at the Lewis and Clark Trail Heritage Foundation of Great Falls, Montana; Bryan Craig, Research Librarian at Monticello in Charlottesville, Virginia; Mimi Jackson at the Lewis and Clark Visitors Center in St. Charles, Missouri; Daniel "Pierre Cruzatte" Slosberg in Los Angeles; historical artist Michael Haynes in Wildwood, Missouri; historic fort builder Steven M. Lalioff in Cicero, Indiana; Karine Schmidt and Anousheh Mahmoodi in Paris; and Steven Gerlach (aka Theophratus von Gerlach, Apothecary and Doctor of Physick) in Sparta, Illinois; Barbara Samuels in Anchorage, Alaska.

For friendship and keelboat advice, thanks to boatwright Butch Bouvier and his wife, Katherine, of L&C Replicas in Onawa, Iowa. And thanks to the late Glen Bishop, Joanne Bishop, and the Bishops' Newfoundland dog, Merri, all of St. Charles, Missouri.

Thanks to all the competent folks at Candlewick Press in Cambridge, Massachusetts, especially designer Sherry Fatla, copyeditor Hannah Mahoney, and that keen and insightful editor, Liz Bicknell. Thanks also to Malcolm Cullen in Toronto for creating the book's unique maps, and to Martin Plamondon for checking them.

For their thoughtful comments on early drafts, I thank Mark Stephens and his students at Germantown Academy in Ambler, Pennsylvania; Marilyn Hudson of the Three Tribes Museum in New Town, North Dakota; Joseph Bruchac, Hannah Freedman, Ally Fried, Jesse Moldofsky, Mindy Stephens, and Brittany Wolf. For checking my final draft for accuracy, I am indebted to Barb Kubik, historian and past president of the Lewis and Clark Trail Heritage Foundation.

Last, I must acknowledge Poetry Alive!'s Bob Falls of Asheville, North Carolina, who handed me the magic bean of an idea. Four years later, I descended from the resulting beanstalk with this book in hand.

A century after Lewis and Clark's voyage,
the world's largest and most luxurious ship is at sea.
In the distance, shrouded in darkness, an ancient iceberg lies in wait.

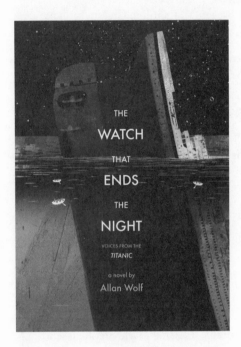

The Watch That Ends the Night
Voices from the *Titanic*

A novel in verse by Allan Wolf

★ "A masterpiece.... Everyone should read it." —*Booklist* (starred review)

★ "A richly textured novel." —*Publishers Weekly* (starred review)

Available in hardcover, paperback, and audio